SUNRISE AT TEN

(Johnstown—Another Age)

by

Marie Morgart

This is historical fiction. No fictional characters were meant to resemble living persons; those who were involved and living at the time, are quoted accurately.

FIRST EDITION

UNIVERSITY EDITIONS, Inc.
59 Oak Lane, Spring Valley
Huntington, West Virginia 25704

Cover by Amy Harold

Copyright 1991, by Marie Morgart
Library of Congress Catalog Card No: 90-71995
ISBN: 1-56002-093-8

DEDICATED TO

MARIAN

WHO HAS ALWAYS BEEN

"THE WIND BENEATH MY WINGS"

SUNRISE AT TEN

FOREWORD

In the 1800s, Johnstown, like its sister city, Pittsburgh, Pennsylvania, had become a Mecca for immigrants as a mining town. Remarkably, these hard-working individuals, with a myriad of disparate backgrounds and cultures, managed to develop the wealth of ores beneath them into a prosperous, flourishing city.

For the most part, these were moral people, generally devout in their religion, and passionately protective of their youth. Their innate flaw was prejudice, which took many forms. Generally, they shared a common antipathy for Hungarians. Apparently, a casual life-style which often included fortune-telling and spiritualism, caused suspicion of witchcraft.

Shona's story has a basis; so-called witches had been driven out of the city before her birth, and people knew nothing of what was later called "extra-sensory perception."

As for the growth of Johnstown and its ultimate destruction, all is factual. Here, the infantile Red Cross made a respected name for itself, through Clara Barton's magnificent handling of this, the nation's greatest calamity. And the city came back—these were indomitable peoples.

* * *

FIRST

Living in the heart of Johnstown, Pennsylvania, could give one the sensation of occupying a vast, green bowl, completely shut off from the outside world. In October, the bowl flaunts a great salad in russet, gold and bronze. Now, in the early days of May, 1872, it stood more timidly, with its hesitant offerings of pale, delicate morsels of white, yellow and chartreuse.

The town's most enthusiastic supporters were sometimes carried away in describing its uniqueness. One popular remark of the 1800s was that "The town is set so deep in the valley that the sun rises at ten and sets at two."

Newcomers sometimes found it easy to believe this patent nonsense, for in the early morning, clouds of smoke from the sprawling iron works often kept the sun from making its appearance much before the indicated hour.

There were mornings, though, like this one, when the air had been washed clean, and vivid sunlight bathed the valley, showing off its neat, copy-cat mill houses with their maple trees and white picket fences.

The MacDonald mansion stood at the lower end of Main Street, near the point where the Conemaugh and Stonycreek rivers join. There were about a half-dozen elegant homes at lower Main and Washington, the only paved streets in the town. All of these were owned by executives of the mill.

Today, Sophie MacDonald was enjoying the sight of the burgeoning hillside, having pinned back the lace curtains to get a better view.

Tiny Shona, in her arms, was unconcerned. Too young to share the view from the master bedroom, she contented herself with the new-found joy of living. Truly, existence was a wonderful thing. Delightful, finding her mother's breast and pressing her hungry, searching mouth to it. Gulping in the sweet, warm liquid, she let her tiny fingers and toes flex in ecstasy. This was a warm soft world. It was a gentle, quiet world. It was a lavender-scented, loving, secure, blissful world.

From the beginning, Shona was an enigma to her mother. Her eyes gave no hint of the green they would hold in later life. They were so intensely blue that they sparkled like jet in her small, ivory face. Her blonde, wispy hair, which would give way to red-gold curls, kept its secret, too.

Later, when Shona had begun to distinguish faces, she would respond to everyone with charmed delight, stretching her tiny arms to them and dimpling. Outsiders saw no mystery, but from the beginning, it was there. Shona's small, excitable mother would catch many a glimpse of this in the infant's look of ancient wisdom which, to her, was almost frightening.

Sophie had called Will's attention to it. "Look at her, Will.

See what I mean? She's so thoughtful, and so . . . wise. I get the oddest feeling. Do you suppose there's such a thing as reincarnation? If . . ."

"Stuff'n nonsense, Sophie," he had interrupted without delicacy. "Where in tarnation do you get these ideas? She's jest a plain baby, like anybody'd have."

Nevertheless, at the mill, where Will MacDonald sometimes ruled with a verbal whiplash, he took a proud stance. Belatedly passing cigars around one day, he took advantage of a chance to do a bit of bragging.

"Yep, she's good-lookin' as a Palomino filly. None of that red-face stuff. She'll be sharp, too. My wife was jest sayin' how much she takes notice already."

As for Cassie, the colored cook, she, too, exulted in the delicacy and charm of this child. "Minds me of l'il Jasper, my chile what die' of the fever," she observed one day, putting Shona in her crib.

Sophie raised her dark, curly head with a start. "In what way?"

Cassie laid a dusky finger against the baby's cheek. "Guess his skin was pinker, but it felt like rosebuds, too. And his eyes was jest like this, black and shiny. Made ya feel like he already knowed ever'thing there was to know."

Sophia relaxed in her wing-back chair and smiled. "I'm glad you said that, Cassie. I've been a little worried about that look. Maybe all babies have it."

Cassie stroked Shona's silken head. "Yes'm, I believes they does."

Sophie watched her as she moved out of the room. There was grace in her walk and a suppleness in her tall, slender figure, that Sophie envied. Although her own five-foot stature would have been considered feminine, sometimes she felt the lack of the dignity that seems to accompany height.

She had no sooner come downstairs than the front door opened. It was Will.

He tossed his hat on the clothes-tree and entered the room, grinning. "Where's the little one?"

"Cassie just took her up."

In two leaps he was out of there, springing up the stairs.

Sophie sighed. It had been ten years since Will had shown such enthusiasm. If it was natural for a wife to be taken for granted, it must be equally human for her to feel the loss. The ardent, smooth-faced lad she married had been ever affectionate, highly solicitous. But in the fifteen action-packed years of his career, this be-whiskered steel magnate had lost those qualities while gaining his fortune. That, of course, was before Shona.

* * *

One warm spring evening just after sunset, Sophie lifted the shade of the smaller of matching white parlor lamps and applied a match to its wick. The light flared, died down, then brightened into a steady glow.

Strong and sharp came a dog's bark, just outside. Sophie crossed to the window and pushed aside the heavy, green brocaded drape. One lone buggy was moving briskly over the cobblestones, with Pat in hot pursuit. Sophie ran, threw open the door and shouted, "Pat!"

At the sound of her voice, he stopped, turned and came back, tail tucked under, head hanging.

"Pat, one of these days, you're going to get under those wheels. Then, maybe, you'll give it up."

Ears flattened, Pat crept past her into the kitchen, seeking the comfort of his basket in the corner behind the enormous coal stove. In the protecting shadow of Will's high-backed rocker, he settled down to brood over the lack of empathy in humans.

* * *

Months later, Sophie looked across the luncheon table at her mother-in-law and smiled. Margaret MacDonald, gentle, white-haired, and as dainty as the bluebells of her native country, was easy to love.

Shona, propped in her high chair with pillows, was trying her best to say so. She gurgled and held out tiny, round arms to her grandmother. Margaret began to rise, then hesitated.

"It's all right, Mother," said Sophie, jumping to her feet. "I'll be happy to have you take her. Will wants raisin pie for supper, and Cassie won't be back until evening."

Margaret's smile faded. "Oh, Sophie, pet, it's too hot for you to build that much fire. For your own good, I dinna think you should." She remembered Shona and caught her up, to the infant's crowing delight.

Sophie began to stack the dishes. "I'm used to it, mother. Anyhow, you're the one who spoiled him. How many days have you spent in a hot kitchen—and for how many years?"

Margaret kissed the baby's neck. "I could'na keep track. But it's rememberin' those times that makes me know how hard it is. Now, if you'll take the little one, I'll do the dishes and the pies in no . . ."

"You'll do no such thing. When you came here to live, I told you that it was my turn to take care of Will. 'It's a poor house that can't afford one lady,' they say."

Margaret smiled, held the baby up and nuzzled her stomach. Shona laughed, deep down, with a hearty chortle that curled her fingers and toes and closed her eyes.

"She adores you," flung back Sophie, breezing away with the last of the dishes.

Margaret carried Shona to a high-backed cane rocker in the living room and sat down. Suddenly she didn't feel well. She had a pain in her head, and her hand prickled. After a moment, the feeling passed. She cradled the baby in her arms, and in a sweet, delicate voice, as fragile as its owner, she began to sing:

> "Hush ye, hush ye,
> Little pet, ye—
> The Black Douglas
> Shall not get ye."

For a while, Shona relaxed, then she stiffened herself; her eyes were wide and searching. She looked up at her grandmother and an anxious expression creased her brow.

Margaret stopped singing and laid a gentle hand over the baby's eyes. "Close them, pet. You're tired, I know." To her amazement, Shona resisted. She grasped Margaret's hand and pushed it away. Then she began to cry, softly.

Sophie looked in from the doorway. "That's odd. You know how seldom she cries. Do you suppose she's sick?"

Margaret laid a practiced hand on the baby's brow. "I dinna think . . ." she began, then paused. "She doesn'a have the fever, and her appetite has been good. If she were not such a wee one, I'd say she had a great worry."

Sophie's eyes widened. "Thank Heaven, I'm not the only one who has foolish ideas. Will thinks it's ridiculous, the way I attribute such feelings to that child. You see it, too, don't you? There's something different about her."

She came to take the baby, who stopped crying in little, jerky sobs and looked around apprehensively at her grandmother.

Margaret reflected. "I hope she's not ill. A bairn should have but comfort and pleasure."

Sophie smiled and glanced at the baby leaning against her shoulder. "Don't worry, Mother. She's just sleepy, I guess. Look, her eyes are closing. I'll take her up. Don't you dare finish those dishes. I'll be right down."

* * *

Late that night, Sophie wakened, without knowing what had roused her. She held her breath and listened. Instinctively, she knew that a sound had come from Margaret's room. She slid her legs over the edge of the bed and felt for her slippers with her toes. Will was snoring.

Margaret's bedroom door was ajar. Sophie pushed it open wider. In a shaft of moonlight, she saw a motionless heap on the floor.

"Mother, dear . . ., Margaret, what's the matter?" she cried, kneeling beside the limp body. There was no response. She tried to feel for a pulse, but her hand shook and she gave it up. Somehow, she got to her feet to call Will.

Having verified the fact that his mother was alive, Will took charge at once, settling her comfortably in bed and riding for the doctor at breakneck speed without stopping to hitch up the buggy.

Dr. Reese was sympathetic, but concise. "Stroke," he told them, at the door. "She's in a bad way. I'm sorry; there's not much I can do." He shook his graying head. "I'll be back in the morning. You folks try to get some rest."

When Margaret wakened the next day, her face was twisted, and it was difficult for her to speak. Sophie and Will bent to catch her words. "My Will . . . the carpetbag . . . Not much—Shona . . ." her voice trailed off, and her eyes closed.

Sophie patted her head. "Mother, dear, don't worry about your Will. You're going to get well. Don't give up."

Almost imperceptibly, a smile curved Margaret's lips, on the right side. Her eyes opened. "No, Shona ken . . . remember, Shona . . ."

Will frowned. "I can't make head or tail of it. What's she talkin' about?"

Sophie looked up at him in distress. The color had drained from her face. "She's delirious, I think." She stroked Margaret's hand. Stooping low, she whispered, "You're going to be just fine. Shona needs you; you've got to get better." Overwhelmed, she wanted to rush from the room. She thought she heard Shona crying, but she shut out the sound.

The cool hand under hers shuddered once, then lay quite still. Sophie's eyes went to Margaret's face. The twist had disappeared, and a half-smile remained, as though she were glimpsing something lovely.

Sophie turned to Will, who was standing at the window. "Will," she called in a low voice, "come here."

He turned; her eyes spoke for her. Rushing to the bedside, he took one look and sank to his knees, one arm flung across her body. For the first time, Sophie realized the depth of her husband's devotion to his mother.

Sophie couldn't bear to see his sorrow. She slipped out of the room.

Later, he found her in the nursery, rocking Shona. Both were crying. He glared at his wife. "Now, you've got the baby upset. Why didn't you leave her alone."

"She was crying," Sophie answered truthfully, "so I came in and picked her up."

"I don't believe it. She don't cry. You got no call to lie to me." He went off in a huff, and Sophie was glad of it. She put the sobbing, hiccoughing baby to her breast, but Shona refused to nurse.

The infant's grief could not have been translated into

thought. Her tears came, not in sympathy with her mother's sorrow, but because she had been enveloped in a series of unhappy sensations. The first had come as Margaret had been holding her. A dark mist had blotted out the loving face. She had experienced a sensation of falling—of the security under her being snatched away. It was her fear that had cried out then, and a sharper recurrence of these feelings had caused her tears now.

Naturally, Sophie did not understand any of this. Yet from Margaret's last words, she sensed something more than cooincidence in the child's behavior.

Controlling her own emotions, she tried vainly to soothe the baby. Shona continued to cry with a woe which could not be alleviated. Her tiny face, wet and swollen, became distorted and crimson.

When Dr. Reed arrived, Shona had lost the battle. Exhaustion had taken over. He examined the sleeping child carefully, and gave his opinion.

"This baby's in excellent health. There's absolutely no reason why she should have been crying like that. Unless, of course," he cast a wry smile at Sophie, "she could be just a tiny bit spoiled?"

Far from resenting his words, Sophie grasped at them. Of course—waiting for fifteen years for a baby was bound to make one over-solicitous. That was it!

Although she recognized her rationalization, that was better than living with the fears she had for her child. Gratefully, she beamed at the doctor. "You're probably right; I don't know why that didn't occur to me."

Looking down at the tiny, flushed face, she let her love overwhelm the fear. God had blessed her with a strong, healthy infant, and she would forget foolish ideas that she might be different from any other child.

* * *

A week later, at the supper table, without an apparent reason, Shona jerked in her highchair as though someone had struck her. Then, she began to cry. Sophie started to rise, but Cassie got to her, first. "There, there," she crooned, cradling the baby in her arms. Shona was not to be consoled. She stiffened, and continued crying.

At that moment, Will, who had worked later than usual, opened the front door, tossed his hat on the hall table and rushed into the dining room. He glared at his startled wife, and then at Cassie. "Where's Plato?" he barked, as though she were responsible for hiding her husband.

Over the baby's crying, Cassie shouted: "He's feeding the horses."

Will turned and dashed through the kitchen to the back yard not noticing the baby.

"What do you suppose is the matter with him?" said Sophie, puzzled. "Let me take her, Cassie. Maybe you should check." She carried the wailing baby to the living room and sat down to rock her. Shona quieted.

Cassie returned in a moment, her face pale under its dusky tan. "Honey," she whispered, so quietly that Sophie could hardly hear. "It's Pat."

"Pat?" repeated Sophie, vaguely. "What about Pat?"

"He's . . . he's been . . ."

Sophie jumped to her feet, gave Shona to Cassie, and rushed through to the back door. There was no one in the yard. She came back to Cassie, who was standing where she had left her. "What about Pat?"

Cassie shook her head and inclined it toward the front door. Sophie ran out on the porch.

Will and Plato were just disappearing around the house, carrying something between them. She gasped, turning to Cassie, standing in the doorway behind her.

"Was that—Pat?" she faltered.

Cassie nodded. "A junk wagon. Praise the Lord, he got it instant-like. Never felt what hit him, most likely." She wiped an eye with her apron.

Sophie's own eyes filled with tears. She had often predicted Pat's demise in this fashion, never really thinking it would happen.

She looked at the quiet babe in Cassie's arms and a thought struck her. Could it be that Shona's upset coincided with the exact moment of the accident? She shook that off, but the thought stayed with her and could not be erased.

The reason for her question was because of the sunny disposition of the child. She seldom fussed; only in times of crisis in her short life had she cried and not been reconciled.

Shona had loved Pat. She had enjoyed getting her tiny hands in his hair, and would flex her fingers, luxuriating in the softness of it. Once, Sophie had put Shona's bare feet on Pat's back, and the baby had laughed aloud. Oh, there had been a definite alliance between Shona and Pat.

Thoughtfully, she took the baby upstairs. This rare gift—or curse—she would watch alone.

She put the child into her cradle, and covered her with a small, pink blanket. Shona gave a quivering sigh, turned over, and put a thumb in her mouth. Her mother stood for a long moment, looking down at her.

* * *

SECOND

Shona was nearly three. A sunny child, with long, golden curls, she was the pride of her father and the joy of the household.

The past two years had been totally without incident. Sophie had almost forgotten the strange episodes which had worried her so. She simply felt gratitude for this happy, well-adjusted little girl, with a joyous smile and a seemingly endless zest for living.

The June evening was quite warm. Sophie sat on the porch swing with the child in her lap, waiting for Will, who was attending a meeting. Shona relaxed, but would not let herself sleep. Papa was coming!

As dusk was falling, a white moth circled Sophie's head. She eyed it with speculation, always appreciating the perfection of the living creatures with which she shared the earth. To her, God was a vital and mysterious power, capable of creating magnificent worlds which lay beyond the knowledge of man.

Will sometimes chided her for being a dreamer. His stolid Scotch background and unimaginative nature deplored his wife's flights of fancy.

He was coming, just now, up the sidewalk in long, easy strides, turning in at the white gate to the well-scrubbed boardwalk that led to the steps. Sophie smiled at him, but he had eyes only for the drowsy little girl, dressed for bed, who opened her eyes and held out her arms to him.

He rushed up the steps and took the child, burrowing his face at the side of her neck and blowing, to her great delight. She rewarded him with her infectious laugh, throwing her arms around his neck and crying, "More, Papa, more." He obliged her, tossing her in the air, romping and rough-housing until Sophie protested.

"Will, please stop it. You'll have her so excited that she'll never get to sleep. I've been trying to calm her down."

He didn't seem to hear. He tossed the child into the air again, and caught her, holding her to him roughly and rumpling her curls.

Suddenly, for no apparent reason, Shona's laughter stopped. She stiffened, struggled out of his arms, and ran to the door. "In, Papa, in." She fumbled vainly with the latch on the screen door.

With a worried glance at her husband, Sophie ran to open it. Shona, serious now, hurried to slam the inner door behind her father as he entered.

He tried to pick her up, but she went to her mother, instead. Sophie took her hand and turned toward the stairs, casting a wordless, mystified look at her husband.

Will followed, somehow feeling cheated. "What's the matter with her—she ain't sick, is she?"

Sophie sat down in a low rocker at the nursery door. "No,"

she said, rocking slowly as she smoothed the rumpled blonde curls. "Something has upset her—it's something we can't understand."

He stared as though she had gone out of her mind. "What goldern thing you got in your head now? This young'un ain't gonna get temperamental with me. First, she's havin' the time of her life, then she gets uppity 'n wants none of it. I won't have such shenanigans. I'll take it out of her, I swear." His angry face was black in the lamp-light.

"You won't do any such thing, Will, and you know it. And Will," she cast a beseeching look at him, "why does your grammar get so bad when you're upset?"

"The devil with my grammar," he mumbled, striding out of the room.

Shona did not cry. She twisted in her mother's arms to get a look at one of the windows, her small body trembling. Sophie began to croon a lullaby, which gradually took effect. Finally, exhausted, Shona fell asleep.

With a sigh, Sophie put her into her bed and blew out the lamp. Telling herself that her little daughter had been over-tired, she knew that was not the answer.

An hour later, lying beside her snoring husband, Sophie was still wakeful. She imagined she heard a sound in the nursery, and lay still, listening, but it did not recur. As far as she knew, Shona had never talked in her sleep.

She turned over to dismiss the thought. She had been working with Cassie on the silverware that day, and her right shoulder ached. Sleep would not come.

At last, she decided to check on the child. Quietly, so as not to waken Will, she slipped into the hall, lit a lamp, and crossed to the nursery.

She pushed aside the half-open door and held the lamp high. Shona was not in her bed. Alarmed, she moved the light to illuminate all corners of the room. The window, which had been partly raised, was now open wide, its curtains waving in the warm, summer breeze.

Sophie rushed to look down into the moonlit garden. It burst into her senses with fragrance, but the stillness was frightening. Shona was gone!

THIRD

High on the mountain, in the "hogback" area above the city, stood a decrepit, forgotten little shack, once used by miners. With the coal seam exhausted, the shack had been abandoned. Mines now operated deeper into the heart and the hills of Johnstown.

The dirty, shifty-eyed little man pacing the floor of the old shack was certainly not a miner. As a matter of fact, he had never found a station in life, save that of an itinerant.

That would be changed now, he thought grimly, striding across the warped, squeaking boards, muttering to himself, and casting a jaundiced eye on the tiny, golden-haired girl trussed up in a pink blanket on a rude cot. She was quiet, but her blue-green eyes flashed defiance.

He circled the room uncomfortably, glancing often at the window. Sunlight had begun to sprinkle light among the trees, and, somewhere, he heard a rooster crow. Too close for comfort, he told himself. People must be living nearby—this was not a place to be hiding out.

Worried, he opened the door and peered through the underbrush, at the narrow trail so recently broken. Then, a large, pleasant-looking fellow came into view, panting a little with exertion, but smiling with satisfaction.

Cheerfully, he called, "Hello, Pete; I'm back."

"Hesh," hissed the other. "There's people in these here parts. Whatever took ya so long?" He shooed the large man into the shack and bolted the door in haste.

"Pete, that farm's a couple of miles from here. It's these hills that carry the sound. And, what do you mean, what took me so long? Did you ever try walkin' from here to the Point? As the crow flies it's five miles—and I'm not a bird." He grinned.

Beaming with satisfaction, he explained. "I couldn't get near the house—people all over the place. So I sneaked into the mill office. All I had to do was slug the night-watchman. I put the note in MacDonald's desk."

"Lucky thing ya used to work for him. Ya sure ya put it where he'd see it, first thing?"

Sam shot him an impatient look. "I'm not stupid, Pete. Whose idea was this, anyway? Don't worry, the first thing on his mind will be to check there. All we have to do is sit and wait."

"Wait? For how long?"

"Just till midnight. I told him to meet me in the clearing at the far end of the park—and to come alone. He's to bring ten thousand dollars in small bills. Then you deliver the child."

"Ya mean I'm stuck with the kid? Why don't *I* collect the money, and *you* bring her? I don't like it—I don't trust you." He glared at the cheerful one.

"Yep, I knowed I shouldn't have did it," he continued, half to himself. Then he roused. "What about the police?" he blurted.

"No police. He wouldn't dare risk that. I warned him. What's this about trusting me? You're the one with the record."

Pete decided to drop that for the moment. He glanced at Shona, who favored him with a glare. "I sure don't like that one. She gives me the creeps. Looks like she's seein' right through ya."

Sam gave her an affectionate look. "You're nuts. Boy, what

I'd have given for a baby like that. Maybe, if Minnie hadn't died . . ." Shaking it off, he barked, "Well, anyhow, it's your turn. How about getting us some grub? And get some . . . things for the little one."

"What's she wear? Didies? How's it goin' to look—me buyin' didies? Next thing, you'll want milk."

"Right. Milk and crackers. She's too old for didies. Get underthings and a dress. Steal them, of course. You can't afford to be seen buying that kind of thing."

When Pete had gone off, mumbling, Shona brightened. She smiled at Sam and made little, whimpering noises. He crossed the room and untied the knotted blanket.

"No sense in tying you up like a mummy. It's not likely you'll try to escape." He tousled her curls and put her down.

Shona ran to the door and tried to reach the knob, set too high for her. Sam watched her with amusement. Smart little codger; no cry-baby, either. He held out his hands.

She frowned at him and went to the window. A rickety chair stood near it, and she climbed up to look out. Sam stretched out on the bunk and watched her.

* * *

Two hours later, Pete returned. He had dried beef, bacon, eggs and bread, as well as the milk and crackers. He chuckled over his experience. Apparently, he had approached a storekeeper with a plea for a job. The kind-hearted fellow had taken pity on him and given him charge of the store while he went to pick up some produce.

"I'll bet he sure was surprised when he got back," chuckled Pete, making a sandwich of beef and bread. "Pretty sharp of me warn't it?"

Sam snorted. "Seems to me if you were so all-fired smart, you wouldn't have brought bacon and eggs. How in hell are we going to cook them?"

He poured some milk into an old tin cup for Shona, but she refused it. She came close to him and whispered, "Potty."

Sam laughed, turning to Pete, who was sulking. "Hey, Pete, we forgot the potty. Incidentally, how about the underthings and the dress?"

"Didn't have none," mumbled Pete, munching his food. He sat down on the flimsy, ladder-backed chair and shook out a stolen copy of the daily paper.

Sam held Shona's hand and took her to the door. "Got no potty, honey. You go over there in the bushes, see?"

He thought she wouldn't understand, but she backed up to him. She was wearing a pink sleeping suit, buttoned at the waist. Flushing slightly, he unbuttoned the small trap-door and shooed her off. She left promptly.

After waiting for what he considered ample time, Sam called to Shona from the doorway, "Honey."

There was no response. In a few minutes, he went outside and called again. Pete came to the door. "Cut out that yellin' around. Someone will hear. Where is the kid, anyway."

"I don't know. Just around here, somewhere. She had to go, so I sent her over behind those bushes."

"Aw, c'mon, that couldn't take long."

It hit them at the same time. They started out in opposite directions, poking the thick bushes frantically. There was no sign of the child.

They met at some distance from the cabin. Pete glared at Sam. "It's your fault. You'd better get busy and find her. How in Tophet we going' to collect a ransom when we ain't got the kid?"

Sam tried to soothe him. "I'll find her. You know damn well a little kid like that can't get far. Now, let's go over this thing right. We did all the easy paths; we'll have to go over the whole hillside. You take everything around the old mine, and I'll climb to the top and look along the stream."

This time, they searched more thoroughly, exploring some small caves and probing thickets carefully. It was no use. Shona had disappeared—without a sound, without a trace.

They returned to the shack in thoughtful silence, both unhappy at this turn of affairs. Strangely, it was Pete who proposed a solution. "If we don't have her, neither does MacDonald. So, he'll pay the ransom, anyhow. Hell, we can be out of here before they find her. Say, what did you tell him about getting the kid—after he handed over the money?"

Sam sighed. "That's all wrong, now. You were to have left her at that big church, just off the park."

For the first time, Pete was pleasant. "Hey, maybe this is the best thing that could have happened. We'll go on with the plan."

"You fool, you don't think MacDonald is going to pay off without knowing that his baby is okay?"

Pete resented that. "I'm sure as Hell goin' to try. I'll get the money and be gone before he can check."

"What do you mean *you'll* get the money? How do I know I'd ever see you again if he did decide to pay off? Ah, no—you're not going without me."

Sam entered the cabin in angry silence, but his mind was racing. He bit his lip, made a sandwich, and flung himself down on the bunk to eat.

* * *

It was an enormous bush, as strong as a tree under Shona's light weight. An ancient lilac, it branched out as though begging to be climbed.

A veteran climber of crib and balustrade, Shona had no

trouble getting high off the ground. She grasped the limbs carefully, and swung her small legs up and around them as though this were an everyday occurrence. There was no fear; the sense of adventure took over, outranking all else.

Settling herself high in a crotch, she peered down through the leaves. Pete was coming through the woods, grumbling to himself, and poking a stick into all the bushes.

When she saw him, she froze, not allowing herself to breathe. He passed by the bush, brushing so roughly that she rocked with it, but she gave no sign.

Later, when Sam came by, she almost called out, but remembering that she didn't like the shack or Pete, she kept quite still and let him pass.

* * *

Will MacDonald paced the floor in angry strides, chewing on a cigar which had long ago exhaled its last, noxious breath.

"Take my baby, will he? The fellow responsible for this will damn soon wish he'd never been born." He gritted his teeth so violently that the cigar dropped to his feet. He picked it up and flung it into the fireplace.

Sophie looked up from the davenport, where she had been sobbing like a child. She wiped her eyes. "Oh, Will can't we do something? I mean—midnight, and then what? Who knows what he, or they might do to you. Maybe the police should handle it."

He glared at her. "The police? What good would that do. This fellow is already in trouble with them, most likely. The best thing to do is what the citizens around here are doing' right now. They're searchin' the town with a fine-tooth comb. What in tarnation could we do? We gotta be here when they find the baby, don't we?"

"Yes, Will, but what about the hills? There are all kinds of places to hide. Shouldn't? . . .

"Lord, woman, they know that. There's a search party up there on both sides of the town."

She had more concerns. "I just thought of something, Will. They won't hurt this man, will they? If they do, we may never see our little girl again." She buried her face in her handkerchief, and turned away.

Her husband shook his head. He had no answers. The note had warned him to keep police away from his home, if he hoped for his child's safe return.

Thinking of his midnight rendezvous, he stepped out on the porch. The hot breath of the summer day hit him. Except for the drone of a bee on the nasturtiums at the steps, there was no sound. It was as though the whole town had joined in the search. For the first time, Will knew what it was to be grateful.

Dropping to the front steps, he slumped like a tired, old

man. He could not allow his thought to express itself, not even to his wife. There would be no point in living, without that baby.

Strangely, his thoughts turned to his wife. Poor girl, this was just as hard on her. How long had it been since he had shown her any real affection? He would get up and go to her.

He entered the house and took her in his arms, still wondering at his own thoughtless cruelty.

Somewhat incredulous, but intensely comforted, Sophie snuggled against him, leaning her head on his shoulder. Her breath caught with the remnant of a sob. Will brushed her dark hair back from her damp, white brow and kissed her.

"I oughta be kicked, Sophie. I ain't the only one sufferin' around here. When this is over, I ain't gonna be that kind of a fool again."

With adoration in her eyes, she looked up at him and returned his kiss. I didn't mind, Will. Your loving her was loving me, too, in a way. Oh, Will, if . . ." He stopped her with a finger on her lips.

"No 'if's' like that, Sophie. It's gonna work all right. I've got the money all ready for tonight."

Just then, someone ran up on the front porch and knocked on the door. Will leaped to answer it.

A little boy of about ten, stood on the porch. He was panting, and his blue shirt was splotched with moisture. He ran one hand through his damp, brown hair.

"Mr. MacDonald?"

"That's right. What've you got to say, son?"

"They sent me—nobody's supposed to be around your house, so they . . ."

Will leaped out on the porch, and grabbed the boy by the shoulders. "I know all that—who sent you? For the Lord's sake, son, what do you know?" He released the boy, who took a step backward.

"The police, sir. They found a li'l old shack up on Hogback, where somebody's been stayin' but they was gone. There's some food they left, and a baby blanket. The police want to know if you heard anything."

Will's face had blanched to a pasty white. He tried to speak, then whispered, "No, we ain't heered nothin'. Go on back, boy. Be sure to let me know what they find out, you hear? I'll pay you handsomely." He pressed a silver dollar into the boy's hand.

The child nodded, and took off like a flash, in the excitement of high adventure.

Will looked after him, and then at Sophie, who was standing in the doorway. A new emotion had replaced his original anger—dark and engulfing. It was fear.

* * *

Nearing the appointed hour, Will set out with his package of money, to the concern of Sophie, who was both eager and apprehensive. She urged him to carry a gun, but he ruled that out as asking for trouble. He kissed her, and started out casually, portraying a confidence which had long taken flight.

Coming upon the clearing, Will discovered that the trees surrounding the area had been cleared of underbrush. One could see from quite a distance in every direction. There was no sign of life, except for the persistent hoot of an owl.

A full moon cast silvered streaks through the branches and across the grassy land. For a long time, he stood waiting, watching, and becoming more nervous. Where was the kidnapper? Could it be that the police had caught the fellow? What if the note had been a hoax? His mind raced, but could reach no conclusion.

Finally, he crossed the grove and sat down against a tree. Come what may, he would not leave until he had some answers.

* * *

Just after dawn, Sophie roused from her place on the sofa to see who was coming up on the porch. The strain of the watchful night gave impetus to her movement. She dashed to the door, just as Will put his hand on the knob.

"Will, what? . . ." she gasped, seeing that he still had the money.

He shook his head. "The fellow never came. That note must have been a bad joke. If I ever get my hands on the one who done this, I swear, I'll . . ." His face reddened, and he threw the package on the chair.

He had no idea what he would have done. Anger, suspense, fear and frustration had taken their toll. Will took Sophie in his arms and wept for the first time.

* * *

Two days later, early in the morning, the boy came again—this time in great excitement. Sophie let him in, and Will came downstairs three steps at a time.

"Will, Tommy says he has some news. Tell us, child—is it good news?"

"I guess it's pretty good. But not real good, if you know what I mean."

Will glared at him. "No, we don't know what you mean. Come, boy; out with it."

Tommy gulped. This Mr. MacDonald, with his orange mustache, grizzled beard and sharp, black eyes, wasn't easy to talk to.

He tried again. "Well, they found two fellows not far from

here, just above the Point. One was dead from knife wounds, and the other one's beat up. He ain't said nothin', though, 'cause he's half dead, too. Anyhow, the police think these are the guys they're lookin' for."

MacDonald gave Sophie a frantic look. "I'm goin' up to the station, Sophie. If these are the fellows, where is our baby? When Cassie and Plato get back, send Plato to the station right away."

Forgetting the boy, he rushed through the house and out the back door. In a moment, his horse rounded the house, clattering away on the cobblestones. Sophie got a coin for the lad and went back into the house. She felt sick, and empty, and hopeless. The thing she had not been daring to put into words now faced her.

* * *

FOURTH

Shona shifted her position in the bush. The men weren't there any more, and she decided to go home and see Papa. However, getting down from her perch was another matter.

After grasping several nearby branches, seeking a foothold, she put one foot in a crotch, but the branch was slender and bent under her weight.

She felt herself falling, and grasped vainly at some small branches, but the leaves came away in her hands, and she somersaulted onto the forest floor, where she lay quite still. A black-and-yellow striped bee droned about her golden hair for a moment, then soared away.

* * *

That afternoon, an ancient, wrinkled woman in a black dress and a pink sunbonnet, came into that part of the woods to dig for ginseng. She nearly stepped on the tiny girl, before seeing her. Kneeling, she put her gnarled hand on the child's chest; then nodded to herself. Gently, she lifted Shona and trudged through the forest, a white rabbit hopping at her heels.

It was an arduous climb to the log house where the woman lived. She hadn't realized that a small child could be so heavy. Ordinarily quite strong, now she had to make several stops to rest. With a sigh of relief, she approached her home. She backed through the half-open doorway and placed the child on the bunk along the wall.

Shona lay still, one tiny hand falling over the side of the bunk. She was very white; the only sign of life was the slight rise and fall of her small chest.

Before the woman could do more than close the door, she heard the sound of men's voices, not far from the cabin.

Alarmed, she grabbed the checkered tablecloth from the table and flung it over the child. Footsteps approached the door and halted. For a moment, there was no sound; then a loud knock came at the door. She crossed to it and opened it a crack. A half-dozen men stood outside. The bearded man in front spoke.

"Kate—we'd like to talk to you."

"I've got nothing to say to you—not to any of you."

"But, Kate . . ."

"Can't you people be satisfied with driving my parents out of town? Why do you persecute me?"

A younger, blond man stepped forward. "We're sorry about that, Kate. You know that was done by another generation. We never did you any harm, did we?"

"That's no guarantee. I could be tarred and feathered any day, if you got some notion in your heads. State your business and get out of here."

The lead man regained his voice. "We only want to know if you've seen a little girl—hardly more than a baby—in these woods?"

Suddenly she realized that if they were to find the child in her present condition, her own life would hang in the balance. She took a deep breath, and stepped outside, closing the door behind her.

She drew herself up, and the men stepped back.

"Now, you listen to me. I have no intention of being involved with you barbarians in the valley. You need my herbs, and I take your money, but that's as far as it goes. Don't come up here and accuse me of kidnapping. I've no use for you or your children. Now, get out of here, and don't come back."

Her deep-set black eyes flashed, and for a moment, her wrinkled face glowed with a semblance of the strength of her youth.

Almost as though in a drill, they stepped backward. Someone mumbled, "Sorry," and with one accord, they turned back to the rocky path down the hill.

Her heart still pounding, Kate watched them go, then went back into the house.

She lifted the tablecloth away. Shona had not stirred. Kate put one hand on the small head, frowned, and went to her great cupboard. Within it was a vast supply of home-canned food, apothecary jars of leaves and seeds, and innumerable swatches of dried herbs.

Working for a minute to loosen a cinnamon-colored piece of root, she broke it up, threw it into a pot and set the pot in the glowing coals of the fireplace. Adding some water from a brass teakettle hanging above the coals, she stirred in a few drops of liquid from a small brown vial. Now, she must wait.

The white rabbit hopped up to her, and she stopped to give

it a pat. From its cage in a corner, a crow squawked its disapproval. Kate grinned, took a handful of corn from a sack in the cupboard, and flung it into the cage. "Jealous, are you, Edgar?" she quavered. "Maybe you wouldn't have to be shut up there, if you weren't so ornery."

Croaking a retort, the crow gobbled the corn, hopping around the floor of the cage, dragging a splinted wing.

The cabin's interior consisted of one large room, with a combination of facilities. Double book shelves and a fireplace took up one complete wall;the hanging bunk stretched the length of the second, and the enormous cupboard occupied most of a third. On each side of the door, a large window, heavily curtained, let in faint light. In spite of the low fire, the house was comfortably cool.

In the center of the room stood a large, round table, with an oil lamp on it. Two ladder-back chairs and an ancient hickory rocker made up the remainder of the furniture. The plank floor was scrubbed almost white, but corners were heaped with boxes and empty cages, and the ceiling above the fireplace was hung with new bundles of drying herbs.

Kate arranged the tablecloth on the table and went to inspect her concoction. She tested it, nodded and poured some of the liquid into a cup.

When it had cooled, she took some on a teaspoon and lifted Shona's head.Carefully, she put a few drops between the child's half-open lips. There was no response. She did it again, several times. At last, Shona's lips moved.

Encouraged, Kate continued the treatment, drop by drop. She noted with pleasure that the little girl was swallowing. However, there was no other movement.

It was not until the next morning that Shona opened her eyes. Kate hobbled to her side and stood over her. Shona had been staring at the rude beams above. When she turned her head and saw the old woman, her eyes flew wide.

Kate gave her a crooked smile and crooned: "It's all right, honey—everything's all right."

The child tried to sit up, but a pain in her head changed her mind. She dropped back and whimpered, "Papa—Shona wants Papa."

Kate smoothed her rumpled golden curls and murmured, "Papa will come, dear. Don't worry. Want some breakfast?" There was no response.

Suddenly, Shona began to cry, a heartbroken wail that would have gone to Kate's heart, at another time.

"Shona sees Papa. He's cy'ing. Mama's cy'in, too. Shona mus' go."

Far from being touched, Kate was electrified. Unless she had psychic powers, like herself, one so young could never be aware of another's grief.

More determined than ever to keep the child, Kate reviewed her course of action while preparing breakfast.

"It's all right, dear. Of course, they miss you. They will be here for you, very soon. Try some of this gruel. It has honey in it."

Reassured, Shona suddenly knew that she was hungry, and nothing had ever tasted so good as this.

Meanwhile, Kate had remembered a book of her mother's entitled "Directory of Herbs and Their Uses." She took it down from the shelf, and found what she was looking for.

The procedure for controlling a person called for a skillful blend of rauwolfia and hemp, used in conjunction with something called "Animal Magnetism," as explained by an Austrian doctor, Franz Anton Mesmer.

Kate settled down to study the procedure carefully. It didn't seem to be particularly difficult. She felt no consciousness of wrongdoing; she had saved the child's life. Certainly, she owed nothing to the villagers below. Because of their prejudice, she had been unable to live as other people. Of course, by now, she was not without her own prejudice.

Kate's grandmother came to Johnstown as a widow with a young daughter. After an enraged mob stormed her home, she drowned herself. Kate's mother was reared by God-fearing folk who loved her. Soon after she was married, the populace discovered that she, too, seemed to have psychic powers. They invaded the home, naming the couple "witch" and "warlock," and driving them out of the city.

The happenings which caused these incidents were innocent indeed. A boy, dying of snakebite at her grandmother's door; a child succumbing to croup in her mother's care, after being neglected for too long . . . These were simple tragedies which sometimes befall even the most virtuous.

At any rate, Kate had no allegiance to anyone in the valley below, and the loneliness for which she blamed them had been almost unbearable, at times. When the child had gone to sleep, she thought of these things, and knew that she was justified.

* * *

FIFTH

Kate found Shona quite suggestible. She accepted the fact that Kate was her mother, and that all was well. With only an occasional twinge of headache, she was able to get up and run around.

Now, she began to enjoy the white rabbit, which she dubbed "Squee," for no special reason.

Today, she was tagging after Kate as she prepared supper.

Kate had been cutting up vegetables for a "Potage du Jour," a meal in itself. She had eaten sparingly in these latter days of her life, but now, she was cooking for a growing child, doubly thankful that she had a large vegetable garden.

She paused. The soup should have been allowed to stand overnight, but there was no time. Shona was at her side.

"What's that?" She pointed at the kettle which Kate was hanging over the fire.

"That's our supper. It's soup. Do you like soup?" Kate gave the mixture a little stir.

Shona frowned. "Don't know soup."

Kate stooped to kiss her. "You'll like this soup, I promise." Shona drew away, questioning. "What's your name?"

"I'm Kate. Can you say that?"

She smiled. "Kate. Now, what's my name?"

Kate sighed. "You're Shona, and you're right here in your house, where you live with me."

She had thought that everything had been cleared up, but there seemed to be some reservations in the child's mind. Besides, she had another worry. How does one keep an active child hidden? She decided that she would have to teach Shona to hide herself if anyone came near the cabin.

That night, Kate remained sleepless, trying to figure out what she could possibly tell the child to impress the importance of this action. In the morning, still thinking about it, she scrambled some fresh eggs from her own hens, and an idea blossomed.

The "animal magnetism" had worked. Why not take it further?

Shona was receptive again, as she had figured. Kate couched her idea in the most elementary of thoughts: bad men might come to take Shona away—she must hide in the big cupboard.

After that, it remained to be seen. Whether or not Kate had achieved her desired aim, would be proved under some particular circumstance.

* * *

Chaos reigned at the MacDonald household. Sophie had taken to her bed and would see no one, except Cassie or Will. At times, she babbled in delirium. Cassie hurried about, bathing her fevered face and arms, and rolling her in wet sheets, as the doctor had recommended.

"You don't have to do this, Cassie," whispered Sophie, one evening. Cassie's white, ruffled cap was askew, her apron was rumpled, and her placid face, drawn.

Cassie patted her hand. "I wish you'd stop talkin' 'bout a nurse. There's plenty of time for more'n jest cookin', 'n I'se sure you don' want no strangers hangin' 'round."

This was one of Sophie's more lucid times. She smiled her gratitude. "Oh, Cassie, you're right. I'd hate having anyone but you trying to keep up my courage. I think I could get up right now..."

"Jest wait a bit, Miz Sophie. It's almost time for bed. In the mornin' I'll he'p you, 'n we'll see about sittin' in the chaise."

Cassie felt relief—perhaps her patient was really going to be well. Yet, she knew there were hopes in Sophie's mind which were only fancies.

* * *

As for Plato, the fourth member of the household, he alternated between worry, work, and staying out of Will's way. Desperately, he needed a formula to placate a man torn between solicitude for his wife and raving anger at the world.

There was no news about Shona. The second kidnapper had recovered, and was in jail. His protestation of innocence was credible in one respect: he had no idea of what had happened to the child.

Meanwhile, Will had identified the dead man as Sam Gaylord, whom he had fired several months before for petty larceny. The police had established that the two men were the kidnappers, and the miner's shack bore mute evidence.

However, there were no other clues. Several times, groups of searchers had combed the area, each probe proving quite as fruitless as the last.

Nevertheless, unsatisfied, MacDonald called some available men on a new quest. This time, it meant climbing an unusually steep section on the opposite side of the hill where Kate's cabin stood.

There were nine of them; MacDonald divided them into three groups, to branch out and meet at the starting place in an hour. He, himself, with two companions set out in a nearly vertical climb to the most inaccessible section of the hillside.

Casting a furtive look over his shoulder, one of his men whispered, "Somewheres up there, they say, the 'Hogback Witch' is supposed to live. I shore don't want nothin' to do with no witches."

"Me neither," mumbled his partner.

MacDonald heard them. He snapped, "What's the matter with you fellows. There's someone livin' up here, and this time, I'm sure as Tophet gonna find out what they know. Go back, if you've a mind to."

Glaring, he continued to lead the way. His timid friends followed meekly. Suddenly, they came to a path leading over the top of the hill.

It was easier going, now, but the men were winded when they reached the log cabin nestled among the pines. They circled the building and discovered a high board fence.

Instantly, MacDonald was skinning up into an enormous maple tree overhanging the wall.

The men followed him. They dropped quietly into the cleared area and made a thorough inspection. Off to one corner was the vegetable garden, its pole beans forming green tents like miniature wigwams. Will stooped to peer into each one. The men looked at each other, and made their way back to the fence.

Kate was completely aware of the search in the garden. It was evident from Shona's behavior. Some time before the men had come into view, she had sensed impending danger and run to the great cupboard for protection.

Smiling to herself, Kate was pleased that her "animal magnetism" had worked so well. When the men reached the front door, she was waiting, the door open wide behind her.

MacDonald approached the cabin with a blustering attitude which faded as he came face to face with the old woman. She stood amazingly erect, her black eyes sharp and cold.

Will stopped short, peering beyond her, into the gloom of the house. "You know anything about a little girl, no more'n a baby, who was kidnapped? We know for sure she was in these parts." His gaze met hers, accusingly.

Kate stepped aside. "You gentlemen have already inspected my garden. If you care to make a search . . ."

MacDonald frowned, and took a step backward. "If she was here, you wouldn't be so all-fired anxious for me to inspect the place. All we want to know is if you can tell us anything."

Kate shook her head. She wanted the men to leave quickly, for she feared that the spell might not hold. Drawing the door a little, she said, "If it's any help to you, I'll go out myself and search. I know these woods better than anyone else."

MacDonald's tension eased a trifle. "We'd appreciate it, ma'am. I'm Will MacDonald—she's my baby. There's a handsome reward for whoever finds her."

Kate viewed the grizzled face. She could see the fear and worry etched in the deep lines around his blue eyes, but she did not soften. Without a trace of sympathy, she watched the group turn away. Troubled, were they? Well, so be it. These high and mighty people in the valley, with their superstitions, deserved to suffer. Maybe it was old Kate's turn to be happy.

She entered the house. Shona was still in the cupboard and did not venture out until Kate opened the door and held out her arms.

The child ran into them, crying, "Shona hide. Did the bad men go away?"

Just for a moment, something gave Kate a twinge of compunction, but she threw it off, settling herself in the rocker with Shona in her arms.

"There, dear, she crooned. "Mother will take care of you.

They won't come back. Shall I tell you a story?" It was an unnecessary question; the child sat up, beaming with anticipation.

"Oh, Mother, please, please," she urged.

Kate frowned a bit at that. "Why don't you just call me 'Kate'? I like that better." She couldn't rationalize the feeling, except that she had encountered a vague sense of gross dishonesty.

Her story was a simple one, about a little girl and a white rabbit, couched in words which her charge could understand. Within her, a fierce, possessive love had come to life; as she spun the yarn, she formulated a plan to be forever safe from search or invasion.

That day, while Shona napped, Kate removed the little pants from her sleepers, and took them far down over the hillside to the edge of a stream. A thorn bush jutted out over the water, and she dragged the garment over it, leaving a jagged piece of material hanging on the bush. Then she threw the torn pants into the stream.

Pleased with herself, she came back to sew a pair of blue overalls for Shona, reflecting on her own cleverness.

However, now it was time to go down into the valley. Doctor Reese had ordered garlic (which he used for poultices and dressings) and thyme for a patient with chronic bronchial asthma. She should have made the trip several days ago.

She hesitated; here was the question of leaving a small child in safety for an hour or so. The house would not do. There were coals in the fireplace—besides, there were too many interesting seeds, plants and roots which might fascinate a child.

Her answer came quickly. At the lower end of the garden, she had constructed a wire enclosure for the purpose of caring for a wounded animal until it could be returned to the forest. The cage was empty now, and clean. Besides, in the corner was a large box of white sand, which she used for scrubbing the plank boards of the cabin. Along with a few dishes, the set-up was ideal for a small child.

Shona was ecstatic: "Shona likes this." Then, she added, as an afterthought, "The bad men won't see me here, will they?"

Kate reassured her. "No one will know you are here. Just don't make any noise, and if you hear anyone calling, keep very quiet. When I come back, I'll bring you into the house to see what I have for you."

Satisfied with her arrangement, Kate turned her thoughts to other things. While she was in the valley, she would steal some clothing for the child. It seemed natural enough to Kate that the people of Johnstown should provide for the little girl. Although it was a somewhat incoherent type of justification, it satisfied her. Perhaps, for the first time in her life, she was content.

* * *

Cassie crept into Sophie's room quietly, wondering whether she should break the news, or whether Will should be the one to tell his wife. She decided on the latter course, all at once sure that she lacked the courage to do it.

Sophie turned her head toward the door as Cassie entered. When she saw Cassie's face, the color drained from her own.

"What is it, Cassie? What's wrong?"

Cassie turned away from her, crossing to the window to fuss with the drapes.

"Nuffin' wrong, Miz Sophie. I reckon I got a bit o' dyspepsia. Don' feel too good . . . no, ma'am." She kept her face away from Sophie's searching gaze.

Not entirely satisfied, Sophie struggled to sit up. "Cassie, will you help me? I'm going to get up."

Cassie rushed to her side. "Oh no, Miz Sophie. You ain't done that yet. Better wait, till . . ."

"I think I've avoided reality long enough," interjected Sophie. "I'm not going to see my baby again, and I certainly can't spend the rest of my life in bed." She cast a penetrating glance at her companion. Let it come, she thought; it's something about Shona.

Cassie helped her to the lounge and plumped the pillows around her. She could restrain it no longer. Big drops began to slide down over her satiny, brown face.

"Don' talk like that, Miz Sophie," she choked. "We'll see our chile again, I jest know we will. I did hear some talk that didn' soun' good, but on the other han' . . ."

"Cassie," rapped Sophie. "Stop beating about the bush and tell me what you've heard. I have a right to know."

"But, Mr. Will, he'll want to be the one . . ."

"Will's staying late this evening. How long do you think I can stand this?"

Cassie looked around desperately, as though searching for an escape. Then, wiping her eyes with a corner of her ruffled apron, she faced her employer.

"They foun' a piece of her nightie," she gasped, sinking to the side of the bed. "I didn' want to tell you—jest didn'."

Sophie whitened again, and a cold feeling came over her. She drew herself up and went to the sobbing girl to sit beside her. "Cassie, stop it. I must hear about this. Where did they find it? Why, just a piece? It could have been torn as they carried her through the brush." Oddly, it was Sophie, the tiny, the weak, who lent the encouragement, trying desperately to face the truth.

Startled, Cassie endeavored to pull herself out of it. "Miz Sophie, you's not strong enough. You shouldn' get upset."

With a trace of impatience, Sophie snapped, "Then don't upset me. Tell me what I need to know. Don't bother to sugarcoat it—just tell me."

Cassie got to her feet and began to fold a blanket aimlessly. "Well," she began, not looking at Sophie, "they foun' this piece of pink cloth on a bush by," she gulped, "by the side of a stream. Then, they foun' some more of it about a half-mile farther on, caught on a stone."

Sophie had been listening, determined not to become emotional. She gazed at Cassie's mournful face for a moment, and the cold feeling returned. Cassie's face, the bedspread, the room—all seemed to blur into one gray mass, and she fainted.

* * *

When the news was broken to Will, he did not, as one might have expected, explode. What he felt was a deep despondency, a slipping away of the powerful hope which had been sustaining him, day after anxious day. He said nothing, but put on his hat and took off for the home of Zeb Walker, the search party leader. There, the story was corroborated. Zeb tried to be comforting.

"That fine stuff could tear easy, Will. Don't mean that the baby—that the baby . . ."

Having ignored the invitation to be seated, Will paced the floor. "That the baby—what, Zeb? That the baby's dead? You know damn well that's what you think, and all the others, too. Well,l I ain't one to give up so easy. Mebbe someone jest wanted us to think that . . ."

It was his friend's turn to interrupt. "Will, we must face it. The kidnappers lost the little one, and probably, that poor lost child wandered off and fell into the stream."

His words, so calm and reasonable, struck clear, cold panic to Will's heart. Without another word or backward glance, he opened the door and stalked out, slamming it behind him.

Zeb spoke to his wife, who was knitting in a rocking chair by the stove. "Lord, I feel sorry for that man."

She nodded, shifting her needles. "We never had no kids, Zeb, and maybe it was God's blessing. I don't think I could take a thing like that."

* * *

SIXTH

Days were long and sunny for Shona. She helped gather peas and beans in the garden, collected eggs, and tried to train her rabbit, Squee.

With the advent of the hunting season, Kate began to make daily searches of the forest for wounded animals. In a week, she had collected a raccoon and a fawn.

Shona was puzzled. "Why did the bad men hurt the doggies?" she asked.

Kate smiled. "I guess they're just bad men. Don't worry, dear. Kate will fix them up."

She was as good as her word. Larger animals were kept in the enclosure, for mutual protection of plant and animal life; smaller ones, in roomy cages set in the garden.

After suturing, or removing pellets, Kate anointed most of the wounds with garlic poultices. Shona's assignment was to feed the animals and watch that wrappings were not chewed off.

By winter, Shona knew the names of all the animals. They had been treated and sent on their way, with no casualties. Only Edgar, the crow, given his freedom many months before, continued to return to the cabin for his daily handout. He would stay for an hour or two, exploring the house and squawking approval. Sometimes, he permitted Shona to stroke his shining feathers, as he gobbled the corn.

With the passing of winter, Kate began to transform the log cabin into a home. She made up pretty flowered curtains and a tablecloth to match, buying some material when she visited Dr. Reese in May. In June, she took some of her dried cooking herbs to Jamie Burns, who ran a grocery and provision store on Washington Street.

Kate felt justifiable pride in her collection. There was no other source of herbs so complete anywhere near the city of Johnstown. Today, she had sage, tarragon, basil, marjoram, chives, parsley, oregano and caraway.

Jamie gave her a toothless smile, and tucked a small, extra bag of flour into her basket. He liked Kate, and if it had not been that he was a bit afraid of her, she might have had a suitor on her hands.

"Company comin'?" he grinned, folding the flowered pink material she had chosen for Shona's dress. Kate glared at him. "If a body wants to improve her situation, what business is it of anyone else?" she snapped, testing a piece of cream-colored leather which was exceptionally soft. She was formulating a solution to the problem of shoes for Shona. Moccasins, of course. Comfortable, soft, and ideal for growing feet.

She bought the leather, and paid for her purchases from a long, red reticule, structured like an oriole's nest. There was little to pay; Jamie had been generous.

He wanted to talk now; there had been times when she had stopped to chat, but this was not to be one of them. She arranged her purchases in her basket, tucked the muslin cover in carefully and hurried out, to the bewilderment of the storekeeper.

Jamie began stacking boxes on a shelf. Not good for people, living alone. One had a tendency to get peculiar. He thought of his own solitary state, and wondered whether he, too, seemed odd to those who came in contact with him.

***

Kate arrived home with her purchases, including a small set of gilt-edged dishes and a blue vase to hold Shona's constant offering of flowers. Things were strangely quiet. There were no coals in the fireplace now, so Shona should have been in the house.

Kate took off her bonnet, hung it by its looped ribbons on a hook behind the door, and threw her shawl on the bunk.

"Shona," she called. There was no response. She crossed the room to the side door leading to the garden and opened it. "Shona." she called again, more anxiously.

Squee came hopping up to her, then passed her by and went into the house. Kate made a tour of the winding path, down through the bushes to the vegetable garden, around the animal enclosure and across to the chicken coop. There was no sign of Shona.

Puzzled and alarmed, she went into the house and found Squee sitting beside the cupboard door. She hastened to open it. There in a small, unconscious heap, lay the child.

Thinking that she might be asleep, Kate patted her face, but she did not waken. The old woman gathered her up and carried her to the bunk. Then she hurried to her herbs for help. Down over their various attributes she went: basil, caraway, chervil, sage . . . That was it! Sage, salvia—the cure-all. "How can a man die, if he have sage in his garden?" She hastened to brew a concoction, and put a few drops between Shona's lips. There was no response.

Kate tried again, and again. Cold dread clutched at her, and there was a strange tightening in her chest. For a moment, she feared that she, herself, would die, leaving the child to an uncertain fate. She sank into the rocker, lifted the cup she was holding, and took a drink of her own medicine. She breathed deeply; gradually the knot in her breast loosened, and her dizziness abated. She got up to try again.

This time, Shona's lips moved. She opened her eyes wide, with a frightened look, and struggled to sit up.

Kate took her in her arms and returned to the rocker. She was weak, and the child was heavy, but amazing strength was returning to her.

Tears filled Shona's eyes. "There were bad men out there. They hurt a nice turkey. I think it's dead."

Kate was impressed. She couldn't help wondering how Shona could know that the shot had found its mark. She soothed the child. "Perhaps the men were hunting food for their families, dear. Don't you know—sometimes we eat one of our chickens?"

The little girl stared at her. She had never seen Kate kill anything, and couldn't understand.

"Listen to me," explained Kate. "Every living thing has to eat something to live. Even if one eats nothing but vegetables, it's often necessary to kill the plant to get food."

Shona was taken aback. "But you take care of animals, you don't shoot them."

"Of course," agreed the old woman. "It's wrong to allow a creature to suffer, if one can do something about it."

She knew that a discussion of ethics was impossible, but her mind was on something else. The cupboard lacked air space, but there was no need for Shona to hide, now. The house and the yard were secluded, and the only hot coals were in a small, pot-bellied stove, used in summer.

She had the problem though, that undoing her mesmerism might be difficult.

Later, she had no idea whether or not she had succeeded in reversing the spell. Then a solution came to her, that could solve it if she had been unsuccessful.

She got an auger out of her father's tool chest and began to drill small holes through the lower part of the door, in an almost artistic fashion. This section of the cupboard had a relatively slim door, and was constructed of soft pine.

Shona watched with interest. "Why are you doing that?"

"I'm making the door pretty."

"I don't think it's pretty."

Kate gave her a beatific grin. "Wait until you see the nice design."

After a tiring half-hour, she got up from the floor and inspected her handiwork. It wasn't too bad. Maybe she had some hidden talent.

Pleased with herself, she swept up the sawdust and took Shona on her lap for a story.

* * *

That year, the second Christmas without Shona came to the MacDonald house with no voluntary attention. Even so, the frequent strolls of carolers sent the convalescing Sophie back to bed with sudden headaches, and set Will to storming.

Not daring to use Christmas wrappings, Cassie had placed little knitted gifts on the dinner table, and fled. Later, Sophie had drawn her aside and pressed ten silver dollars in her hand.

"Don't say anything to Will, Cassie. Just tell Plato I have something for him too. Tell him to come in before Will gets back."

For Will had gone again, spending his holidays like his Sundays, tramping the woods. He always returned in a dark mood, and retired early.

That night, Sophie sat at her window, watching the icy stars in a black void until sheer weariness overtook her. She fell asleep, sitting bolt upright.

* * *

Springtime in Johnstown came awake as usual, with promise and beauty. Peach, pear, cherry and apple trees in nearly every yard, perfumed the air with their pink or white blossoms, and the hillside, too, misted with them. Here was pink and white dogwood, wild lilac, and the pale yellow-green of a profusion of maples.

Both Will and Sophie missed the beauty, however. Spring showers brought mud and dampness, and somewhere in the warm, pregnant earth lay a secret too terrible to bear.

There was some gray in Will's hair now, and Sophie's once clear blue eyes were ravaged and sunken by tears. Cassie, herself a bit drawn, attempted vainly to bring some cheer to the devastated household.

"There's a robin, buildin' a nest above the kitchen window," she announced cheerily, one morning.

Will put down his copy of *The Johnstown Democrat*. "Tell Plato to take it down."

"Oh, but Mr. Will . . ."

"Have him take it down, I say. Now!"

Cassie subsided. When Will had stalked out of the house, she explained to Sophie, "I thought it would be nice to watch the little ones; you can see directly over from your bedroom window."

Sophie gave her a vague, melancholy smile. "Do as he says, Cassie. This isn't a happy home for little ones, anyhow. They'll find another place."

Cassie found it difficult to sleep, that night. All her solutions had been exhausted, all efforts to bring things back to normalcy, had failed. The burden was too heavy. She waited until she heard Plato snoring, then got out of bed and knelt beside it. This is what she had been taught to do. How could she have forgotten?

* * *

May of 1878, perhaps, bloomed a fairer lady in the woodlands than in the city below. May apples spread their small umbrellas over the forest floor. Above them, wild fruit blossoms competed with each other, and small crystal streams gurgled under graceful yellow willow branches.

This was Shona's sixth birthday. She sensed that it was a special day—also that it would mean something to her. Here, in a rare trek into the woods with Kate, it seemed that the beauty around her had been spread for her benefit.

Kate had discovered a formula for changing Shona's hair from its golden color to a dark brown. She regretted her action, but it was necessary.

She watched the child's joy in silence. Within her, a great struggle was going on. Her deed could never be rectified—nor could it be absolved by giving up the little girl. In that case, she would be tried and convicted of kidnapping. With her reputation as a witch, death would be inevitable.

Kate brought herself up, sharply. How could she have even considered giving up the child. She would rather forfeit her own life.

* * *

Shona's penchant for clairvoyance grew stronger each year. Kate gloried in it. "I may not be a full-fledged witch, my dear," she told Shona one day, "but you're going to be. I see the signs."

She looked at the old woman, wide-eyed. The witches I read about are bad. I don't want to be a witch."

"You can be good, child—if you're a white witch."

"What's a white witch?"

"She's a person who does only good for people, who heals illnesses and helps get rid of troubles."

"I'd like that," Shona observed. That's what you do for the animals. When I grow up and you grow down, I'm going to take care of the animals, and of you, too. (She had persisted in the notion that the aging process worked in reverse, after a time.)

Kate proved to be an apt teacher. She had begun teaching Shona to read and cipher at the age of three, charmed by the child's natural intelligence. While Kate was cooking, Shona would spell out the long words she encountered.

"What's p-e-r-s-e-c-u-t-i-o-n?" she asked, looking up from an ancient book, *Demonology and Witchcraft*.

"Persecution. That's a number of cruel things that were done to witches when the leaders of the church decided that all witches should be wiped out."

"Would they per-se-cute the good witches, who helped people?"

"Those, too. It's like this," said Kate, tossing a heap of bread dough on the table. "When the white witches heal someone, the churches claim that's the work of the Bad Man. They say that this is to make people turn to him, instead of to the Good Man. So, there must not be any witches at all."

Shona digested this. Kate kneaded the dough and put it into a wooden bowl. She covered it with a white cloth and set it on the top of the stove.

Then she looked at Shona, sprawled on the bunk of her stomach and saw the book. She came over and took it away. "Get something lighter, child. This is nothing for you to worry your little head over."

The child sat up and put her hand to her head. "How did

you know about my head?"

"What do you mean? Kate stopped halfway to the bookshelf.

"It hurts. Something's going to happen." She ran to the door and opened it, peering down the shaded path.

Alarmed, Kate hurried over to close the door. This new action of Shona's—going to the door, when she sensed danger—worried her. For the first time, she spoke sharply to the child.

"Get away from this door. If there's danger, and you feel it, why would you open the door? Go to the garden and stay there until I call you."

Crushed, Shona obeyed. This time, she hadn't been fearful. A strange bond had seemed to reach out to her. Now she felt a sense of loss.

Actually, exposure had been closer than Kate had imagined. Along with his friend, Brewster, Will MacDonald had decided to make a different call on the "Hogback Witch." Someone had spread the rumor that the woman had extraordinary power, with an insight into both past and future.

Although Will claimed he didn't "hold with such stuff," he retained a childlike hope of finding out something —anything—about his little girl.

They were nearly up to the cabin, when a pang struck Will in the chest. Jim sympathized, "Must be indigestion. Let's sit down here for a while." But the pain did not ease. His discomfort became so intense that he had to move. With Jim supporting him, they crept back down the mountain.

* * *

Shona gloried in Kate's library. Her fantasy world began with Perrault's FAIRY TALES, which she had discovered in a large box. There was also a book of AESOP's FABLES, and several versions of the doings of the Knights of the Round Table, and life in King Arthur's court. All of these impressed her greatly.

Later, she found TALES OF THE ROMANS, a pagan book, which Kate found, too late, that she couldn't approve.

Feeling guilty about neglecting all spiritual training, she presented a POCKET BIBLE FOR LITTLE MASTERS AND MISSES, filched from a local book store.

"It's for you, she announced pleasantly, handing the simplified Bible to Shona. I think it's time to know more about the Good Man, than just to pray, 'Gentle Jesus, meek and mild . . .''

Eager for any book, Shona beamed. Some time later, she crossed the room and put the Bible in Kate's lap. "It's not very interesting."

She realized that Kate was annoyed, but decided to ask,

anyway. "Why don't we ever go to church?" Suddenly, she wondered why she had always been hidden.

Kate made no response. Instead, she reached for the fairy tale book on the table. "Shall I read you a story?"

Still wondering, Shona agreed. Nevertheless, she couldn't seem to keep her mind on the tale. Now occupied with a great conundrum, it kept returning—there was no answer.

* * *

In two more years, Shona was eight. Squee was gone and she didn't want another pet. Routinely, she did chores, collecting eggs, cleaning cages, and helping with feeding and treatment of wounded creatures. Evenings, however, always found her with a book.

The child had grown so swiftly that Kate had difficulty in keeping her in clothing and in shoes. She was taller now, and exquisite, with golden curls framing a delicate face. Today, she was wearing her new white pinafore, with the lace trimming. Kate admired her, not noticing that the brown dye had washed off.

For a long time, Shona had been thinking—pondering her life, and her cramped existence. There was the scent of autumn in the air. She stared at the red-yellow flare of a giant maple, above the animal pen, but did not see it. Suddenly, she ran back to the house.

"Something's happening," she told Kate, who was snapping string beans. She crossed to the front door and opened it. "I must go and see."

Kate put the pan down and jumped to her feet. "Shona, you know better than this. You know you mustn't go out, if you feel danger. Please go to the garden."

Shona winced and backed away from her, blue eyes wide. Putting both hands to her head, she threw herself on the bunk.

Kate went to her and laid a hand on her shoulder. "Shona, I didn't mean to be harsh. What in the world is so pressing that you want to go out there?"

Shona sat up, her eyes pleading. "Kate, there's a man out in the woods. He's in trouble; we must help him."

"We want nothing to do with men. You know that. Let him get out of his own trouble." Kate's face drew longer, and pallor showed through her leathery tan.

"But, Kate, you don't understand. He's hurt. I think he's hurt enough to die, if we don't help."

Kate locked her jaw and went to scrape the flour from her bread board. "You know these men don't care about animals," she flung back, "so why should we care about them?"

The old woman hated what she was doing, but she couldn't risk having someone from the valley see the child. For four years, the story had been spread in Johnstown about Shona's unsolved disappearance, and newspapers had carried her picture and description. It would be easy to figure out who she was.

Kate decided she couldn't risk it. But, suddenly, Shona wasn't on the bunk. She was at the front door, again.

"Shona, don't . . ." cried the woman, but the little girl had slipped up the latch and was gone.

Panic clutched the old woman. Leaving the door wide behind her, she traveled down the steep path after the child as quickly as she could, holding her long, brown dress up out of the way as she ran.

Shona was fleet, and had already disappeared behind a tangle of bushes. When Kate finally arrived at the spot where Shona had stopped, she discovered a groaning youth, scarcely more than a child. His body was twisted oddly, face and shoulders turned toward them, but his left foot, caught in the teeth of a great, round bear trap, lay doubled under him, in the other direction.

Kate sank to the ground near him and helped him shift his body to a more comfortable position, but she could do nothing with the trap.

"Go up to the house, Shona, and get the poker. Hurry, child," she commanded, all her instincts alert to preserve this man, for some unfathomable reason.

Shona was off like a deer. Kate surveyed the situation. Where the trap gripped the trouser-leg, dark wetness saturated the cloth, brown on the shoe, red-brown on the May-apple leaves where it had run. She knew it was a nasty wound. Possibly, the leg was mangled beyond help.

He moaned again, more faintly. Seeing his smooth, girlish face, and the brown ringlets framing it, she thought what a shame it would be if he should be doomed, at best, to life with a wooden leg. Well, not if she could help it. Oddly, she forgot her fear.

Soon, Shona was back, dragging the poker, her face pink with exertion. "I got it, Kate. Can you get him out, now?" She pushed it into Kate's hand, and turned confident eyes to the old woman.

For only a second, she wavered—then she set to work with the poker, prying the steel jaws apart with all her strength. As she managed to haul the torn leg away from the trap, the young man shuddered and fainted.

"We must get him to the house," muttered Kate, half to herself. "I can't treat him here."

"But, Kate, how can be get him to the house? We can't carry him."

"Of course, we can't. Don't you think I know that?" Kate snapped.

Shona couldn't understand the new Kate. Never had she been anything but kind and loving; this irritable tone of voice was all wrong. Tears blurred her vision as she listened to Kate's plan.

"Go back and bring two bean poles from the garden. After you've brought them, you can get that brown blanket in the cupboard. We'll need five pieces of hemp, too. Make them about this long (she indicated length with her hands) and don't cut yourself with the knife. I'd rather not have you bring the knife to me. You might fall on it." Suddenly, Kate's voice was gentle.

Shona blinked away the tears and smiled. Kate wasn't angry at her. With a bound, she was off, rejoicing in the fact that her job was so necessary.

After constructing the rude litter, it wasn't too difficult to roll the young man onto it. He was slightly built, although fairly tall. Kate and Shona managed to move the litter a foot or so with every tug, but the woman's strength was ebbing fast. Many times, she had to sink to the ground to rest.

Impatient, Shona tried to take over, but to no avail. "I can't even move him, Kate. Isn't that awful?" Perspiration dampened her red-gold curls.

"I know you can't, dear. You're not strong enough. Just give me a breather now and then; we can make it." Kate was strangely pale, and her breath came in gasps.

It was farther than she had indicated. She never knew how they made it to the cabin, but at last, the patient was inside, and the door was bolted.

Without letting herself think about later complications, Kate set about boiling chervil root. The young man was beginning to stir. When the broth had been made, she sipped a bit of it herself, feeling stronger almost at once.

She turned to Shona, who was staring, wide-eyed at the tourniquet which Kate had ripped from her petticoat. It was soaked with blood, as was the torn trouser leg.

Kate saw the look. "Go out to the henhouse and collect the eggs, Shona."

"But Kate, it's not time, yet," protested the child.

A bit of Kate's irritability returned. "I have a reason for wanting the eggs. Will you go, or not?"

Shona flew off, fearing her displeasure.

While she was gone, Kate gave her patient his medicine and set about cutting off the trouser leg. The sight which she had spared Shona was a sickening one, often seen in caring for her animals. White bone of the leg showed through a mangled mass of bloody pulp, and she had to attempt to clean and re-place the flesh. Her one thought was to dress the wound while there was still a chance of saving the leg. She cleaned it as well as possible with alcohol, and applied a garlic poultice.

The young man, who had revived for a few moments, fainted again. Shona, entering with a basket of eggs, frowned. "Why does he sleep so much, Kate? You wouldn't think he'd be so tired, in the daytime."

There was no answer. Kate was tearing more long strips of muslin and wrapping the leg with a firm and expert hand. "We'll have to make him a bed on the floor, child. First, bring me that 'hap' at the far end of the bunk; then get me some clean straw."

Shona obeyed with alacrity. Together, they padded the straw, wrapping it in Kate's heavy, knotted bedspread. The child had always enjoyed helping—this was even better. She had found the man. He was really her own project.

An hour later, the patient opened his eyes again. "You must think I'm a baby," he said, trying to smile. "I guess I've never been hurt that much before. I never thought anything could be so painful."

"It was bad," agreed Kate. "And it may get worse. But I have some pain-killer which will help. Want some, now?"

He nodded, gratefully, and accepted the potion.

"I guess I should tell you something about myself," he said.

Looking at his boyish face, drawn with pain, Kate replied gently, "It doesn't matter who you are. All that's important is that you stay quiet and give that mangled leg a chance to mend. Don't waste your strength."

She helped him move to the bed placed near him, and at last, he dropped off into a natural sleep.

The next day, Kate did some more planting. She left Shona to sit with the patient, who had identified himself as Michael Stewart, but had given no other details of his background. Kate was no longer worried; she had a plan.

Shona enjoyed playing nurse, immensely. She offered Michael sage tea until he could drink no more, and fluffed his pillows with regularity. He bore it pleasantly, in gratitude.

Not being able to think of anything more to do, she came and stood over him. "Shall I get a book? If you want me to, I'll read to you. I read very well, Kate says."

Michael smiled at the little girl with the blue-green eyes and golden curls, and loved her. "I'd like that, Shona."

Immediately, she brought the book which had so fascinated her, but was forbidden. She dropped it to the floor beside him and sank, cross-legged, next to it.

Michael scanned the title, and frowned. Of course—why hadn't he thought of it before? This was the home of the "Hogback Witch."

Shona saw the frown and knew the trend of his thoughts. "It's all right, Michael. Kate's a white witch; she does only good. It's men who are bad . . ." She hesitated. "I don't mean you, Michael. You're not bad, are you? I mean, you don't kill things, do you?"

Seeing the pleading look in her eyes, he knew that he would never hunt again. He thought of his rifle, lying somewhere out there in the forest, and hoped that she would never connect it to him.

"Shona, I swear to you that I shall never kill anything, unless it's by accident. Does that make you feel better?"

She smiled at him and smoothed his brown curls. "Are there any other good men down there in Johnstown? Kate says all men are bad."

"Kate's . . ." He changed his mind and fell silent. This child with the red hair must be the blonde baby which had been abducted some years ago. How many years was it—about four or five? Of course, the witch must have done it. The men, who were said to be involved, must have been innocent. How could she have kept such a secret—and for so long.

An uneasy thought struck him. Kate had been good to him, up to now, but could she turn him loose to tell what he had seen? A cold sweat broke out on his brow.

Shona had forgotten her question. She was reading the cure for toothache:

"Galbus, galbat, galdes, galdat,
Galbus, galbat, galdes, galdat."

She looked up from the book. "Do you have a toothache?"

"No," he smiled, trying to forget his worry.

"See," she said, triumphantly, "it worked."

His twisted grin bore little resemblance to his usual, bright smile. He raised himself on one elbow, and shoved up his pillow.

Shona was at his side immediately, supporting him as she had seen Kate do, and pushing his pillow into place. "I'm going to be a nurse when I grow up," she told him. "Kate's an animal doctor—maybe I'll be an animal nurse."

He tried the smile again, this time, succeeding. "How did you come to live with Kate? She's too old to be your mother."

Shona's eyes widened. "But she *is* my mother. All the children in books have mothers, except orphans, and I'm not an orphan. Kate said so. I belong to her."

Michael grasped Shona's hand. "Shona, you don't belong . . ."

"Yes, she does," broke in a voice from the back doorway. There, straight and tall, stood Kate, her black eyes flashing. "I don't want to hear that kind of talk from you again." She scowled, crossing to the fireplace to hang a bundle of leaves. "Shona is mine, and we're happy. If you want our help, you'll respect our hospitality."

Michael quailed, but persisted, "Kate, you can't get away with this forever. Can't you see that?"

"We won't discuss it," she snapped. "Shona knows she's mine. I won't allow you to put wrong ideas into her head."

Actually, she was not alarmed. Obviously, her plan should soon be put into action. However, it was time to transplant the basil; meanwhile she must think of a way to keep Shona busy as she worked on Michael.

She took Shona with her, to help with the planting. As they

were working, she suddenly began to smile.

Shona looked up and caught it. "What did I do?"

"Not a thing, dear," laughed the old woman. "I just remembered that basil must be planted with curses, and I was thinking what aa poor witch I am. I don't know any curses."

Shona's face fell. "If you don't, the basil won't grow. I'll get the book, right away."

"No, child," Kate explained. "There's no need to worry. The basil's been doing fine for me for many years. That just goes to show how much there is to witchcraft. Don't let them tell you . . ."

She bit her lip. Why was she feeling that, somehow, others would take custody of the child? Strangely, she felt ill again; she fought it off.

"Come," she said to Shona. "I'm going to stir up some pancakes for supper. You can drop them."

The next day, Kate concentrated on finding a garden job for Shona, to keep her out of the way while she worked on Michael. He seemed to be restless. It occurred to her that someone would be looking for him.

The idea set her in a panic. She dropped into the rocker, her heart pounding, and a strange pain shooting from her chest into her shoulder and down her left arm. She took a deep breath and gasped, "Shona—the sage tea—can you bring me some?"

Shona, who had been showing a book to Michael, jumped to her feet and ran to get a cup. Pouring the tea from the cracked, earthen pot, she brought it to Kate, and held it for her. Kate's hands were shaking.

She sipped the tea, leaning her head against the back of the chair. Her worries had intensified. Although she had planned to mesmerize this young man, she had not reckoned with the fact that he could influence the child. The additional worry about searchers, brought an apprehension which affected her whole body.

Shona gave her attention to Kate, now. For supper, she had prepared watercress sandwiches, but Kate could eat nothing. She drank another cup of tea, and asked Shona to bring her pillow, so that she could sleep in the chair.

The child was alarmed. Her head felt as though it would burst, and she had trouble in keeping alert. She wanted to throw herself on the bunk and cry, but that was out of the question. An omen of impending disaster cloaked her in gloom. She knew what it was, and shuddered as she tucked in Kate's pillow and stroked her hair.

Without a word to Michael, Shona escaped into the garden, where he could not see her cry. That night, she lay for hours, trying to penetrate the darkness above her, for a great evil hung there.

Morning dawned, gray and foreboding, sending a shaft of

light across Shona's face from the outer edge of the heavy curtain at the window. She wakened instantly from troubled sleep, and sat up in the bunk.

In the shadows, she could see Kate, still sitting in the chair. She scrambled down and went to the old woman, grasping the gnarled hand which clung to the rocker arm. It was stiff and cold. Shona jerked away, and the rocker swayed, crashing forward with Kate in the same, unnatural, rigid position.

Shona screamed, and Michael sat up immediately. He took in the scene at a glance. Shona had shoved the rocker aside and, sobbing, had thrown herself over Kate's inert body.

Michael crawled to her and tried to pull her away, but she turned on him in anger.

"I hate you. You upset her and made her sick. Why don't you get out of here and let us alone?"

"Shona, Kate's dead. You know I can't walk, so you'll have to go down to the city and bring help." His practical remark made no impression. She sobbed on, prostrate over the dead body.

He couldn't bring himself to anger; grief had overwhelmed the child, but for the moment, he was helpless and frustrated.

When her crying had abated, Michael decided to try again. "Shona," he said, with quiet firmness, "listen to me."

She raised her head and blinked at him through tears.

Encouraged, he proceeded, "Shona, you know what must be done when something, or someone, dies."

Horror showed in her eyes. Looking straight at him, she began to cry anew, tears streaming over her flushed cheeks.

"No, I won't let them put Kate in the ground. She's mine."

She threw herself over Kate's body again, and went into another paroxysm of grief.

Michael waited. She finally quieted, raising herself from the body. No matter what, he had to continue. He spoke in a calm, authoritative voice.

"Shona, there are good men, as well as bad ones. You must go for help, and you must do it now. Kate would expect you to take charge."

He had not been sure that she was listening, but at his mention of Kate, she straightened up, and brushed away her tears.

"She would?"

He nodded, gratified at his small victory, almost afraid to continue.

"What should I do? I don't know anybody."

This was a poser. At seventeen, Michael's sole experience with tragedy had been the death of a beloved dog. He thought for a moment, then spoke carefully.

"Go straight down the path and through the woods to the cleared land. Just below, there are two houses. Stop at one of them, knock on the door, and ask them to help you find a policeman, who will know what to do. The policeman will be one of the good men I'm telling you about."

She knew about policemen, and was comforted. She hadn't known that there were policemen in the valley. Getting to her feet, she looked at the figure on the floor, and then at Michael. "Are you sure this is right?" she whispered.

"Yes Shona, I'm sure. Don't be unhappy; Kate was a very old lady, and God was ready for her. She'll be well, now, and some day you can see her again." He saw her face clouding, and hastened to continue. "Right now, dear, it's important to take care of her. Do you understand that?"

Nodding, she went to the screen in the corner to use the wash basin to bathe her flushed, tear-streaked face. She came out, dressed in a clean pinafore, cast one loving, despairing look at Kate's body, and slipped out of the door.

Michael dragged himself to the overturned rocker and, managing to right it, pulled himself up, into it. Looking down at the still body, he suddenly realized that he was alone—with a dead witch. It was not a comforting thought.

* * *

SEVENTH

Will MacDonald took the last sip of coffee from his white mustache cup, and grasped his napkin, blotting a drop from his tie. Rising, he went around to Sophie's chair and kissed her cheek. She looked up at him in surprise.

He gave her one of his infrequent grins. "Don't know what got into me, Sophie, but I feel good today. Seems as if this is goin' to be a right nice day."

Sophie beamed at him. "It's good to see you like this, Will. Reminds me of the way you used to be, before . . ." She stopped.

His grin disappeared, and he turned away, striding to the hallway, where he snatched his hat from the clothes tree and went out, slamming the door behind him.

Sophie sighed. She had forgotten how careful she must be. Just for a moment, there, she had grasped at the idea that they might have reached a turning point, but now she realized that could not be.

Today, Will would be off again, on his weekly tramp through the hills. He would be grumpy when he returned. He would read the newspaper, and she would continue knitting Cassie's purple shawl. They would retire early, he, undressing in the bathroom, she, under her nightgown. They would crawl into opposite sides of the great bed, after having knelt at its side for a few moments.

It was a monotonous pattern of life for Sophie, broken only by an occasional visit from a friendly neighbor.

As for Will, he was sometimes impatient with his wife, but perhaps, subconsciously, annoyed with himself even more. Some driving force caused his continued treks through the forest; he did not know why. Perhaps finding a set of tiny bones would have put his mind at rest.

It was not a search; he had scheduled for himself a systematic pilgrimage, covering only one area each week. Linked together, he could cover the entire circle of mountains in a year.

Today, he took the horse-car to Moxham, and from there, he intended to cover the hogback mountain, which he had traveled more than a year before.

Will had barely entered the wooded hillside when he heard men's voices and saw a group of about a dozen men, up ahead. He rushed toward them.

The men stared, as he came toward the clearing where they stood. He looked from one to another. "What is it," he gasped. "Is this another search party for some unfortunate child, or . . ."

"It's a search party, all right." The leader, a burly lumberjack in a green jacket, stepped forward. "Three days ago, a young fellow by the name of Michael Stewart disappeared somewhere up here. His Pa and Ma's about crazy. His Pa was hurt in the mill, or he'd be up here, too."

Will nodded. "Believe me, I understand. I'm Will MacDonald; my little girl . . ."

"I remember you, MacDonald," spoke up another man. I'm George Pierce. Remember, I went along with you, once, to see the 'Hogback Witch'? Let's see, that must have been about four years ago."

"Five," Will cut in. "That was right after, after . . ." He couldn't continue.

"Say, MacDonald," the leader said, suddenly. "You know these woods. How about joining us?" As an afterthought, he added, "I'm Zeb Walker. I run the hardware store."

He turned to his men. "Let's go on up to the witch's place and see if she knows anything."

"Not me," piped a slight, blond man, with a long face and a reddish beard. "I was up there once, and I tell you, she gives you the chills."

"Now, look here . . ." Zeb began, then broke off, staring into the woods above them. All eyes followed his gaze.

Running down the hill, dodging the trees and slipping on leaves, came Shona, her golden curls flying. Just as she came in sight, she tripped, and came rolling down the hill to their feet.

Zeb stood her up and brushed clumsily at her blue pinafore. He had a black beard, but kindly eyes, and Shona didn't fear him, as she did the staring group. She clung to his hand and began to cry.

Will MacDonald seemed to be in a stupor. He shook off the idea which had occurred to him. Shona had been blonde, but so tiny . . . there could be no reason to think . . . But the uneasiness persisted. He rushed forward.

"Who are you, little girl? What are you doing in these woods? Don't you know there are wild animals here? What's your mother thinking of, lettin' . . ."

At the mention of her mother, Shona began to sob more bitterly. "My mother's dead. She's up there at the house; I have to get a policeman."

Zeb patted her shoulder. "Don't you worry, we'll take care of things for you. I'll take you with me, but first, we're out to find a young man who's missing. Didn't happen to see someone, did you?"

Shona gazed up at him; she liked him very much. This must be one of the good men.

"Do you mean Michael? He's up at our house. He got caught in a bear trap, and my mother is . . ." she caught herself, "*was* taking care of him."

MacDonald intervened. "Who is your mother, little girl? There ain't no houses in these parts, except that shack where the witch lives."

Shona's blue-green eyes flashed at him. "It's not a shack. It's a beautiful log house, and my mothers' a white witch, not a black one . . ." She broke down again, still clinging to Zeb's hand.

"My God," exclaimed Will, reverently, "It's my Shona. How I've lived for this day." He knelt and tried to take her in his arms, but she backed away.

Shocked, he remained as he was, holding out his hands. "Is that your name honey? Shona? I'm your father; don't you remember Papa?"

She backed to the other side of Zeb. "I don't have a father."

Zeb tried to draw her out. "What's your name, honey? Nobody's going to hurt you. Don't be afraid."

She looked up, trusting him. "My name's Shona, but I don't have a father. I just have Kate . . . I mean, now I don't have Kate any more." She swallowed hard. She mustn't let Zeb see her cry.

He stooped and whispered to her, "This man is your father. He's been looking for you for a long time. He loves you a lot. Go with him now, while we go up and take care of things at your house."

Frightened, she clung to him, but he was disengaging her hand. In a flash, she was off, running back up the hillside to the only security she knew. Now, there was no one she could trust.

In four strides, MacDonald caught up with his daughter and scooped her up in his arms. She fought him with the unnatural strength of fear, using her nails like little claws, and almost succeeding in biting his arm through his plaid jacket.

MacDonald's heart leaped in an odd combination of excitement and uneasiness. His daughter—but had he really recovered the child who had been so completely his? She stopped struggling; he saw the trapped look in her eyes. He set her down, but held tightly to her hand.

Speaking softly, he said, "We're going home, Shona. You got no call to be afeered of me. I'm your Papa; your Mama's been sick ever since that witch stole you."

The men were beginning to mount the hillside. Zeb waved to her, and continued to lead the way.

Shona scanned Will's face, not wanting to trust him. Unaccountably, she decided in his favor. "Kate didn't steal me, she found me. She told me about it, one day. I don't want to live anywhere else. She's my mother."

Will reasoned with her. "Shona, child, she's dead. You can't go back there and live alone. Think of your real mother, and how much she misses you. Don't you want to see her?"

She looked up at Will. "Will you bring me back? We have a baby fox and a sick possum up there. Someone has to take care of them. I have to feed the chickens, too, and gather the eggs."

He promised, glad to be able to strike a bargain so easily.

Thus, they set out for the MacDonald estate—Will a bit uneasy, but encouraged and feeling more like himself than he had in five years, and Shona, a bit apprehensive, yet expectant.

She marveled at the ride in the horse-car, and wondered at the many people, who didn't look at all like Kate. When the pair finally turned in at the gate, something told her that this, indeed, was her home.

* * *

EIGHTH

Cassie held back the heavy, green brocaded drape at the front window, and scanned the sidewalk.

"My laws, Miz Sophie," she exclaimed, "Mr. Will, he got a child by the han'. Now, where do you suppose he picked her up?"

Sophie looked up from the shawl she was knitting as Cassie's birthday gift. Cassie was unaware of the fact, and had praised it with enthusiasm.

"Maybe the child was lost, Cassie. I'm glad he could bring himself to notice it. He's been so hostile to children, ever since . . ." She sighed.

Cassie was studying the approaching pair with a puzzled expression. "It's a l'il red-headed chile, jest 'bout the age . . ."

She smothered a gasp. "Miz Sophie, don' you get excited now. You know that ain't good for yo' heart."

"Why would I get excited? What's wrong with you, Cassie? You look as though you'd seen a ghost." Sophie put the knitting aside and went to the window.

Cassie pointed a trembling finger at the pair entering at the front gate. "It's l'il Shona, that's who it is. Oh, Lordy me, it's our chile." Tears began to stream down her face.

Sophie ran to the front door and threw it open. When Shona saw her, she stopped and drew back, but Will picked her up and rushed up the steps.

"I've found her, Sophie. It's hard to believe, but this is our baby."

With tears in her eyes, Sophie held out her arms, but before Will could reach her, she crumpled in the doorway. Will set Shona down and swung Sophie into his arms. "Take care of her, Cassie," he flung back over his shoulder, indicating Shona.

Cassie stooped and held out her arms. "Yo' Mama goin' to be all right, honey. Come to Cassie—I ain' held you sence you was a baby. You use' to like Cassie, in dem days."

Shona looked at her doubtfully, but kept her distance. "Do you have anything to eat? I'm hungry."

Cassie straightened up and took her hand. "Jest you come out in the kitchen with me, 'n we'll see what's there. I got some fresh-baked bread, and the bes' butter you ever tasted."

Somehow, she reminded Shona of a young Kate, with her deep suntan and slender body. Even now, her kindness and stability gave the child something to cling to.

And so it happened. By the time Will and Sophie had become acquainted with Shona, they were almost outsiders.

Early the next morning, someone rapped at the door. It was Zeb Walker, asking to see the little girl. Shona, already dressed, came up behind Cassie and peeked around.

Zeb gave his message uneasily. He had hoped that she would be asleep, hating to face her. "I just wanted to tell the little lady that everything's been taken care of. The lad's resting in the hospital, and the animals are fine. Both of them were set free, and I'm temporarily taking charge of the chickens, until we know what to do."

Shona came around Cassie, wide-eyed. "But that baby fox," she protested. He's too little to be alone. What will happen to him?"

Zeb grinned. "I wonder if you've taken a good look at that little fellow, lately. He's just about as big as he's going to get."

Relieved, the child smiled back at him. Her confidence in Zeb had returned. She didn't ask about Kate—that was something she didn't want to think about.

After a week, true to his promise, Will took Shona back to the cabin, but the windows were boarded up, and the door was locked. Zeb had given him the key, but he would not enter, until he had some authority to do so.

* * *

Naturally, the news of Shona's return got to the Press. The searchers were full of their own versions of what had happened. One story was that the kidnappers had sold the child to the witch; another, that Kate had been the kidnapper.

Trying to get MacDonald's version, two reporters hung around the house—outside, after a cold reception from Cassie. When Will came home, they pounced on him.

"Tell us about the child. How did you come to find her? Is it true that she's been living with the 'Hogback Witch'? How did she get there? Why was there no sign that the witch had her?"

Maintaining a stony silence, MacDonald pushed his way past them and went on up to the door. He was so infuriated that, later, he would slam the door at the sight of any stranger. At work, upon questioning, he said nothing.

Eventually, Sophie told the story, or as much of it as she knew. Although this was against Will's wishes, she had no choice. The police wanted to know. Of course, the real story never came out—that of Kate's ploy to keep the child. "Animal magneticm" was not a household term.

Neighbors were more or less afraid of Will. Only the chubby, friendly Amanda Davies ventured next door to visit.

"I'm so happy for you, dear," she beamed, taking Sophie's hand. "When can I get to see the child?"

"Shona's upstairs, dressing an old doll of mine," said Sophie, withdrawing her hand. "She's never seen a doll before, and I'm afraid she's quite absorbed. Perhaps, she'll be down in a little while."

Much as she would have liked showing off her lovely child, Sophie hesitated to introduce her to anyone. They would be sure to have questions; no one could be sure how that would work out.

As relieved and happy as the MacDonalds were to have their little girl safe and sound, they were at a loss as to how to handle her. If they were a bit envious of Cassie, there was a certain relief in having someone near to whom the child could relate.

Tiring of the doll, Shona had discovered Plato. At the time of Amanda's visit, she was in the chicken coop with him, helping to feed the chickens. She was in deep conversation with this new-found friend.

"I have—had—chickens, too. I had a special one," she told him, choking a little. "I hope someone's good to her. You could hold her in your hand. She was a Bantam—you know—a tiny chicken."

Plato, a muscular man with an unusually gentle manner, gave

her a smile. "I know jus' where I kin git a Banty fer you."

"You do?" She clapped her hands in delight.

"Yep. Count on it."

Late that afternoon, Plato made good. He tapped at the kitchen door, where Shona was reading to Cassie. (Since her discovery that Cassie was intelligent, she had appointed herself as a teacher.)

"Miss Shona, come on out 'n see what I'se got fer you." Even the sound of his voice was excitement.

She rushed outside. There on the porch, in a small cage, were two beautiful Bantam chickens: the tiny brown hen so small she could almost fit in a child's hand; the rooster a miniature too, with a rainbow tail, a blue-green ruff, and two-inch spurs.

Shona's delight was beyond expression. She breathed deeply. "Oh, may I hold them? Are they really mine? If she lays eggs, may I have them for breakfast?"

Plato was almost equally pleased. He nodded to every question, and she flung her arms around his neck. "No wonder Cassie married you—you must be her Prince Charming." The compliment was agreeable—no one had ever portrayed him in such glowing terms, before.

Several days later, on an exceptionally warm afternoon, a stern lady, with high-piled hair and a pancake hat, came to the door. Shona greeted her; her mother, still in delicate health, was lying down.

The visitor looked down on Shona with disfavor. She had not come to deal with the child, herself. She glared. "I'm Miss Farris Chandler, and I must speak privately to your mother, at once."

Shona's training came into play. She didn't care for this overbearing lady, but it was important not to show it. "Please have a chair. I'll call mother, right away." She hurried upstairs, glad to be leaving.

Sophie entered the room courteously, having been briefed on what to expect. "I'm Mrs. MacDonald. Do you have something to talk about?"

"Indeed, I do. Apparently, your child has never been registered in the free school. Has she been attending a private school?"

"No, Shona has never been registered. We intend to enter her, this Fall, right in this neighborhood. Why, is there some question?"

The woman dropped her business-like facade. "See here, Mrs. MacDonald, we know why the child has never been registered. She has been in an unsavory, heretical environment, and it is our duty to see that whatever injury she has experienced, will be rectified."

Sophie couldn't help bristling. "You're wrong. Shona reads beautifully; she has had training. Nor is she an heretic; she says her prayers each night, without coaching."

Miss Chandler drew herself up. "You need not try to cover for her, Mrs. MacDonald. Here is her appointment card. Unless you want to hear from the school authorities, you'll see that she arrives for testing in the morning."

Sophie didn't trust herself to speak. She accepted the card, and ushered the woman to the door, still not knowing who she was or whom she represented.

* * *

Shona's tests proved, not only that she was up to her grade, but that she was far beyond it. When it became apparent that the problems were too simple, others, more comprehensive, were introduced. Proceeding to the high school level, she did even better.

By this time, Sophie knew Miss Chandler as a representative of the school board. When she came with the test scores, her lips were taut.

"We find Shona to be unusually well-versed in most of the subjects. Therefore, in spite of her age, it will be necessary to enter her in school, in the Fall. She will need to take these papers with her."

With no change of expression, the woman minced out of the door, leaving both Sophie and Shona speechless.

Nevertheless, Shona did not go to school that Fall. She wanted to; other children fascinated her. Only since coming down from the mountain had she actually seen a living child. She had a lot to learn about them.

Clutching Cassie's hand, she was on her way to the provisions store for the first time. Her brain was not acting properly; it surged with anticipation, but was also flashing a danger signal to which she would not give credence.

It was still a thrill for her to view her contemporaries. She tugged at Cassie's hand, urging her on.

"Land sake, chile, don' pull like dat. We's got plenty time to git there."

"But I want to catch up to those little girls," she explained, pointing to a pair ahead, one with long, black braids, the other with two tiny blonde pigtails.

Cassie hastened her step and they caught up.

"Hello," said Shona, eagerly. The pair turned around.

"Oh, hello," said the dark one. "What's your name? I'm Grace, and this is Janie."

Shona looked up at Cassie. "This is my friend, Cassie. I'm Shona MacDonald."

The pair exchanged glances. "Shona MacDonald," they chimed together. Then, with one accord, they caught each other's hands and raced off, as fast as their black-stockinged legs could carry them.

Open-mouthed, Shona stared after them. She had a dark, sick feeling inside. "What's the matter, Cassie? Why did they run away?"

Cassie held her hand more tightly. "Honey, chillen kin be cruel. Don' let 'em bother you, nohow. Seems the word's out that you been livin' with a witch. Folks are afeered of witches."

"But, don't they know she was a white witch? She brought medicine to the town, that helped cure sick people. Don't they know that?"

"Sweet chile, they don' know nothin'; that's why they afeered. People are always skeered of things they don' know about."

The excursion had now lost its excitement; the store meant little. Shona knew that she was scheduled to enter high school, soon. It took no special sense for her to see that she would have trouble.

* * *

It was one of those rare days when Johnstown's air was clear, and the sunrise burst early, in radiant gold. Arrayed for the first day of school, the maple trees were highlighted in red and yellow, arching over the streets.

However, the beauty of the day was lost on Shona. She walked along beside Cassie, grateful that other children, too, were being escorted by mothers or friends. Nevertheless, she planned to leave Cassie before entering the school yard.

The high school was on the upper floor of the building; the playground accommodated all grades. When Shona approached the school, she quailed at the number of children swarming over the grounds.

Shona detached her hand from Cassie's and walked toward the line-up with a smile, but her expression changed at the last second. She had suddenly become aware of danger. A moment later, a small stone hurtled over the heads of several small children and struck Shona on the temple.

She dropped to the ground and lay still, a trickle of blood running down on the bricks. As Cassie rushed to lift her, a teacher appeared to admit the lines.

"What happened," she asked, startled at the whiteness of Shona's face, and the expression on Cassie's.

Cassie glared in the direction of the older children, who were suddenly hushed. "Some young upstart hit this chile with a rock, 'n I'd advise you to to fin' out who. 'Cause, if you don' I will, 'n he'll be sorry he was bo'n, sho' nuff."

Having issued her pronouncement and ultimatum, Cassie turned and carried off her charge with dignity.

The agitated teacher shooed the children indoors, without regard to the formation of lines. She had an idea of the reason for the assault, and had no concept at all of a way to cope with it.

Shona wakened in her own bed, and immediately became unhappy. "Why am I here? Why did you bring me home? I want to go to school. Please, Cassie, I want to go to school."

Cassie' anger had not abated. "Yo' Mama don' lak you goin' to school wif roughnecks. Miz Sophie goin' get you a tutor. If we was to tell Mr. Will, we don' know what might happen, so don' say nothin'."

"A tutor? What's that?"

"A teacher to come to the house," put in Sophie, who had just entered the room. Her dark hair, just washed, lay in damp ringlets, cascading to her shoulders. She was trying to smile, but her eyes were tragic.

As Cassie left with some clothing, Sophie came over and sat at the foot of the bed. Before she could speak, Shona cried, "Oh, Mama, please let me go to school. I want to have friends and be with other children."

She stretched a pleading hand to her mother, who caught it, her eyes brightening with moisture.

"Dear, we're afraid you'll be hurt. The people here in Johnstown have come from nearly every country of Europe. Many of them are quite superstitious. Some of them may be afraid of you."

"Why would anyone be afraid of me? Please, mother."

Sophie sighed, put an arm around Shona, and kissed her. "Whatever your father says," she agreed, feeling guilty. Well did she know what Will MacDonald would say.

For a few days, Sophie avoided telling him what had happened. Meanwhile, she was searching for someone who could tutor the child at home.

Shona soon forgot the school incident. Drying dishes, one day, she remarked to Cassie, "There's something in my house that I want."

"Well, mebbe we kin arrange to git it, chile. What is it?" Cassie was scrubbing the sink.

"It's my book, called DEMONOLOGY AND WITCHCRAFT."

Cassie's jaw dropped. "Somehow don' soun' lak a good kine of book, chile. I don' hol' with no kine of witchcraft."

Shona's blue-green eyes widened. "It's not a bad book, Cassie. It's wonderful. It tells you how to cure all kinds of things. Kate . . ." her voice broke, then recovered, "was a good witch, she fixed up hurt animals, just like the doctor fixed up your cut finger. If you had let me, I could have done it, just like Kate."

Cassie regarded her soberly, turning to carry flowers in to the dining room table. "I sho' hopes you ain' got witchcraft in that li'l head, honey." Shaking her head, she disappeared through the swinging door that hung between the two rooms.

Shona climbed into the big hickory rocker beside the stove, and began to sway gently. Her disappointment at Cassie's attitude gradually gave way to the conviction that she would have a chance to show Cassie some good witchcraft.

Her presentiment was soon fulfilled. That evening, Cassie picked up the teakettle, which had been bubbling on the stove for Sophie's tea. The plaited rug which lay before the stove had been kicked up, and she stumbled, causing the boiling water to slop over her hand.

Tears came to her eyes; she dropped into a chair, clenching and unclenching her fist.

"Bring me that lard, honey," she moaned to Shona, who stood, frozen. At her words, Shona sprang into action.

"We don't need lard, Cassie, I can blow the fire. Let me fix it for you." she implored.

"Chile, I don' want none of that witchery business. Jes' give me the lard, like ah ax you."

But Shona was already at her side, mumbling something that sounded like words from the Bible, and blowing the injured hand.

Fascinated, Cassie watched. Surely, there could be nothing bad in such an angelic child, but then, she had been exposed to . . . She stopped thinking about it, for at the touch of the cool breath on her hand, the pain had melted. The angry-looking scald had subsided, and she could not really be sure that it had hurt so.

She looked down at the golden head bending over her injured hand, and laid the other hand on it.

"Chile," she said in awe, "Ah don' know how or why, but you got some mighty powerful stuff there."

Shona was radiant. "You see, Cassie? I can do it. I can cure people. I told you I could."

It was not until she was in bed that night that an uneasy feeling came to Cassie. Had the child somehow precipitated the accident, in order to show off her skill?

Angry at herself for even that moment of doubt, she turned her back on the sleeping Plato and tried to sleep. In spite of herself, an uneasy feeling kept her awake for a long time. When she finally slept, her rest was troubled.

* * *

When Will discovered what had happened at school, typically, he was furious. He contacted the teachers, the principal, and the school authorities, but it was impossible to discover who had injured Shona.

To add to his anger, one morning, Cassie had discovered strange yellow marks on the stone porch wall, and several on the window.

"It was eggs, Mr. Will. Eggs all over the place. We heard 'em last night, when you was at the meetin', but when we went out, nobody was aroun'."

In high dudgeon, Will went to the police station. Partially soothed by the promise that the house would be watched, he went home to lay down the law.

A tutor would be hired; Shona would not leave the house, except to play in the new sandbox he had bought, or to visit Plato and her pet bantams. Sophie brought up the question of playmates.

"Don't need 'em. I never had playmates. All she needs is right here. She has books, don't she?"

Shona seized on that. "Please, Papa, may I have the books I want from my old house?"

He looked at her, this lovely, porcelain child, with the golden curls, and his pride swelled, as it always had. "You want your books—we'll get 'em. Go with Plato tomorrow, and pick out what you want."

Having settled matters to his own satisfaction, Will was in an amiable mood. He decided that when Shona had what belonged to her, he would hand over the key to the police.

The police, however, didn't want the key. Their view was that Shona, as the sole occupant, owned the house—until claim was made to the contrary. So, the key to the old log house was hung on a hook in the kitchen, and forgotten.

* * *

It was the kitten that started the whole thing. Of course, it was black. That was not clever for a person who was believed to be a witch. But how could an animal lover ignore an adorable kitten with big blue eyes—especially when it cried?

Cassie went along with it. She heated milk for the tiny animal and made a bed for it in the summerhouse. Will never went there; besides, at the worst, he would chase it away.

Shona was sitting on the porch steps with the kitten, when a little girl with short, curly brown hair saw her. She came over and sat down on the steps.

"My name's Alice; what's yours?"

Shona hesitated. She remembered the other girls' reaction to her name. "My mother calls me 'Honey,' she hedged. You can call me that."

Alice was not to be put off. "That isn't your real name, is it?"

She gave up. "Well, no; it's 'Shona,' but I'm not a witch—you don't have to be afraid."

You don't look like someone to be afraid of. I like you. Can I play with you?"

And so they became friends. Alice showed her how to play

jacks and rummy; they played in the sandbox and played "house" on the porch. Saturday was the only day Alice was free to play.

The tutor, Sten Weston, gave Shona daily play hours. From eight o'clock until noon, her time was her own. After lunch, there was study time, which didn't end until suppertime. It was a long day, but Shona loved studying.

This particular Saturday morning, Alice was showing Shona how to jump rope. She caught on swiftly, but Alice was distressed by her lack of agility. She must be shown.

Now, Alice, the expert, was counting: One hundred three, one hundred four, one hun . . ." She clutched at her chest.

"I have a pain. I'm not supposed to jump rope. The doctor says I have something called 'leakage of the heart.' "

Shona was alarmed. "Then, why do you do it?"

"Because, I . . ." Alice fainted.

Shona stood undecided for a minute. She didn't know which house Alice lived in. It was strange—she had not perceived any warning.

As she hesitated, holding her kitten, two women rushed up and came in at the gate. One woman stooped to the prostrate child. "My Lord, I think she's dead. What have you done?"

The other woman grasped Shona's arm. You won't get away with this, do you hear?"

Frozen, Shona felt too much emotion to notice threats.

"Please, get Alice's mother. I don't know where she lives."

By this time, Cassie had rushed out, and a crowd was gathering. "What's going on, here?" came a voice from the rear, and Zeb Walker pushed his way through.

Several people began to talk at once. "It's that girl, the witch-child. She's put a hex on this little girl . . ." "She oughtta be . . ." "Why don't they put her away, she . . ." "We knew it all the time . . ."

Zeb reached Shona, who stood motionless, Cassie's hand on her shoulder, clutching the black kitten. He nodded to Cassie, and faced the crowd.

"Why don't some of you idiots get the child's mother? You don't make sense, blaming someone for an illness and maybe causing a death, by neglect." He picked up Alice, and nodded to Shona. "Don't worry, honey. You just go in and keep the doors locked, till these folks get their senses back."

Cassie led the child into the house, inwardly upbraiding the ignorance of the crowd. Surely, Shona couldn't have . . . Realizing the implications, she put that nonsense out of her mind. Shona was a loving, caring little girl—nothing more.

Sophie had seen it all from the upstairs window. Now, she was waiting to take the child in her arms. Too ill to study that afternoon, she sat with her mother.

"Mama, what can I do? They all think I'm a witch. I can't

even explain. Nobody wants me to explain. The worst part is, they think I'm a black witch—not a good one." At last, she broke down and sobbed.

Sophie put her arm around her. "We'll just have to show everybody that they're wrong. Nobody could be around you without knowing that."

"But, Mama, I'm not 'around' anybody. I'm here at home, where people don't get to know me. I think I should be going to school."

"Don't bring up that subject to your father, dear. He just wouldn't understand. I worry about his anger when he finds out what happened today."

As she expected, Will's reaction took the form of raging at the ignorance of people. Then he turned to storm at his daughter.

"What's this about a cat? You know how stupid these people kin be, yet you take a dang black cat for a pet. Who's been causin' trouble? Did Cassie get you the cat?"

"Oh, no, Papa. It just came up on the porch, and I liked it."

"Well, it has to go. Plato will get rid of the cat."

"But, Papa . . ."

"Don't question. We've gotta have nothin' about you to suggest . . . anything of your life—up there." He had trouble saying it. He had always kept her past as indistinct as possible.

Seeing her pitiful, crestfallen face, he relented. "Don't worry, I ain't goin' to tell Plato to destroy the animal. He'll have to find a new home for it."

* * *

When the morning paper came out, Will was jubilant, but Shona was in tears. Alice had died. The thing that pleased Will was her mother's statement. "Yes, I knew she was playing with Shona. She's a sweet child, and I want people to know she had nothing to do with Alice's . . . death. Alice was very ill; she deliberately disobeyed me by jumping rope. The doctor had warned us that any strenuous exercise could be fatal."

A week later, Mrs. Parks came to the house with a gift for Shona. It was the life-sized doll which had been with Alice constantly. "I want you to have it," she smiled at Shona. "You made these last days happy for Alice. She had no other friends . . ."

Choked with emotion, she made a swift exit. Shona looked at the doll, without feeling. She would put it away—far away.

* * *

It was a gray day; there had been no sunrise at all, and Shona had the unpleasant feeling of living in a dark world.

She was sitting on the side of the bed, watching Cassie's deft fingers flourishing the button-hook over her new, patent-leather-champagne leather shoes.

NINTH

Sophie gave her young daughter a weak smile. For fifteen years she had believed that she was to have no children. Then, a daughter; now, a son. God had been good to her, after all.

She beckoned to Shona. "Come here, dear, and see what I have."

With some curiosity, Shona crossed to the bed, dreading what was now a certainty. Her mother turned to a blanketed bundle, and lifted a corner. A tiny, red face screwed itself into a grimace in its sleep, and relaxed at once.

She stared for a long minute. "Whose baby is it?"

"Why, it's ours. Yours, Papa's and mine. Oh, and of course, Cassie's and Plato's, too."

"But it's not yours, is it? Are you going to adopt it?"

Sophie hesitated. She didn't know just how to handle this. "Of course, it's mine. Didn't you want a little brother? Papa and I thought . . ."

"Oh, Mama, I used to want someone to play with. I don't need anyone now. Please send him back."

Her mother sighed. "Dear, we can't send him back. He's really ours."

"You mean—forever?"

"Yes."

Shona gave her one unhappy look, and fled.

Sophie's eyes filled with tears. She tried to sit up; Cassie restrained her with a gentle hand.

"It's all right, Miz Sophie. She'll be fine, once she gits used to the idea. Ah'm afeered we should've got her prepared." Sophie nodded, too upset to speak.

Although she had reached the age of ten, Shona hadn't really known the facts of procreation, except in a vague, story-book way. Nevertheless, she had lived with a finger on the pulse of life, since she was born. Today, she knew that this heartbeat was wrong. Her little brother's birth was a disaster.

She went to her book. Perhaps there was something here that could help. Not knowing just what she needed, or what she was looking for, she studied the herbs used for achieving health.

There was basil, to avert the evil eye; chervil, good for the aged; caraway, for love potions; mustard to resist poison, and sage, protector against black witchcraft. All the others seemed to be less appropriate.

She decided that she would have to study the problem; the trouble was, she didn't really know what the question was.

Sadly, for the time, she gave it up.

She was sitting in the den, one day, at the close of the school year, waiting for Mr. Weston. Her tutor was seldom late.

The room was pleasant, furnished with several lovely Hitchcock chairs, Will's mahogany desk and chair, two oval drop-leaf tables, and a row of glass-fronted bookcases. The den, on the eastern side of the house, was cool.

She did not wait long. Mr. Weston tapped on the door and rushed into the den, as usual. This time, however, he had a sheaf of papers in his hand, and seemed to be unusually cheerful.

"Sorry, I'm late." He laid the papers on the desk and sank into the swivel chair. "I have some great news for you." He smiled, showing perfect, even teeth. With his shining brown hair and small, neat mustache, Shona could picture him as a fairy-tale prince.

She leaned forward, expectantly. "Don't keep me guessing—is it really good?"

"Good? Your final test was a triumph. You earned a 98; that's better than anyone in your class at school."

"What does that mean?" She felt rather let down. Accustomed to making high grades, such news was of no particular value to her.

"I must talk to your parents. I hope it means that you'll be allowed to go to school. You need to be with other students, even though you're younger than your potential classmates."

Shona gave him a thoughtful look. "You know, Mr. Weston, I don't know whether I really want to go to school, now."

"Now? What do you mean? Isn't this what you've been wishing for, all these months?"

She leaned toward him. "Promise you won't say anything to my folks, or to Cassie. They mustn't know."

He frowned. "Of course, I promise. It must be serious, to make you want to give up going to school."

"It's *very* serious. I don't belong in this valley. People don't want me. They think I'm a witch. Someone hit me with a stone, someone else threw eggs all over the front of the house, and when my playmate died, the people wanted to blame me for it. This city hates me. So, I've changed my mind about going to school."

Her tutor thought about this. He knew something of her problems, but she had always seemed to be so self-reliant.

Thinking about it, he realized that what he told her now, might possibly affect her whole future. He would have to be careful.

He opened his mouth to speak, but she held up a hand. "Wait; there's something else. I have a little brother now, and he's going to need a lot of help. I should be here for him."

Weston tried again. "Shona, running away from your problems only makes them chase you. Stand your ground. You're sure to make friends; other people don't matter. As for the baby,

I'm sure, between his mother and Cassie, he'll have the best of attention."

Shona listened seriously, but now it was evident that she would have to explain. "Mr. Weston, there's a special reason why the baby needs me. There's something wrong with him—very wrong."

"What does the doctor say?"

"He doesn't say anything—he doesn't know."

Perplexed, he stared at her. "You mean, you know something about the baby that the doctor doesn't know?"

She nodded.

"How can that be?"

"You see—that's why I can't say anything. Everyone thinks it's weird that I know things when nobody else does. Now, you probably think I'm a witch."

He frowned. "I'm not superstitious, Shona. No, I would never think that of you, Shona. Certainly, I don't see any valid reason for you to be denied the fellowship of your peers."

She tried another angle. "Anyhow, Papa would never agree. You know how he feels about me."

"I do and for that reason, maybe I can convince him, and your mother, that this will be best for you."

Privately, at that moment, he decided it would be more productive to see her mother. He regretted his promise. An explanation could have helped.

Helplessly, she looked at him. "Mother's in the parlor."

He found Sophie doing a needlepoint picture. She greeted him warmly. She was a pretty little woman, he thought—but Shona bore no resemblance to her.

He took the chair she offered him, and came straight to the point. "Mrs. MacDonald, Shona has made astonishing progress in her studies. She's far above students of her age. I'd like to see her attend the public high school, with her peers. I realize that they're older than she, but she needs to get to know people. I recognize your reason for her seclusion, but I'm hoping that it's no longer necessary."

Sophie smiled, thoughtfully. "You're probably right, Mr. Weston. We haven't been as close to Shona's needs as you have. In fact . . ." she hesitated, "we haven't been very close to Shona, at all."

He understood. "That's just it. She's becoming such a loner, these days, that it's necessary for her to broaden her world. She needs younger people."

Thanking him for his concern, Sophie showed the tutor to the door. Having promised to speak to Will, she couldn't help wondering. How would he react?

Fortunately, she was agreeably surprised. Will, himself, had seen it. Shona was moving away from everyone, even Cassie. Plato, along with horses, chickens and bantams, was neglected, and her private scrap of garden had grown up in weeds.

Indeed, shut off with her beloved books, Shona was becoming a recluse, and her father saw it. So it was that Shona signed up for the Fall term. At the age of ten, she would attend high school.

Shona's trepidation eased when she discovered that the 1882 graduating class—Johnstown's first—consisted of seven girls. Evidently, going to high school wouldn't mean being surrounded by a large, hostile class. She pictured a pleasant friendship with someone who could explain life in the city.

* * *

It seemed that nearly every morning's sunrise was belated, this summer. The smoke from the prospering Cambria Iron Company darkened the sky over the city, and sprinkled tiny, black particles over window-sills and gardens.

Few complained. Business was at a new high, fostered by the enterprise of Philadelphia Quakers. Will's boss was Daniel Justin Morrell, the only incorporator who lived in Johnstown. As a popular general manager, he brought leading metallurgists and technicians of the iron industry into the city.

There was a great deal of praise for Morrell, in many areas. He had sponsored the building of the Bessemer Converter, first in the nation to be constructed. Now, streets, often muddy, were being paved with stone or brick. Wooden bridges were replaced with iron, and attractive public schools and buildings were being built.

As a department manager, Will MacDonald did his part in improving the Cambria mills. He aided in the construction of the rolling mill, and now held a position which the company was reluctant to broadcast. Competition in the mills was at a peak.

With Will only briefly at home, Sophie had more time to herself. Today, it was incredibly hot upstairs, but Shona found her mother in the bedroom, making a dress. She had just cut out a piece of pale, green voile.

"It's for you," she smiled, in response to the silent question. Her upswept, dark hair lay in damp ringlets around her face. "I'l like you to stand with us at the christening."

"Mama, you know how I feel about that. Those religious people are ready to tear me apart. I don't want to go."

"But, dear," Sophie protested, "I thought you'd do this for the baby, and for me. Please, Shona."

She relented. "I guess I could." It was difficult to refuse her mother anything.

Shona loved the baby's dress. It was a long, white silk robe, with a double flounce of skirt, and a quilted bib. There was a quilted bonnet of the same material.

"It's beautiful, Mama. You make such nice things. But, tell

me, don't you ever want to get out of the house?"

With a patient smile, Sophie said, "I think I have enough to keep me busy. What more can a body want?"

Shona gave up; it must be good to be content. She crossed the room to look at Ian.

"Mama, why does he sleep constantly?"

"All babies sleep a lot. It helps them to grow."

She studied the baby again. Surely, he was a beautiful child, with his curly hair the color of a new penny, and his skin so fair. Was there really anything wrong with him, or was the trouble with her mind?

* * *

This was an extraordinarily hot summer. Shona watched Cassie packing her freshly churned butter into brown crocks for storing in the springhouse.

"I'll take them down, Cassie," she urged, eager to get into the chill air of the building. Much of their food was stored in or near the icy water. "It will be a treat."

Cassie, grinned, wiping her brow with a corner of her apron. "Since I got too much to do to be coolin' myself off, I'd be obliged, honey."

Carrying the crocks into the garden, she came upon Plato, hoeing weeds, and perspiring. He wore long trousers, turned up to his knees, and no shirt. His muscular brown body glistened in the sunlight.

He beckoned to her, and she crossed to him. "Miss Shona, sumpin' gotta be done 'bout Billy. He gotta go."

"Go?" What's wrong with him?"

"He' a little devil, that's what. Po' Brigham Young, he' dyin. Look at him. We ain't goin' get no baby chicks that way."

Shona stared at the white leghorn rooster, standing in a corner of the chicken yard, head down, wings drooping. Then, she saw Billy, strutting around, pecking any hen that happened to get in his way. Fortunately, most of the hens were inside the coop, trying to keep cool.

She hated it, but there was no choice. The white rooster must be in charge of his flock. Sadly, in a lowered voice, she said, "Can you find him a good home? Do you have to take Milly, too?"

Plato convinced her that they should be together; this made sense. She had no idea what was in store for Billy.

It was not until afterward that Will talked to her about it. "That banty of yours—he's makin' a pile of money fer the guy that bought him. Too bad Plato couldn't have kept him."

Shona stared at him, wide-eyed. "What do you mean? How could he? . . ."

"The banty's been winnin' big. Seems, he's such a little

fellow, the bets are always on the other one. But Billy wins; he's won twice, now."

"Wins—what? I don't know what you mean."

Cock fights, honey. Don't you know about cock fights?" Obviously, she didn't. Suddenly, Will was ashamed. He never should have mentioned it to a little girl. He tried to skirt the issue.

"Makes no difference now. They'll probably retire him. They never keep that up very long."

Shona's eyes filled with tears. "He's been hurt—I know it. Why would Plato? . . ."

Will cut in. "He didn't do nothin' wrong. I told him to sell the banty. Thought this fellow was raisin' them. Neither of us knowed he was goin' to . . . do what he did."

She was off, running to her room. Later, when she came downstairs, composed, Will eyed her keenly. He would never mention the subject again.

* * *

Ian's christening took place in the First Presbyterian Church. Will and Plato wore double-breasted reefer suits; Sophie and Cassie wore dresses which Sophie had made, in almost identical styles, with yoked bodices and draped skirts.

Shona's dress was much like what the other little girls were wearing. Her light green dress had a smocked, fitted bodice. Its calf-length skirt had three tiers of ruffles at the bottom. She made a lovely picture: golden curls caught up in the back and topped with a tiny, pork-pie hat.

These days, the fashion world was topsy-turvy; women were dissatisfied, and were making their own outfits. Their call was for anything unique; garments not seen before.

Naturally, there was whispering as they trooped into the church. Will had never been in this church; now he began to wonder whether they accepted colored people. Sophie had other worries, but looking at Shona, she felt better. Surely, no one could think evil of such a sweet, lovely child.

As for Cassie and Plato, they were slightly uncomfortable. They preferred their own Methodist church. However, they felt indebted to Sophie and Will. After the Civil War, they had fled Georgia and its chaos, and had found a haven in the MacDonald household.

Fortunately, the christening went on without incident, and members of the church were pleasantly civil.

As for the baby, he slept through the whole thing, as Shona knew he would. Yet, her worry was for him. Even with nothing in the world to concern her, the foreboding remained.

Later, Sophie went to help Cassie prepare vegetables. She needed someone to talk to.

"Cassie, what do you think about Ian?"

She gave Sophie a startled glance. "Honey, there ain't no better, healthier, good-lookin' chile than Ian, 'n that a fact." That was unconvincing; she began again.

"You know, ever since that baby be bo'n, our chile has a notion that he' sick. You axed the doctor, 'n he say everythin' fine.

Sophie relaxed. "Right, Cassie. I shouldn't let it bother me. Shona hasn't actually had an explanation. We'll forget it—she's only a child."

* * *

TENTH

The beauty of autumn delighted Shona. Traveling to school, she thrilled to the red and gold of the maples arching the street above her. This was one of those rare mornings of normal sunrise; the walk to school was a lovely adventure.

It was a new school building. Shona was impressed by its size. The 60-foot structure accommodated two stories of classrooms. A long portico covered both entrances, where doors and staircases communicated with other rooms. She gazed at the golden maple trees shading the veranda, then looked about. No children were in sight.

Her watch gave no clue. It showed 8:30; that was plenty of time to get to her nine o'clock class. To her surprise, the session had begun.

"Miss MacDonald, I suppose you have a reason for being late?" The voice was familiar. She stared at the man, then ran and threw herself at him.

"Oh, Michael, Michael, how glad I am to see you. Why are you here? Do you? . . ."

Gently, he disengaged her arms from their clutch. The other students were gaping; his face was scarlet.

"Shona, I'm your teacher. I need to know the reason for your tardiness. Unless there's a good excuse, I'm afraid you'll be scheduled for detention."

In a flash, she was back to reality. "Oh—my watch . . ." She looked up at the clock on the wall. It was 20 minutes after nine. "I guess it stopped," she told him in a muted voice.

He had regained his composure. "Since your watch let you down, I suppose we'll have to forgive the offense, this time." He motioned to a front desk at the window.

"That will be your place, Shona. I think you'll find all the necessary materials inside. We'll begin again, with introductions. Several of you don't know each other. So, beginning with Daniel Dayton, tell us something about yourself." He nodded to the boy in the front seat at the other side of the room.

Unhappily, Shona conformed. There were so many things she wanted to know; there was so much to tell him.

She had hoped to talk to him after school, but before she could get to him, he had gathered up his papers and disappeared.

Several days passed before Shona had an opportunity to talk to Michael. She faced him. "Why didn't you come to see me? I don't know where you live—everybody knows where I live."

"I'm sorry, dear." His voice was gentle. How could she know that he cared for her in a way that he, himself, couldn't understand. It wasn't that she had helped in caring for him; there was more to it than that. There had been a bond between them.

He tried to explain. "Shona, when you knew me, I was in Normal School, studying to be a teacher. Last year, I was graduated; this is my first job."

"Weren't you glad to see me? I'm sorry; I forgot there were people in the room." Her blue-green, expressive eyes filled with tears.

He stared at her; the loveliest thing he had ever seen. If only she were older; if there were some way to bring their ages together . . . He chided himself for being ridiculous, assuring her that he was happy to see her. Angry with himself, he shut out all foolish, unrealistic thought of Shona.

As for Shona, she was not defeated. Somehow, Michael would be part of her life, even if he didn't know it. Many times, his enchanting smile flashed to mind when she was studying. She would stop and dream. At school, she kept her eyes on her books and tried to pretend he wasn't there.

School was better than Shona had expected. Two boys snickered to see this young child as a Junior in high school, but that stopped with her first recitation in class.

No one seemed to notice who she was. Borrowing a pencil, one day, Peggy Dayton, sitting next to her, spoke for the first time.

"How did you come to be in high school? You're so young."

"I'm almost eleven, Peggy," Shona responded. "It's just because I've had so many books to read, and my mother was a teacher."

"But, your mother . . ." As soon as she said it, Peggy wished she hadn't.

Shona gave her an unhappy look. As she was about to say something, Michael rapped on his desk. "Too much whispering, over there."

They didn't have another chance to talk, until after class. Explaining her life with Kate was difficult, but in a way, pleasant. She couldn't recount experiences at home.

Peggy was fascinated. This was a better story than the newspapers had printed. "You said she wasn't a witch. Didn't she heal the animals with witchcraft?"

Shona shook her head. "That wasn't witchcraft at all. It was just using special herbs to cure illness or injury. Kate wasn't a witch, the way people think of witches."

"It must have been hard on her, not being able to live in town. People did terrible things to witches. I heard that they hanged some of them right here in America. In Europe, they even burned them."

"I know. When I came here, I was afraid they were going to hang me." She told Peggy about the stone, and the egg incident.

Peggy's sympathy ran high. "Believe me, I'll tell anybody who talks against you, just what I think of them."

And so, Shona enlisted an ally—a friend in whom she could trust and confide. However, the disparity in their ages didn't occur to her, until it began to make a difference.

Talking to Peggy one day, Shona invited her to come over to study with her. Peggy declined. "I can't—I have a date."

"A date?" This contingency hadn't occurred to her.

"Not what you think, silly. Peace Rhodes and I are going to a concert with two of the fellows from the senior class."

Gloom prevaded Shona's world. Her age had been causing unhappiness, just as her background had. Was there to be nothing for her, here in Johnstown?

More and more, she yearned for the old log house—the chickens, the garden, the animals. Why couldn't she take care of it all, herself?

And so, she began to dream.

Happily, though, school was going well. She studied with Peggy, and often with both Peggy and Peace. They were fond of her; to please her, they referred to themselves as "The Three Musketeers." It was kind, but somehow, the barrier was there.

She had another concern, these days. Ian was walking, and had begun to call for his mother. Shona watched him—a beautiful, curly-headed baby who attracted attention every time she took him out in his carriage.

Sometimes, she wondered just what she was looking for. Then, at a year and a half, he was running. Could she have been wrong? The ever-recurring question had never been answered.

* * *

One day, at the close of the term, Michael came to visit. He knew he had to do it, but couldn't put his finger on the reason. As an excuse for the call, he pretended a need to talk to Shona's mother about the senior year.

Shona sat, facing him, on a straight chair. For some reason, Michael selected the piano bench. Perspiring, and ill at ease, he flattened both hands on the bench and didn't move until it was time to leave.

The reason for Michael's visit finally became clear to him.

He wanted to observe Shona in her home setting, to see her parents, and what sort of influences she was having in her life. Although speculating on what possible damage the old woman might have done, he couldn't help marveling at the education she had given the child.

Because of fearing to show too much interest, Michael was uncomfortable. He knew that the kind of affection he felt was improper. The MacDonalds must not have reason to suspect him.

Across from him, near her mother, Shona sat in admiration. How could she have compared anyone else to a prince in a fairy tale? His wavy brown hair and winning smile made him so lovable that she wanted to rush over and kiss him—well aware that she couldn't.

After he had gone, she made a discovery. There, plainly showing on the mahogany bench, were two hand prints, just a body's distance apart. She touched them, tentatively. Then, she sat on the bench and put her hands on the prints. Hers were much smaller—his, so strong and capable.

Delighted, she went to Cassie and explained about the marks. "Don't polish them off, Cassie. Promise me you won't take them off."

"Cain't promise no sech thing, chile. What if yo' Mama say clean 'em off? Why you want marks on the bench, anyhow?"

"Oh, Cassie, it's all I have to remind me of Michael. I love him, and he doesn't love me. He thinks I'm a child."

Cassie softened. She knew something about "puppy love." Smiling, she said, "Okay, honey. I promise."

Two weeks later, Sophie came to play the piano. She was horrified to see two large prints on the bench. Then, she justified Cassie's neglect. It was too much; Cassie had been working too hard.

In a surge of sympathy, she decided to help out. She had been working Cassie too hard, and not doing her share, as she always had.

Not long afterward, Shona came into the sewing room, almost in tears.

"Why, dear, what's the matter?"

Shona sniffled. "I never thought Cassie would let me down."

"Let you down? You must be mistaken. Cassie wouldn't do that."

"I'm not mistaken. She promised to save the marks on the bench for me—and now she's cleaned them off."

"Are you talking about those hand prints?"

She nodded, wiping her eyes with the handkerchief her mother handed her. "I never thought . . ."

Annoyed, Sophie remarked coldly, "I cleaned them off. I thought Cassie had too much work, so I did it. I can't see any good reason why you'd want to preserve them."

"Oh, Mama, why can't you see—they were beautiful."

Sophie sighed. She couldn't see. Finally, she dismissed the matter as one of those childish foibles which a parent must expect.

* * *

And so another year went by—too slowly for Shona, and too swiftly for her parents. She was doing well with her school work, and was sorry for that.

Michael was proud of her. "If you keep up this excellence, you have a good chance of becoming valedictorian," he smiled.

Shona registered shock. "Please, I don't want to be a valedictorian."

He couldn't get her to explain, but she managed to show that she meant it. Bewildered, he watched. She neglected her projects, skipped test questions, and never raised her hand in class.

Now, he questioned her more closely. "What's going on here, Shona. Why are you putting on this act?"

She gave him a wide-eyed stare. "What act?"

He could have shaken her. She was so irritating, so unpredictable, so . . . lovable. Now he wanted to shake himself.

"You know very well what I'm talking about. Why are you putting on this act of ignorance?"

She wouldn't lie to him, nor would she tell him the truth. "I don't want to study any more." That was all he could get.

He never got his answers. Shona made her purpose less obvious, but she achieved her goal—to keep out of the limelight.

* * *

It was Ian's second birthday. Surrounded by the family, which included Cassie and Plato, he was seated in his high chair with his cake before him. Shona lighted the candles, and Cassie turned out the gas light.

The two small candles lighted his face, just enough to make his copper-colored ringlets form a halo. Shona gave him an admiring look. "Blow, honey; blow out the candles, see?" She illustrated with puffed cheeks.

Ian hesitated. Then, with a powerful effort, he tried to blow. The candle remained lighted. When he refused to try again, Shona extinguished the candles. She had never approved of blowing on a cake, anyway.

Shona's feeling of uneasiness about Ian's failure, was put down. For too long, she had been worrying. Her small brother was as hearty and healthy as a two-year-old could be.

Nearly a month later, Ian came running toward her, and fell. She picked him up, stood him on his feet, and he tumbled again.

Sophie saw the fall, the rose from her sewing machine. Shona was holding him in her arms, her ivory face, oddly white.

"I don't know what happened," she said. "Maybe he's just tired." She put him down again, and this time, he stayed on his feet, swaying a little.

"Come to me, dear," called his mother, reaching out to him. He tottered toward her, and with a supreme effort, fell into her arms.

Understandably, Sophie wasn't long in contacting a nurse friend, who gave her the name of a prominent doctor, reputed to be excellent with children.

Now, in Dr. Ferguson's waiting room, Ian seemed to be as active as usual. Holding a stuffed cloth bear, which his mother had made, he clung to it, singing to himself and swinging his feet.

Looking at him, Sophie began to regret this move. The doctor would wonder why she had pressed the need for an early appointment.

As he examined the child, she tried to explain. "I don't know why I was so worried. He's perfectly all right—I can see that. It's just that he was so unsteady . . ." She groped in vain for an excuse.

Dr. Ferguson didn't answer for a few minutes. Then he looked at her gravely. "You were right to come—although I can't be of much help. The child is seriously ill."

Sophie gasped. "How can you say that? Are you sure? What is it?" Her questions tumbled out before he could answer.

He held up one hand. "If you'll listen carefully, I'll try to explain. This is a rare problem, and there's much yet to be learned about it."

She quieted, alarm in her eyes, and in the stiffness of her posture. "Yes, doctor; I'm listening."

"How old is the boy?"

"He's just had his second birthday."

"And he's been normal in every way, until now?"

She nodded. "Yes. In fact, he's been ahead of some other children I've seen, of the same age."

The doctor's lips tightened. "It's really what I suspect. This is an infantile type of dystrophy—usually caused by malnutrition."

Sophie's face reflected indignation. "Malnutrition? This child has had only the most wholesome types of food—he hasn't wanted for anything."

He spoke gently. "Not that kind of malnutrition, Mrs. MacDonald. This is a metabolic disorder. It's a degeneration of nerve cells—sometimes a degeneration of the optic pathway, as well."

"Optic pathway?" Sophie interrupted in a frightened voice. "Does that mean he could become—blind?"

"Possibly." He went on to explain the deterioration of all neurologic function, such as blindness, incontinence during sleep, and perhaps, seizures. When he came to "degeneration of tracts of the spinal cord," she could bear it no longer. Sobbing, she faced him.

"Is there *nothing* you can do?"

Dr. Ferguson gave her a sympathetic smile. "Mrs. MacDonald, we may be helpless at the moment, but there's always research. Possibly, in the next few years, we'll know a lot about this, and can treat it with success."

She wiped her eyes. "Doctor, will you be honest with me? I can take it. I need to know. Tell me what to expect."

Dr. John Ferguson was not one to dissemble. When a patient asked for honesty, he gave it. At this moment, he was feeling acute sympathy for Sophie.

"Mrs. MacDonald, you can see that the prognosis is poor. Death is caused by complications within a few months or years of the onset of the affliction."

Stricken, she gazed at him. "Doctor, what shall I do? What *can* I do?"

He rose, and put a hand on her shoulder. "Give him a great deal of affection, and—be patient with him." He patted boy's head, and Ian gave him an angelic smile. Swiftly, the doctor left the office.

Grief-stricken, Sophie went home to tell Will. As for Shona—the dreadful prognosis must not be given to her daughter.

* * *

Shona's reaction to the news that her little brother had a serious illness, was to get out her book to find out what to do about it. The search wound up with no clue as to the nature of the sickness.

Sophie spoke softly to her. "Dear, it's very serious. The doctor says the best thing we can give him is love. That means patience. We can't become irritated or impatient."

Shona didn't understand, so her mother attempted to give her the main points of difficulty that Ian would be having.

Stunned, she stared at the child, happily sitting on the floor with his blocks. "Mama, I don't see how any of my herbs, or all of them together, could cure all that. Maybe we should find another doctor."

Her answer was echoed with a roar, when Will came home. "So that's what the specialist says, is it? Well, we'll see what other doctors say. Seems to me doggone funny that nobody ever heered of such a thing. I'll git to the bottom of this."

And thus began the quest.

At once, Will and Sophie took the baby to every successful doctor in town. After that, dissatisfied, they went on, away from the city. There were two railroads: the Pennsylvania Railroad and the Baltimore and Ohio, which connected with its main line, 45 miles away, at Rockwood.

The MacDonalds traveled on both railroads, canvassing the state and going further, on to Baltimore. Unfortunately, the responses to their questions were even less comprehensive than the disclosures of Dr. Ferguson.

Apparently, only one doctor contacted, had ever seen a case; he knew of no cure. As far as that was concerned most of the physicians had never studied the malady; some had not heard of it.

Frustrated, the couple returned home to a hopeful Shona. She saw them arriving in the buggy with Plato, and ran to meet them, curls flying.

"Oh, Papa, Mama—what did the doctors say? Do they have a cure? Is Ian going to be all right?"

Dismounting, they had no opportunity to speak. Ian leaned to Shona from his mother's arms for a kiss. Sophie set him down, but he hung onto her skirt and didn't try to walk.

Shona was still talking. Will gave her a glare. He glared at everyone, these days. "We'll do our explainin' in the house. No need to tell all the neighbors our business."

Indoors, Cassie and Plato were invited to learn, along with Shona, that there was no help for the baby. It was a dismal little group. Shona grieved with them for a while, then her optimistic spirit took over. None of the doctors knew much—maybe what they did know, was wrong.

The next day dawned in gloom. Chilly breezes blew faded leaves in tiny whirlwinds over the front lawn. Only a few days ago, Plato had been raking diligently. Shona surveyed the deserted street with distaste. Somewhere, up there, the sun was trying to get through.

Except for a few mill workers who were on an odd shift, the street was deserted. She sat on the porch swing, and pushed gently. Moving slowly back and forth, she meditated. Today, she was to take Ian to the park for an outing. But, somehow, something was different.

An ominous feeling had wakened her that morning. At the time, it was no more than a chill. She had gotten up and closed the window, but the mood remained. It was a sense of foreboding, as strong as any she had felt about Ian.

Her mother was at the door. "Honey, Ian is ready for his walk; are you prepared to go?"

She got to her feet. Yes, she supposed she was prepared—for anything the fates would give.

Ian loved his walk. Usually, he trotted along with Shona, sometimes declining her hand and running ahead to explore. Today, however, his mother put him in the stroller, taking no chances on sudden weakness. She had tied him in with a strip of muslin, which made him unhappy, indeed.

They had not gone far, when he revolted. "Ian want . . . out." He tugged at the cloth. "Out, Sona, det me out."

Suddenly, his words became indistinct and his hands dropped. When Shona looked at him, his head had fallen back, and his small body was racked with convulsions.

Across the street, two women, out to do their Saturday shopping, saw Ian's strange behavior. They rushed over to see what was wrong, and were aghast to see the active little boy, tied in his seat, and obviously in trouble.

The women screamed at Shona. "Why do you have him tied? What have you done to him? How can you be so cruel to the child? The questions continued, but Shona wasn't listening.

"Please, get out of my way. I must get help; Ian's very ill." She tried to get around them, but they blocked her way.

The taller woman, with the pince-nez and the feathered hat, took command. Addressing the younger woman, she said, "You get the police; I'll wait here. I don't know what her mother means, trusting the child with this . . . this . . ."

"Witch," supplemented Shona, angrily. "Why don't you say it? Get out of the way, so that I can get help for this child. If you don't . . ." She stopped, unhappily. What could set do?

The woman was glaring down at her; the other woman had gone. "If I don't . . . what? Will you put a hex on me, or what? Be careful of threats—they can get you in trouble."

Shona ignored her. She untied the muslin and lifted Ian. He wasn't moving now; he appeared to be asleep. Leaving the cart where it stood, blocked by the woman, Shona dashed around her and back down the street to her home. The woman called after her, but she didn't hear.

Safely at home, Shona sobbed out the story to Sophie, who took Ian up to his bed and dispatched Plato to get the doctor.

Although Dr. Ferguson wasn't accustomed to making house calls, in this case, he had a professional interest. This unknown, undetermined disorder had an apparent relationship with several other degenerative diseases—yet it was unique. Caught up in his personal theories, he came, almost eagerly, to see the boy.

He found Ian, sitting up in bed, trying to take off one sock. Frustrated, he began to scream. Shona removed both socks and smiled at the doctor. "He hates to wear anything on his feet. We've always had trouble with that."

Dr. Ferguson was using his stethoscope. He smiled at Shona and prodded the little boy's abdomen. "How long did his seizure continue?" he asked.

"Only a few minutes, Doctor. Then, he seemed to sleep."

The physician nodded, patting the curly head. "Unconsciousness usually follows. Don't be too much alarmed. We don't know enough about this trouble to judge its course accurately."

Sophie put out a shaking hand to grasp his arm. "Doctor, can you tell me . . ."

"I told you everything I could," he said, patting her hand. It's always best to prepare a family, in such cases. However,

sometimes things aren't as bad as they might seem."
That would be her only consolation, for a long time.

* * *

Soon after Dr. Ferguson's visit, the doorbell rang. Shona ran to the door, beating Cassie by a few seconds. From the dining room, where she had been setting the table, Sophie heard a gruff voice.

"Young lady, is your mother at home?"

She hurried into the living room. A tall, overweight policeman stood just inside the door, facing Shona.

Sophie interposed her frail body between them. "I'm Mrs. MacDonald; this is my daughter, Shona. What can I do for you?"

The policeman gave her an admiring look and an apologetic grin. "I'm afraid you'll both have to come down to the station with me. There's been a complaint."

"It's about your baby. You do have a baby?"

She stiffened. "We have a two-year-old son. What about him?"

"Seems your daughter here, was doin' something to him. These people seem to think it was some kind of witchcraft."

Shona stepped up, shaken and white. "How could they say that? I was trying to take care of him. He was . . ."

She was crying now. Her mother put an arm around her shoulder. "Don't worry, dear. We'll straighten it out."

Sophie wouldn't allow such a thing as suspicion to cross her mind. Didn't she know her daughter better than anyone else? She was sure that the child loved her little brother with all her heart.

Dressed for the trip to the police station, she was almost calm. Her daughter was a picture in the cobalt blue dress she had made for her, with its embroidered collar and cuffs and ruffled hem. Surely, the sight of this lovely child would avert all question of such guilt.

However, questioning at the police station was not so simple. A homely, burly officer listened to the accusations with a seemingly sympathetic ear.

The women were the Misses Sara and Lucy Rearick, sisters, who lived halfway up Main Street in the old family home. Sara, the tall, angular woman, did the talking; Lucy, short and stout, seemed to be accustomed to listening.

"Officer, we know that this little girl," she threw Shona a look, "lived with the 'Hogback Witch' for some years. We've seen this little brother of hers many times, but never in the shape he was in when she was fussing over him. He was having some kind of attack. Since her mother doesn't seem to worry, we think the situation should be looked into."

The officer looked at her sister. "Do you agree with what Miss Rearick says?"

"Of course, I do," spoke up Lucy, glad to have a chance to give her opinion. "I think this girl should be sent to a mental hospital or be locked up. There's no place in this city for witchcraft."

Sophie and Shona had been sitting on a bench near the policeman's desk; now he turned to them.

"What do you have to say?" He addressed Shona with a sneer, far from the admiration her mother had anticipated.

She looked directly into his eyes and said, "The ladies are right; he was having some kind of spell. I wanted to help him. That lady," she indicated Lucy, "wouldn't let me pass her to take him home. I just picked him up and went around her. There was no witchcraft. I'm not a witch."

He wasn't impressed. Looking at Sophie, he snapped, "Well, what do you have to say? I'd like to know something about this strange illness of your son."

Sophie hesitated, not knowing where to begin. Then she said, "Sir, my son has a rare affliction. Shona has nothing to do with it."

The officer gave her a skeptic smile. "And was your child born with this "affliction,' as you put it?"

"No, he . . ." She broke down and sobbed.

A sudden disturbance rose in the outer office, accompanied by loud shouting. Will MacDonald burst into the room, followed by an apologetic officer.

All speech was drowned out by Will's angry diatribe. "What in tarnation are you doin' to my wife and child? My man tells me you've got'em in custody. Custody for what? You better have a good reason, or by jumpin' Jupiter, I'll know why."

He stopped for a moment, to glare at the offending officer. "What's your name?"

"I'm Officer McDevitt, sir." Suddenly apologetic, it occurred to him that this intensive questioning might be beyond his duty. He added, hurriedly, "The chief wanted me to check on this complaint. I'm sorry, if I . . ."

MacDonald assured him that he would, indeed, be sorry if he detained his family for one more moment. He turned to shout at the ladies who had caused the problem, but they had gone, quietly slipping out of the room as he bellowed.

Plato was waiting with the buggy to take them home. He was indignant about Shona's arrest. "It ain't right to be causin' trouble fo' l'il Miss Shona. Where they git these notions, anyhow?"

Will knew full well where people got their ideas, but he refused to talk about it, dismissing the incident as the work of some busybody women with nothing better to do.

* * *

As for Shona, she was crushed. Must she forever be haunted by superstition? What could she do in order to prove that she posed no threat to anyone?

Impulsively, she thought of Michael. She had been thinking of him a lot, these days. Michael would know what to do. He could go to the police station and tell them . . .

Arriving at the apartment building, she almost forgot what she had come for. She had been here once before, with some extra credit work. Climbing to the second floor, she rapped on the door.

Michael greeted her with affection, even daring a peck on the cheek. He wanted to hold her—how incongruous it was that he loved her so, and must keep her at arm's length.

Under his kiss, she glowed, thinking how wonderful it would be if . . . Trying not to think about that, she told him her story. When she had finished, he patted her shoulder. "Don't you worry about it. If there's any further trouble, I'll be at your side. I promise."

Now, she must leave. It wouldn't do, having anyone see her here. He moved to the door. "Shona, you'd better go. Your mother will be wondering. Does she know where you are?"

"No, Michael. I didn't tell her. I went to get her some material, and I just stopped by. That's all right, isn't it?"

She wanted him to tell her how much he had wanted to see her, but that was wishful thinking. It was clear that he was anxious to be rid of her.

She looked at him sadly. "I was hoping you wanted to see me, Michael. You hardly notice me in school."

He tried to explain, without encouraging her. "Of course, I'm glad to see you, dear. However, I don't think you should come here. People might talk."

"It seems to me that they've said about all there is to say. What would they talk about?"

He hesitated, at a loss for words. This slender child was a woman in so many ways, that he felt cheated. Looking at her now, loving her, he knew that he must not encourage her.

Shona had no reservations. "Michael, do you have a girlfriend?

Startled, he said, "No. Why do you ask?"

"Because, if you don't, I want you to wait for me. I'll be older, soon. You do love me, don't you?"

"Of course," he said easily, glad to be able to say so without making any commitments. "But you'll find someone your own age, and can make plans for the future. Then, I'll be happy for you."

She gave him a look of disillusionment which he would not forget, and dashed out of the apartment. From his second-story window, he watched her, golden curls flying, and longed to go after her. When she was out of sight, he turned away, sick at heart.

* * *

That Sunday, Shona was playing with Ian. She had stacked pillows around him, for he had difficulty in sitting alone. He was stacking his blocks; failing entirely to place a chosen block, he let out a scream of frustration—and the doorbell rang.

A spectacled young lady with tightly drawn hair, greeted Shona pleasantly. "I'm Mary Jane McKay. I represent the Tribune. May I speak to you for a few minutes?"

Busy quieting the child, Shona motioned her to the striped satin settee, and went on putting the block in Ian's hand and helping to place it in the wall he was building.

The reporter ventured a look around. Never had she seen such luxury. The shining hardwood floors, the Persian carpet, the heavy drapes and delicate lace curtains; it was a dream home. Obviously, this girl had everything.

When Ian had quieted, Shona rose to face her visitor.

Almost apologetically, Miss McKay stated her mission." I wanted to ask about your little brother. What kind of disease does he have?"

Reluctantly, Shona tried to describe Ian's condition, avoiding her recent session with the police.

Miss McKay listened patiently, but she seemed to be more interested in Shona. "Can you tell me something about yourself? They say you were kidnapped by a witch."

Shona flared. "That's not true—you shouldn't repeat it. Kate found me, and took me to live with her."

"At any rate, she should have brought you home. Didn't you miss your parents?"

"I don't know. I was so small; when Kate said she was my mother, I believed it. Actually, she *was* my mother for about five years, I think."

The reporter changed the subject. "What about yourself? It's said that you can see the future. Is that true?"

Shona was angry again. "Who told you that? I haven't had much to do with people around here."

"It seems that you predicted, since the birth of the baby, that something would be wrong. Is that true?"

"No, it's not true. I was wondering, but when he was healthy for two years, I thought I was wrong." She was at a loss—who could have told the reporter this story?

Miss McKay wasn't to be put off. "You say you were wondering? Was the baby sickly when it was born?"

Before she could answer, Sophie came into the room. She had purposely stayed away, so that Shona could speak for herself, but when she entered the dining room to put away some embroidered napkins, she heard the last remark, and intervened.

"Young lady, I think you've asked enough questions for today. This ailment of my little boy was not evident until recently. It's a progressive disease. My daughter is in no way responsible."

She was exceptionally pretty that day. Her dark, shining hair was caught back in a cluster of short curls, and her blue eyes matched her simple print dress. Right now, her eyes were flashing. Shona felt a surge of pride.

Embarrassed, the woman got to her feet. "I wasn't accusing Shona of anything, certainly. I was just interested in her seeming ability to foretell events of the future. Perhaps . . ."

"We don't believe in fortune-telling, Miss; Shona has always been a dreamer. Is that any reason to stigmatize her for life? She loves the boy and would do anything for him. There's really nothing more to be said."

Strangely, as Sophie came to the defense of her daughter, she strengthened her own belief in the child. She was convinced that, aside from the strange, psychic powers with which Shona had been born, she had been innocent of all charges.

* * *

ELEVENTH

Soon after that, the "Three Musketeers," as they called themselves, were trudging home from school. They made an interesting study in contrasts: Peggy, a serene girl, with short, black hair; Peace, baby-faced, her hair in long, blonde plaits, and Shona, much younger, a porcelain doll, with red-gold curls to her shoulders.

Without warning, a half-dozen teen-aged boys jumped out in front of them from an alley between stores. One of them grabbed Peace by her pigtails, and another tripped Peggy, sending her sprawling. Laughing, they turned to Shona, but she was too quick for them. As she helped Peggy to her feet, she was facing them with blazing eyes.

"What do you think you're doing?" she flared. "You ought to be ashamed of yourselves, picking on girls."

One of them, more brazen than the rest, stepped forward. "We got nothin' against the others—let 'em go home. We want to talk to you, witch."

The girls looked at each other—then at the spokesman. Peggy stepped forward. "We're staying. No one is a witch, anyhow."

A short, stout lad with a pleasant face, said, "I think she's right. I don't see anyone here who looks like a witch."

Another, agreed. "I never did believe that stuff about this MacDonald girl. "C'mon, Isaac, let's call it off. She can't show us anything about witchcraft."

Isaac bristled. "You fellows don't know anything, do you? I read—that's more than some of you do. Some of the worst witches, the Sirens, would lure men at sea, to their deaths. They were beautiful, too."

He stopped explaining, and turned to Shona. "Listen, you. We all know you was raised by a witch; you've got to know some tricks. We want to get even with old 'Bulldog', and I think you can help us. I'll even pay you."

Shona tossed her head. "The principal never did anything to me. Even if I were a witch, I wouldn't help you to do anything. I'm going home, and so are my friends. Please let us pass."

"Not so fast, witch. I told your pals they could go. I've got other plans for you." He indicated the other girls with a jerk of his head, but no one moved.

Irritated, he stepped toward Shona with an upraised fist. "You'll be sorry, if you don't get rid of these . . ."

With one accord, Peggy and Peace flew into action. They knocked Isaac down; Peggy sat on him, banging his head on the brick walk, while Peace defied the other boys to stop her.

Amused, the five other gang members were quite satisfied to stay out of the fray. After all, they weren't too fond of Isaac, and had only come along for fun.

After flattening Isaac, Peggy got up, took Shona's hand, and said, "Let's get out of here."

Together, the girls trooped away, leaving Isaac lying on the sidewalk. He wasn't moving; the boys were beginning to be apprehensive.

Then, a quiet little fellow piped up, "That's a good idea."

"What's a good idea?" asked the chubby one.

"Let's get out of here." With that, they took off, leaving Isaac to whatever fate was in store for him.

* * *

Shona arrived at home, distraught. Cassie met her coming up the street, alone. "Where's yo' friends, chile? Don' you know tain't safe to be on the street alone? I come to look—yo' Mama, she done worry, when you late."

Being in no mood for a sermon, Shona ran ahead of her, into the house and up to her room, without looking for her mother.

Sinking down on the pink chaise lounge, she looked about. It was a lovely room, she thought. Pink rosebuds on the bedspread and bolster, pink ruffles at the windows. Why couldn't it be a pink life, pleasant and beautiful, with nothing to do but enjoy its loveliness?

She knew that it wasn't to be. The grim facts of her existence cast purple shadows, and a deeper darkness seemed to be facing her. An omen, so familiar to her lately, cast its shadow over her, but she could not cry.

Cassie came in, just then. After one look at her beloved child, she took Shona in her arms. "Ise sorry, chile. I jest came by to tell you I didn' mean to be cross. Cain't he'p worryin' honey. Too many bad folks, wishin' you harm."

Shona responded with a hug. "Cassie, when you stop worrying, I'll know you've stopped loving me. I did have a bad experience for a while, but everything's okay, now."

Aware that things were not right, Shona pushed the omen far from her conscious thought. Whatever was to happen, she would deal with it.

* * *

Shona wakened to a dark Saturday—one of those mornings when the sun hadn't yet shown its face at nine o'clock. Of course, from Will's point of view, since the mills were going full blast, it was going to be a pleasant day.

But with Shona, things were not well. She stayed in bed much longer than usual, but she was unable to sleep. The pain in her head was usually bearable; in fact, she had learned to ignore it. This morning, oddly, it was there in full force.

She had just finished dressing, when she heard a loud rap at the door. She couldn't hear what was going on, but there was a man's voice, shouting, angry. She sat down on the bed. There was no point in going down. Whatever it was, it wasn't good.

Cassie tapped on the bedroom door. "Honey, maybe you should come downstairs. "Yo' Mama don't know what this man sayin'."

She rose from the bed with a sigh. Somehow, this was no surprise. She glanced in the mirror of her vanity dresser as she passed, not remembering combing her hair. It was all right; she was very pretty in her lilac dress with the smocked bodice. That was no asset. Witches come in all shapes and forms.

There was more than one man downstairs. The room seemed to be filled with people. Facing the large, red-faced individual in its center stood Sophie, trembling.

The florid man was bellowing: "There's to be a town meeting tonight. You and your husband had better be there. If you're afraid of what your witch daughter might do, better leave her at home."

Shona pushed through, to rescue her mother. "What is it I'm supposed to have done, now?

He glared at her. "Injured my son, and left him for dead; that's what you did, you . . ."

"I never touched your son. If you don't believe that, I have witnesses to prove it."

For a moment, he seemed to be uncomfortable. Then, his confidence returned. "Maybe you didn't do it yourself, but you made that girl injure him. That's what witches do—they make things happen."

Shona looked him over. Suddenly, she felt very adult. This man must not be allowed to dominate the room. She faced him with a frown. "Just who are you, sir? How dare you come here and bully my mother? If you have a complaint, take it to the authorities. We don't want you in this house."

Staggered by the flashing eyes and flushed face of the little girl, he flinched. "I'm Josh Carpenter, and Isaac is my son." Recovering some of his anger, he turned to Sophie. "We sure do have a complaint. You'll be hearing about it tonight at seven. See that you're there—city hall."

He turned to the men standing behind him, and the group left at once, as though glad to get away.

Shona sat down beside her mother, who had dropped to the settee. "Are you all right, Mama?" She put her hand on Sophie's brow.

Annoyed, Sophie faced her. "I'm just fine, Shona. Now, please tell me what's been going on. It looks as though I don't really have a daughter. You don't confide in me; I don't know what you're doing, and, worst of all, you get into trouble."

"Mama," Shona's voice was low, "I only wanted to spare you. Some boys caught us coming home from school and tried to make me do some witchcraft. When this man's horrible boy threatened me, Peggy beat him up. Then we left. I didn't do anything."

"You left? The boy was hurt, and you left him? Shona, that's not the kind and loving girl that you used to be. What were you thinking of?"

"I was thinking of getting out of there—that's what I was thinking. Peggy and Peace were in danger; especially Peggy. What if those boys decided to punish her?"

Privately, her mother agreed with her, but she couldn't let the matter rest. "But, now you could be in some trouble. Was the boy badly hurt?"

Shona gave her a sheepish look. "I think he was unconscious; he wasn't moving. Peggy banged his head on the bricks pretty hard."

Horrified, Sophie tried to explain that this was not a simple occurrence. If this action were to reflect on Shona, it could change the whole course of her life. Later, telling Will about it, was her next worry. Oddly, he did not explode. Instead, he decided on a session with his daughter.

Shona was almost afraid of Will, when he was angry. Now, he was probably angrier than he had ever been with her. For years, he had been scolding Sophie for her crazy ideas of Shona's strange powers. But ever since Shona's return to her home, she had been in trouble with someone. Were the stories fiction or fact? By Jupiter, he would find out.

In a harsh voice that sounded through the house, he called

for Shona.

She found him in the study; sitting in his swivel chair and elbow-deep in papers. The roll-top desk was loaded; there were long, narrow account books written in his elaborate cursive hand, and reams of purchase orders and receipts.

He looked at her over his half-glasses and snapped, "Sit down, young lady." This wasn't a friendly greeting. She felt chilled. He hadn't even turned his chair.

Dropping into a large, leather rocker, she waited for him to speak. There was a low fire in the fireplace, casting a shimmering light over massive seascapes on the wall, and model ships on a shelf.

She had always considered this a pleasant room. Now for some reason, it loomed ominous as a cave. Will wrote two more entries, and finally swung his chair around.

"Daughter, I have some questions to ask, and I expect some dang straight answers. Understand?"

Wordlessly, she nodded.

"This—woman . . . What kind of witchcraft did she do?" His dark eyes searched her face as though looking for denial.

She gave it to him. "Papa, she didn't do witchcraft. If they believe someone is a witch because she has herbs and the wisdom to cure wounds and illness, then, I suppose she was a witch. She always said she wasn't."

"Well, this woman that wasn't a witch—what did she teach you?"

Shona forgot fear; she was angry. "She didn't teach me anything that wasn't good. I learned how to care for the animals when they were injured by cruel men. I learned how to plant things, and how to cook. I learned about the Good Man, too. Does that make her wicked?"

He ignored her defiant tone, and tried another angle. "Your mother's been telling me for most of your life that you can see things—before they happen. Where's she get this notion?"

"Papa, I do see things. Sometimes I see clearly what will happen; other times I just see blackness, and I get an awful headache."

He pondered that, and couldn't deal with it. "That's nonsense," he sputtered, rising from his chair and pacing the room. "It's also the kind of foolishness that gives you trouble. Don't you dast tell anyone such a story."

"But, Papa, some people do know." She hadn't wanted to say that Miss MacKay had been asking about it.

"They know? You been tellin' that around?" He stopped to glare at her.

"No, Papa. I think Miss McKay heard it somewhere. Maybe one of the neighbors . . ."

"Neighbors? What neighbors? We don't have nothin' to do with no one but Sadie Owen, and she ain't likely to carry tales."

"There's Amanda Davies," Shona reminded him.

"She don't count. She's always around, borrowin' sugar or somethin' but your Mama don't talk to her, much."

Tired of the discussion, Shona blurted, "I don't know then. All I know is that I'm being blamed for things that I haven't done, and I want to die."

She flew out of the room and up the stairs. Flinging herself on the bed, her mind filled with ideas to escape all this harassment. It came to her that the key to the old cabin was still hanging in the kitchen. There was some place to go, after all—away from Johnstown and its horrible people.

Slipping down the back stairs, she crossed the hall and peered into the kitchen. Cassie was standing at the stove, with her back to Shona. Could she reach the key, around the corner, without making a sound? She moved toward the key rack, and picked off the key, inadvertently touching some other keys, which jingled.

Hurriedly, she replaced the key, and stood there, not knowing what to do, or say.

"Lan' sakes, chile," Cassie beamed, coming to put her arms around Shona. "You been so busy with school 'n other things, that you don't seem to have time fo' Cassie 'n the kitchen. Now, you jest set in that rocker, 'n Cassie'll give you a warm cinnamon roll."

Shona dropped her head. "No, thanks, Cassie. I couldn't eat anything. In fact, I think I'll go upstairs. I don't feel very good."

Alarmed by Shona's dismal attitude and her pallor, Cassie went to Sophie. She was very pretty, in the lilac printed dress which Sophie had made, and her spotless white apron and frilled cap. Sophie, sitting on the porch swing smiled her admiration.

Cassie had not come for praise. Before Sophie could speak, she blurted,, "Miz Sophie, what's wrong with Miss Shona? She's white as a ghos'. Won't even have a cinnamon roll, jes' out of the oven. Say she goin' to bed."

"Dear me," sighed Sophie. "I hope Will wasn't too hard on her. He wanted to talk to her alone, and I don't know what went on." Noting Cassie's worried expression, she soothed, "I'll go to her, Cassie. I'm sure there's nothing to worry about."

Just then, Will came out on the porch, and Cassie beat a hurried retreat. She didn't like the look in his eyes and the set of his jaw.

Will sat down beside Sophie; she was a comfort to him. Looking up, she touched his face. He gave her a despairing look, and took her in his arms.

* * *

That evening, the city's council chambers were packed; those attending were the angry, the fearful, and, of course, the curious. As a matter of fact, the latter made up the majority.

Uneasily, Shona looked around the room with no idea of what she would be facing. What more could she explain? Just as she was about to sit down, she saw him. It was Michael.

Her transformation was barely short of miraculous. Her eyes shone like sapphires, and her delicate face glowed in sheer radiance. Watching Shona, her mother, who was accustomed to the child's beauty, gasped.

Her eyes followed the direction of Shona's gaze. She caught a glimpse of him as he sat down in the rear section of chairs. She knew that young man from somewhere. Yes, she remembered, he was Shona's teacher.

Now, she recalled, it seemed as though Shona had known him in the past. Sophie had paid little attention to the story. She regretted that. Obviously, this young man meant a great deal to her daughter.

The president of the council was George Thatcher, a bald-headed man with a luxuriant brown beard and a kindly face. He had no idea why this beautiful child was the cause of controversy. With a tap of his gavel, he called the unruly meeting to order.

"Due to the fact that this is a special meeting, there will be no business tonight. There seems to be a complaint for the council to address. Who has the complaint?

At that, Josh Carpenter was on his feet. He described the attack on his son as being entirely unprovoked, and blamed, not Peggy, but Shona, for the damage to the boy.

Thatcher frowned. "How is your son, now? What is the extend of his injury?"

"He's got a concussion, that's what he's got. His head's bruised real bad. Something's got to be done about that girl."

"I suppose you mean Shona MacDonald?"

"Whatever they call her. I call her '*witch*'."

The chairman's mouth tightened. "Mr. Carpenter, there will be no name-calling. You'll have to be more explicit. Just what is it that you think Shona MacDonald has done to your son?"

Josh exploded. "She put a hex on him—that's what she did."

"And how do you know that?"

"Why, everybody knows she lived with the 'Hogback Witch.' She got that stuff by bein' around that old woman."

Patiently, Mr. Thatcher heard him out, as well as the testimony of the Rearick sisters, about the baby. Here, he seemed to be impressed.

Aloud, he reflected. "Couldn't this have been an illness, which the girl was trying to alleviate?"

Sara, who had done most of the talking, looked at her sister for support. Lucy had never spoken in public, and her voice quavered. "We did see the girl fussing with the child. And a lot of people believe that she's a witch."

Thatcher rapped his gavel. "Miss Rearick, I'm afraid that, too, is hearsay. Have you anything concrete to submit?"

She shook her head and sank into her chair, embarrassed to have spoken at all.

Before the chairman could call for another witness, Mary Jane McKay, reporter for the *Johnstown Tribune*, stood up, asking to be recognized by the chair.

Recognition granted, she smiled. This was her repayment of a brush-off.

"Sir," she clipped, "Shona admitted to me that she knew there would be something wrong with her brother, before he was born. He was a fine, healthy child, but at the age of two, he developed a strange disease. What would you make of that?"

"Pure coincidence," snapped Thatcher. Actually, he didn't know what to make of it. "Are there any other complaints?"

No one stood up. He smiled at Shona. "I guess it's your turn. Seems as though you might have a lot to say."

Shona rose to her feet, reluctantly. "Not too much, sir. The boys jumped us. Peggy here," she cast a grateful look at her friend beside her, "saw the boy threaten me, so she grabbed him. Peace, over there, watched to make sure that the other boys didn't do anything. I had nothing to do with it. I'm not a witch."

"Why did the boys accost you?"

"This boy said they wanted me to help them do something to the school principal, to get even with him. I refused."

"And what about this other thing about the baby?" His voice was gentle.

Just then, a voice from the rear spoke up. "May I explain this, sir."

The chairman nodded.

The man came to the front of the room. "I'm Doctor John Ferguson, specializing in metabolic disease. The MacDonald baby is under my care—such as it is. This small child has a rare form of infantile dystrophy, a progressive illness. This never becomes evident much before the age of two. There is little hope for the child. Certainly, Shona had nothing whatever to do with his trouble."

Shona brightened. Things were better now, since the doctor's explanation, but how did he know to come? She had no idea that her father had made a visit to the physician, pleading for help.

Apparently, Chairman Thatcher was assured of Shona's innocence, but there was still the question of her life with the so-called "witch," and of her psychic ability.

In a flash, Shona knew that Michael was going to speak.

She had barely caught the thought, when Michael was on his feet. "Mr. Chairman, there have been many unfounded charges here. Before you adjourn, I would like to say some things. I am in a better position to know Shona than anyone, even her parents."

Given permission, he came forward, a fair-skinned, blue-eyed, young man, with sort, curly brown hair. All Shona could think of was a picture of Michaelangelo's *David*.

Usually at ease in public, Michael found it difficult to express himself when it came to Shona. Somehow, he collected his thoughts.

He looked around the crowded room. "You probably know that I was lost, up in the hogback, and that a search party found me days later. What you may not know is that the 'Hogback Witch' rescued me. I was caught in an abandoned bear trap. She saved my leg—also my life. She did all this with simple herbs. There were no incantations."

There was a stir in the crowd; then everyone was quiet, hanging on his words.

He continued. "As for Shona, she helped nurse me when I was almost completely helpless. She applied poultices, brought me soup, and ran errands for Kate. She fed the chickens, gathered eggs, and weeded the herb garden. It's incredible that anyone should accuse her of witchcraft."

Pausing, he looked at the chairman. "I guess that's it."

"Then, I suppose we must have a vote. Will the secretary poll the council, individually? It may be a standing vote. The question is: Do you believe that Shona MacDonald is responsible for the injuries to Isaac Carpenter?"

"The 'nays' were unanimous. The room cleared quickly, except for the MacDonalds, and Michael.

Shona brought so close to Michael, felt a weakening of her knees which she had never experienced before. She wasn't sure that she could remain standing. A warm feeling came over her; all she could think of was getting away. Nevertheless, she had to face the fact that she owed him a great deal.

Politely, she murmured, "Thank you, Michael, for standing up for me."

Will brushed by her and grasped his hand. "Young fellow, if you ever need a job in the mill, it's yours. I do thank you for what you done."

Sophie nodded. "Indeed, we do sir. I wonder if you would come for dinner on Sunday? We're having the usual chicken, if you'd like that?"

He was about to decline, politely, when he saw Shona's face. It was so full of hope and expectation that he knew he was trapped. There was no way to deny those eyes.

"Thank you very much, Mrs. MacDonald. I'll be happy to accept, if it won't be too much trouble."

They turned; the room was empty, except for Mr. Thatcher, who was waiting to lock up.

Leaving the building with Mr. Thatcher, Michael and the MacDonalds noticed a group of people almost encircling them. That corner of Main and Market streets had newly installed gas lights, and the cluster of faces seemed almost ghostly.

No one moved toward them, but a sudden barrage of tomatoes, eggs and stones pelted them from all directions. A voice they all recognized as that of Josh Carpenter, yelled, "You're all in cahoots—don't think we don't know that. But you won't get away with it, you'll see."

At that, a stone flew by Shona, grazing her mother's head. She dropped to the ground; Will and Shona knelt beside her. Michael took off after the assailant, and as suddenly as the crowd had appeared, it dissipated. Only a few aghast pedestrians stood on the opposite corner.

Sophie's cut bled copiously. Will stanched it with his pocket handkerchief and looked up at Thatcher, who stood helpless. "Could you get some help? I live right down there . . ."

Before he could say more, George Thatcher was off, calling back over his shoulder, "I know where you live . . . and I know Plato. Right back."

In a few seconds, he was out of sight, just as Michael came running back. Sophie was sitting up, dazed and smeared with blood and egg yolk.

"Couldn't catch him," he gasped, panting for breath. "But he won't get away with this, believe me. We'll have that Carpenter fellow behind bars, as soon as they catch him."

Will was too angry to respond. Michael looked around at the others, and could barely suppress a smile. He, himself, like them, had great splotches of egg and tomato on his clothing. He would have made a remark, but when he saw Will's face, he decided that any attempt to lighten the situation would make it worse.

The police, it appeared, had their sympathies in another direction. Both Michael and Will were given a series of intensive questions about their complaint. Afterward, it was decided that there must be a valid reason why so many people believed that Shona was a witch.

The upshot of it was that they refused to arrest Carpenter. There was no proof that the assault was his work, or had anything to do with him. The fact was mentioned that the new gas lights cast eerie shadows on faces. Perhaps, Carpenter wasn't in the crowd at all.

By this time, Will seemed to be a good candidate for apoplexy. His face was turkey-gobbler red, and he constantly paced the floor. However, he did have a plan.

The idea was, with the help of Jim Brewster, to organize a vigilante committee to round up the perpetrators of the wrongdoing, and bring them to punishment.

He found Jim in the Bessemer mill, where the roller-driver table pushed the ingots with an hydraulic pusher. Jim was substituting for the supervisor, watching the rolling of the steel blooms.

He spotted Will, and came forward, jabbing at his forehead

with a blue handkerchief. "Will," he grinned. "What brings you here? I haven't seen you in a coon's age."

His smile faded, seeing the grim expression on Will's face. "What's the matter, Will? I hope it's nothing serious."

"Are you with me? I need someone to help me with a project."

"Of course, Will. I'll do anything I can."

But, after he heard Will's intention, he withdrew. "That's not a good idea. What would we do with these fellows, even if we could catch them? We can't do anything illegal."

Will gave him a crestfallen look. "What then? The police are no help, and this Carpenter shouldn't be allowed to injure other citizens and get away with it."

"I agree. But there are other ways to punish him, and any others who aided in his crime."

MacDonald brightened. His friend saw the hopeful look, and raised a hand. "Not so fast. It may not be possible."

Eagerly, Will pressed him. "Give it to me. Why wouldn't it be possible. What is it you're considerin'?"

"Well, other than his family, what is it that means more to a man than anything else?"

He reflected. "His job, I guess."

"Exactly. That's where we may be able to get him. I've seen him around the mill, and I suppose this is where his friends work, too. First, I have to do some checking."

Seeing Will's puzzled expression, he explained. There had been a great deal of stealing going on; most of it just small items. Men had been forging their own tools: hammers, screwdrivers, and other implements. If Carpenter could be caught making off with anything, he could be blackmailed into confessing his deed—perhaps naming his fellow thugs.

MacDonald didn't think much of it. "Ain't that chancey? How do we know he'd do anything like that? And what good would it do us?"

Jim showed some impatience. "Can't you see, if a fellow doesn't mind breaking the law in one place, he'll break it in another. If he's caught by us, he'll know it will cost him his job not to cooperate. Get it?"

Now, Will was elated. "I always admired you, Jim. You're a good man. Now, how do we go about catching the fellow?"

"You just leave that to me. I'll contact you—but first I must find out where he works."

* * *

TWELFTH

Sunday dinner at MacDonald's home proved satisfactory to

Shona's parents—tragic, to the little girl. Throughout the meal, Michael avoided her eyes, and soon made his departure with the excuse that he had papers to grade.

That was true enough, he thought, walking home. And from now on, he would dodge any personal contact with Shona. If he couldn't look at her without the sort of thoughts which a man shouldn't have about a thirteen-year-old girl, he wouldn't see her at all.

Shona, on the other hand, was so crushed that for a little while she decided on hating Michael. Why was he so cruel to her? He was courteous; that was it.

That afternoon, she felt abandoned. Even Cassie, who was so busy helping Sophie with the baby, and the many problems he was causing, had little time for her. Beset with the notion that no one needed her, she decided to leave.

This time, she found the kitchen empty. She took down the keys and stuck them into her reticule. It was real silk; a gift from her father on her thirteenth birthday. She had loved it, seeing this as a sign that he recognized her adulthood. Now, she thought, he would probably be glad to be rid of her.

With a few personal belongings and two neatly folded dresses in her small carpetbag, she set out to find her old home.

It was early evening, darkened prematurely by thick clouds, rather than mill smoke. The gas lights had not yet been turned on. Keeping out of sight as much as possible, Shona moved through side streets toward the mountain.

Once up among the trees, her sense of adventure took over. She knew the general direction she must take, for the sun had set near her home, and the hogback rose east of Johnstown.

Climbing carefully and steadily upward, to lessen chances of discovery, she was fascinated by the number of small woodland creatures scurrying by. It didn't occur to her that night was falling fast, and she was a long way from her destination.

Suddenly, she heard an ominous sound. Looking down, she saw an enormous rattlesnake at her feet. Swiftly, she leaped over it, just before the snake struck.

Shona moved faster now. She had recognized that, as Kate had warned, the forest is not always kindly to poachers.

Tonight, the moon was full. She was grateful for that. Her heart was pounding, almost as though it couldn't hold out at that rate. Upward through the trees she sped, now beginning to wonder whether she could find the house. The stream she was looking for must have changed, for there were several streams, branching out, probably altered by the latest spring flood.

Climbing around a clump of rock, she came upon the clearing which was only about a mile from Kate's. They had found a baby skunk there once, the only time she had seen the glade.

It was just a matter of traveling that mile. Shona had been

weary of climbing; now she found extra strength, and soon reached the house.

There were boards across the windows. Using a heavy stick as a lever, she pried the boards off, but the house was still very dark.

She unlocked the door and let it stand open. Moonlight shot through the doorway and across the room. She headed for the lamp on the table, and lighted it. With a sense of nostalgia, she sat in Kate's tall rocker, saddened by a deep sense of loss.

Then, she realized that someone, seeing the light in the abandoned cabin, might come to see what was going on. She closed and locked the door, and made her bed hurriedly.

Climbing into the bunk where she had slept for those years, Shona was happy for the first time in many months. She turned her face to the moonlight, then, remembering, slipped out of bed to say her prayers.

* * *

All was not well at the MacDonald household. With the morning had come the disturbing fact that Shona was nowhere to be found.

Cassie had gone up to waken her for school, and came back with the news that her bed had not been slept in. Sophie was more puzzled than worried. "Where could she have gone?"

Cassie thought for a while. Then she said, "Mebbe she done made her bed and took a walk."

"But why?" asked Sophie. "Why would she go alone? She knows that's not safe."

Cassie chuckled. "Ah don' reckon there's much Miss Shona's afeered of. She did tell me she had to do some naturin' fo' school."

Shona had been gathering leaves for a community science project, and was also making a collection of seeds. It all made sense to Sophie, but by evening, when no one had seen Will's daughter, he exploded.

"It's that Carpenter, that's who it is. He's got my child, and by Jimminy, he'll pay for it. If he touches a hair of her head, he'll have some answering to do."

Sophie soothed him. "Don't blame Carpenter. I could see things heaping on her, till she's tired bearing them. Let's check with the YWCA. She might go there, to get away, where no one could get to her."

But there was no such word from the YWCA, and Will was off to the police, to attempt to organize a search, although he knew what the answer would be.

Unfortunately, Sophie had other problems which were keeping her mind so occupied, that she left the recovery of her daughter to Will. Little Ian could no longer walk; but that was the least of his problems. The worst part of the illness was the incidence of his tortured seizures. Even under kind, gentle hands there was no release. Moaning, he jerked and twitched, until at last he would drop into an exhausted sleep.

Today, Sophie and Cassie were having a session of massage for the little fellow. This was intended to prevent deformities of his wrists and ankles by manipulating and exercising the controlling tendons. The doctor had encouraged it, but they had noted with dismay continuing areas of atrophy in the tiny limbs.

"Cassie, this isn't helping," Sophie cast a despairing look over the child, who was quite relaxed and calm. Mutely, Cassie agreed. Sophie's eyes filled with tears.

For a moment, they stood silent; then Cassie swept the stricken Sophie into her arms. Stroking the dark, curly head, she murmured, "Honey, ah knows you'se got jest about as much trouble as a body kin stand. But you got to go on, don' you see? Cain't let up, nohow."

Sophie straightened and took a handkerchief from her bosom to wipe her eyes. "Cassie, what would I do without you?"

"Lord knows, honey—Lord knows."

They laughed together, freed for just a second, of all the consternation that surrounded them.

Then it was back to Shona, and the anxiety returned.

* * *

As for that little girl, being in the old house was a dream come true. Loving every corner of it, she explored. In the great cupboard, and the adjoining smokehouse, she found enough provisions to last an entire family for a long time.

There were dried apples, dried apricots, prunes, and raisins. Heaped in bins, she found navy beans and peas, and, in a row of jars, every kind of cooking herb she would need. The smokehouse contained smoked ham, bacon, and a store of beef jerky.

Suddenly, returning to the house, she felt a chill. Not daring to light a fire in the fireplace, she built one in the little stove, once used for summer cooking.

Realizing that she was hungry, she brought in some bacon to fry, and a cupful of raisins. It was not exactly the kind of breakfast she was accustomed to, but that didn't matter.

Shona looked around the house, Apparently, there was a great deal of work to do. That was fine. Work would prevent thinking of the people for whom she had made so much trouble. For a moment, her thoughts drifted to Michael, but she stopped the fantasy. Angrily, she shut him out.

* * *

Not having touched his supper, Will got up, threw on his

coat and hat and stalked toward the door.

"Where are you going, Will?" called Sophie. "You haven't eaten a bite. Surely . . ."

"I'm goin' to see Carpenter—that's where I'm goin'. And when I get done with him, he won't have no appetite, neither."

"Will," she remonstrated, dismay in her voice. "Please don't go. I know Shona left on her own. Two of her best dresses are gone—so is her carpetbag."

That almost stopped him. Still, he wouldn't be denied the privilege of letting this fellow know what would happen if he ever did anything to Shona.

His tension easing a bit, he turned. "Sophie, I got to see this fellow. If for nothing else, he has to know that he won't get off Scott-free with his crimes. It won't hurt to threaten him, a bit."

She remonstrated, but he was gone. It would be so much easier, she thought, if Will were not so impulsive.

Somewhat calmer, Will took the walk to the Carpenter home. Jim had told him where it was located—in Woodvale, right in the heart of the city. He had also discovered that the man worked in the wire mill.

On the way, Will considered his wife's comment. Had Shona run off? Why? Where would she go? He had no time to ponder; the Carpenter home was just ahead.

He noted with surprise that this was not the usual millworker's house, with white picket fence and tiny yard. Set back some distance from the street, it was a stone mansion as large as his own, with neatly manicured shrubbery, and oval beds of flowers, glowing with chrysanthemums and asters of all colors.

Will entered the gate thoughtfully. How could this man, not an executive, have the kind of money to manage this type of estate? He became more convinced than ever that the fellow was crooked.

Grimly, he rapped on the door. A maid answered it. She was dressed almost identically like Cassie, with a frilled cap and apron.

"Is Mr. Josh Carpenter at home?" he inquired, trying to peer around her at the luxurious living room.

She blocked his vision. "No, sir, he's at work. He's on the three-to-eleven shift."

Frustrated, he was about to leave, when a pretty young woman appeared. "It's all right, Jane; you may go."

The maid left, and she opened the door wider to let him in. "May I ask your business, sir?" Entirely at ease, she had a dignified air which Will had to respect.

Not knowing just what to say, he mumbled, "I came to see your husband. I'm Will MacDonald, and my daughter is missing. I'll admit, Mrs. Carpenter, I thought he might know something about it."

She dropped some of her aloofness. "Sir, are you insinuating that my husband would stoop to kidnapping? I consider that an insult." She tossed her pretty head with its upswept brown curls, and her blue eyes flashed.

Will had regained some of his own composure. "See here, ma'am, what about the insult when he threw a stone and hit my wife? What about the insult to my family and some friends when he organized a mob to pelt us with eggs, tomatoes and rocks? Let me tell you, lady, he got away with that stuff for now, but I ain't finished with him."

There being little more to say, he turned to leave; she put out a staying hand. "Mr. MacDonald, is it true—what you say about my husband?"

He came back to her. "Every blessed word. If I'd had more proof, beside us only hearin' his voice, he'd be in jail right now." Mollified, he was glad to be able to tell the story. Obviously, Carpenter hadn't confided in his wife.

Her chin trembled. Lord, he hoped she wouldn't cry. He never could cope with a woman in tears. He needn't have worried. As swiftly as she had lost her serenity, she regained it.

She extended her hand. He didn't know why, but he took it. "I'm so sorry, Mr. MacDonald. I do hope you're mistaken. It doesn't seem to me that Josh would be capable of such things."

Gratified to have found a willing ear, Will left, rather pleased. He couldn't help wishing he could be around when Josh's wife asked him about the incident. Of course, he would lie.

When he opened the gate, to his surprise, Plato was waiting for him, with the surrey, Fearing trouble, Sophie had sent him.

Pleasantly, Will climbed into the coach. "What's the news, Plato? Have you heered anything about my Shona?"

Plato shook his head. "Don' know nuttin'," Mr. Will. I'se certain there be news today. Miz Sophie's expectin' her to come back."

"Pray she's right, Plato. Lord, what worries we've got. Is Ian all right?"

"Yassuh, Mr. Will. Leastwise, he no worse."

He had to be satisfied with that.

* * *

Surprisingly, to Sophie, Will leaped into the house in a good humor. His meeting with Mrs. Carpenter had been highly satisfactory. This would be the kind of revenge that could make things pretty uncomfortable for a man, at home.

She was relieved, but reproving. While thankful that her husband had not committed the crime of attacking Carpenter, she didn't like his joy.

"Will, you must realize what you've done. This will probably cause a lot of trouble in that home."

"What in tarnation has that fellow caused me? Grief, that's what. You got no call to be takin' his part."

Annoyed, he sat down in his easy chair and picked up the paper.

Plato had been in the kitchen, getting the key to the tool house, when suddenly he let out a shout, and came rushing into the room.

"Folks, I got some good news." In excitement, his breath came out in little gasps.

Will and Sophie both jumped up. "Is it about Shona?" asked Sophie, nearly as breathless as Plato.

"It sho' is, Miz Sophie. Ah knows where she is."

Will grasped him by the arm. "How do you know? What do you mean? Where is she?" Questions came out in a torrent, without giving him time to answer.

Plato grinned. "Jes' be calm, Mr. Will. She in a safe place. She up at her ol' homestead."

"How do you know that?" pressed Will, giving his arm a shake.

Plato pulled away. "When I come to git the key to the tool shed, I see the place empty, where Miz Shona's house key use' to be. So, I put two and two together."

He expected Will to be relieved, and was not prepared for his reaction.

"Get the buggy, at once. Lord, who knows where she is? Move, Plato!"

Plato gave him a bewildered look. "But Mr. Will, I jes' said . . ."

"You said she's safe. What gave you that idea? How do you think she'd ever find the place? If she took off to the hill from here . . ."

Suddenly, Plato realized what he meant. The forest west of Johnstown constituted a favorite hunting place. Its luxuriant vegetation housed creatures, large and small, some of them dangerous.

But, Plato had been hunting, too. He knew that few, if any wildcats and bears remained here. That kind of game was to be found in Richland or Jackson township, or perhaps Laurel Ridge, where a hardier type of hunter was apt to go.

As they drove, he pointed out the facts to Will, who, nevertheless, sat tight-lipped and shaken, beside him. Pity Miz Shona, he thought to himself. Mr. Will was going to be furious.

Climbing the steep part of the Hogback was difficult for Will. Not accustomed to as much physical activity as Plato, he had to stop occasionally. That was not for long. He pressed on; there was no time to be lost.

When they reached the cleared area where the cabin stood, he breathed a sigh of relief. Obviously, the boards had been pried off the windows. They had been propped up, to prevent light's showing through. He noted a tiny wisp of smoke coming through a small pipe on the roof.

Will was so relieved that he almost forgot to be angry. He ran to the door and tried the knob. The door was locked; he banged it with his fist.

Inside, Shona was quaking. Who could know she was here? What kind of person would do such terrible pounding? An old reflex almost took over. She turned toward the cupboard, then shook herself, mentally. What was she thinking of?

Will kept pounding. She would open this door, or by golly, he would break it down.

Standing far back from the door, she called, "Go away. I'm not going to open the door."

To her surprise, she heard her father's voice. "Gol dern it, you'll open this door, or I will."

Her relief was so great, that she unlocked the door and threw herself on her father. "Oh, Papa, I'm so glad it's you. I was frightened." She gave him a kiss, but he held her off.

"What do you think you're doin', young lady. Git your clothes and let's get out of here."

She stepped backward. "I'm not leaving."

Grabbing her arm, he growled, "Yes, you are, or I'll know why."

She wrenched herself away and backed up further. "Papa, I'm staying. This is my house, and I have a right . . ."

Will glared. "I don't care whose house it is, you're my daughter, and you're goin' to stay under my roof until you're of age."

"But why, Papa? I can take care of myself."

He tried a more gentle approach. "Shona, use your head. How could you keep yourself warm in the winter? Winters are bad up here. You'd have to carry water—mebbe you couldn't even git out of the house. And what if someone broke in and . . ."

She hesitated. "Maybe Cassie could come up for a while?"

At that, Plato stepped forward. Before he could speak, Will roared, "Are you crazy, child? Ain't Cassie got more 'n enough, trying to keep up her work and look after li'l Ian? Seems you could help—not leave her high 'n dry."

That struck Shona like a blow. Her shoulders sagged, and she whispered, "You're right, Papa. I shouldn't have deserted Cassie and Mama, when they have so much to do. I thought it would be easier, without me to cause trouble."

He put an arm around her shoulder. Never had he seen her quite so dirty, or so lovable. Her golden curls had become a mass of fluff, her face was streaked with coal dust, and who knew what had happened to her pink pinafore.

"Come on, honey," he said. "Let's go home to Mama."

Willingly, she let Plato take the carpetbag, which was still unpacked. As he led the way down the old path, she was thinking. She wouldn't be a child forever. When they no longer needed her, she would come back to stay.

On the ride home, Will chided himself. Shona should have been punished. Why had he been so lenient? He chuckled to himself. She always could get around him. But, that wasn't really it. Deep down, he realized what she had been going through; although he wouldn't admit it, he pitied her.

Sophie, on the other hand, was so happy to see Shona, that she cried. This was more punishment than the little girl could bear, so they cried together.

As for Cassie, she did her weeping out of sight. Her empathy with Shona came from a deep perception, which no one, who has not been persecuted, could understand.

* * *

THIRTEENTH

The pettiness which Shona had encountered in Johnstown, was not an example of the city in general. In spite of the large number of people employed in the mines and iron works, there was little crime.

Naturally, there were many workers who enjoyed stimulating drinks, but brawls were exceptionally rare. About half of the population was of Welsh origin. These people were naturally orderly, even under the influence of liquor.

As for the other half of the inhabitants, they were well mixed as to heritage. The majority of them were recent immigrants, needing their jobs. With large families, it was expedient to be hard-working and sober.

There was another factor in the peace and prosperity of the Cambria Iron Company. The mills were under the patronage of Philadelphia Quakers.

Under this long-distance direction, Johnstown had prospered. From 1850 to 1880, population statistics had leaped from more than one thousand to more than 20 thousand.

Department managers like Will, with devotion to their jobs, made Johnstown's mills famous. During the Civil War, as loyal citizens, they had subscribed thousands of dollars in Pennsylvania war bonds.

Now, Will faced a dilemma. In spite of his successful career, he wanted peace for his child. Should he leave the city and start anew, somewhere where no one knew Shona's background? She had good reason to be miserable. Was it fair to make her come home to prejudice?

He didn't know that prejudice was only part of Shona's problem. There was no way for him to understand the grief that tortured her.

Shona, so much in love with Michael, had no hope of his ever returning that affection. He would certainly never have a love affair with a child. He had made that clear.

Unhappily, she understood this. What she did not understand was the reason for his avoidance of her. What had happened to their friendship?

Now, another hope had been dashed. Michael didn't come to see why she hadn't been in school for so long. Apparently, he had been unaware that she was missing. Or, was it that he didn't care?

Today, she made her decision. She would never return to school, not even for her coveted diploma. The reason, she wouldn't admit, even to herself. She was afraid of saying goodbye.

To prove that Michael meant nothing to her, Shona set to work with a will. There were household chores to be done for her mother, and she liked helping Cassie prepare vegetables for cooking.

What was more difficult, was assisting in the care of Ian. His plight broke her heart. The once beautiful little boy, half-lying, half-sitting, propped by pillows, was a pathetic sight. He had lost interest in the toys around him, and clung only to his little, satin pillow.

Ian was now sightless—his beautiful blue eyes blank and staring. Perhaps that was the worst thing she had to endure.

Running into the sewing room, one day, Shona threw herself on the floor near her mother. Startled, Sophie put a hand on her head. "What is it, child?"

"Mama, I just can't bear it. Don't make me help with Ian any more. I just can't . . ."

"Of course. And you needn't. I realize that we've been expecting too much of you." Her voice was soothing.

"No, Mama, it isn't that. I can't take seeing him like that." She stopped, then started to say something, and changed her mind.

By this time, Sophie was deeply interested. Shona, so enigmatic, had something on her mind. "Please, dear, tell your mother what's bothering you."

"Mama, I don't like to say it. It's just that lately, when I look at Ian, he isn't there. He just disappears."

Then impatient with herself, she said, "Mama, sometimes I think there's something very wrong with my mind."

Sophie caressed her curly, tousled head. "Honey, I'd give a lot for a mind like yours. Don't worry about anything like that—sometimes one's mind plays tricks."

Mollified, Shona went down to the kitchen to see what Cassie was doing. She found her shelling peas, and sat down to help. Cassie had been wiping her eyes. She hastened to put her handkerchief in her bosom. Shona caught the movement.

"What's wrong, Cassie? Are you having trouble? I know you've been working very hard."

Cassie shook her head and managed a smile. "No, honey, it's jest that li'l Ian seems gettin' worse. Yesterday, he had three of them spells, one right after the other. I's afeered for him."

Shona sobered. "I know, Cassie, I know."

They commiserated with each other, both aware that there had been nothing but increasing debilitation for the child.

Further, Shona's confession to her mother was still in her mind. Somehow, she knew—Ian was going to die.

* * *

Early next Saturday evening, the doorbell rang. Cassie opened the door to a young man whom she had never seen before. He was nicely dressed in a double-breasted reefer suit, and held a nosegay in his hand.

To her inquiring look, he almost whispered, "Is Shona in?"

"Yassuh," said Cassie. "And who might you be?"

"I'm Danny Dayton. I'm Peggy's brother."

Her worry dropped away. At least, this young man was from a respectable family. "Jest set there a spell, sir. I'll call Miz Shona."

Cassie's call alarmed Shona. Something must be wrong with Peggy. She went flying down the stairs, and burst into the living room.

Danny rose from his chair as she came in, and she nearly ran into him. "What's wrong?" she gasped. "Is Peggy all right?"

He smiled, sheepishly. "Yes, she's fine. I came because . . . because . . . Well, there's a lecture at the library tonight. I thought you might want to go. I know I'm seventeen and you're younger, but I've admired you for a long time."

His words spilled out, almost as though he had memorized them. He thrust the nosegay at her, somewhat clumsily. Shona gasped, automatically accepting the flowers. Why would he think she would want to go out with him? And to a lecture?

Tact wasn't necessary; she told him the truth. "I have a headache, and was lying down. I wouldn't be good company, I'm afraid. Thank you, though, for the flowers."

Telling her mother about it afterward,, brought about a strong reaction. Sophie knew that Shona was mature for her age, but certainly, thirteen was too young an age to be dating. She said so, firmly.

However, Shona, who previously had no interest in the young man, was certain that it would be quite proper for her to accompany him to a lecture. Or anywhere.

She would have argued, but when Will came into it, she knew she was defeated. Anyhow, Danny didn't come again.

* * *

A week later, Cassie burst into the dining room in excitement. "Miz Sophie—Mr. Will—come quick! Sumpin' wrong with li'l Ian."

They rushed to the nursery, Shona with them. Ian seemed quite peaceful, one lock of copper hair curled on his forehead, and a half-smile on his pale face.

Sophie caught him up, but he was limp. She listened to his chest, and shook her head. To check his breathing, Will went for the mirror on the small dresser. Holding it to the child's lips, no moisture appeared.

There was no doubt; Ian was gone.

Although the MacDonalds had been fully apprised of the fact that their son had but a short time to live, his death was no less traumatic for the couple.

Will could take anything, no matter how unpleasant, if he had a chance to fight. This was out of his hands. For the first time in years, he was moved to pray. As for Sophie, she was devastated.

Shona, on the other hand, even in sorrow, felt as though a burden had been lifted from her. She had joined in his suffering, perhaps more than the others. The pain of caring for his helpless body, and looking into his beautiful, sightless eyes, at times, had been almost unbearable.

She took to her room, declining both consolation and food. Her only thought was to be alone.

Ian's body had been sent to Henderson, the family undertaker, for care. Sophie had chosen the small white casket, and Will had belatedly purchased a cemetery lot in Grandview.

Shona took no part; lying in her room, she was not sure of her own identity. Although not aware of it, the accusations of the Rearick sisters were there, in the recesses of her mind. From the time of his birth, she had predicted trouble. Was this a tragedy which her negative thinking had brought about?

In the midst of Shona's agony, Sophie came into the room. At first, her own grief had shut out all thought. Now, as she began to regain control, she knew instinctively that her daughter needed her.

Sitting on the side of Shona's bed, she stroked her daughter's hair. Shona, lying face down, lifted her head.

"Oh, Mama," she began, and then the tears came.

Sophie remained silent until she had somewhat recovered. Then, with a break in her voice, she said, "You wouldn't have wanted him to suffer needlessly, in order to keep him, would you?"

Shona wiped her eyes and sat up. "Of course not, Mama; that's not what's bothering me. What if I caused Ian's illness?"

Sophie straightened. "What do you mean, child?" There was alarm in her voice. For years, she had tried to put down the worry that Shona might have some strange power which she, herself, did not understand.

"Mama, I predicted trouble when Ian was born. I don't know why. Maybe it was jealousy, and I did something to him with erroneous thinking. Oh, please, Mama, tell me I'm wrong." Her eyes were shining with tears.

Sophie breathed her relief. The child had no conscious guilt. This psychic gift was just that; there was no way her foreknowledge meant malice.

She looked directly into Shona's eyes, and gave her the assurance she was feeling. "Honey, listen to me. You are not responsible for Ian's illness. You have been given a great gift. Some day, you will be proud of it."

Immensely relieved, Shona went to her mother's arms. For a short time, they comforted each other.

Suddenly realizing that there was much to be done, Sophie stood up, smoothing her rumpled hair. "I had forgotten. Both of us need some clothes. We must buy black dresses."

Unwillingly, Shona acceded to her wish. Not concerned about her beauty, she disliked the formality of wearing black. The Japanese custom of wearing white for mourning, was more to her taste.

At any rate, the gowns were pretty: Sophie's of silk, full-sleeved, with yoke and gored skirt, and Shona's in chiffon velvet, a shorter version of the same style.

It was not that Sophie was attempting to be more than she was. They were not rich—just well off. But important men would be coming with their wives, and for Will's sake, she wanted everything to be right.

Now, with the tiny white casket in a corner of the living room, and the chairs, settee and lounge ranged around the wall, she hoped the spacious room would be adequate. There were flowers everywhere, but the piano in the center gleamed bare, except for the silver candelabra. Cassie refused to endanger its polished surface.

Shona knew few of the people she greeted. It was gratifying to see a few familiar people, like Jim Brewster, Sadie Owen, and Amanda Davies.

There were, indeed, men from the mill. Not only were there supervisors and directors, there were pattern makers, laborers, and janitors. Evidently, Will had been well liked in his dealing with fellow workers.

Will had been shorn of his beard for some time, now. He had only a small mustache, and his face appeared much younger. As he moved about in his simple, dark suit, Sophie thought he had never been so handsome.

As for Shona, she felt the burden of being forced to be

friendly and grateful, when she wanted only to run up to her room. There were always more people. They spilled over into the dining room and even in the hallway.

Now, the Daytons were arriving. Peggy ran to throw her arms around Shona; Daniel stood there, wishing he had such a privilege. However, there was no awkward moment; there were more friends to meet.

Will and Sophie were gratified to see Dr. John Ferguson. His kindly preparation for their ordeal, had saved them much worry and wonder, and Sophie told him so. "Doctor, you don't know how much we appreciated your help."

He smiled, taking her hand. "I know how hard this must be for all of you. However, it's remarkable that his illness didn't continue for several more years. We should all be thankful for that."

Shona left to meet a group of men, entering. A large, bearded man stood out from the rest. She ran to him.

"Mr. Walker, how nice of you to come. Mr. Pierce, too, and all of you."

Her pleasure was genuine. She had a soft spot for the men who had taken care of her trouble, and Michael's.

Thinking of Michael, she turned her head; there he was.

Startled, she moved off, not wanting to talk to him. Her knees were weakening again, and her heart had begun to pound.

For a moment, Michael was awed by her loveliness. He had always appreciated it, but as she stood, golden curls swept up, her face and throat ivory above the black velvet, she was exquisite.

Impulsively, he crossed the room and took her in his arms. For just a moment, she thrilled; then she pulled away. "Why are you here?"

Suddenly chilled, he clipped, "Do you ask that of everyone who comes to pay his respects?"

She hedged. "I had the idea that you didn't want to see me, anywhere except in the school room. Anyhow, thank you for coming. I'm sorry if I was impolite."

Just then, Mrs. John Parks, Alice's mother, came up to Shona. She spoke to the lady briefly; when she turned back to Michael, he was gone.

Her pang was greater than if he had not come. That fleeting moment in his arms was more of a thrill than she wanted to admit to herself. She kept re-living it in her mind as she greeted guests with polite, automatic responses.

Sophie noticed her change of attitude, and attributed it to exhaustion. "Honey, I think you'd better go to bed." Grateful for the suggestion, Shona slipped away. She wasn't tired at all. The greatest thrill derived from his caress was the realization that he was not nearly so indifferent as he wanted her to believe.

Unfortunately, with that recognition came the fear that

perhaps she had destroyed his interest.

She slept fitfully that night, alternately dozing and walking until morning. Opening her eyes, she had an uneasy feeling. Today, even as the sun was unwilling to rise, so it could be a very long time before she would really see a dawn.

* * *

Shona did not attend school again. Peggy visited her often, bringing her the news. In the spring, she brought Shona's diploma, with a note from Michael that Shona had many more credits than she needed; enough to admit her to Normal School, if she chose to go.

It was a formal note, with no sign that he had missed her attendance. She was crushed, but tried to hide it.

Peggy didn't notice. "I have news for you. Peace eloped. Right after graduation."

"Eloped?" Shona was stunned. "I didn't know she was serious about anyone."

"Neither did I. Burton Galloway's been chasing her, but she always seemed to hate him. I don't understand it."

Shona thought about it before saying, almost to herself, "Maybe things work out better if you don't love someone too much."

But there was no point in imagining how things could have been. Although Michael had always liked her, the realization suddenly came that he would never allow a romance to develop between them.

And so, it was over. With the disappearance of the fantasy which had invaded so many waking hours, Shona unexpectedly experienced a sense of freedom. It was good.

* * *

FOURTEENTH

Christmas came and went without generating much attention in the bereaved MacDonald home. The nursery had been converted into a library for Will. All reminders were gone, with some careful engineering by Cassie.

Although his study, or "den", as Shona called it, had been adequate, of late years Will had become an history buff. He had begun amassing all types of books dealing with the history of Pennsylvania and the origin of Johnstown, carefully delving into the personal life of Joseph Johns, (or "Schantz"), the city founder.

In addition, there were law books, statutes of city, county and state. He read constantly; Shona wondered what could possibly be so fascinating.

What neither she nor her mother had any inkling of, was that Will had an eye on politics. More than anything, he hoped to become a commissioner of the new Cambria County, and thus gain the potential for becoming state senator.

* * *

That year, as usual, there was a great deal of snow. Shona enjoyed winter. She would walk through the yard and the garden beyond, to drink in the beauty of the white carpet on each side of the shoveled path and admire the pure white winter blossoms heaped on trees and shrubbery.

She had discovered that she couldn't be accepted at Normal School, because of her extreme youth. The dean had been firm about that. So, another year slipped by, and Shona began to lose incentive.

At first, she had considered being a teacher; then, it seemed more appropriate for her to become a nurse. She had always liked caring for animals, but somehow, in the light of experience, she had an uneasy feeling that perhaps she liked animals more than people. It bothered her, a little.

* * *

The year 1887 brought the usual spring freshets to the city. A number of small streams had overflowed—perhaps more than usual. The MacDonald basement was flooded. Plato was taking no chances with the first floor, either. He spent most of a day lugging furniture upstairs, before Sophie put a stop to it.

"Plato, this isn't necessary. You know our house is set higher than most because of our high basement. There won't be any water up here, I promise you."

"But Miz Sophie, you kin never tell for sure."

"Well, we'll just take our chances, won't we?" Sophie didn't realize it, but she was relying on Shona's talent to protect them.

Shaking his head, Plato retired. He was certain, as were many of the townspeople, that some day there would be a major flood.

* * *

The cause of this concern was an old dam, twenty miles up the Conemaugh river, situated about three hundred feet above the city. It has been a small, natural lake, converted into a reservoir to supply the Pennsylvania Canal system, which ran from Philadelphia to Pittsburgh. Johnstown lay in the western division of the canal.

It was a remarkable transportation system—its boats were not always in water. At times, in order to cross the mountains, they were mounted on rails. Naturally, with the building of the Pennsylvania Railroad, the canal had become obsolete.

However, after the abandonment of the canal, there was little attention given to the dam. Farmers in the valley below became increasingly fearful that the dam would collapse.

Will, too, had his concerns, one of which was that part of the mill in the Woodvale area. He knew that the South Fork Hunting and Fishing Club had made some drastic changes, after buying the property. They had increased the size of the dam until it was three miles in length and a mile and a quarter in width, representing an immense volume of water.

He made a point of seeing a friend, J. B. Montgomery, who was also an engineer. "J. B., I understand that this here dam ain't got no sluiceway. How do they keep it from bustin' out in one of these dang spring floods?"

J. B. wasn't alarmed. "It's not hard to see that after stocking the dam with bass and trout, the Club wouldn't likely make a means for them to escape. They have three waste-gates at the bottom of the dam which can be raised when there's too much water in the lake."

"Do they do that?"

"I don't think they've done it for a good while."

Will became more nervous. "You mean to tell me that they don't use anything to let the water out? That there dam's made of shale and clay, they say. It's gotta give, sometime."

Montgomery's voice was calm. "It's secure enough. They're scheduled to make some repairs this year. As long as water doesn't go over the top, it's perfectly safe."

Will had to be satisfied with that, but his uneasiness did not entirely cease. Arriving at home, in spite of Sophie's protests, he enlisted Plato to help move everything to the second floor. Tactfully, his wife kept silent when the water didn't rise.

As for Shona, life was a bit tiresome, but she was grateful not to be embroiled in one of the unhappy events which had been so much a part of her life in Johnstown. More and more, she gravitated toward Cassie, her mentor and friend.

One day, shelling peas with Cassie, she came up with a startling comment. "Cassie, do you suppose I'll ever get married?"

Shocked, Cassie almost lost the pan which she was balancing on her knees. "Honey, chile, you cain't be serious?"

"Indeed, I am. You don't see anybody beating down my door, do you? No one wants a witch."

Cassie consoled her, pointing out that there had been no problems lately, and that, pretty as she was, there would surely be suitors.

A few days later, her prediction came true. Danny Dayton, after waiting patiently for two years, had decided to try again.

Actually, he had been very busy working as an apprentice to J. Swank & Company, manufacturers of stoneware. There were various kinds of earth used in making pottery, but the Swank Company specialized in an unusual blue clay.

He stood waiting for someone to answer the door. His palms were sweating; he looked at his nails. To his horror, he saw little rings of blue clay under the edges.

Shona, herself, came to the door, showing no sign of surprise. At her invitation, Danny came in and sat awkwardly on the ege of a chair.

"Miss Shona . . ." he began.

A smile crinkled her blue eyes. "Just call me 'Shona,' please. 'Miss' sounds too prophetic." Before he could say anything, she explained, "I guess I've been expecting to be missed. I was telling Cassie, one day, that everyone's afraid of me. People think I'm a witch."

He gazed at her with adoring eyes. There were pretty girls in his class, but none of them were *that* pretty. Her red-gold curls were resting on her shoulders, and her blue (or were they green?) eyes were as lovely as he remembered. Witch, indeed!

At last, he got around to stating his purpose. "Shona, I have tickets for the Washington Street Opera House, for tomorrow. The play is 'Uncle Tom's Cabin.'' Will you go with me?" (He crossed his fingers behind his back.)

To his amazement and joy, she agreed. "That is, of course, if my mother allows me to go."

Sophie was not so easily persuaded. "I don't know what your father will say. You wouldn't go anywhere else, would you?"

Accordingly, Danny assured her that they would come right home—unless it would be all right to stop at Joe's Pharmacy for a soda.

Perhaps grudgingly, Sophie gave her approval. After all, Shona was fifteen, now. They couldn't keep her at home, forever.

And thus it happened; Shona had a boy-friend. She did like him, but sometimes his presence weighed on her. There were countless walks, tiresome lectures, and Saturday band concerts. In bad weather, there was nothing to do but stay in the house and play checkers or parcheesi. As in so much of her life, she had a sense of being trapped.

Also, there were times when she did not enjoy their togetherness. Somehow, touching annoyed her, and when he attempted to take her in his arms and kiss her, she would laughingly slip away.

Ceaselessly, now, haunting her, there was Michael. She wanted to forget it, trying not to speculate on what he was doing. She could not imagine that he would find a girl; the idea was too painful to think about.

The horrible truth came out by accident. Shona, Danny and

Peggy were playing parcheesi at the Dayton home. Peggy, elated at being on vacation, felt exceptionally cheerful.

"Guess what?" she chirped. "I just saw that reporter, Miss McKay. You remember—the one who gave you so much trouble?"

As if she could forget. Impatiently, Shona urged, "So what? Why should I care about her?"

"Well, I was just surprised. She was with our teacher, Mr. Stewart. I thought he'd have better taste than that."

Shona could feel the blood rising to her face. She hoped no one would notice, and they didn't. Soon afterward, she pleaded that she had a destructive headache, and the game ended.

Arriving at home, stricken, she went straight to Cassie, in her woe.

* * *

Quite by accident, Sophie found out what was in her husband's mind—his plan to enter politics.

She was straightening up the study, which had a way of becoming an incredible clutter. Opening the top drawer to put away some newly sharpened pencils, she made a discovery. Crammed into the narrow drawer, was a heap of petitions, all signed. A notice on the top of each one stated his name and intention to run for the job of county commissioner.

After recovering from the shock, she gathered up the papers and took them with her. That night, she let him read the evening paper before disturbing him. Thus, he would be less liable to be crotchety.

At last, he put down his paper, and she launched her attack. It must be kind, but firm. She picked up the papers, which had been lying, unnoticed, on the table by her chair.

"Will, dear, what is all this?"

Startled, he jumped to his feet and picked them up. "Where in tarnation did you git these?"

"I was straightening your desk. After all, Will, don't you think you should have told me? Why, the secret?"

"I was goin' to git around to it. I don't like you gettin' into my desk. Can't a man have some privacy?"

"Will, I could have saved you a lot of trouble. I know you're well liked, and would probably have backers, but, dear, I don't see how you could make it. Why go to the worry and expense of a campaign?"

He bristled. "And jest tell me where you got this idea?"

She didn't want to tell him her real reason, but there was one angle which she could explore. Her voice was soft, "Will, have you ever made a speech in your life?"

" 'Course, I have. Didn't I tell those miners to git back to work and fergit that strike nonsense, or they'd be out? Didn't I save the company a lot of gol dern trouble with my speeches?"

She gave up; the truth would have to come out. "Will, that kind of talk made sense to the miners. It would show something else to the educated men who are looking for an orator to win an election for them."

If Will lacked ability in that field, he was certainly not unintelligent. "I git it," he snapped. "It's that business of yours with grammar. Why don't you let up on that?"

"Because, dear, language is so important. This country was founded on the ability of learned men to put its precepts into words. You know that a great speaker can sway a nation."

He glared at her. "Ain't I successful? You seen how the fellows at the mill respected me, didn't you?" Then, he saw her pained expression, and backed down a little.

"Tell you what. I'll ask Jim if he thinks I ain't got enough education to make a good county commissioner. He's a smart fellow."

Will's bluster was not anger; it was a deep, inner hurt that his wife would not support him in this project. He had been reading and studying for months, learning about federal, state and county law. When it came to politics, he was sure that he had covered every angle, even making a study of prominent legislators and their successful projects.

Ironically, Will had given no thought to the fact that he still talked like a backwoodsman. Although he heard his well-educated wife's speech every day, he had never absorbed it.

However, he did go to Jim Brewster. As gently as he could, his friend pointed out that one's language could make a great difference. Perhaps, Sophie . . .

"Nope," Will cut in, defensively. "I don't need no one to learn me grammar. I'll git a book and do it myself."

Off he went to the library, and again his evenings were taken up with reading. Sophie sighed. He hadn't told her what was going on, or what he had decided about his campaign.

* * *

That Sunday, Danny came to take Shona for a walk. He had something specific in mind. Danny always loved being mysterious.

"Come on, Danny, stop being coy. Tell me what it is you want me to see. It couldn't be much, or I'd have seen it already."

He grinned. "Maybe you have, maybe you haven't." Noting a flicker of irritation on Shona's face, he sobered.

"The thing I want you to see is the new Cambria Hospital. Remember when they built it, last year?"

"Of course, I remember." She didn't know when she had been so impatient with him.

"Well, it seems to me that you said you always wanted to be

a nurse."

"Certainly, but there isn't any nursing school in this city, so..."

"That's what I wanted to tell you. The hospital has only one doctor and two nurses. They need some girls to be, well, nurses' aides. You could learn nursing and help do it at the same time."

All at once, Shona caught his enthusiasm. "Do you suppose..." She stopped. "Where did you get this information?"

"Peggy, of course. She keeps in touch, even though she's busy with her studies. She wanted me to take you up there, to talk to someone in charge."

Shona brightened with pleasure. "Peggy is the best kind of friend, anyone could have. I'm so lucky to know her."

He faked a wounded air. "Guess I'm no kind of friend at all. Guess I'll go jump in the river." He stuck out his lower lip and pretended to be leaving.

She caught him by the arm. "Danny, no one could have a more loyal friend than you. Thanks for bringing the message."

He brightened and almost tried again to kiss her, but her mother walked in.

After hearing Danny's proposal, Sophie had a dubious look. "You'll have to ask your father. I don't think you want to get into that kind of work."

Shona pressed her. "Mama, why not? What's wrong with my learning to be a nurse?"

Sophie sighed. "Dear, do you know what sort of work they do up at Cambria Hospital?"

"Of course. They care for sick people. What do all hospitals do?" She stared at her mother, wondering what objection she could possibly have.

"Honey, it's a dispensary for wounded mill workers. There are some terrible accidents in the mills. You'd see some pretty fearful sights. I don't think your father will approve."

Undaunted, together they went into Will's study. Danny, always cowed a bit by Will, but now accompanied by Shona, felt strong enough to talk. He explained what he had learned, and suggested that this was an excellent opportunity for Shona.

Contrary to Sophie's opinion, Will approved. "Guess you do want to git out of the house some. Mebbe this is a good chance. If you don't like it, you don't have to stay."

With her father's blessing, her mother withdrew her objections—at least, outwardly. Inwardly, she quaked. This could be hard on the child.

Shona, on the other hand, had no negative thought. The next day, with Danny at her side, she was off to the biggest adventure of her life.

The new, brick hospital had barely been established. Its shrubbery was little more than a foot high, and its trees were no more than plumed sticks. Indoors, the walls and floors were shining white. It looked as a hospital should look, and it smelled like a hospital. Shona loved it all.

A secretary ushered them into the large, nearly empty office. Miss Chandler greeted them warmly. Through newspaper publicity, she knew of Shona's exceptional high school record. The girl could be invaluable.

Smiling, the nurse began to explain. "We need someone badly. There is so much to do around here. You can wrap bandages, make up, or clean beds, and take care of linens. I can promise you, you'll be busy."

Shona's face shadowed. Danny saw it, and spoke for her. "But Shona was hoping for training, so that she could become a nurse. This seems more like housework."

Miss Chandler smiled, undisturbed. "I understand. But a lot of nursing *is* housework—a hospital must be clean, first of all. The nursing part, learning about medications and procedures, will be taught, largely by observation and study. We have some excellent books."

Delighted, Shona cast her doubts aside. She knew housework, and was thrilled with the opportunity to observe real nurses in action. It was a made-to-order job.

Later, Will didn't agree with the pittance she would receive as compensation for her work, and said so.

Wanting to convince him, Shona urged, "Papa, don't you see? Getting a chance to learn—to become a real nurse, is better than money. Please, please say it's all right."

Since he had endorsed the project, earlier, Will was not one to go back on his word. "Well, I guess I got to stick to what I agreed. But if I see it ain't workin' out . . ."

"It will, Papa, it will. I know it. Something tells me I'm really going to be needed."

He shot a worried glance at her, but she didn't see it.

* * *

From the beginning, Shona enjoyed her job. Each weekday, she got up at six, bathed, dressed, and climbed the hill to Prospect, where the hospital stood.

Days which she had thought would be routine, were invariably different. There were small injuries or illnesses: a chip of steel in an eye, or perhaps, a case of food poisoning.

But the arrivals she dreaded were the bleeding and the burned—and they were many. Kate had shielded her from the most graphic injuries to the animals—even from seeing Michael's deep wound until it had been sewn and covered with herbs.

Nevertheless, she had seen enough to stand up well under circumstances which would have been sickening to the uninitiated. Lorene Chandler was pleased with her. She said so to Dr. Galloway, one day.

"We have a gem in little Shona. She's so helpful, and so bright. She seems to learn without being told. In fact, it's uncanny, the way she handles a patient."

Robert Galloway looked up from his paper work. "That's fine. Helps me a lot. I just had to tell that little Mary what's-her-name to go. Now, we'll have to find another Shona, I guess."

"That won't happen, I'm afraid." Lorene sighed and left the room.

However, Shona did have some problems. Bandaging, in particular, was something of a chore. She mastered it, though, after concentrated effort and trials on various inanimate objects.

These days, Lorene was the only nurse. Mrs. Jackson had taken a leave of absence. Being "with child," she was subject to a host of maladies, some of them imaginary. A new nurse would be coming; meanwhile, Shona was asked to do some things which had been out of her sphere.

As a result, she was allowed to bandage a head injury caused by a workman's brush with a crane. It was only a graze; Lorene had shaved the area and anointed it with an ointment, as Shona watched.

She gathered up her equipment and turned to Shona. "You know how to bandage this; I must see to another patient. Be very careful."

Thrilled, Shona was indeed careful. She made the bandaging as neat as possible, and just before taping the end, used her scissors to cut off excess material.

To her horror, she saw blood on the piece of bandage. Not only that, there lay an ear lobe. Shaking, she held out the fragment of bandage. "Mr. Ridley, I don't know what to do. I've cut off a piece of your ear."

Jack Ridley, a tough foreman with a unique sense of humor, winked at her. "Didn't feel a thing. Put it back."

"Put it back?"

Grinning, he whirled off the meticulous bandaging and took the ear lobe from her trembling hand. He stuck it on his ear, holding it tight with the particle of bandage.

"Now, bandage me."

"But Mr. Ridley, I wouldn't be allowed . . ."

"I'll take full responsibility. Don't look at me like that. It will be all right."

Hesitantly, Shona checked to see that the ear lobe was in the proper position; then, holding it as tightly as possible, managed to repeat her bandaging.

During the procedure, she apologized again. "I'm so sorry. I don't know how that happened. Dr. Galloway will be angry; surely, he'll fire me."

Ridley sobered. "You're not going to tell?"

"Certainly, I must."

"If you do, *I'll* tell. He was grinning again. "I'll tell them you did it on purpose."

She didn't appreciate the joke. "Mr. Ridley, I can't see why you would do that. You know it's not true."

He settled down. "I was only kidding. Please don't tell."

Quietly, at home, talking to Cassie, she did tell. "What shall I do, Cassie? If he has trouble with his ear, I'm responsible. I think Miss Chandler should know. She'll know what to do about telling the doctor."

Cassie hesitated to advise her. She thought for a moment, then looked directly at Shona. "Honey, you already knows what's right. You do whatever that is."

Shona decided not to tell her parents, but she realized that there was no choice . . . In the morning, she must explain the accident. There could be no excuse.

The worry was groundless. At first, when Lorene heard the news, she was shocked. Then, hearing of the man's reaction, she was relieved. "It isn't everyone who would have taken it like that. Our only hope is that the ear will heal."

"Do you think it will? Is it possible for it to grow fast? The lobe was completely cut off."

"Well," the nurse reflected, thinking aloud, "there's a good supply of blood in that area, and there will probably be little, if any, pain."

She smiled at the woebegone face. "Shona, I think we have a good chance. At least, the workman isn't angry at anyone. We're in luck."

Shona was thinking: *You're* in luck. *I* may be in trouble. She didn't say it aloud. At least, she could be grateful that there had been no mention of her losing her job.

That week, the new nurse came. Lorene introduced her to Shona. "Shona, this is Miss Jean Bovair, a registered nurse. You will take instructions from her, so I can be released for other work. I'm sure you two will like each other."

It wasn't difficult to like Jean. She was modest, kind, and extremely helpful. Busy, Shona scarcely noted her beautiful blue eyes and her shining brown hair braided like a coronet around her head.

However, Jeans attractiveness wasn't lost on Danny. From the moment he saw her, something struck him—almost as the feeling he had gotten when he had seen Shona for the first time.

Perhaps her attraction was heightened by the fact that Shona had discouraged all romantic attention so many times. By this time, he almost viewed Shona as a sister. Jean, on the other hand, didn't make him feel like a brother at all.

Something of his mood caught Shona's attention, and she saw Danny with a new awareness. His shining brown hair and smooth, lightly tanned face gave him an immaculate, well-groomed appearance. It could well be that Jean would be just as much impressed with Danny as he apparently was with her.

She was wondering about it one day, making up a bed. Danny came in, passing by the door without seeing her. He headed for Jean, seated at a small desk in the hall.

Shona stayed out of sight. Unhappy as she was at the thought of losing her only companion, she understood.

What she could not know was that Jean's charm was affecting Danny in a different way. If she had recognized his project, she would have been outraged. And even as Danny was planning, he had an uncomfortable sense of being a traitor to Shona.

Later, he found Shona in the office, making notations. She was particularly lovely in her light blue uniform and crisp, white cap. He paused for a moment, then blurted, "Shona, do you care at all for me? Do you believe that Jean and I . . ."

She beamed at him. "Of course, I care for you. You're as dear as a brother to me. I'm happy for you and Jean."

He began to pace the floor, avoiding her eyes. "My future isn't with Jean, Shona. Can't you see, I'm in love with you? You ought to know it. Shona, I want to marry you."

Her eyes widened, seeming to flash a deeper blue. Should she have foreseen this? At any rate, there was no point in taking him seriously.

She spoke casually. "Danny, I'm only sixteen. I wouldn't know the first thing about being a housewife. Besides, maybe I have a dream of my own."

He gasped. "You mean, you've been seeing someone else?" His tone was almost threatening.

Shona stood up and touched his arm. "No, Danny, you old dear, I haven't been seeing anyone else. A girl is allowed to dream, isn't she?"

As she moved to leave the room, Danny grabbed her and turned her around. "Shona, I've got to know. Who is this 'dream' fellow? What did you mean?"

She wrenched her arm away and faced him, angry at him for the first time. "I don't think my dreaming is any of your business, or anyone else's." She flounced out of the room, golden curls bouncing.

In dismay, he looked after her, realizing the enormity of his own deception. However, there was no turning back.

* * *

Things were going smoothly at the hospital, but Shona had a constant worry. It was a week past the time for Jack Ridley to return for the removal of his bandage, and he had not shown up.

Almost as though she had willed it, he put in an appearance. There he stood, still bandaged, with the dirtiest bandage anyone could imagine. With a bountiful smile on his face, he sat down in the examination room and beckoned to Shona.

She came running into the room. "Mr. Ridley, where have you been? This bandage should have been removed a long time ago."

He grinned. "I wanted to be sure my ear wouldn't fall apart when we took off the bandage. Aren't you grateful?"

"It may fall apart yet," she whispered, cutting off the material with shaking hands.

As she worked, Ridley studied her exquisite profile and slender body, and something struck him. It had been with him from the first time; now it came back sharply. He had an idea.

The bandage, stiff, and grease-laden, came away easily. For a second, Shona held her breath. There, with no sign of injury, was a perfectly normal ear, with a tiny pink line where the lobe had been severed.

Her anxious look flashed into a smile. "Oh, Mr. Ridley, it's all right. Your ear healed. Isn't it wonderful?"

He grinned with satisfaction. "I knew it. Can't see what you had to worry about."

Shona was so relieved, that she didn't notice the fact that Ridley had not moved to leave. Instead, he sat there with a fatuous expression which puzzled her.

"Miss MacDonald, are you involved with a young man? I mean, are you serious about anyone?"

She gave him a quizzical glance. Was he joking again?

"I can't see why that would be of concern to you," she retorted stiffly.

He shifted, uneasily. "Well, you see, I have a son, who hasn't been, well . . . selective, in choosing his friends. I thought, maybe, I could introduce him to you. He's a bright lad. I think you'd like him; he's sure to be a lot of fun. Takes after me."

She shuddered at the picture he painted. Nevertheless, she felt obliged to be tactful.

"I'm sure your son must be all you say he is. But, you see, I am very much 'involved,' as you say."

His jovial expression changed to one of disappointment, but he didn't quite give up. "But, if you'd just meet Jackie . . ."

She shook her head, and he rose stiffly. "Well, I guess it's no use. If you change your mind, you have my address. Maybe you owe me a favor."

For a second, that parting remark flashed an alarm, but at once, she realized that no harm had been done—and she *had* reported the accident. Nevertheless, she returned to her work a bit shaken.

* * *

Several weeks passed before Danny came again. Somewhat sheepishly, he arrived at her home with a pair of tickets to the circus. Each spring, Barnum and Bailey brought their attraction to town, but Shona had never seen it.

This was the right thing to do. Danny congratulated himself. If there had been a breach in their relationship, this should mend things.

For a time, his strategy worked. Enchanted, Shona walked in awe, exclaiming at the fairy-like costumes, thrilled by the sparkle and glitter of the settings.

Danny exulted in her pleasure. He had been sure that her love of animals would make the circus enjoyable. To his chagrin and surprise, Shona's joy soon faded.

She looked at him with tears in her eyes. "Danny, I can't bear it. Look at these magnificent animals, caged for life, just for the pleasure of crowds of humans."

Shocked, he remonstrated. "But Shona, these animals are safe and well fed. They don't have to fight for their food. If they are sick or injured, they have the best of care."

She wiped her eyes. "Does all that compensate for their loss of freedom?" Without waiting for an answer, she went on. "Why, then, don't we commit a crime and get ourselves thrown in jail? Then we'll be well fed and cared for. Shall we make it a big thing, and try for a life sentence?"

Shaken, Danny stared at her. He took her arm, held the pink parasol over them both, and said nothing.

Soon after that, they watched the animal trainer cracking his whip at an elegant Bengal tiger. The cowed animal obeyed his complicated orders well, with only an occasional, insolent swipe at his master.

Shona had seen enough. "Let's get out of here," she whispered. "That's all I can take."

Still wondering, Danny took her home.

* * *

FIFTEENTH

It was a brilliant day in October, with the sun rising at the proper time, and the hillside ablaze with color.

All through the summer, the waters of the Stonycreek had been so shallow that boys ran across the river on dry stones. The Conemaugh, a mountain stream joining it at the foot of three hills, was also nearly dry. Together, the rivulet ran for a hundred miles, into the Allegheny river and on to Pittsburgh.

Certainly, there was no inkling of a threat to the inhabitants of the valley on this pleasant morning.

Today, as Shona walked up the hill to the hospital, she breathed in the beauty of the scene. Dominated by red-and-gold maples, and supplemented by the mauves and yellows of oak and buckeye, against the dark green of pine and hemlock, it was a living picture.

Nevertheless, incongruous as it seemed, this was the day when Shona had her first warning. It came as a dark cloud, in an otherwise clear, blue sky. No larger than a kite, it moved overhead, seeming to cast a shadow over her. She shivered, in the warm sunlight.

Shona had been crossing the wooden bridge to Prospect when the shadow appeared. Looking down at the small, sparkling stream below, she experienced a feeling of being carried away by a great force, into a dark maelstrom. For just a second, she encountered an unfathomable terror.

The darkness and chill passed so quickly that for a few minutes, she was disoriented. Making her way on to the hospital automatically, her mind whirled.

When she arrived, Jean was in the office, preparing new charts. Looking up, she started, seeing Shona's wide-eyed, worried expression.

"What is it?" she gasped. She might as well have been talking to herself. Shona dropped into a Morris chair near the desk. After a long silence, she roused, as though from sleep.

"Jean, I can't explain it, but something may destroy us. I've had a warning."

"A warning? What do you mean? Who is 'us'? When?"

"Don't ask. I don't know. It doesn't seem to be an imminent danger, but somehow, I must get my family out of this city."

Puzzled, Jean did not press the matter. Nevertheless, as Shona gathered up her records, Jean shot an occasional glance at her. Could Shona be having mental problems?

She voiced her worry to Miss Chandler, who scoffed at the idea. "Jean, that girl has the soundest mind of anyone I've ever know. Don't worry about it. Everyone has strange feelings, at times."

As for Shona, she went about morning chores as usual, but her movements were mechanical. She must speak to her father. This would be the great hurdle. Although her mother would agree to anything she proposed, convincing Will was another matter.

All the way home, she was thinking . . . thinking . . .

Naturally, Shona immediately went to Cassie, her dearest friend. She related her experience and waited for the result. It was not long in coming.

"Shona, honey, seems like you jest over-tired. You been workin' at that hospital 'n helpin' me at home, with never a thought of relaxin' or seein' yo' friends."

"Oh, Cassie, please take me seriously. I tell you, I felt something ominous. I'm sure there's going to be a great disaster. The trouble is, I haven't a clue when or where it's going to happen."

Shona's eyes were pleading, her voice trembling. If Cassie

didn't believe her, she must be wrong.

But, Cassie did believe. Far in the back of Cassie's mind were registered the times when Shona had known about things before they happened. Now, as they were emerging, she, too, was frightened.

If this prediction were to be spread abroad, there would be more accusations of witchcraft, and possibly more persecution. Somehow, she must convince the girl that her concept was unreal.

She tried another tack. "Chile, why not wait 'til you see what happen? Mebbe that feelin' was jest some food what didn' digest proper, or lak ah say, mebbe you jest too tired."

Somewhat soothed, although not convinced, Shona decided to take her advice. Without a sharp awareness of the problem, there wasn't much chance of convincing anyone to leave the city.

She remained determined to work on her father, however. Why not convince him that living on the hill was expected of him, due to his position at the mill. Surely, he would want to do the proper thing.

Her plot failed. Will had no intention of living on the hill, and said so in explosive terms.

"Why in tarnation should we move up to the hill? This is where I make my livin', dad burn it! What do I care if the high-'n-mighty look down on me? I'm proud of what I do, and by darn, I'm stayin' right here to do it."

Shona said no more. To Cassie's delight, she seemed to be content, and didn't mention the matter again.

* * *

A day or so later, the rains came. The original, heavy, pelting drops soon changed to a steady downpour. It flattened the neighborhood geraniums, turned the side roads into mud, and stripped the bright leaves from the trees along the sidewalks.

Shona watched the streams with some trepidation. They did rise, to some extent, but later in the day, the rain slackened, and did not come again for some time.

Now, business fell off at the hospital—a relief to Shona. She had been constantly running, sometimes for Jean, sometimes for Miss Chandler. There were also periods when the doctor called for her.

Today, her gratitude for the respite became obvious. She had a headache—always a bad sign. She alternately dawdled and worked on completing forms, with the accent on loitering.

Jean noticed her lassitude and came over to inquire. "Aren't you feeling well, Shona?"

Shona's head, which had been drooping over her papers, jerked up. "I'm just fine. I didn't sleep well last night. That always makes me groggy."

Unconvinced, Jean said no more. Still worried, and sensing that here was some deep trouble, she decided to make things easier for Shona. She would not call on her that day, if that were possible.

Unfortunately, near the end of the day, the horse-drawn ambulance delivered its burden. The blanket-wrapped patient was soaked in blood. Shona rushed to help, but Jean had already turned down the blanket and was wiping the blood from the man's face. Shona let out a little gasp. It was Michael.

He was unconscious. Jean directed her to staunch the blood while she went for antiseptic and bandages. Shona had difficulty in controlling her hand. Setting her jaw, she took a firm grip, and the bleeding stopped.

Looking at his pale, blood-stained face, a sudden flash came to her. Maybe this accident was the outcome of the warning she had worried about. She shook it off—the omen had been clearer than that.

Suddenly, she became aware that Dr. Galloway and the ambulance driver were having a conversation in the doctor's office. She strained to hear, but their voice were low, and the snatches of dialogue were unintelligible.

Helping Jean dress the wounded head and shoulder, Shona had some questions. "Jean, how could this man have been wounded so? He was my teacher—how could he have been in the mill? Or do you suppose a horse . . ."

"No, Shona, it wasn't a horse." Dr. Galloway stood in the doorway. "And he *was* in the mill."

"But . . ."

He tolerated her impatience with a gesture. "Mr. Stewart had taken his vocational class of five boys to see the workings of the mill. Apparently, one of the boys strayed beyond the ropes and into the path of a crane. Stewart lunged to push him away. That's about it. He was struck by a steel beam."

Shona would have been impressed by Michael's heroism, but right now, she had but one thought. "Will he be all right?"

After making an inspection of the damage, the doctor looked up and announced, "Physically, these wounds will heal. We have no way of knowing what injury has been inflicted on his brain."

Inwardly, she shuddered. Her dearly beloved Michael, to live with a damaged brain? That was unthinkable.

When it was time to leave, she wanted to scream that she belonged at his side—that she would stay. But a night nurse had been hired, and she had to go home.

That night, she spent hours alternately dozing and waking, focusing on worry. In the morning, she forced herself back to reality. Brooding could do no good; Michael needed her.

It was raining again as Shona climbed the hill to the hospital. The dreariness continued as she entered the building. Quietness hung over the room where Michael lay, white and still. He had shown no signs of consciousness, and his pulse was low.

Shona looked at Jean, who answered the unspoken question. "Shona, he's had a serious blow to the head. We just can't tell very much about such injuries."

Later, the doctor gave no more encouragement. As Shona made her rounds, giving medication to several patients and checking various dressings, it was all she could do to stay away from Michael's room.

She need not have worried about leaving him. Rounding the corner to enter his room, she stopped short. There, holding his hand, was Mary Jane McKay.

After a brief pause, Shona crossed to the bed to take Michael's pulse. It did seem to be somewhat stronger.

She looked at Mary Jane. Today, she wasn't masculine, or intimidating. Her chestnut-brown hair lay in waves to her shoulders, and her sensitive face was filled with concern as she bent over him. Shona softened.

"Has he shown any sign of consciousness?"

The girl shook her head, pensively. "No, he hasn't. I can't get the doctor to give me any information. Do you know what happened?"

As Shona told her of Michael's heroic act, at that moment, somehow they were drawn to each other. After all, both of them loved Michael.

That evening, the *Tribune* carried a front-page article, beautifully written, with a by-line by M. J. McKay.

Several days passed, with no change in Michael's condition. Mr. and Mrs. Stewart visited regularly; one day, they asked to see the doctor.

Shona was filing in the room when they came in, and Doctor Galloway motioned to her to continue. Mr. Stewart came to the point. "Doctor, I can't see any change in my son's condition. Do you?"

"Frankly, Mr. Stewart, I don't. He's stable—his heart is good, but there's no way of predicting the outcome."

Mr. Stewart lifted his black-bearded chin as though to gain strength.

"Dr. Galloway, we want to send Michael to the general hospital in Pittsburgh, where he can get the care he should have. This thing's gone on long enough. We want to see some results."

The doctor rose and bowed stiffly. "Sir, of course, that is your privilege. I should warn you, however, that I think it inadvisable to move him just now."

Stewart held his ground. "We'll see that there's a consultation about this. You'll be hearing from us in a day or two." He picked up his hat and stalked out. His wife began to follow, then hesitated. "You understand, Doctor—we think you've done everything you can."

"Of course—I understand." The doctor bowed again and sat

down.

Shona, who had been listening with dismay, followed Mrs. Stewart out of the room. "Oh, please, listen to me. I think you'll be having some good results very soon. Our hospital has a wonderful reputation, and together with the loving care Michael is receiving, he'd be much better off here."

Mrs. Stewart took a closer look at her. "Weren't you the child who was living with the witch up on Hogback?"

Shona's heart sank. "Yes, ma'am." In a desperate burst of confidence, she went on. "I helped Kate take care of Michael when he was caught in the bear trap. When he wakens, he'll tell you . . ."

Michael's mother, smiled at her. "Dear, Michael has told us about you—many times. He is very fond of you. After all, you and Kate did save his life. We owe you a great deal."

Shona seized the opportunity. "Then don't take him away. We can give him everything he needs. Dr. Galloway is wonderful. He . . ."

Mr. Stewart cut in. "Of course, you'll defend the doctor. The fact remains that my son isn't responding to his treatment. We have no choice . . ."

Now, it was his wife who interrupted. "Oh, yes, we do have a choice. It's better to have him here with dedicated friends than to take him away from his home. John, please!"

"All right. But if he doesn't come around soon—that's it."

Shona's relief at the respite dimmed by the fact that there was so little chance of an imminent recovery. She began searching her mind for Kate's teaching.

Remembering something called by Kate, "Laying on of hands," she pondered the explanation. "Practically anyone can promote healing this way. Let them call it 'witchcraft' or 'mumbo-jumbo'—it works. That's what I've done with Michael."

She recalled the swift improvement of their patient. This was it. Saying nothing to anyone, it was time to make use of Kate's teaching.

The opportunity came earlier than expected. The next morning, she was placing linens when Miss Chandler came in.

"Shona, we have two new patients, but they have superficial wounds. I'd appreciate it if you would stay pretty close to Mr. Stewart. The minute he shows signs of coming around, the doctor must know."

She tried not to show her joy, as she rushed off. There was no clear-cut idea in her mind as to where she would begin. Kate had often used scripture, but that had not seemed to be important.

She remembered learning one thing from the Bible: the twenty-third Psalm. That seemed to be a likely beginning, comforting and peaceful. And so she began, stroking his hand or cheek, and reciting, "The Lord is my shepherd . . ."

Jean came into the room as Shona was reciting. She backed out quietly. Although practical and worldly, she couldn't help being impressed by the dedication of her student. Perhaps this constant stimulation could get through; at any rate, it could do no harm.

Sophie found Shona in the bedroom that evening, curled up on the chaise lounge, reading the Bible. It was a leather-bound, gilt-edged edition, still new, one of those gifts which is appreciated only for the thought.

"Shona, honey, she ventured. "It's so nice to see you reading the Bible. I think you'll find it interesting. How far have you gone?"

Her daughter frowned. "Oh, Mama, I don't intend to read it through. I'm trying to find certain passages."

Sophie sighed and left the room. There was no accounting for Shona.

* * *

Morning brought rain, again. Sloshing up the hill, as mud poured down over the brick sidewalk Shona looked up at the slate-colored sky. If this weather was any indication of the coming winter, there would be a lot of snow.

This wasn't much of a worry. Looking back at the past dry, hot summer, and the present trickle of water in the river bed, even a spring freshet seemed unlikely.

Suddenly, the darkness seemed to deepen, and Shona had a chill. Heavy snow in the mountains nearly always meant flooding in the valley. It suddenly came to her—the meaning of the omen. Their home was in danger. Where she had felt secure because of the lack of evidence, now it had become quite clear.

And yet, the optimist in Shona would not be denied. Why not wait and see? There was plenty of time. Spring was far away, and besides, this could all be imagination.

Forgetting it, she spent the next three days in constant attendance on Michael. At times, he would stir, or move his lips, and she would hold her breath, press his hand and pat his cheek. It would pass.

She voiced her frustration to Jean. "It's so hard. I can't bear it. There doesn't seem to be any way to break through."

Jean consoled her. "Keep at it, dear. I think his color is better. And, yesterday, when you were out, I saw him move his right foot."

Seeing Shona's gratification, she nodded, smiled, and slipped out of the door.

From then on, Shona worked more feverishly. She stroked his hands and feet regularly, and talked to him as though he heard every word.

When the turning point did come, she was not there to see it.

She had slipped out of the room, quietly, when she saw Mary Jane coming down the hall. Tired to the point of an exhaustion born of frustration, she went into the ladies' room to splash some water on her face.

Emerging, Miss Chandler met her, with an excitement not typical of her professional manner. "Shona, Michael opened his eyes. Miss McKay was talking to him, and he smiled at her. Isn't that wonderful?"

The bitter-sweet news came to Shona like an electric shock. How could this be? Why couldn't she have been the one to break through? She rushed down the hall to the room.

Mary Jane was stooping over Michael, kissing him. Shona backed off, feeling like an intruder—a very distressed one, indeed.

However, Mary Jane had heard, and motioned to her. "Oh, Shona, isn't it wonderful? He opened his eyes and smiled at me."

Shona rushed up to the bed. Michael's eyes were closed, and he seemed to be unchanged in both position and expression.

"Michael dear," Shona whispered, patting his cheek. "Do you hear me? Let's see you smile again. Please, open your eyes . . ."

There was no response.

By this time, Jean and Dr. Galloway had joined Miss Chandler as onlookers. To everyone's disappointment, Michael did not respond to anything, by word or by touch.

As they had given up and were preparing to leave, Michael opened his eyes again. He stared at the group. "I give up. Who are you people?"

He was looking at Mary Jane when he said it, and she hastened to reassure him, introducing each of them.

The formalities over, he closed his eyes again. "I don't know any of you. Why don't you leave me alone? Can't you see I'm tired?"

They stared at each other—Mary Jane even more horrified than Shona. "He doesn't even know me, and we're engaged to be married. Doctor, do you think this is permanent?"

He reassured her. "We must be grateful for his recovery to this point. I'm sure his memory will return at some time in the future. At least, I hope so."

Shona's own mind was reeling. Michael—engaged! How could this be? Hadn't he loved her for most of his life? And why wouldn't he remember . . .

Looking across at Mary Jane, suddenly, she felt herself thrust into an emotion she had never felt before. It was hate, a most unpleasant sensation. Almost instantly, it began to drain her.

Resolving to put the evil thought behind her, she stayed away from Michael, completely.

When the Stewarts finally came to take Michael home, still

under amnesia, Shona was nowhere in sight.

It was time to put all thought of Michael out of her mind, and to begin thinking of her own life. Reflecting on it, she discovered that Danny hadn't been around for a long time.

No sooner had she missed him than he was there. Popping in casually, in his usual, carefree manner, Danny was ready for a Sunday walk.

Shona felt such pleasure in seeing him, that she greeted him happily. Danny had a way of cheering her up. Packing a picnic basket was out of the question, and he knew it. The dark skies were, as usual, threatening rain.

"Danny, could it be that you came for a game of parcheesi, because you had nothing else to do?"

Sheepishly, he admitted it. Shona laughed and brought the box. Her mother had discreetly disappeared. Danny raised a leaf of the drop-leafed table, and moved two chairs into place.

"Sure you don't want a walk?" he kidded her, taking a seat.

Shona instantly sobered. "Danny, if there's this much rain now, imagine how heavy the snow in the mountains will be. It frightens me."

He was preparing the board. "There's no doubt about it; we'll have another Spring flood. I just hope the rain keeps up."

"You hope the rain keeps *up*? What's the matter with you?"

"Well, if it keeps up, it won't be down here."

"Danny, forget the old saws. Aren't you alarmed about what could happen next Spring? That old dam above the city has frightened the people here in Johnstown for years. And it's getting older."

Seeing her anxiety, he leaned toward her. I have an idea. Since you're so concerned, let's go up and take a look at the dam. Maybe you'll stop worrying, once you see it."

Plato obligingly saddled the horses while Shona changed into her riding habit. Then, they were off together, traveling more than a dozen miles to the breast of the South Fork Dam.

It stood, peacefully, about three miles above South Fork, not really appearing as a threat to anyone. Although its breastwork rose for nearly an hundred feet above the river's natural bed, the water was at least fifteen feet below the breast. There seemed to be small likelihood of its ever overflowing.

The pair rode along the water toward the South Fork Fishing and Hunting Club's main house. There were no boating parties today, but several fishing boats idled nearby.

Shona was not assured. She insisted on traveling back to inspect the breast of the dam. What she saw was discouraging. There was a myriad of small leaks; one of them shooting out for several feet. In other places, one could see chunks of straw stuffed into its surface.

Danny refused to share her alarm. "They're been working on this, that's obvious. This embankment is made up of shale and clay. Straw is always used to stop leaks while the work is being done."

When she heard that, Shona's resolve deepened. "We're going to the sheriff. We have to find out whether they're really working on this."

He teased her. "Can't it wait until tomorrow? I don't think very much can happen overnight. Besides, I doubt if you can reach the sheriff today. Anyhow, I don't think anyone's very much worried about a flood, right now."

That evening, Shona went to her father's study. He was looking at a grammar book, and mumbling to himself. Almost as though he were caught in a devious act, he slapped the book shut.

Smiling to herself, she ignored it. "Papa, have you heard anything about those dam repairs that were to have been made this Fall. If we have a lot of snow this Winter, that dam should be repaired."

"See here, child, you got nothin' to worry about. Last week, I talked to J. B. myself, and he tells me there ain't—isn't any danger. That dam's about to be fixed up any day now, so it'll be ready for winter. Stop fussin' about such little things."

"But, Papa, it's not a little thing. For years, people have been worrying about that dam, and . . ."

"That's it. Nothin' ever comes of all those warnings. Don't give it any more thought."

He looked toward his books, as though eager to get back to them, and she took the hint.

Quietly, she left the room.

* * *

Although Shona loved snow, the Winter became everything she dreaded. It began in the mountains as though rising from the ground, covering all, bending trees and shrubbery to the earth. It seldom ceased—each time the snow began again, it did so with a violence rarely seen in a Pennsylvania snow storm.

The trek to the hospital each day was arduous. At times, Plato could use the horse and buggy to take Shona up but there were days when no vehicles got through. There was a great deal of strength in Shona, but sometimes, getting up the hill was more tiring than a days' work.

She arrived one morning, exhausted, but trying not to show it. Jean met her with some news. Apparently, Michael had regained his memory. "I hear that he and Mary Jane are planning to be married."

That was hardly a shock to Shona. Idly, she asked, "When?"

Jean hesitated. "I hate to say—I may be wrong. Someone said it would be next June. Anyhow, maybe we'll be invited to the wedding. Certainly, you should be, after all you did for him.

Shona rose to leave. "I did nothing special. Everything I tried to do, failed."

"I'm not sure of that," said Jean. "It was your constant encouragement that brought him out of his coma. Maybe he would still be unconscious . . ."

"Jean, dear, don't be so noble. That's not likely, and you know it." She didn't mean to be irritable—somehow, talking about Michael was unpleasant.

Speculating, Jean watched her go. She had long ago sensed the fact that Shona had more than a cursory interest in Michael.

* * *

SIXTEENTH

Christmas Day of 1888 barely dawned at all. Through the night, the whiteness of the snow had lent the city an unearthly glow. Street lights, heavily laden, gave off only tiny pin-pricks of illumination. With the daylight, whitened clouds, heavy with their burden, continued to heap snow on every immovable object.

Early in the morning, a few people ventured abroad with shovels. Unfortunately, the depth of the continuing snowfall rendered such projects practically worthless.

Indoors, the MacDonalds, Cassie and Plato, were set for a day of rest, peace and contentment.

The Christmas tree was a perfect spruce, set in a corner of the living room, gleaming with fragile, glass ornaments. Gifts were heaped neatly beneath it, the wrappings already disposed of by a meticulous Cassie.

Early that afternoon, Sophie began to play the piano. As they joined in "Adeste Fideles," someone rapped on the door.

It was Danny. A brown woolen cap over his head, and bundled to his eyes with an enormous knitted scarf, he was scarcely recognizable.

Apologetically, he stooped just outside, unfastening large buckles on his high galoshes.

"Come in, come in," roared Will, holding the door open. "We don't need snow inside, yet."

In a jovial mood, he shook Danny's hand. "Merry Christmas, son. We're having some music here. You sing?" He was taking Danny's ulster.

Danny shook his head. Still a bit shy of Shona's father, he moved over near Sophie, at the piano.

"That's all right." Sophie patted his hand. "You stand here with Shona, and maybe you'll want to join in. We're no singers, either, but we do fancy our music together."

Danny could have enjoyed the carols, but his mind was on

something more important. He held a small package in one hand, behind his back. How Shona would view this, he had no idea, but it was something he had to do.

He grasped Shona's hand with his free one. As her mother searched for another sheet of music, Shona whispered, "What's wrong with you? Are you ill?"

Danny shook his head and moved toward the settee. "I think I'll sit down for a while. I've been shoveling—or trying to. Kind of tired."

Indeed, he appeared to be just that. However, it was not the snow which had wearied him. It was worry.

Shona came and sat down beside him, to listen. Her mother was playing Gounod's "Ave Maria."

They were scarcely seated, when Shona rose. "Just a minute, Danny. I have something for you." With that, she ran upstairs. Always lovely in Danny's eyes, today, she was entrancing, and he hadn't really noticed.

As she returned, breathless, he did notice. Her dress of Christmas green silk, was modestly low cut, and shirred. The skirt, draping gently across the front, and gathered tightly at the back waist, emphasized her slender figure.

Coming near, she was even prettier, her red-gold hair a coronet of plaited braids, with tiny curls escaping around her face. Somehow, he had a strong urge to kiss her.

She advanced, holding out a small, silver package. "This is for you. I hope you like it."

As he couldn't take her gift and open it with one hand, he slowly brought out the present he had been hiding. She hesitated, then took it, soberly. "Danny, you know what I . . ."

"Yes, I know, but . . ." He looked around. Everyone was watching and listening.

Cassie stood up. "I think we better go." Plato rose.

Suddenly, Danny found his voice. "No, please stay. You're family, too. I'd like you to see."

There was nothing for Shona to do but open the tiny box. It contained a diamond, beautifully cut, actually quite expensive, for one of Danny's means.

She was at a loss. Speechless, she looked at him. Then, in front of everyone, he caught her by the shoulders and kissed her.

Shona did not resist. Before she could say anything, Will stepped forward.

"Welcome, son. It's about time this girl of mine did something sensible. I hear you're doin' well at J. Swank and Company—movin' right up."

Embarrassed, Danny joked, "Oh, yes. I don't get blue clay under my fingernails any more."

Will's intrusion irritated Shona. "Papa, aren't you jumping to conclusions? I haven't said I would accept such a gift."

"Are you crazy, daughter? You mean to say you've been

stringin' this boy along all this time, and now you're goin' to tell him it's all off?"

Looking around at her shocked family, she backed down. "No, Papa, I don't know what I'm going to say. I haven't been 'stringing him along.' I've already told him . . ."

She couldn't go on. How could she mention someone else, when there was no one? Michael was a dream—not someone to claim. Suddenly, she blurted, "Yes, Danny, I'll accept the ring. Just so you know, I love you, but I'm not *in love* with you."

He was satisfied with that, and accepted everyone's congratulations happily. He never doubted for a minute that Shona would soon be in love with him.

One little thing bothered him. His fidelity to Shona had not been complete. There were a few episodes with Jean which would have dismayed, and probably alienated her. All he could do was hope against hope that she wouldn't find out.

SEVENTEENTH

Spring arrived as usual, the next year. On reflection, there was nothing ordinary about the season. The rain fell more often, and with increasing force. Grass grew more luxuriantly; flowers bloomed earlier.

All that was in the valley. However, Winter refused to leave the forests on the hills. In the frigid air of the mountains, the refrigerated snow receded slowly, imprisoning the wild flowers which ordinarily would have been in bloom.

Later, early in May, the season changed. Warm weather, along with ferocious rainfall which pelted hill and valley alike, brought a sudden thaw.

In the beginning, the people of Johnstown were not unduly alarmed. They were aware of the roaring streams teeming down from the hillsides, and those near the rivers prepared for another spring freshet.

One dark day, in a cold drizzle, Shona met Mary Jane at the market. The woman greeted her kindly, and Shona softened. This was the one Michael loved; there must be a bond between them, somehow.

Her thoughts sprang to the fact that the newspaper had the strongest influence on the population. Maybe she could send a message. She knew by now that the warning she had received, the constant headaches, the fear that refused to be put down, all were part of a great, incipient danger.

"Mary Jane, may I speak to you about something that I believe you'll think is important?"

The reporter smiled. "I'm sure it must be—and now I'm curious."

Shona hesitated for a moment, but she must risk it. "Last

fall, I visited the South Fork dam. I don't like what I saw there. Unless there's been some major repair work, it's in bad shape. Shouldn't the people be warned that this Spring could bring more than the usual flooding to the city?"

Instantly, Mary Jane agreed.

She had lost some respect for George Swank, editor of the *Johnstown Tribune*, because he had taken all alarms about the old dam lightly.

"He's maintained for several years, now, that the breaking up of the old dam (if it did occur) would occur gradually, not causing any trouble for the city. Now, he's planning to write an editorial. It's to be published on May thirty-first."

"But the crisis is now."

"I know that. I wanted to write something two weeks ago, but he ignored my concern."

"Try to get through to him. There's going to be a real disaster. I'm sure of it."

Mary Jane studied Shona's earnest face critically. She remembered their earliest meeting—almost a confrontation. This had been the witch-child.

Carefully, she worded her question. "Do you sense something which you think everyone should know?"

All the terror of that first warning flooded back to Shona. "Mary Jane, I can't describe the feeling that came to me sometime ago, looking at the river. I was being swept into a dark void. There was untold danger on every hand."

"Do you really think this was anything more than the uneasy feeling most of us get, looking at the river, these days?"

"Definitely more. This was in October—the river was very low."

She stopped. This had become an interview. The enormity of what she had done hit her. Mary Jane had always been interested in her background.

Sick at heart, Shona answered no more questions. Now, she found herself trying to bring the encounter to a polite conclusion.

Mary Jane was intrigued. She wanted to know more about this strange person, who, clearly, had a power which the ordinary mortal did not possess.

"Tell me . . ." she began, but Shona was already on her way.

"Give my regards to Michael," she flung back over her shoulder, bitterly sorry that she had been so explicit.

At home, she went straight to Cassie, and told the whole story. Cassie was rolling out pie dough. She threw up one hand and made a white streak across her forehead.

"Lan' sakes, chile, why didn' you tell us you had sech feelin'? You knows how yo' Mama sets store by things lak dat."

"I didn't want to worry anyone. I spoke to Papa about moving to the hill, but he wouldn't hear of it. What are we going to do?"

This time, Cassie didn't have an answer.

Almost to herself, Shona said, "I guess we'll just wait until the flood warning comes, and do whatever's necessary. One thing I'm sure of, somehow. There will be no way of saving this house."

Under her satiny brown skin, Cassie paled. "But, honey, dat means we might have trouble savin' ourselves, too."

"Cassie, we're going to have a whole lot of trouble. But, somehow, maybe we'll make it. Don't worry too much."

Leaving Cassie in a daze with two conflicting statements, Shona went to the cellar with the apples and potatoes she had bought. In her imagination, she saw them bobbing around in water. Closing her eyes, suddenly the up-and-down movement in the water was neither apples nor potatoes. It was people.

Frightened, now, she went to her mother. "Mama, did you ever have a daymare?"

"A daymare? What in the world is that?"

"The opposite of a nightmare, I suppose. I made that up."

Sophie smiled at her daughter—sometimes the child, although usually the most mature type of adult.

"No, dear, I've never had a daymare. Tell me about it."

To make it easier on her mother, she spoke of the apples and potatoes, without mentioning the people.

Regardless of that, Sophie was alarmed. "Darling, we must tell Papa."

Shona frowned. "You know Papa never believes that I have such feelings. If he does, he attributes it to passing fantasy. No, I don't think he should be told."

"Then, what can we do?" Sophie sniffed, and reached into her bosom to draw out a lace handkerchief.

Shona's fright had passed. There would be a way of handling whatever was to come—why else would there have been a message? She patted her mother's shoulder. "I guess we'll have to read our Bibles and pray a lot."

That pleased Sophie. She had been worried about her daughter's indifferent use of the Bible, and had wondered whether living with the witch had corrupted her in some way.

As for Shona, she had decided to warn anyone who would listen. There was no doubt at all that the dam would collapse this year.

* * *

Several days later, the *Johnstown Tribune* carried a news item which created a sensation among readers of the paper.

Entitled "A POSSIBLE TRAGEDY," and bearing the by-line of M. J. McKay, it warned of a conceivable disaster.

The story began: "A young woman of some notoriety in this

city is warning its citizens of the danger inherent in the unsafe condition of the South Fork Dam.

"Shona MacDonald, who made headlines when she was kidnapped by a woman known as the 'Hogback Witch,' has evidently acquired some strange powers. At this time, she is seeing visions of a great disaster in Johnstown.

"Just how she is able to do this, and whether any credibility can be given to the portent, is not clear. One thing is certain—it would be well to consider this so-called 'omen' as a very real possibility."

That much of the account seemed to be innocuous enough. The remainder of the article was rife with innuendo.

One of the most character-damaging references stood in regard to the illness and death of the MacDonald baby. Other incidents, paled in the light of the facts. Shona had predicted the baby's illness—subsequently, the baby had died.

If Will MacDonald was angry, Michael Stewart was livid. He put down the paper, resolving that Mary Ann had better have a good reason for her unconscionable action.

Grabbing his hat, he strode out of the house to the small frame house on Market Street. Accustomed to walking in, now he rapped on the door.

Although dressed for the evening, Mary Jane had not expected to see him so early. She beamed at him.

Ignoring the fact that she wore a captivating pink dress, and her brown hair lay in waves to her shoulders, Michael glared at her.

She stared at him in amazement, as he raged.

"What do you mean by slandering Shona like that? Her power of clairvoyance has been with her since she was a baby."

Mary Jane greeted that with a sneer. "That's not likely."

"Then you're not ashamed of defaming the girl?"

"Certainly not. It was a good story. Besides, the people of the city needed a warning."

Shocked, he gazed at her cold manner. Could this be the loving, caring woman he had believed her to be?

Equally upset, Mary Jane glared back at him. Why should it mean so much to him that she had made a few observations about Shona? She motioned him into the living room and faced him accusingly.

"Seems to me you're unduly disturbed. Do I get the impression that there's something going on between you and this girl?"

" 'This girl' means a lot to me. I've known her since she was a child. She's suffered a great deal of prejudice here, for no valid reason."

She threw him an angry glance. Choosing to dwell on his first remark, she shouted, "So, she means a lot to you. I wonder just what *I* mean to you. How dare you come here to berate me for an article that is doing a service to the people?"

It was Michael's turn to sneer. "What kind of service do you think you're doing to Shona?"

That enraged her. "Shona, Shona . . . She seems to be the focus of your affection. Why don't you get out of here and give her this?"

She took off her ring and threw it at him. He didn't pick it up.

Turning to the door, he said, "If I gave her a ring, it certainly wouldn't be one of yours."

With that, he left the house, slamming the door.

Walking swiftly down the street, his anger did not diminish. All he could think of was Shona, and how much he cared.

* * *

As for Will, he wasted no time. Donning ulster and hat, he strode to the newspaper office.

"I want to see Mr. Swank," he blustered to the girl at the front desk.

"I'm sorry, sir. Mr. Swank is not in. If you'll leave your name . . ."

Will cut in. "When *will* he be in? I've got to see him."

"Mr. Swank will not be in the office for a few days. There's been a death in the family."

Will hesitated. "Then, who can I see about this darn article in the paper?" He waved the clipping.

"I could let you talk to the reporter, but she must be out on assignment. I haven't been able to reach her."

This was a ploy. The secretary had been trained to prevent any and all confrontation.

Will gave up, temporarily. Giving the necessary information, he strode out of the office, mentally cursing the workings of such organizations.

Sophie awaited him, worried more about his health, that the effect of the newspaper item on Shona. A man given to such rages could be a prime subject for apoplexy, and the thought frightened her.

Happily, when he arrived, she could see that some of his anger had worn away. She kissed him.

Oddly, the person least disturbed by the appearance of the news item was Shona. Although unhappy about Mary Jane's betrayal, she gave it little thought. The furor over witches had long since passed; apparently Johnstown had matured.

What was important was the communication to the people of the city. This warning would carry more impact than if she were to shout from a soap box. There were at least 28,000 residents of Johnstown. Surely a majority of them read the paper.

She tried to soothe her father. "You see, Papa, I don't mind the insinuations. We've been through this 'witch' business before. What's important is that people have a substantial warning on the condition of the dam. I'm sure it's unsafe."

"Well, Miss Know-It-All, how do you know that?" He put down his book and leaned back in the swivel chair.

"Danny and I were up there, some time ago. We saw the shape it was in. Apparently, someone was working on it. We saw tufts of straw here and there, which Danny said were used as temporary stops for leaks. But there were many other places spurting water. It just can't be safe."

Slightly convinced, Will reached for the telephone, which had been newly installed. "I'll just call J. B. Montgomery. He'll know what's goin' on." He leafed through the directory.

But J. B. didn't know. He maintained that the dam had been built of wood and stone, rather than shale. Water must not be allowed to go over the top of the dam, but, he reiterated, water could be released through three waste gates at the bottom. He assured Will that repairs had probably been made.

Not satisfied with a supposition that work had been done on the dam, Shona talked to Danny about it, that evening. "Let's go up again, and see for ourselves," she begged.

Although thinking the issue unimportant, Danny agreed. On Sunday, they took the horses and drove to South Fork.

The wind was chill—there was no rain, but the clouds were smoky and dark, and the sun had never shown up. As yet, the clubhouse was deserted and all the cottages were closed. There were no boats.

Carefully, they inspected the breastwork. Someone had been working on it, if crudely. Fishguards of heavy wire screen crossed its crest—ostensibly to keep fish from leaping out. Logs floated on the water to keep fish away from the spillway, which had finally been constructed.

"That could be a hazard," Shona pointed out. "Couldn't the logs force the water higher? That would erode the breast of the dam."

"I suppose it could." Danny's perfunctory agreement stemmed from the fact that he couldn't see any real reason for worry. Now that the largest leak had been stopped, he could see no justification for concern.

They rode home in silence. Waiting for Plato to take the horses, Danny finally said, "What are you planning to do?"

Shona looked at him speculatively, not seeing him at all. "I'm going to get my family out, soon. I'm not sure how, but I can't let them die."

"Oh, come now, Shona . . ."

She turned on him. "If you care about your family, you'll do something about them, too. I don't think you're taking this matter seriously."

He almost pouted. "Of course I do. I just don't see . . ."

"You don't see? Well, I've been doing some checking. Do you realize the size of that waterway? It's nearly three miles long, and in some places it's a mile wide. It covers 50 acres. At the dam itself, it's more than sixty feet deep."

"You've really looked into it." He was impressed.

"I certainly have. Can you imagine what that amount of water, rushing into a deep valley, would do? There could be untold loss of life. The question is, how do we get people to believe the extend of their danger?"

They could come to no conclusion. Eventually, Shona, tired of his lack of support, decided to wait until later, and discuss the matter with her parents.

Danny's folks lived away from town, close to the hill, in Woodvale. Their house was on fairly high ground—they had never suffered more than basement flooding.

When Danny finally got around to studying a map, he discovered that their home lay directly in the path of the possible dam overflow.

His belated alarm to his parents didn't frighten them. Mr. Dayton explained, "Dan, for seven years we've been hearing about the danger posed by that dam. For many of those years, we've had spring floods—some of them heavy. Somehow, the dam has always held. Why is there any reason for fear, now?"

Danny kept still, not wanting to implicate Shona.

The next morning, when Shona went to the hospital, she saw no difference in the attitudes of her fellow workers. She had no idea whether they had read the article, or whether it had bothered them in any way.

Side by side with Jean at the linen closet, Shona brought it up. "Have you seen the article in yesterday's paper about the dam—incidentally, about me?"

Jean responded pleasantly. "I have, and I think it's brave of you to allow her to say the things she did. After all, everyone should be aware of the danger; heaven knows we've been warned often enough. But who's to know whether it might happen?"

This wasn't what Shona had expected. Her mind began to sort out Jean's possible thoughts. "She's reflecting what most of the people say. My warning means nothing—she thinks I'm a fake, seeking publicity."

All this, she didn't say aloud, but it rang in her mind as though she had. After all, it was a logical assumption.

Later, when they were stacking the crisp, white sheets in the closet, Jean spotted Shona's diamond.

"Shona, you didn't tell us. When did you get that? Who's the lucky fellow?"

"It was a Christmas gift. I haven't been wearing it to work. I just forgot to take it off."

"But you haven't answered my question. Who is the guy?"

Forcing herself to face Jean, she said, "Danny Dayton." She

expected to see pain in Jean's sensitive face, but, happily, there was no change of expression.

Pleased to see that there was no deep involvement between Jean and Danny, Shona went about her duties with a sense of relief.

Late in the afternoon, Lorene Chandler called Shona aside.

"Has Jean confided in you, lately? Apparently, there's some sort of problem."

Shona's eyes widened. "No, she hasn't. She seemed to be perfectly all right, this morning."

Lorene came closer and whispered, "I found her in the broom closet, crying."

At once, Shona knew. The discovery of Danny's engagement had been more of a blow than Jean had shown.

She hedged. "Perhaps there's trouble at home—an illness, or another concern which she doesn't want to discuss. Why don't you talk to her?"

"That's just it. I tried to draw her out, but she's tight as a clam. That's why I came to you. You two seem to be quite close."

Glad to make a forthright statement, Shona said, "I'm sorry; I wish I could help. She hasn't said a thing."

Shona stayed away from Jean that afternoon, unsure of a proper approach. As for Jean, her composure seemed to be unchanged. If she felt turmoil, there was little indication of it. She went about as usual, quietly affable and communicative. The only clue to the possibility of a dilemma was her unusually pale face.

Shona faced Danny that night. "Danny, please tell me the truth. How much were you involved with Jean?"

Her mouth had a determined set; her blue-green eyes seemed to be looking directly into him.

Inwardly, Danny squirmed. "Lord, Shona, I haven't promised her a thing. We had some dates, that's all. I thought you knew that."

"It looked that way. Then, there was nothing romantic between you?"

He had to avoid her eyes at any cost. Staring at the floor, he mumbled, "You know, you're the only one I ever wanted."

Dissatisfied, she pressed him, but he refused to commit himself. There would be no confession—not from him.

* * *

Several days later, Michael came to the door. Shona hadn't come home yet, and Sophie invited him in to wait. She had always admired him—now she was curious about his amnesia.

"I understand you've completely recovered from that terrible accident. They say your memory has returned." It was more of a question than a statement.

"Yes," he grinned. "No side effects, they tell me."

She couldn't help asking, "Do you remember being in the hospital?"

A strange expression crossed his brow. "It's funny, no matter how I try, I can't seem to recall a thing. From the time something hit me, until wakening in my own bed, I don't know what happened. They say that Shona was one of my nurses."

Sophie smiled. "And a dedicated one. She sat with you nearly all the time."

He was pleased at that. "She a dear. I came by to apologize for that item in the paper. The reporter was a good friend of mine. Who knows what possessed her to write it like that. Shona's had enough prejudice to bear."

"You know—it would seem so. But apparently, Shona is so gratified to get the message to the people, that she no longer frets about injustice. She's not angry at all.

Just then, the telephone rang. Sophie went to answer it, plucking the receiver off the wall carefully, fearfully, as though it were alive.

"Yes, yes. I understand. Thank you."

Returning to her chair, she smiled apologetically, "Shona's employer called. She wants Shona to stay for an hour or so. They've just taken in a seriously injured workman."

Michael got to his feet. "Well, I just wanted to tell her how sorry I am. Now that you have a telephone, I can call her. Thanks for telling me what you did."

Sophie never delivered Michael's message. When Shona arrived, she was already behind in the planning so carefully begun. There was a new road to Hogback. It wound along the side of the hill, in the exact path shaped by Indians more than a century ago.

Shona intended to ask Plato to chance the fact that this road could bear a wagon, and take some of their possessions up, almost to the cabin on Hogback.

There was no time for supper. "Mama, we don't know when the storm will hit. Heavy clouds are hanging up there, right now. Can you help?"

Although shaken by the urgency of the matter, Sophie dug in. She wrapped each piece of Limoges china diligently in newspaper, and covered the silver chest with a baby blanket for protection.

Shona occupied herself with clothing, packing it in an old chest, meticulously, so that it would not wrinkle. Heaping a carboard box with shoes, she set it down.

Looking around, Shona decided that they would need another oil lamp, so she wrapped the prettiest one. Whatnots weren't important.

Rushing with the work, a helpless feeling pervaded the

household. Will looked at the project as unnecessary and foolish, but somehow, subconsciously, he was relieved to have the others make the decisions.

As for Cassie, she had no doubt whatever that the disaster Shona had predicted would happen. Returning from a trip to the provisions store, she flew into action at once. What about Plato? Would there be time for him to get there?

She could picture imminent disaster for all of them. There was one thing to do. Pray!

However, the act of praying could go on along with the work. Cassie was not one to sit and pray when matters were to be taken care of.

And so, at last the wagon was loaded. Shona went with Plato, giving her mother and Cassie instructions to go up to the hospital and wait for them. As for Will, he had a great deal to do at the mill. Of one thing he was sure—there *would* be a flood.

Fortunately, the road had been built of cinders, and wasn't muddy. The wagon climbed easily, without too much strain on the horses. Of course, there was the steep path above, but it posed no challenge to Plato.

After he had placed things in the cabin, Shona locked it, and they hurried back to the wagon. She climbed up with Plato. "We've got to get down fast, so that you can get the horses to safety."

He nodded. That was what had been worrying him. He had made arrangements for the animals at a public stable on the eastern hill.

It was May 29. Dark storm clouds hung over the mountains, ominous in their density, but somehow, Shona's sense of urgency had diminished.

"Don't worry, Plato. There won't be much rain tonight; I can tell—the pressure in my head has disappeared."

He frowned. There was no accounting for this child. For a while, she had been wildly excited; now, for some reason, she was calm.

* * *

EIGHTEENTH

As they left Hogback, a light rain began to fall. Ordinarily, it would have amounted to nothing, but with the ground already saturated by a combination of heavy rains and the excessive melt of spring thaws, the cinders of the road began to slide. Heroically, the horses stalled with their hind legs, holding the wagon back.

When they finally reached town, the rain had diminished. Contemplating the threatening level of the raging river, Shona could hardly believe that this had been the tiny rivulet of last summer.

Lights in the houses showed people busily moving their furniture and carpets upstairs. Shona wanted to run through the town, telling them not to do that—just to get out of town. Now convinced that the entire city, in that point between the two rivers, would be lost, she agonized in frustration.

Meanwhile, that evening, the downpour had eroded much of the work at the dam which the men had been doing —constructing sewer trenches. By morning, the lake had risen two feet. At seven, it had risen a foot each hour, and was now within three feet of the dam's breast.

At first, the men attempted to create another spillway. The shale was almost impenetrable. As a desperate measure, they heaped stones, logs, and other blockage—anything to keep the water from the top of the dam.

Now, water was spurting through the shale-and-clay front in all directions—mute evidence of the frailty of that surface.

* * *

Having failed to get in touch with Michael on the evening before, Shona set out again to find him. Apparently, he had not come back to his apartment. There was no one else to contact, but Mary Jane.

She went to the newspaper office, which had moved its main operation upstairs. The secretary greeted her pleasantly.

"Miss McKay isn't in yet. She had an assignment which kept her out for most of the night. These are hectic times, around here."

As Shona left, she smiled to herself, sadly. These were indeed hectic times—she wouldn't allow herself to dwell on what would happen. The only thing left to do was to prevent some of the tragedy. She went on home. The MacDonald family had permission from Dr. Galloway to stay at the hospital, but there seemed to be no imminent danger.

In the morning, Shona went about her chores perfunctorily, wondering how to find Michael. At least, she thought, he knew of her intuition, and would act on it.

Jean called attention to her distraction. "Shona, what is it? You go around as though you had heard the last trump. Are you really so worried?"

She roused herself to answer. "Jean, I'd give anything to be able to warn the whole city of the condition of the dam. They've heard—but they don't believe it. All they can think about is moving things up out of the flood waters."

Jean nodded. "I know. They've heard that warning too often."

After her chores were done, Shona asked to leave the

hospital. There were only a few patients, and Miss Chandler had been kind.

"I assume you're going to the Memorial Day activities?"

"No, Miss Chandler, I'm going down to warn some of my neighbors. I'm sure it will rain soon, and from seeing the condition of that dam, I'm also certain that it won't hold."

Miss Chandler spoke of Shona's obsession to Jean. "She's under such a strain. She really believes that the dam is going to collapse."

Jean looked out the window at the heaping black clouds. "Maybe she's right. She's been up to the dam recently, and she says it's leaking heavily. The engineers say only that it must not go over the top. A lot of rain might do the damage."

Smiling, Lorene clapped Jean on the shoulder. "Now you're doing it."

"Doing what?"

"Getting all worked up over something that is not likely to happen. You don't think those rich men up there are going to lose their fish and their playground if there's any way to prevent it?"

Feeling a bit foolish, Jean smiled.

As for Shona, the question was not whether, but when, the dam would collapse.

She began a house-to-house canvass, before realizing that most of the citizens were probably at Sandyvale Cemetery, honoring their dead.

Hurrying in that direction, she met a large group of people moving away from the scene, where small American flags had been placed on many graves.

Her first contact was Mrs. Parks, whose child, Alice, had been her playmate. The woman was wiping her eyes, having just placed a bouquet on Alice's grave.

Shona rushed up to her. "Mrs. Parks, I have to tell you, in case you haven't seen it in the paper. I've had a warning. At first, it wasn't clear, but now, I know it presaged the collapse of the South Fork Dam."

Mrs. Parks drew back as though doubting her sanity. "You've had a warning? What do you mean?"

Not wanting to take time to explain, Shona turned away, calling back over her shoulder. "Believe me, your life is in danger. Get your family out of the city! Go to the hills."

She warned some other wondering people, who also seemed to doubt her sanity, and then ran almost into Sara and Lucy Rearick. Meeting them was a welcome surprise. When she repeated her warning, they showed complete respect.

"We'll certainly do as you say," Sara cried. "Naturally, you're in a position to know." They had reached their home and were dashing up the steps.

Others were not so amenable. Those whom she encountered

were usually skeptical, or they laughed.

After a few more unsuccessful warnings, Shona went home, mentally exhausted. She found her mother and Cassie sitting calmly on the displaced furniture. They had made no preparation to pack.

"Mother—Cassie—what are you doing?" she gasped. "You're not even ready. You can't stay here tonight. Who knows when it will happen?"

Sophie spoke softly. "Honey, we can't impose on the hospital without good reason. We'll go at the first threat, I promise."

"Mama, it's just too dangerous here. When that dam breaks, it's going to come right down this valley. Can't you see? There may not be time to get to the hill."

Banking on Shona's perception, Sophie couldn't be persuaded. At last, everyone agreed to wait—at least, until morning.

By this time, the rain, which had been falling steadily, was a downpour. The river had overflowed its banks. Now, with water seeping into the first floor, Will rushed in to support Shona's plea.

"Take your mother and Cassie up to Prospect. I have to see that some rolling stock is moved; I'm takin' Plato with me."

Noting Sophie's pained expression and Cassie's fear, he added, "No need to worry. We ain't—aren't goin' to be in danger. That part of the mill is set pretty dang high."

And so they separated, the subdued women walking with Shona to the hospital. The rain had slackened for a time, but the wooden bridge, over what had been a peaceful stream, now spanned a ferocious, swollen river. Somehow, it stood. They crossed it, thankfully.

* * *

Up at the lake front, things were getting worse. At some time in the night, the rain had become a cloudburst. The lake continued to rise about a foot an hour. This morning, Henry Weber, an employee of the Sportsmen's Club, was working at another camp nearly a mile away.

Suddenly, he noticed that the lake seemed to be lowering. He made a mark on the shore. That confirmed his suspicion.

Rushing as swiftly as possible to the dam, he studied the face of it. Water welled out beneath the foundation of the dam, and spurted all over its breast. That was about two o'clock. Forty-five minutes later, the stones in the center of the dam were undermined, and in eight minutes more, a gap of twenty feet appeared in the lower half of the wall. At about three, the rest of the masonry fell in.

Weber's description of the destruction said that the remainder of the wall "opened outward like twin gates, and the great storage lake was foaming and thundering down the valley of the Conemaugh."

With a tumultuous clap that echoed and re-echoed in the hills, the water shattered and tossed houses, trees and rocks high in the air and a torrent roared down the mountain, overwhelming everything in its path.

Shortly after the collapse of the dam, from his vantage point at South Fork, Freight Agent Deckert telegraphed a warning "begging the people of Johnstown to take to the hills."

Someone else saw what was happening. Standing near the Woodvale Bridge, David Lucas and a friend were considering the bridge's strength, when they saw something in the distance that seemed to be dark smoke. David knew instantly what had happened. In another moment, he was on his horse, pounding down the valley, crying, "Run for your lives, the dam has broken."

There were people who ran; most, did not.

* * *

In the city, a low, rumbling sound brought the suspicion of danger to people who had been skeptical. They climbed on rooftops, lumber and anything available that floated, but when the great wave swooped down at locomotive speed, those in its path were swept under to certain death.

South Fork and Mineral Point had been annihilated, just before that—houses, trees and logs were swept along with the monster wave, which had not yet shown its real power.

In the yard of the Pennsylvania Railroad, it tore up the buildings, and carried off locomotives, digging their graves and burying them as it went. Woodvale with its population of about 3,000 people was wiped out. The Gautier Barbed Wire Mill of the Cambria Iron Company was leveled, as was the Woodvale Horse Railroad Company. The stables swirled on the water, along with every horse and car they had sheltered.

Approximately eighteen miles below the dam, high on Prospect Hill, the telegraphed news came to the hospital. In tortured anticipation, the staff came out on the hillside, along with Shona's family and a few patients.

Not realizing the distance the water would travel, they waited for what seemed to be an interminable time. Gradually, everyone began to suspect another false alarm. Everyone, that is, except Shona.

At about four o'clock, they glimpsed the beginning of the colossal disaster. Like a great black cloud of dust, it advanced. Nearing, it became far more hideous than Shona's "daymare". A frenzied black wall of water hurtled into the valley, shredding houses and tossing people, animals and trees like match sticks on its foaming crest.

The crashing noise of the tons of rubble, and the cries of

humans and animals made it all too horrible to bear.

Shona felt a chill and closed her eyes. Only determination kept her from fainting. Where were her loved ones? Were they safe? Were they, indeed, alive? She must do something —anything . . . In a panic of conflicting emotions, she started running down the hill.

They screamed at her, but she didn't hear. Part way down, she stopped. A section of town on the far side, although deep in water, had escaped the path of destruction. People were in boats, on housetops or swimming to the hills. They were safe.

Then she saw that these, too, were doomed. The deluge, forty feet high, but only an eighth of a mile wide, had been slowed by friction. But when it burst against the waters of the swollen Stonycreek, the two clashed. Then, joining, they created a vast whirlpool, smashing the waters back into the valley to finish the destruction.

Out of her sight, a massive build-up of debris at the hillside and the Stone Bridge, rose at least ten feet above the masonry, effectively damming the raging water. It was that enormous obstruction which had turned the flood back into Johnstown.

It was impossible for Shona to realize the terrific force of the giant whirlpool. Weighing tens of thousands of tons, it crushed everything beneath it. Of one thing she was sure. Her home, and the entire central section of the city had been wiped from the earth.

However, little time could be wasted in speculation. Refugees who had been clinging to the hills were climbing up toward the hospital. Except for some small injuries, they did not seem to be disabled, but many were weakened by their ordeal.

Shona came back to reality, relieving a mother of a crying child, and carrying it up to the hospital. The act of helping soothed her anxiety.

Dr. Galloway met his challenge gallantly. He had no idea how he was going to care for these people. But right now, it was paramount that they find a place of refuge, and some surcease from terror.

Shona was off again, this time, with Cassie at her side. Together, they supported the weak or the aged on the trek upward, grateful for their combined strength.

When, apparently, the last fugitive from terror had appeared at the hospital, the doctor's count had reached 71. That did not include three patients.

Now, it was evening and no one had been fed. Lorene came to him, as he treated an injured leg.

"May I speak to you for a moment?"

The doctor nodded. "I'm just finishing this bandage. Now, I think our friend here can be on his feet, to join the others."

She watched, noticing the deftness of his hands, which she had envied at other times. The thought came over her that he should have been a surgeon. Of course, she had entertained other illusions, less logical.

"There you are, good as new." The doctor placed the last piece of adhesive, and the man stood up, smiling.

As he left the room, Lorene was startled from her reverie. She dropped her eyes, fearing that he would read something there. "Doctor, I was wondering what we would feed these people. There are so many."

He patted her shoulder. "We'll have to ration what we have, and hope for the best. Maybe you girls could help the cook to make up a dish that goes a long way."

She reflected. "We do have a lot of potatoes. Maybe soup, or salad . . ."

"I knew you'd come up with something. That's why I depend on you so heavily." He smiled, picked up his stethoscope and headed for the doorway.

Thrilled by his praise, she turned toward the kitchen, beckoning to Shona in the hallway, holding a baby. Shona handed the child to his mother. "He's just beautiful," she remarked.

Tears came to the woman's eyes. "He's all I have—now."

* * *

Organizing the care of a large number of people posed more than one problem. There were the aged, the infirm, five infants and eight children, in addition to more than 50 distraught adults.

Dr. Galloway had it all thought out before nightfall. The old folks and children would get beds insofar as possible; blankets were available for issuing to the adults; the babies were another matter.

Searching in the storeroom, he had discovered a half-dozen large boxes, not too deep to serve effectively as cribs. He issued orders to the nurses.

As for Sophie and Cassie, he accepted gratefully their urgent offer of help. In awe, he saw his plans fall into place. Truly, these ladies were a godsend.

The original hubbub had now quieted. Except for a few weeping women, the assemblage had settled down.

Gathering them in the entry way and the adjoining hall, the doctor made an announcement.

"I have something vital to say. Our water comes from a deep well, but it may be contaminated. Do not drink any water unless you know that it has been boiled for at least five minutes. Milk must be saved for the infants. Food will not be as plentiful as we would like, but no one will starve."

He took a handkerchief from his white coat and blotted his brow. "I guess that's the message. Try not to worry; get some sleep. You will need your strength."

Somehow, the night passed. Now and then, a baby cried, or a

child called out in its sleep; otherwise an uneasy peace reigned.

And yet, the atmosphere was heavy with sorrow. Hushed sobs and sniffles breathed in the air. Once, a woman screamed. She continued shrieking until the doctor brought a sedative. It took some time for the wakened sleepers to settle again.

Shona spent the night pacing the corridor or resting in the office's Morris chair. Worry over her father and Plato, as well as Michael and Danny, kept her in a state of constant apprehension.

* * *

She need not have fretted over Will and Plato. They had gone to an upper section of the Cambria Iron Works, which stood on level ground, looking down toward the great Stone Bridge.

Ready to return, that afternoon, their raincoats soggy and cold, Will pulled out his gold watch, beautifully etched, its cover depicting an oncoming locomotive. To his dismay, the watch had stopped at three.

Looking down at the stinking brown floodwater rolling below them, only a few feet away, Will frowned. "We'll have to go up, toward the hill. There's no way we can cross, here."

As they climbed higher, a thunderous sound overwhelmed them. Coming from a distance, it became a continuous roar, crashing and reverberating through the valley.

Turning, they saw a sudden rise in the river, and understood what it was.

In another moment a giant wave came into view—brown tide, crested with a mammoth cloud of white spray. The force of it crashed against Westmont hill in black fury, almost as high as the elevation itself.

With it came a gigantic heap of people, animals and debris, smashing into the stone bridge, which miraculously held. The two rivers clashed with a deafening roar, and the backwash swirled into that part of the city which had escaped the tide. In a few seconds, the people who had been out of the path of the wave, disappeared in a giant whirlpool.

The men stood in awe, unable to take their eyes from the scene. When he could speak, Will gasped, "Judas Priest, did you ever see anythin' like that? It throwed box cars around like nothin'."

Plato, overwhelmed, agreed. "Look at that heap, boilers, machinery, telegraph poles and all kinds of wood, over there. Funny, something seems to be holding it together."

Will took a closer look. "Looks like the wire mill's gone. That's barbed wire. Too bad. Biggest commission they ever got. Darned shame!"

Plato had been listening intently. "Do you hear that?"

"Hear what?"

Lowering his voice in awe, Plato said, "Sounds like people,

screaming."

"Fer gosh sakes, Plato, how can you tell, with all that noise?" Listening intently, he heard it, himself. He nodded.

Soberly, he said, "You're right. There's humans in there, along with their smashed houses and the junk. The worst thing is, there's not a dang thing we kin do about it."

As the crashing abated, the cries of the doomed people grew louder. An acrid smell rose from the heap of corruption.

Will sniffed the putrid air. "I smell smoke. I'll jest bet some of them coal stoves and such 've set fire to that heap."

Plato turned away. "Let's get out of here. That screaming is getting to me, and the smoke is coming this way."

Will agreed with alacrity, and they sprang up the hillside, moving quickly, as far from the disaster as possible.

Then he stopped short. "I guess I got no sense of direction. Do you know . . . which way is Prospect?"

Plato pointed toward the east. "Over that way, I think. We'll have to go far around, to stay out of the water."

It was twilight when they finally decided to find a place to spend the night. By now, they had no idea of their location. They were still in the forest.

Finally, they came to a clearing, where a small house stood near a barn. Behind the house lay several fields, standing in muddy water.

They looked at each other. "Do we try here?" ventured Plato. Will hesitated.

At last, he agreed. All they needed was a floor, indoors. It wasn't as though they were asking for charity. He knocked on the door.

A tiny, mouselike woman answered it, stepping backward when she saw them, and nearly closing the door. "Yes—what is it?"

Will licked his lips. This was difficult for him, asking help from a stranger. "We can't get back to our folks. We thought you wouldn't mind if we slept here on the floor tonight."

Before she could say anything, a burly man moved behind her, pushing the door open so that he could see. After one glance, he shouted, "We *would* mind. We want no truck with strangers. Just get off of my property, or I'll have the dogs . . ."

They waited no longer. Rushing off, they suddenly discovered that there was no place to go. Will had an idea. "They don't have to know; let's sleep in the barn. We can be out of there before it's light."

Plato demurred. "It's me they don't want. Iffen they catch me here in the morning, no tellin' what they'll do."

Scoffing, Will put down the thought. Sure that Plato and his good manners would be welcome anywhere, he dismissed that idea.

Nevertheless, Plato was firm. He wanted nothing to do with

the farm or the people on it.

And so, they moved on. At the top of a hill, they came to a barroom. The bartender was cleaning up, and chairs were upended on the tables.

Will approached the man. "Sir," he ventured, not wanting a recurrence of hostility, "we need a place to stay for the night. I can pay . . ."

The proprietor gave him a pleasant look. Sweeping his hand about him, he laughed. "Help yourselves—I don't know what you'd pay for. Not a cot in the joint."

Will set down two chairs, and dropped onto one. "We're plumb tuckered out. Been walkin' for hours. We jest appreciate havin' a place to light."

"What brings you here? I've had no business all day, so I decided to close."

"Don't you know? The South Fork Dam broke. Johnstown is gone."

"Gone?" The idea took some getting used to. "You mean . . . it's flooded?"

"Worse than that—there's nothing left. Not in the center of town, anyhow. From what we could see, that blasted water just took away all the houses, people, and everything." Talking about it, Will became nervous; his voice shook.

Plato took over. "We'd been up on the hill when it happened. I tell you, it was awful, the terrible noise, the screams . . ."

It was the bartender's turn to shake. "I have a daughter living down on Locust Street. I must get down there right away . . ."

"Down, where? There's no place to go."

No logic would dissuade him.

"There's no money in the cash box, so nobody will rob you. I'll be back—you'll be well paid." He was gone.

"Didn't even leave the key," grumbled Will. "What in tarnation do we do now?"

Plato took off his coat, turned the dry side out, and made a pillow. "We get some rest, I guess." With that, he stretched out on the floor.

Hesitating for a moment, Will turned the "Closed" sign toward the street, and followed suit, leaving the lights blazing.

* * *

Shona's concern for Michael was well-founded. If she had known what he planned to do, she would have been frantic.

His parents had called to tell him that his favorite aunt was dying. They had gone on to Pittsburgh to see her, and would await him there.

Walking toward the Pennsylvania Station, he met George Johnston, a Pittsburgh lumber merchant. Johnston asked him if he had read the notice posted at the telegraph office.

Slightly alarmed, Michael asked, "What was it?"

"It was feared that the three-mile dam (they call it) would give way. I know enough about Johnstown to know that my life is not worth a snap, once that dam gives way."

Michael tried to show no agitation. "Then, you're on your way to Pittsburgh, too. Looks as though there aren't any other passengers."

They were walking up the steps to the depot when they heard the thunderous roar of the advancing water. Rushing onto the train, they boarded, just as it pulled out, with the conductor tugging frantically at the bell rope.

Sitting at the car window, with a sinking feeling, Michael could see the frothy, yellow wall advancing. His first impulse was to jump and run, but better judgment made him stay in his seat.

Below, the nearby mill yards were a turbulent, dirty ocean, where pieces of houses and barns rode like ships in the current.

At the mill, when the water rushed in on molten steel, it caused a series of explosions, but the noise was almost covered by the roar of the flood.

On the other side of the train, he could see men and horses floundering in the wild water, housetops carrying whole families, which clung to each other in terror.

The train was on the bridge now. Buildings and debris spun through the structure. It seemed to both Michael and his new friend, George, that it would not possibly hold much longer.

When the train finally dashed into the hillside forest and slackened, George breathed a sigh, looking at Michael. "That rate of speed made me think the engineer had gone mad."

Michael agreed, looking back through the trees at the city. The entire valley had become a roaring maelstrom; only the standpipes of the mills stood above the raging water.

As the train continued at a normal pace, the two, still shaken, discussed their experience.

Michael speculated. "At least two-thirds of the town is probably now gone. When I left, everyone had climbed to the upper floors of their homes. Many of them did not know, or wouldn't believe, that the dam would break."

George questioned him about this.

"Well, you probably know the Aesop fable, "The Boy Who Cried Wolf?"

He smiled, inclining his head.

"Well, the people of this city have had dam scares for about seven years, now. For three of those years, there has been heavy spring flooding. The dam was supposedly repaired; anyhow, it has always held."

The pair became suddenly silent, still agitated by their experience.

Michael fell into a reverie. When would he see Shona again? Was she safe? Somehow, he had every confidence that she would be.

They were in Pittsburgh, now. George gave Michael his card, and Michael grinned. "Seems I don't have an address any more. Guess I'll have to get in touch with you."

They parted as friends. A common fear had brought them together, uniting them in a lasting kinship.

* * *

All that weary night, Shona, beset with worry, fretted over the fates of her loved ones. Danny, however, was the least of her concerns.

She knew that Danny's family lived in Woodvale on Maple Avenue—the main street, directly in the path of the river below the dam.

However, she was also sure that Danny, well aware of the danger, would take steps to get them to safety. But in her confidence, there was one thing she did not consider. Would Danny's parents listen to him?

They would not.

"Why should we leave?" Daniel, senior, objected. "We're close enough to the mill to get there. I'm staying right here, in my upstairs, with my household goods. Looters won't be taking over this house, like they always do in some places."

There was no moving him. In desperation, Danny rushed to his mother. She was sitting in a hickory rocker, looking down at the raging water, and knitting.

Danny dumped the knitting on the floor and grabbed her arm. "Mama, we've got to get out of here. We have the word: the dam is going!"

She drew away from him, stooped to pick up her yarn, and sat down. "Your father doesn't believe it—neither do I. Please, Danny, don't be melodramatic."

At that moment, David Lucas dashed by on horseback, yelling, "Run for your lives—the dam has broken."

Finally, the Daytons realized that they must go. Braving the already flooded street, they made for the hillside, Danny supporting his frightened mother. Then, a tremendous roar hit their consciousness, and before they could turn, the colossal wave of water and debris closed over them. All three disappeared, not to be seen again, even in death.

* * *

NINETEENTH

The next morning, the hospital came alive early. The children, less frightened than they had been, were noisy and sometimes quarrelsome. Dr. Galloway set some of the more able parents to keep a peaceful atmosphere by inventing games.

Approaching Miss Chandler, he laid out his plans. First, he must go out for provisions. He knew that he would probably need to travel for some distance, but the refugees must be fed.

"You'll handle things, I'm sure, Lorene. I don't know what I'd do without you."

This unusual praise was music indeed. She smiled and gave him a peck on the cheek. "You know I'd do anything for you, doctor."

Quizzically, he glanced at her, but she remained expressionless.

Breakfast was served early, so that the doctor could have something before he left. Sophie and Cassie helped with the serving, and he sighed with gratitude that they were there.

They served oatmeal and coffee to the elderly, and toast to children who didn't like oatmeal. With no milk for the cereal, Shona found some honey, which seemed to make it much more attractive.

When dishes had been cleaned up, beds made and blankets folded, Shona realized that there was very little to do.

She went to Jean. "I'd like to go down the hill part way and see whether there's anyone stranded. When I went down yesterday, I saw that the bridge had gone."

Jean acquiesced. "I'd go, too, but I don't think Miss Chandler would like it if I left her. Go on; you can report back to me in an hour or so."

Moving cautiously now, for the ground was slippery, Shona ventured down the mountain. Just above the swollen river, she stood aghast. The heaps of debris she had expected, were not there.

Ahead, lay a vast wasteland, so smooth that not even a bump could be seen. The violence of the whirlpool had scoured the land.

The bare ground stretched on and on, bounded only by a distant hillside, where the yellow-green of young maples stood against a silver sky.

At once terrible and beautiful, the scene brought back some of her fear. She took a deep breath, and a mixture of odors drew her attention to a black, smoking mass, almost out of her sight around the hill. The stench was so sickening that she didn't have to be told. This was the scene of a horrible tragedy.

Searching through the trees on the hillside where she stood, she was relieved to see that there was no one needing help. Turning back to the hospital she noted a road leading on, over the hill. For a moment, she wanted to travel that road, hoping to get to the mill to find her father and Plato.

Then, reluctantly, she returned to responsibility.

Back at the hospital, she found that those who had come for refuge needed more than food and shelter. They were distressed; some, nearly to the point of suicide.

One particularly difficult case was that of the woman who had screamed in the night. Now, she sat in the long hall, on a chair. Other people had moved away, farther down the corridor.

Shona found her looking straight ahead, and not showing any recognition or awareness of her surroundings.

Some distance away, a year-old baby sat on the floor, playing with a dirty rag doll. A blonde, curly-headed child, it had become the center of attention.

It struck Shona that perhaps she could bring the silent woman out of her depression. Hesitating, she went to the baby's mother and asked to take the little one for a few minutes, promising to feed her. Granted permission, she took the child to the unhappy person.

Standing before the woman, she held out the baby. "Would you take her for a little while, until I get some milk?"

For a moment, the woman's arms began to reach out; then they dropped. She covered her face with shaking hands.

"That's not mine. Take it away. Oh, Lord, where's my baby?" She broke into hysterical sobbing.

Alarmed at what she had done, Shona took the infant back to her mother. "I'm sorry; I thought the little one would cheer her."

Taking the child, its mother gave a tremulous laugh. "It's all right. I'm glad she didn't take Betsy. We might have had a time, getting her away."

Shona hadn't thought of that. She looked back toward the woman, who was weeping quietly, now. Instinctively, she knew that this could be infinitely better than frozen silence.

Nevertheless, that would be the end to playing doctor. For the first time in her life, Shona's confidence in herself had been shaken.

An hour later, Cassie, who had been working feverishly in the kitchen, came to talk about Sophie.

"She's layin' on a bed, 'n jest won't get up. She's not cryin', jest lookin' at the ceiling. Don't seem right to me. Will you come 'n talk to her?"

Shona rushed to the room where Sophie lay. Sure enough, she was greeted with a blank stare.

"Mama, dear, what's the matter? Don't you feel well?"

Suddenly, she began to cry. "I've been so worried. What will we do if Papa doesn't come back? I don't see how Cassie can be so brave about Plato."

She wept for a little while. Shona sat down on the edge of

the bed and patted her shoulder.

"Mama, you've got to hold up. There's no reason to think Papa . . ." She hesitated. "That is, we know they weren't down in the path of the flood. More than likely, it's going to be difficult for them to get to us."

That was logical. There had been only one negative thought in her mind. Oddly, it didn't relate to her father.

Sophie sat up, comforted. "I should be ashamed. Of course, they had been warned. Besides, they were going to that upper mill. Forgive me, Shona."

"There's nothing to forgive. We're all on edge. If you could see the disaster below . . ."

That was a mistake, she thought, instantly. Some things are better left unsaid.

Amazingly, Sophie had regained her calm. "Yes, I've got to see. We've probably lost our house, but at least we have our lives, and even a place to stay."

She stood up in her white uniform, suddenly remembering her dress hanging on the clothes rack in the office. Looking down at rumpled clothing, she said, "I'll get dressed. Will mustn't see me like this."

Somehow, Shona persuaded her to put on another uniform. The best thing for her mother would be to forget herself.

It worked. In a short time, Sophie was moving around among the refugees, giving extra attention to a few most in need of it.

Then, those not traumatized by frightening experience began recounting witnessing of the unspeakable horror sweeping the valley. Some said the wave was thirty feet high; others insisted that it was at least forty.

One gentleman remarked on the fact that huge locomotives were tossed around like chips on the great wave.

Modestly, he recounted his story. After the surge, a section of roof had been floating nearby. On it clung a woman and a young girl. He swam out, to bring them in, one at a time. The odd thing was that neither one had any idea of the identity of the other, nor of how they came to be on the same piece of roof.

Eagerly, a woman told of heroic Dr. Lowman, who had saved his own family and then worked diligently to save others. She had been rescued by the doctor. Sadly, her husband had refused a proffered hand, insisting that he could make it on his own.

Thinking of it, she began to cry. "He was such a proud man. Look what it cost him."

Tales went on, until, late in the afternoon, Dr. Galloway returned. On the road above the hospital, a wagon stood, loaded with provisions. Most of the able-bodied men ran to help.

Amazed, Lorene collared the doctor. "Where did you get all this? I mean, how . . ."

He gave her an enigmatic smile. "You know, Lorene,

everyone wasn't flooded out. Up over the hill, I found a provisions store which supplies farmers."

"But what about money? You certainly didn't have enough for all this." She waved a hand toward the wagon, which the men were busily unloading.

He grinned. "Seems the hospital has a good reputation. Not a word was said about money, except that the time for repayment didn't matter."

Satisfied, she pressed his arm. He was everything a man should be: resourceful, confident, strong. His attributes were many—at least in the eyes of one who had decided to list them with love.

* * *

Early that evening, there was a noise at the door, which had been locked. Then someone began to pound. The nurses looked at Dr. Galloway, who went to open it.

There stood Will and Plato, dirty; unshaven, and disreputable—the most wonderful sight in the world to their family.

Everyone talked at once. The stragglers were too weary and hungry to go into detail. Will dropped into a chair and unlaced his heavy boots.

"Judas Priest, how my feet hurt. How about you, Plato?"

Plato was already removing his own shoes. "Cain't hardly feel 'em no more, Mr. Mac. Reckon my blisters got blisters."

It developed that the pair had been traveling all that day, believing that their movement was eastward. Then the sun set. They discovered that they had made a wide sweep of the mountain, which had taken them in the wrong direction. There was no way to estimate the mileage covered.

By this time, food had been prepared. Famished, they attacked large pancakes with gusto, washing them down with a great amount of coffee.

That night, the MacDonald family slept well. United at last, there was no thought of the losses which had been sustained. Since everyone was safe, nothing else mattered. Everyone, that is, except two young men whose fate was important to one of them.

* * *

Several days passed, and people were restless. Some of them had already departed, bent on finding relatives or friends who lived on the mountain above the valley, or on the outskirts of town.

As for Shona, she decided to make an exploratory trip to find a way to get down the hill. A crude footbridge had been erected, which enabled her to descend to Washington Street.

Long before she had reached the spot where the Stone bridge came in view, she smelled the noxious odors accompanying the smoke. The fire, which had raged in fury for some time, now burned low. Several firemen were shooting water on the gigantic, smoldering heap. They might as well have been squirting water pistols. The fire burned from somewhere deep inside.

A mass of rubble spread out for acres above the bridge, where the furious water had tossed it and departed. Just below her, on the river bank, a heap of debris, buried in mud, seemed to have an odd shape. Looking more closely, she recoiled in horror. Protruding from the muck, were limbs, hands, and several naked bodies.

Across from her, men were digging along the hillside, about 500 feet away. They were removing bodies, trowelling off the mud, and pushing them into canvas bags.

Shona turned and fled. There was nothing she could do, or wanted to do, to help.

Back at the hospital, she sought out Cassie. "Cassie will you speak to Mama for me? I thought maybe you and my mother could continue to help here, and I could go down to the valley. Yesterday, the doctor said the Red Cross was coming. I don't know when, but I can find out."

Cassie gave her a doubtful look. "I don' lak you runnin' around down there, in all that filthy stuff. First thing you know, you'll get some bad disease."

"Oh, Cassie, I'll be careful. The Red Cross knows how to take care of such things. All I want you to do is to convince Mama that I'll be all right."

"Honey, that'll take some doin'." Cassie turned sharply and went to the kitchen.

Shona sighed. Cassie would do her best, but she had already voiced the fear that Sophie probably echo. Nevertheless, Shona had decided. So . . . she went to the valley.

Dr. Galloway gave her his blessing. He had no choice. Looking into her lovely, earnest face, it was evident that she would not be denied.

"You're not leaving us—permanently, that is?" He searched her blue eyes for assurance.

"Oh, no, Doctor, I love it here. But this is something I want to do. I know my mother would have been there to help."

He smiled, assuming that she was talking about Sophie, yet, somewhat puzzled. There was no way for him to know that Shona's mind had been almost constantly on Kate, these days. Kate would have expected her to be on hand.

Happily, she kissed them: her mother tearful; Cassie, stoic.

Leaving the problem of Will for last, she was prepared for his reaction. "What in tarnation do you want to go down there for? There'll be plague and the Lord knows that else. Ain't you got no . . ." For a moment, he hesitated, then decided to ignore his lapse in grammar. "No sense . . ." he concluded, lamely.

"Papa, if I know you, you'll be helping, too. I'll give you one more day, maybe." She cajoled him, stroking his cheek. Naturally, he gave in.

"Well, me and Plato jest found out that they're goin' to blast that mess at the bridge. No help for it. Things is so solid that blastin's the only way. We thought we'd go and give a hand."

"See, what did I tell you?" She kissed him and was off.

That day, the sun had risen brilliantly, properly. Even so, Shona was wearing a long coat. These days, the weather had a nip in it, like the chill of late Fall—a blessing in staving off disease.

In the bleak area below the hills, activity ran high. The dead were still being recovered—a steady line-up of wagons took them to various morgues for identification.

Temporary houses in each suburban district were jammed with people, attempting to find loved ones. Shona moved toward a special one and tried to enter. A uniformed sentinel with a musket stopped her, to ask her mission.

Taken aback, she hesitated. "I . . . that is, some friends of mine are missing. May I come in, please?"

Shona had no idea of finding Michael or Danny here. But somehow, forcing a positive attitude, she found herself subconsciously thinking the unthinkable.

She moved through, along with others. To the right, twenty bodies had been washed, identified, and covered with sheets. Bits of paper bearing their names were pinned at their feet.

To the left, bared faces of those still unidentified, lay in pathetic rows—most of them unrecognizable.

The thing that had drawn her to the central morgue was a vague combination of loyalty and melancholy. Michael had taught her here. This was the school-house.

Just then, startled out of reverie by a sudden commotion, she hurried to see what was happening.

Outside, the gruff voices of the sentinels were shouting, "Move on." A group of thieves, collared by vigilantes, was putting up a fight. Evidently a citizens' arrest was in progress. In the midst of it all, the sheriff appeared.

Shona moved off, looking up at the hillside, where people had come from miles around, to view the disaster. How incongruous, the cheerful thrill-seekers, compared to those below, the weeping women and unhappy mean, with their quiet, beaten faces.

She turned. Someone was standing in her way. The person facing her said casually, "Do you have relatives here in Johnstown?"

From his polite manner and gentlemanly attire, he must surely be a stranger. He carried an ebony walking stick, with a carved, golden handle. It was easy to suspect that he could be one of the owners of the dam.

Abruptly, she retorted. "My folks were not in the flood, thank goodness. A thousand people must have drowned."

If that had been an accusation, he ignored it. "I hear they expect to find twice that many. More than a thousand were probably swept to the bridge; hundreds have been found on the hillsides."

Shocked at his callous remark, Shona turned away, her anger tempered by worry. She had no word from either Michael or Danny. Annoyed with herself, she let it happen. Panic.

Unhappily, she headed for home. She had seen no sign of the Red Cross. She thought about it, and turned back to the guard at the door.

"I had heard that the Red Cross is coming here. Do you know—is that true? I haven't seen anything that looks like a Red Cross headquarters."

The guard, trained and expressionless, said, "Yes, Miss. The Red Cross is here, but not *here*. Miss Clara Barton arrived on Tuesday, and they pitched her tents, but she wasn't satisfied with the location. Now, she's down on the plateau. Just go across that foot-bridge to Kernville. Some old buildings block the view from here, but you can't miss it."

Gratefully, she thanked him and turned away. Less than a quarter of a mile away, she discovered the camp.

A large imposing hospital tent stood in the center, with eight smaller tents. Entering the large tent, Shona stood in amazement. There were innumerable cots, heaps of supplies, and Miss Barton sat at a desk in the center, giving instructions to what seemed to be a horde of people.

She approached, timidly, and waited. Seeing her white uniform under her coat, Miss Barton beckoned to her. "Are you a nurse? Have you come to help us?" Her smile was kindly, and Shona began to relax.

"I'm not really a nurse, yet, but I've been learning, up at the Cambria Hospital in Prospect. Yes, I'd like to help."

It turned out that all of the smaller tents held beds, too. The Red Cross corps had been sent out to find persons who were severely injured, or traumatized, and now many of the cots were occupied.

She was put to work, at once. While preparing bandages, she couldn't help noticing the cleanliness of her surroundings. The boards of the tent floors were as white as the scrubbed floor of her cabin, and the linens on shelves and beds were snowy.

What a contrast to the filth outside! Impressed, Shona did her best to make the neatest possible wrappings. Perhaps, that way, she would be allowed to do something else.

Opportunity was not long in coming, but it appeared as a mixed blessing. Miss Barton called for Dr. John Hubbell, field agent for the Red Cross, who would explain.

He was kind, but suddenly, she wondered whether this

proposed position was desirable. It meant entering and visiting private homes, to find anyone who might need assistance.

Faced with Hubbell's clean-shaven face and earnest blue eyes, Shona was suddenly ashamed of her reluctance. What would he think to hear the announcement that she didn't want the job?

She soon discovered that there was no problem. A physician was to accompany her, so that prospective patients could be diagnosed swiftly.

Armed with additional support, her qualms disappeared. She liked the man at once. Dr. Winston was a thin man with a pleasant face—a volunteer, like herself. It seemed natural to trust him.

Their first stop was at a home nearby, on the hillside. Shona knocked on the door. There was no sound from within.

Noticing that the door was unlatched, Dr. Winston pushed it, and they entered.

There was no one downstairs in the barren living room or the kitchen. Motioning to Shona to stay, the doctor slipped upstairs. A few minutes later, he returned, alone.

"There's a woman up there, rocking a dead baby. I can't get through; she doesn't hear me, and she clings to the infant. We must report this, at once."

However, as they were leaving, they were to see something even more urgent. Next door, children and adults packed a small house, spilling over onto the porch. All, even the children, were sluggish, moving as though they were drugged.

Shona rushed to pick up a tiny child, lying on the porch floor. It moved its head to look at her and closed its eyes.

"Doctor—this little boy—I think he's dying."

Doctor Winston took the tot. Putting a hand on its head, he frowned, and looked at the other languishing youngsters.

"These children are all very ill. Help me, and maybe we can persuade everyone to come with us. There's some kind of poisoning here—perhaps the water."

A little girl, livelier than the rest, spoke up. "We have lots of water. Mama put a bucket out for rain water, but that wasn't enough. So I got some of the boys to go with me, and we got water."

"Where did you get it?" Dr. Wlinston dreaded the answer.

She pushed stringly brown hair back from her face, and said, proudly, "We got it from that stream, up on the hill. There was lots of it there, and it was nice and clean."

He shuddered. Perhaps, in comparison with the murky water of the nearby river it seemed to be clear, but the stream had been washing through outhouses as it overflowed.

"Child, that water, like all the water around here, is not fit to drink. Everyone who drank it is in danger."

Moving into the house, he spoke to the adults sitting or lying on the floor in lassitude. "Will you all please come with us?

We're from the Red Cross, and we can help you."

The little girl, right beside him, shouted, "Mama, we'd better go. We're all going to be very sick."

Her mother rose from a chair, to appeal to Shona. "There's nothing here to eat; that's why we're weak."

Shona tried to explain about water contamination. "If you've been infected, there will be medical treatment at Miss Barton's camp. They also have plenty of food."

They murmured among themselves. Some dreaded hospitals; others disliked asking for charity. Dr. Winston stood silent, knowing that hunger would take over. At last, they agreed to go to the center below.

That evening, Shona headed for Prospect, tired, but somehow fulfilled. They had aided several families. Already her work had brought satisfaction, and worry had been pushed into the background.

Suddenly, near a refugee house, she encountered a line set up by the National Guard to curb vandalism.

A young officer, obviously inebriated, staggered into her path and bowed deeply. "May I have the pleasure of your company? You're the best, best . . . prettiest lookin' thing I've seen . . ." At a loss for words, he waved his arms.

She sidestepped him, appealing to a sober deputy, who blocked the officer, attempting to follow. Facing him, the deputy drew himself up. "You can't pass, sir."

"Can't pass?" He gestured threateningly. "Do you realize you're talking to a Lieutenant of the National Guard?"

"So—I talk to an officer of the National Guard. I, who have lost my wife and my children. I, who have seen our dead mutilated, their fingers and ears cut off by dirty looters for a little gold. Why should I not talk for the right, even if you are an officer of the National Guard?"

Shona stood riveted where she was, listening to the powerful plea.

But the lieutenant was too drunk to be lectured. He spotted Shona again, and started toward her. The sentinel, holding up his musket, stopped him. Furiously, he shouted, "You dirty, drunken cur. I ought to lay you out, where you stand."

"C'mon, try it," roared the officer, swinging at the guard. He slipped, staggered, and almost fell.

Suddenly, a large man, who had seen the episode, rushed forward, his face red with rage. He shot out a violent blow, potentially lethal, but at that moment, the officer slipped, and it barely clipped his chin.

Irate now, the Lieutenant seemed to recover his senses. He took off his military coat and dropped it to the ground. Then he stepped forward, bristling. The big man was waiting for him, but two privates and a newsman blocked him. The officer used the extra time to get a weapon from his pistol pocket.

At that point, the deputy rushed up, knocking the lieutenant to the ground. With a snarl, he got to his feet and lunged at his opponent. The privates caught him, and he finally gave up.

In order to report the incident, the deputy picked up the coat and weapon which had been dropped.

Pleading, the privates and other members of the Guard gathered about him, begging him not to report their officer. "He's a good fellow," one of them said. "It's just what he can't drink. He doesn't do it, as a rule."

The others seemed to concur. Reluctantly, the sentinel gave in. Throwing the coat to them, and handing over the gun, he said, "Here, then. But if he doesn't go immediately to his quarters I'll take him there—dead or alive."

Shaking in alarm, Shona had been glued to the spot. All at once, someone gently took her arm. She started, and turned. It was Michael.

He held out his arms, and she threw herself into them. "Oh, Michael, Michael . . . I thought you were dead. Tell . . ."

He put a finger on her lips. "Not now, darling; you can't know how I've worried about you. I . . ."

He broke it off, clasping her so tightly that she could scarcely breathe. (Or was it that the function of breathing had already stopped?) Together, they clung as though they would never let go. When they finally kissed, Shona understood passion.

Still holding each other tightly, the pair was suddenly aware of the spectacle they were presenting. Shona could feel the heat rising in her face. Looking on with interest stood the characters of the preceding drama, excepting the lieutenant, who had been escorted away.

Embarrassed, Michael drew her off, and they began to walk. After traveling a short distance, he looked down at her. "Why are you venturing out alone? Don't you know how dangerous it is, these days?"

She countered. "That was just an unfortunate incident. I don't think things like that happen often."

Michael was continuing. "I just read in the Pittsburgh papers . . ." He saw her question, and said, "Yes, I was in Pittsburgh. I'll tell you about it. Anyhow, the item said that barrels of whiskey are constantly being found in the wreckage. Men are fighting ferociously to hang onto such treasure. That's probably why that young officer was in such a condition."

Shona smiled vaguely, not wanting to talk about anything except Michael. "I'm sorry I threw myself at you like that. What would your fiancee have thought?"

"What fiancee? That's over."

Excitement clutched at her chest. "I don't understand. How could that be?" This was a fairy tale.

His anger at Mary Jane flared anew. "She . . ."

"You don't have to tell me, if you don't want to. I can't say

I'm sorry, because I'm not." Shona's interruption stemmed from suddenly remembering his distaste for unpleasantness.

He smiled, and kissed her. Tentatively, he approached the question. "What about you? Seems there was a boy-friend. Where does that stand?"

She held out her hand. At that moment, the moon broke through, striking the diamond. In the semi-darkness, it sparkled like another star.

She didn't see his face fall, but felt his unhappiness, almost as a physical blow.

"Michael, I can break it off. I don't really love him—that way."

"Shona, surely you wouldn't make someone believe you loved him enough to marry him, and then . . ."

"Darling, you don't understand. I've always told Danny that I loved him, but I wasn't *in love* with him. There is a difference."

"Then, why . . ."

"He took advantage of the fact that it was Christmas; my family was there—he had bought me a ring. I didn't want it Michael, but my father was so excited and happy, that I didn't know what else to do."

It all spilled out in a torrent, much faster than her usual way of talking.

Michael was skeptical. "You mean to say, he was willing to marry you, even though you weren't in love with him?"

She nodded. "There is one thing, though. Someone else is very much in love with him, and maybe if I withdraw, she'll have a chance."

They had reached the hospital. In the bright light of the doorway, he studied her lovely, earnest face. Could all this be true, or a figment of her active mentality? It didn't seem to him that Shona would lie.

"And who is this person who's in love with Danny?" he asked, just as Jean appeared at the door. She had heard his question.

Flushing angrily, she answered it. "Shona, what have you been saying? I never told you that."

"You didn't have to—I could tell," retorted Shona. With that, she flew into the building, leaving Michael and Jean staring at each other.

Perhaps because of intense preoccupation with work, Shona's perception of the future had diminished to an occasional headache. Unfortunately, she learned to ignore these.

Of those who had taken refuge in the hospital, few remained. These were the ill and the injured. However, there were new faces. Some of the patients, taken from trees or found in debris, had been brought in because of proximity to the dispensary.

The next morning, before leaving for the Red Cross, Shona

made the rounds of the beds, hoping or fearing to see Danny.

He was not there, but she came to a badly injured man who had been a neighbor of Danny's. She went over to him. His head, and most of the upper part of his body was swathed in bandages; one side of his face showed a large, purple bruise.

Hating to disturb him, but anxious about Danny, she approached him.

"What happened to you, Mr. Jones?"

He looked at her, dully. Then his good eye opened wide. "You're Danny's girl."

"Fiancee, Mr. Jones. But I haven't heard. Do you know anything about him?"

"There's not much to know," he gasped. Collecting himself, he went on. "I was climbing with him—he was pushing his mother to move faster. Then that . . . thing came down on us. I grabbed a tree . . ." His breath gave out.

She didn't want to hear, but she pressed him. "What about Danny and his family?"

He recovered somewhat. "That big heap of boards and horses came down over them like a wave. I was hit by a log and landed in another tree."

"Horses? I don't understand."

"That horse barn, just above. It must have been wiped out."

He couldn't say more, and Shona didn't press. The shock of discovering Danny's fate made her realize how very much she had cared. If it were possible to be in love with more than one person, perhaps . . .

In her woe, she sought Jean—then couldn't tell her. Jean sensed something as terribly wrong, and insisted on an explanation.

Shona wiped her eyes, gave her a tremulous smile, and looked away. "You won't have a rival any more—neither will I."

Jean grasped her by both arms. "What do you mean? Has something happened to Danny?"

Dumbly, she nodded. "It got him. That monster got our Danny." Blinded by tears, she rushed out of the room toward the office. It was crammed with visitors.

Fortunately, it was time to leave for work. Maybe, on the job, she would be able to forget, just for a time.

That was nonsense. Everything in the world was flood.

* * *

TWENTIETH

Gloom hung over the city. As Shona's mother sometimes said, it was "the kind of day when Dutchmen hang themselves."

Wending her way toward the valley, Shona thought of that. Dark clouds hung low, matching her mood. The world moved in gray and brown. She felt gratitude that her father was too busy to notice her traveling alone.

Today, she chose another route, straight down to the river, away from the crowds.

That was a mistake. Before traveling very far, she came upon a group of masked men, digging out bodies, spraying off mud, and stuffing them into sacks. The powerful scent of disinfectant permeated the air.

She remembered that this was to be her job today—teaching people how to use disinfectants properly. Trying not to think of those bodies, or of Danny, she shuddered.

In passing, trying to fight depression, she looked down at the river, just below. There, caught along the shore, was half of a naked body, face down. Undulating in the water, loosened flesh clung to it, curdled, like sour milk.

A sudden pain caught her in the stomach. Not having eaten breakfast, the effort to vomit brought forth only a little water, and a sickening, continuing nausea.

Arriving at camp, she forced all thought into the neat, well-ordered world of the Red Cross. The cure for pain, particularly this kind of agony, would be work.

* * *

The day had been a frustrating one for Will and the hundred or more workers toiling with increasing fervor to break up the sixty-acre mass of debris at the Stone Bridge.

Sinking into an easy chair in the lounge, strangely, he had no appetite for supper. Sophie came to him and kissed him, stroking his cheek.

"It must have been a hard day."

"Hard? It was the worst, blasted day I've seed . . . seen, yet. We blasted, hauled, lifted and pulled the stuff away, and what have we got?" Glaring as though it were all her fault, he took out his handkerchief and blew loudly.

Sophie smoothed his hair. "You must have made *some* progress?"

"On, we made progress, all right. Now you can see some muddy water, about thirty feet wide, under the center arch. There's a couple of other patches, too, but if you was . . . weren't lookin' fer it, you'd never notice."

"But they said it would only take a week."

"To my way of thinkin' a month would be more like it. That

whole mess is locked together so tight that even crowbars 'n axes is hard put to get out some pieces."

She bent to kiss him again. "I'm proud of you, my dear. The only thing I worry about is the dynamite."

"Fergit that. They don't want to damage the bridge. That's why these little charges don't do the work."

He suddenly quieted. There was something which Sophie must not be told. No use for both of them to worry.

That day, picking his way over some logs, he had seen Joshua moving toward him, menacing. From his grizzled, wild look, Will assumed that he was drunk, but watching his surefootedness on the logs, it became evident that this was not inebriation. It was insanity.

He had approached Will with an ominous glare and gritted teeth. "I still know you, you wretch. Harborin' that witch daughter in your house, after all she did. Seems you got reason for that. I notice you folks are all safe."

Then, he began to cry—big, choking sobs that racked his body.

Seeing Will speechless, Carpenter covered his weakness with more anger. "You see, I didn't have a witch. So, my wife and my son got—drowned. Washed away like straws . . . Never had a chance."

Before Will could respond, the man lowered his voice. "I got one thing to say to you, MacDonald. Get that woman out of town. She caused this flood, and I aim to kill her. I'll give you a week."

Will had been left in a maze of conflicting thought. The speech was extremely lucid—unlike the raving of a madman. Yet, there could be no question. The man was demented.

His concern now became the amount of credence he should give to Shona's peril. Should a threat by a lunatic be taken seriously?

In the end, he decided to wait. He would say nothing.

That evening, Will sent Plato to bring Shona home, but she had already left—with Michael. Will was not a little perturbed; this Michael business was going too far. Shona was engaged, and besides, this man was ten years her senior. There was nothing good about it.

By the time she reached the hospital, he had worked himself into a dither. "Young lady, I don't approve of your actions. Can't you remember you're engaged to Danny? On top of that . . ."

"Papa, there is something you don't know, and I don't know how to tell you. It's about Danny."

"I've got a hunch. Danny found out about . . ."

"No, Papa. Danny's gone."

"Gone? Gone where?"

Will had not noticed, but nearly everyone, including the small children, now referred to the lost ones as "gone." Even as he repeated it, the meaning dawned on him.

"You mean—he's dead?" He said it incredulously. "He was right with you, tellin' everyone to git out."

Shona was weeping now. "I know. He tried to get his parents out, but it was too late for all of them."

Will patted her shoulder. "I'm in the wrong, child. I blew off when I didn't know . . . But what I do know is this: the other fellow's too old fer you."

Through tears, she smiled. "Papa, I don't care if he's sixty. I love him. Furthermore, I've always loved him."

* * *

When Shona arrived at the Red Cross station next morning, there had been another shipment of supplies. There was so much, that the organization had decided to cooperate with the Grand Army of the Republic. Together, they would distribute provisions to various substations, thus avoiding crowds of excitable folk at headquarters.

The GAR had also appointed a committee to duplicate the work of the Red Cross in visitations. Dr. Winston seemed to be happy for the assistance.

He explained the additional help to Shona. "People are starving out there. More than one person has been found dead at home. It's peculiar; there doesn't seem to be any such thing as 'human nature.' One person is so proud that carrying a basket to ask for food would be humiliating. But another, having six children, would send them, one by one to make collections."

She smiled at him. "I guess that's why I like animals.

"Why?"

"Well, I know animals pretty well, and you don't have to guess what their nature is. For example, none of them destroy their own kind. That's not their nature. But people aren't alike. Your nature differs from mine. So, for example, it wouldn't be fair to point out a person who commits a crime and label that as human nature."

He couldn't help smiling at her childish wisdom. Suddenly, it struck him. That's what it was. The lovely, cherubic face, framed with red-gold curls and wide, innocent blue-green eyes, all denoted extreme youth.

Dr. Winston spoke gently. "How old are you, my dear?"

She hated telling him. Her youth had always caused trouble. Looking at the ground, she murmured, "Seventeen," then supplemented, "going on eighteen."

They were heading for the wagon which was to carry them to the station for the disinfectants to distribute. Shona stared at the team.

"That's Blackie and Lady. They're our horses; they weren't drowned." Then her eyes flew open. "Plato, what are you doing here?"

"Helpin' out, honey, jest helpin' out."

Of course, it was nice to see him. But it did seem odd. Why was Plato so often on hand? Apparently, her father intended to give her protection.

Thinking about it, of course her father would worry. In passing, they had noted some drunken brawls. This must be the reason why Papa insisted on having Plato with her in the morning. He knew that Michael took her home.

Now, though, Plato would be on hand throughout the day, and would also be taking her home. No reason, perhaps, on the part of her father. Yet, it seemed peculiar. Besides, she wanted Michael.

Shona spent the day in a house-to-house canvass, delivering household disinfectants, explaining their use and the necessary precautions. The scent of disinfectants was a familiar one—in fact, the area reeked of it.

Later, approaching Prospect, they crossed to the railroad yards to pick up the hospital's share of supplies.

She stared in wonder. She knew that provisions had come from all over the nation, but had never dreamed of the quantity which had been acquired. Provisions were heaped incredibly high, in carload lots. There were rows of stacked barrels of flour, hundreds of hams strung on poles, crackers in great bins, piles of canned goods, and all sorts of dried foods.

At another point, were barrels of kerosene oil, boxes of soap, and candles of every description.

Outside of the yards, a rope line enclosed the entire space. Soldiers, rifles on shoulders, stood guard. A few women, who had not yet received supplies from the relief committee, begged for immediate food to give their children. Small portions were meted out; they would have to wait.

Shona stood thoughtfully, as Plato loaded the wagon with the allotted reserve. "It's too bad," she murmured.

He jerked his head to look at her. "What's too bad? All this be too good to be true."

"Don't you see? People don't have stoves, pans, kettles, or even knives and forks. Some of the food won't be much good, if it can't be cooked."

Plato grinned. "You'se a caution, Shona, honey. You do get the ideas in that curly head."

When Shona arrived at the hospital, her mother was smiling, but her eyes were sad. She drew her into the office. "Mama, please tell me—what's the matter?"

Fumbling in her uniform pocket for a handkerchief, Sophie wiped her nose and tried a better smile.

After some gentle persuasion, finally, it came out. "My lovely home, my furniture . . . It's not that I'm not grateful for our safety, but it's terrible—everything's gone."

Shona patted her hand. "You'll have another home, and new furniture. Compared to a lot of people, we're just plain lucky."

By now, Sophie was calm again. "I just remembered; we saved our pretty lamps and my lovely dishes—even my best clothing. Oh, Shona, can't we go up to the cabin and look at the things?"

Incredibly, her mother had not understood the scope of the flood. Shona tried to be patient. "Mama, we can't go to the cabin for some time. The mountain streams went wild. They washed out the road and a great section of hillside. That was one of the first things I checked."

Seeing Sophie's fallen face, she hastened to add, "Don't worry, Mama. We'll get up there, some day."

That seemed to help. There was no further discussion.

* * *

Payday at the Cambria Iron Company was not quite as usual. When Will went for his money, he discovered that wages were being given out to surviving friends and relatives, without argument. Officers paying out the money attempted to make sure that the persons applying for money had legitimate claims, but there was no red tape.

Pleased at the fact that he was now solvent, no matter what the state of the banks, Will came to the lounge and laid a bag on the table beside Sophie.

She looked up, puzzled.

"Sophie, we ain't—we're not paupers any more. We can pay our own way. I jest got paid."

But, how could they possibly . . ."

"Tom McGee, an assistant cashier, saved the money. It was in a safe in the first floor of the company store. When the water came up, he went to the second floor with it. Then, when that dad-burned dam water came, he got on the roof and jumped to the hill. Ain't that a caution? He guarded that money all night."

Sophie's countenance lighted. "He must be a very special kind of man, this Mr. McGee."

"That's right," said Shona, who had just come in, and was standing behind her father. "We owe him a debt of gratitude."

She was thinking of all the heroes of the past—also including her own special Michael, and the beauty of his rescue.

Shona's wakefulness that night gave her pleasure. Remembering Michael's kisses, she alternately relived then and slept in his arms.

In the morning, when she aroused from a sound sleep, her first awareness was that of a developing headache. Sophie bustled about with trays, having no time to talk, but she did get a glimpse of Shona's eyes.

"What's the matter, honey?" she whispered in her daughter's

ear.

She kissed her mother. "Don't worry about me, Mama. I'm just fine." With that, she left the building to meet Plato, who was just driving down the road.

Traveling through the lower part of the city, the land lay flat and bare to the distant hillside. Plato surveyed it. "It's a desert of hard mud, that's what it is. One thing's for certain: nobody will have to clean it up."

They rode in silence for some distance. They he said, "I'se to pick you up tonight. Yo' Papa don' want you walkin', even with Michael. It's better you ride in the wagon."

That was a blow. If there was ever a time when she wanted to be with Michael, alone, it was now.

* * *

This morning, the Red Cross was jubilant. The early plea for assistance, soon supplemented by President Harrison's eloquent appeal to the nation, had been warmly met.

Carefully holding a professional check, Dr. Winston smiled at Shona. "Money is coming in from everywhere. Large cities, and many small towns, have sent enormous sums. We're also getting contributions from London, Berlin, and other European cities."

She smiled at the doctor. "How much do they have?"

"They've just totaled the figure for these two weeks. It's approximately $700,000."

Before Shona could register shock, Michael appeared at the entrance. He was wearing overalls, and carrying a shotgun.

She rushed up to him. "Michael, what is it? What are you going to do?" The fright he saw made him prop the gun against a table and take her in his arms. Not caring about witnesses, he kissed her.

Still holding her, he explained. "I've got to go with some other fellows to ride shotgun. We're transporting a lot of money to the First National Bank."

"But, they said the bank was destroyed. Besides, isn't it dangerous, with all the vandals, and now, robbers coming in from Pittsburgh?"

"The vaults haven't been damaged. Right now, they're holding about $500,000 in cash. Don't worry about me. That's what I've got old Betsy for."

Someone outside was shouting to him—there was no time for further reassurance. With a swift peck on Shona's cheek, he disappeared.

* * *

Climbing to the top of a mountain which sheltered Johnstown, Mary Jane McKay struggled to hoist her camera, a cumbersome load, along with its tripod, nearly to the summit.

Arriving, breathless, she stood in awe at the extent of the disaster. From the valley, it had appeared that a large portion of the town had escaped damage. Now, she saw two great swaths, one on each side of the city, merging into a desert where not a single building remained. Except for the gutted walls of the general store, and those of the Gautier wire mill at the edge, the entire two-mile strip had been swept clean of everything.

Near her, forming a huge Y, a block of buildings stood, although somewhat damaged. At its upper edge, a Roman Catholic church rose. Although, from the valley, it had appeared undamaged, from this vantage point, she saw a large hole in the rear of the building.

Just then, the bell in the tower struck the hour. In the emptiness, it carried a funereal toll. She shivered. Then she noticed another, and prettier church, not far beyond. Folding up her equipment, she began a trek downward. She had captured the over-view; now supplemental shots could be achieved from below.

After filming a large collection of pictures, she gathered up her materials. Sure that this would be a bonanza for the *Tribune*, she planned to make up a collage which would be eagerly accepted, perhaps nationwide.

Regretting her abrupt rejection of Michael, Mary Ann imagined success as a means of bringing back his attention.

Where Shona was concerned, she viewed no real threat. This was a child, as Michael had explained many times. It would be foolish to let jealousy rob her of the best man in the city.

Thus, her rationalizing, in its own way, produced a fleeting sort of happiness.

To her dismay, her hopes soon faded. The pictures were published, and Mary Ann McKay had been praised for their quality, but there was no word from Michael.

One evening, desperate, she went to see Shona, at the hospital. Sophie opened the door to get a breath of cooler air, just as Mary Ann came up the steps of the portico.

"Is Shona here?" she inquired abruptly, wondering what Sophie was doing there.

Sophie recognized her at once, and was equally cool.

"She's lying down; she's had a difficult day. Do you want me to get her, or can I be of some assistance?"

"I'm trying to get in touch with Michael Stewart. He's my fiance, and I haven't heard from him.

Somewhat at a loss, Sophie hesitated. Then she said, "I'm sorry. We don't know where he's staying. Perhaps, if you contacted the National Guard, or the Red Cross, you could get some information."

Inwardly, she hated to give any clue at all, but realistically, she knew there was no way to keep the woman from finding out.

Sophie remembered Shona's whispered dreams of a life with Michael. Even if Will never consented, if Michael were to reconcile with Mary Ann, something in Shona could be destroyed. This must not happen.

With no idea as to a course of action, she went to the kitchen, drained the potatoes, and mashed them with vigor. Shona must not hear of this.

As for Mary Ann, she went directly to the Red Cross, where she found Michael without asking. He was unpacking a large box of medical supplies. She touched his shoulder. He jumped as though she were an apparition. "Mary Ann . . ." he began.

"Michael, I came to ask you to forgive me. Will you do that? I'm sorry; I was jealous. Please, can't we begin again?" The pretty face that had once been dear to him, almost worked its charm.

Instantly, he thought of Shona, and the sense of fulfillment and joy he had acquired, holding her. Without Shona, there could be no future.

He spoke gently. "Mary Ann, I was wrong to ask you to marry me. Perhaps I can't marry Shona, but I've loved her all of my adult life. You're lovely—you'll find . . ."

But she was gone, with only a trace of a sob.

* * *

Payday for Sophie was an auspicious occasion. Never having been employed in her life, something seemed almost criminal in taking the money.

She hesitated, making no attempt to accept the envelope being proffered by Dr. Galloway.

"Come on, it's yours. I'd say nobody working here ever earned this more than you and Cassie."

Cassie, who had accepted her own envelope gratefully, joined in the persuasion. "Miz Sophie, iffen you don' take your money, then Ah'll have to give this back. You did jes' as much as ah did."

Put that way, she gave in—as she had wanted to do, all the time. How wonderful, her own money! There would be no need to ask Will for anything, for a long time.

Later, lying in bed beside Will, her plans began to develop. Will had promised to buy her a piano, some day. But there were other things, little household treasures which they had not been able to salvage. With this money, there would be no need for consultation on such purchases.

Smiling into the darkness, she dropped off to sleep. The important thing was her new-found realization of self-sufficiency. Somehow, she was freed of the feeling of dependence which a life with Will had engendered.

The next morning, Will made a trip to the doctor's office.

Sophie had not told him of her earnings, partly because she was busy, and later, because he was snoring when she crept into bed.

He walked up to the desk, laying five large bills on the desk. Dr. Galloway looked up. "What's this for?"

"Why, it's to pay fer lodging. We've been eatin' 'n sleepin' here fer a month—it's only right that we should pay."

"Mr. MacDonald, I don't see it your way at all. The work that your two women have been doing here can hardly be repaid. I don't know how we could have possibly handled these refugees—at least not so comfortably. Besides, we've used your wagon and horses, and Plato has been wonderful. How can you think you owed us anything?"

Slightly convinced, Will put the money back in his pocket. He was about the leave, when the doctor called to him. "By the way, I paid your wife and Cassie yesterday. Now, I'd like to reimburse you and Plato."

"You—what!" MacDonald flamed to the roots of his hair.

"I paid your wife and Cassie. They certainly earned it."

MacDonald's livid face could have prefaced a stroke. "See here, sir. My wife don't work for money. She's never worked in her life, and I ain't about to let her start now."

Dr. Galloway looked him in the eye. "Isn't it about time she got some recognition?"

Will said nothing when he saw Sophie, busily making beds. His silence continued while they were eating lunch.

"Will, dear, I have something wonderful to tell you." Sophie's eyes sparkled—gleefully, it seemed to Will. He waited.

"Cassie and I were paid yesterday. Just think of it—the doctor gave each of us a great deal of money." She stopped, thinking she shouldn't have said that.

Will made no comment, so she continued. "I guess it isn't a *great* deal of money, but after all, I never had a payday before."

He studied her happy face with something like compassion. "I guess this means a lot to you."

"Oh, Will, you can't imagine! It's splendid, knowing that one can be worth something . . . Not that I don't appreciate your support of all these years. But there's something about feeling independent. You know what I mean?" Her blue eyes sought his, trying to read his thoughts.

He finished his sandwich and rose. "I've got to get to the mill. We've got the buildings on the west end fixed up—thank God the machinery wasn't damaged. The big trees and the drift is finally out. But this east end is bad. It's about gone, I'm afeered." He kissed her and left.

Sophie looked at Cassie, who sat silently by. "Do you think he was angry about the money?"

Cassie smiled grimly. "Iffen so, he was smart enough not to show it."

TWENTY-FIRST

In the shelter of an ancient brick building near the hillside, a dozen or so bereaved men diluted their sorrows by imbibing the contents of a barrel of brandy. Over the open-topped building, hung a stack of house roofs, piled like a giant card-house, hiding them from watchful eyes.

The mourners sat on the floor, in various levels of intoxication. There were snatches of song from time to time; some cried. A few drowsed in melancholic stupor.

Suddenly, a grizzled, dirty-faced man appeared. There was no doorway, but his body seemed to fill the wide gap in the wall. In a rasping voice, he announced his presence.

"How many of you fellows lost wives, children, or loved ones in the flood? Come on, now, let's see. How many?" His wild-eyed glare penetrated some of the most inebriated. The majority raised their hands.

He followed with another question. "What are you going to do about it? Will you let this crime go by, unavenged?"

One small man put down the can he had been using for a cup. "What do we do, go out and blow up the Lord? You must be crazy, to spout such talk."

"Crazy, am I? Well, I intend to punish the witch that destroyed this city, with or without your help."

"Witch? What witch?" The little man was wide awake, suddenly, intent on hearing the serious charge. In fact, everyone in any condition to hear was listening now.

"I'm talkin' about the girl who was livin' with the 'Hogback Witch'. You remember how old Kate hated us folks down here in the valley? Naturally, she built that hate into the kid."

"Aw, c'mon, Carpenter," dissented George Pierce, who had been one of the searchers. "Shona's a nice girl, pretty as a picture, and real smart. She warned us, didn't she? Why would she do that?"

"Because she *is* smart. That way she could wipe out the city and get away with it, like you're letting her do. Take notice—*her* folks are safe. She's got no worries."

Pierce raised his hand to say something, but Carpenter glared him down. "You want proof? Maybe you didn't read the article in the paper about her strange power. Seems, she said that her healthy baby brother would die—and he did. Can't you see what a monster this girl is?"

"Carpenter, you're crazy." Pierce stood up to leave. "That's pretty flimsy evidence of witchcraft, as far as I can see." He stalked off.

Joshua ignored him. He noted with satisfaction that the men were beginning to talk among themselves, and seeming to agree. He turned and left the scene for a few minutes. When he returned, he had a heavy coil of rope flung over his shoulder.

Wild-eyed, he searched their faces. "I don't know how much you fellows cared for your families, but I, for one, have decided to make this witch pay—with her life. They hanged witches in Salem—and if any of you really cared about your poor, lost loved ones, you'll come with me to avenge their deaths."

Almost to a man, they got to their feet, if more or less unsteadily. Shona's friend, Zeb Walker, who had just arrived on the scene, stepped forward to protest. "See here, Joshua, you can't do that. It would be murder. That girl wouldn't harm anyone. She helps care for people every day, at the Red Cross."

Too stirred up to reason this out, the men were roused to anger. They didn't like Walker's denials, and began to mutter against him. He sighed and walked away, swiftly.

Walker's idea was to go to the nearest National Guard outpost and alert them of the crime in progress.

However, his hasty exit, unnoticed by others, worried Joshua. With a nod of his head, he beckoned to an irate fellow standing nearby. "Get that fellow. He's going to try to stop us, and we've got to do this."

The man he addressed was not wearing a shirt, and his bulging muscles made him right for the job. He left, and in two minutes, he was back.

"That fellow ain't goin' nowhere."

Joshua grunted his satisfaction, and began to give directions.

"She'll be comin' down the other side, so we've got to get over there, and stay on the hillside just above the road. MacDonald's handyman will be driving the wagon, and first, we've got to jump him. That'll take about five of you—he's a powerful man. I'll take care of the witch, personally, but I'll need someone to put up the rope for me . . ."

By this time, the men were aroused to the point where reason had been cast to the wind.

"What are we waiting for?" shouted a pale-faced man, weaving on his feet. "We know where the witch is. Let's go get her, right now!"

As he rushed at Carpenter and tried to clutch the rope, two of his pals held him back. One attempted to soothe him. "See here, Homer, ya don' wanna get yourself strung up, do ya? Jest calm down 'n do as Josh says. We'll get 'er, never fear."

The pale man jerked away, and fell. Helped to his feet, he was angrier than ever.

Carpenter shot him a nasty look. "What are you trying to do—let her get away and get the lot of us arrested? This gang from the National Guard is mean. We don't want to tangle with them."

Then, raising his voice just loud enough to be heard, but not so strongly as to attract other attention, he said, "Just follow me. We skirt the hillside all the way, so as not to be seen. Be careful not to make noise."

Perhaps the alcohol had begun to dissipate; possibly, emotion had brought the men around. At any rate, their arousal to hatred now made them far more dangerous. These men, in their intolerable grief, were out for revenge, strengthened by the knowledge that they were no longer helpless victims.

Cautiously, they crept through the forest, keeping a screen of trees and bushes between them and the few buildings clustered in a Y. Crossing behind these structures, they moved to the opposite hillside.

Arriving at the right spot, Carpenter spoke in a stage whisper. "Which of you men has the guts to lie across the road?"

They stared at him. Someone spoke: "Who wants to be run over by a wagon?"

"Don't be a fool. This fellow's a pushover. He's sure to get down to see what's the matter. That's when you jump him. Who's going to volunteer?"

The pale man seemed to have new strength. "I'm not afeered. We gotta git that wagon stopped. I'll do it."

Evilly, Joshua smiled. Things were working out. "Fine. Now, you two, pick out about three other fellows and jump the driver when he gets to the ground."

"As for me, I'll take care of the witch, personally. Somebody take this rope, and I'll show you the hangin' tree I picked out. Hurry, there's not much time. They'll be on their way soon."

The man with the rope worked swiftly, fashioning the noose almost professionally, testing its security, and approving. There were eight men remaining, all ready and eager to jump Plato.

Carpenter looked them over. "I don't need so many—if any of you want to pull out, that's all right."

They glanced from one to another. No one moved to leave. All the better, thought Carpenter. If they killed the negro, that was a small matter.

With the help of his friend, Homer spread himself loosely across the road, his hat lying a short distance away, as though he had fallen. The intention was to make Plato assume that the man had been beaten and robbed.

Carpenter surveyed it all with satisfaction. Now, it became difficult to wait. He took out his watch. Soon, the sun would set—where was the wagon?

At last, he heard it. The rumbling noise told him that it was an empty wagon—someone going home. With a sharp hiss to his men, Carpenter held his breath.

The wagon came into view, Plato driving, with Shona on the seat beside him. At once, Plato saw the figure on the road, and stopped. "This may be a trap," he warned Shona. "Get down in the wagon, till I see. If a robber is lookin' for money, he'll be disappointed."

Cautiously, he clambered down.

No sooner had he touched the ground than they were upon

him. He made a good account of himself, knocking one of them out with a right uppercut, and doubling up another with a blow to the stomach. Then, they overwhelmed him, beating him into insensibility, as Carpenter was attempting to grab Shona.

That wasn't easy. Like a wild animal, she fought, kicking, biting and clawing. He suffered innumerable small wounds, but persisted, knowing that he was going to destroy her.

Gritting his teeth, he slapped, hard. She bit his hand. Then with an angry, powerful blow, he knocked her senseless.

* * *

As far as Michael was concerned, the day was a complete loss. Shona had worked out of reach, bustling about. Once, in approaching her to make some plans, she didn't even look up. Continuing to pack boxes, she tried to explain.

"Michael, dear, I'm sorry. The hospital on Bedford Street must have this medicine right now. They have an influx of typhoid cases. I can't stop, even for a minute."

Noticing her damp, golden curls and flushed face, he realized her complete dedication. Never had she been lovelier. With a sigh, he went back to his accounting job.

Late in the day, there was no sign of her leaving, but for the loud, empty sound when the wagon moved off. Dropping his work, he ran after it, but other noises drowned his voice.

A bit hurt, Michael returned to consider his woes. Shona hadn't asked him to go along. Obviously, her father had something to do with this. There must be some way to break through that barrier.

Dejected, he finally left for home. Other volunteers had already gone, by a path over the hill. Involuntarily, he began to stroll down the road, walking between the wheel tracks.

Perhaps exercise would help get him out of this blue mood, engulfing him. Straightening up, he began a fast trot, delighted to feel the speed he once had enjoyed as a boy.

Then, far in the distance, he saw a wagon, stopped in the middle of the road. That was odd. Moving up into the trees, so as not to be seen, Michael hurried forward.

Approaching, he could see someone crouched on the ground. A circle of men stood watching.

"Hurry, Carpenter," came an angry voice. "What's wrong with you, anyhow? Get that rope on 'er."

Closing in, Michael was horrified to see Joshua lifting Shona's head. He had a rope, but something was wrong. "What the devil—can't you tie a slip-knot?" he roared at someone.

At that moment, Michael jumped, almost bowling over the men, and assailing Carpenter. Caught off guard in his kneeling position, he jerked once at the blow, then sprawled on the ground.

Angry at the turn of events, the group turned ugly. Two of them grabbed Michael, twisting his arms behind him.

"Let's hang him, too—the witch lover," a voice shouted. Michael swung around knocking down one assailant, and tripping another. Now, ruthless, they closed in.

Before another blow could be struck, there was a sound of galloping horses. It seemed to come from all directions, as, indeed, it did. Turning to flee, the men found themselves surrounded. The National Guard had arrived.

Shona was awake now, but her vision was fuzzy. Michael took a chunk of rag out of her mouth, and held her close.

Above them, a voice asked, "Is she all right?" Michael nodded, looking up. It was George Pierce.

"Looks like we were just in time. Thank God, they were stationed nearby."

Shona struggled to rise, not recognizing Michael. "Plato—we must help Plato. They got him."

A soothing voice behind her said. "Here ah is, honey. Looks like *we* got *them.*

"Oh, Plato, I'm so sorry. Does your head ache very much?"

"Well, cain't say it ain't felt better, but what about you? Did that fella hurt you?"

She tried to shake her head, but a sharp pain made her realize that something did hurt. Suddenly, she saw that Michael was holding her. The ache fled.

Before she could express her joy, one of the guardsmen approached. "You people all right? Need an escort back home?"

Shona smiled, a bit weakly. "Thank you for all you've done. I think we'll be all right, now that you have those men."

And, indeed, they did have the offenders. Carpenter, wild with anger and frustration, screamed obscenities as they tied his hands. Herded, like cattle, the men were forced to march to headquarters under watchful eyes.

Close in Michael's arms, still trembling, Shona whispered, "Papa will have to love you, now. You're a hero."

He smiled at her. "Sweetheart, if the Guard hadn't come, neither of us would have been saved. I'm no hero—and your father will be the first one to tell you so."

She ignored that, and turned to George Pierce to thank him. He had disappeared.

It was twilight; no one had noticed the sunset, but it was a balmy, clear evening, with a brightening moon just above the trees.

Moving over a smooth, new road, not even the familiar odor of disinfectant could deter the joy of the lovers in the wagon. Forgetting her aching head, Shona thrilled to the light, clip-clop of the horses, the subdued moonlight-silvered clouds, and the warm safety of Michael's arms.

She looked at Plato, wistfully. "Do you think we could stop

for a little while?"

Understanding, Plato nodded, obligingly swinging the horses around and over the hill to a grassy mound, untouched by flood waters. There they sat in enchantment, until Shona realized suddenly that they would be missed.

She was instantly remorseful. "Oh, Plato, I'm sorry I asked you to do this. Papa will be angry, and it's all my fault. Let's get back, quickly."

"I'll take the blame," volunteered Michael. His gallant gesture worried Shona.

"Oh, no—probably you shouldn't be with us." Worry increased the pain in her head. "Papa might not give us a chance to explain."

Plato soothed her. "You got witnesses, honey. I believes yo' Papa will be so glad you ain't kill' that he won't be mad at nobody but that Carpenter fellow."

Shona started, looking at Plato. "Killed? What do you mean? You're the one who could have been killed. They must have thought you had money. That Mr. Carpenter hates me, I know, but he wouldn't kill anybody, I'm sure."

Michael and Plato looked at each other. Could it be possible that Shona hadn't realized what the men were intending to do. With one accord, they made a silent pact to keep it from her, if at all possible.

"Never mind, dear. That brute did knock you out, you know." soothed Michael. "Of course, you could have been killed, if you had been hit hard enough. Maybe you shouldn't mention that to your father."

She attempted a grin, and a pain shot through her head. "I think you're right. Papa would get a gun, or something. He doesn't like Mr. Carpenter."

Driving up to the door, they were met by an irate MacDonald, who, with his wife, was standing on the stoop.

"Where in tarnation 've you been?" Will exploded, helping Shona down from the wagon. "If you're goin to be workin' till all hours, I'm puttin' a stop to it, right now."

"Papa, don't be angry." Shona put her arms around him and kissed his cheek. "I was so tired that I asked Plato to stop somewhere, and just look at the grass and sky. I'm so weary of mud and dirt."

He melted, but retained a bit of his glare for Michael's benefit. "Where'd ya' get him? What's been goin' on?"

"Papa, don't be mean. Michael's had a hard day, too. He was walking and we picked him up." She thought this was true.

Will MacDonald wasn't satisfied with the story of the attempted robbery. When Shona and her mother had gone inside, he pursued the matter.

Drawing his black eyebrows into a scowl, he stared from Plato to Michael. "Come on, now. Tell me what really happened.

There's more'n this to it."

To their feigned ignorance, he snapped, "Look here; Plato was haulin' an empty wagon. It wasn't nobody's—anybody's pay day, and no reason for him to be carryin' money. Don't make sense for a band of robbers to attack him."

He looked from one to the other in expectation. Nothing came. Shaking their heads, they seemed to have no answers. Michael turned to leave.

"Jest a minute, young feller." Will's abrupt call made him pause and turn. "Listen, I want to git to the bottom of this. Don't you think I've a right to know?"

Michael finally broke down. "Mr. MacDonald, they were going to lynch Shona. They attacked Plato in a body, to get him out of the way, then Joshua Carpenter was getting a rope ready. If it hadn't been for George Pierce, who overheard the plot and called the Guard, we couldn't have saved her."

Horrified, MacDonald seemed to be in shock. Then, he said, "How'd you git there?"

Michael explained. He could see that the impact of his story staggered MacDonald, and for a moment was sorry to have broken the tacit silence. Yet, Shona's father did have a right... About to leave, he turned back. "One thing," he added, "Shona doesn't know."

"She doesn't know? She *has* to know. What are you sayin'?"

"Evidently, Carpenter hit her; he knocked her out."

Red with rage by this time, MacDonald controlled it by lowering his voice to an ominous whisper. "This man will pay . . . Believe me, he'll pay."

Plato, who had remained silent until now, acted as peacemaker. "Mr. Mac, he's already payin'. They took him off to the jailhouse. He cain't hurt nobody there."

Will shook his head. "That's not for long. I've gotta stop this man." Stalking into the building, he left them wondering.

Michael grinned at Plato. "Looks like we've permanent positions as bodyguards."

"You bet," agreed Plato, shaking his hand. And so they parted.

* * *

As for Joshua Carpenter, defeated for now, he had no intention of discontinuing what he considered as a crusade. The MacDonald girl must die!

Pacing the floor of his small cubicle in the Ebensburg jail, he formulated a plan for his release. The important thing was to make them conclude that he had been drunk and didn't remember anything.

Later, following an impassioned plea, he was called to the desk, assigned a small penalty and released with a warning.

Elated, he paid his fine and departed. Now, his plot would begin in earnest.

* * *

TWENTY-SECOND

The next day dawned without a sunrise. Smoke from night work at the mill had darkened the sky at a time when storm clouds were gathering.

Will was also in an ominous mood. Before Shona could get away, he called her aside. From the look in his eyes, she knew that she wouldn't like what he had to say.

"Shona," he began, and hesitated. He had been much more lenient with her of late. But, for her own good, this must not continue. It was time to put his foot down.

"Young lady, you know that you're still under age, no matter if you're soon to be 18. You're a child until you're 21."

She nodded, wondering what was coming.

"Well, I made a decision for you. You're to give 'em notice at the Red Cross. You're comin' back to the hospital. Today!"

"But . . ."

"No 'buts.' You have a job here, 'n the doctor says he can use you. You're not runnin' over the city no . . . any more."

From the set of his jaw, she could see the futility of trying to argue. Silently, she turned and went out to a waiting Plato. He was driving the buggy, today. Obviously, his mission was not work, but guardianship. He got down to give her a hand. Unhappily, she climbed in.

Having tendered her regrets at giving notice, Shona looked around for Michael. She had expected him to be at one of his regular posts, but there was no sign of him.

Reluctantly, she got into the buggy to let Plato drive her home.

He had a sensitivity, where Shona was concerned. He knew that she was not herself, and felt her depression.

Casting a sidelong glance at her pouting, childlike face, he grinned. "C'mon, honey. Nuthin's as bad as that. You still got a job, and this one, you'll be gettin' a check fo, too."

Shona's smile was almost a grimace. "Plato, you know I don't need money. Papa takes care of me. I liked my work down there; it was exciting. Besides . . ." she paused.

He knew she was thinking of Michael, and changed the subject. "Jest you wait till nightfall, honey. Yo' Papa, he done got sumpin' goin' that boun' to make you happy."

She gave him a skeptical glance. In this present disheartened condition, it would take something very special, indeed, to cheer her.

That evening, when Shona's chores were done, she didn't want to read as usual. Instead, she went out to sit on the front steps, sensing instantly that Plato lurked, just inside.

She took a deep breath and forgot her captivity, aware of an unusual fragrance. A warm breeze caressing night-blooming flowers nearby, touched her cheek. Watching the fireflies darting over the lawn like minute, erratic stars, she suddenly recovered some of her innate joy of living.

Now, she was thinking of Michael. A whole, new world awaited them—a place where they could be forever close. Nothing could worry them; no one could keep them apart.

Someone touched her shoulder, jolting her out of the reverie. It was Plato. "Honey, you want to see what yo' Papa got? He in there, right now, workin' on it."

She jumped to her feet. "Of course, I want to see it. Plato, you've got me so curious, I can't stand it."

He grinned and led the way.

They went down the hall to the exercise room, where pulleys and equipment ranged around the walls. There, in the middle of the room, was Will, making marks on sheets of unprinted newspaper.

Shona stared at the layout of blocks and rectangles which had been spread over two pages. He was working on a third.

"What is it, Papa?" She had seen drawings of floor plans, but had no idea when her father had taken up engineering.

He threw out one hand, proudly indicating his accomplishment. "It's the plans for our new house—even bigger than the old one. See, here's . . ."

Generally, she knew better than to interrupt him, but there was no help for it. She was horrified.

"Papa, you know we don't have the money for any kind of a house, let alone a big one like that."

He ignored her sin, joyous in his new-found information.

"Honey, you don't understand. When Johnstown's banks began doing business, they had this policy of refusing to make loans any higher than what the lot was worth. They wouldn't insure me against destruction of my house, either. "I didn't like it, but I guess that was good business. Anyhow, since the flood, my property is worth twice what I paid fer it, and there won't be no . . . any problem about gettin' a loan."

"But Papa, why would you want to build on the same property? You know how often we have spring floods; don't you want to go higher?"

Suddenly, the joy fled. "Don't mention movin' to the hill again. I belong here, where my work is."

Noticing her crestfallen expression, Will softened. "Don't worry, honey. There's a proposal by a certain Captain Jones, who wants to dredge the river bed about thirty feet lower and add seventy feet to make it wider.

"I hear from my friends in business, that as soon as the debris is cleared off, they're goin' to do it. So, you see, there won't be no . . . any more floods."

Seeing that she was impressed, Will's exuberance rose again. "There's some more good news. They're workin' on gittin' a charter for the town to take in all these little boroughs."

"Is that good?"

Will let his imagination run on. "Good? In ten years, Johnstown will be one of the best cities in the world. Nothin' kin stop it. We're goin' to have the streets laid out, somethin' like Washington City.

Seeing that he had her interest, he continued, happily. "One thing's for sure: with the Cambria Iron Company, the Gautier Steel Works, the mines, and great railroad service, there's no stoppin' this town."

Smiling politely, Shona couldn't share his enthusiasm. Perhaps it was because there was something of the seer in her. She could almost picture the city as it would be in the future.

True, it would probably grow. There was every reason to believe in its prosperity. But a reservation in her mind told her that, regardless of its possibilities, Johnstown was destined to experience some flooding forever, as well as perpetual lack of cooperation from the boroughs.

When they returned from the exercise room, Sophie had already retired. Sitting up in bed, she called to Shona.

"Dear, will you come here for a minute?"

Shona crossed the room and sat on the edge of the bed, wondering. "What is it, Mama?"

"Do you suppose there's a road up to the cabin, by now? Id like to go up there, just to look at some of my things. Do you think I'm foolish?"

"Of course not. I understand; there might be a road which can be used. I'll have Plato check tomorrow, and if it's all right, we'll go up together."

Relaxing, Sophie kissed her cheek and dropped back on the pillow. "I knew you'd understand."

She was so small and frail; Shona wanted to hold her, but she knew that her mother hated showing any sign of weakness. When it came to that, Shona reflected, no such imperfection existed in her mother. A gallant lady, Sophie had done well.

She hurried off, hoping to find Plato and explain her mother's request.

It was too late; Cassie and Plato were in bed. Shona, moved off to her own small cot, ignoring a slight headache. Yet, somehow, a feeling of uneasiness persisted.

Early in the morning, apprised of his mission, Plato took off for the mountain cabin. Shona watched him go, straight and strong, sitting his horse as a knight must have done, in complete rapport with the animal.

More than an hour later, she and her mother were making up a bed, when Plato came to the office. "Please, I gotta see Miz Sophie, right away."

Lorene Chandler looked up from her paper work, wondering at his urgency. "Of course, sir. She and her daughter are working right in the next room."

Trying to calm himself, Plato straightened up, attempting to appear casual. As he entered, they dropped the pillows they were dressing, and rushed to him.

Before they could say anything, he raised a hand. "Now, ladies, I'se got some news, 'n I don' want you to git upset."

Naturally, that upset them.

Shona grasped his sleeve. "Plato, you don't have to beat around the bush. We've been through too much, together. What is it?"

"Ladies, I'se sorry. The road's not in, yet. And ah don' think you wanna see the cabin. It's pretty bad."

"Bad? What do you mean?" Sophie's eyes were wide; she sat down on the edge of the bed.

"Ah hates to tell you this. Somebody blowed up the place." His face contorted with emotion.

Shona gasped. "You mean—with dynamite?"

"Must 'a been. Ain't nothin' much more powerful aroun' here. Besides, it's easy to git. Lots of it, down there in the mill yard."

She glanced at Plato's unhappy face. No longer the assured protector and champion, he seemed almost a child, facing tragedy. Clearly, the loss of his beloved family had struck him deeply.

Strangely, not only Shona saw it. Sophie stood up and put a hand on his arm. "Plato, it doesn't matter. I thank God that you weren't inside when that happened. Maybe this is my punishment for putting so much value on material things. Every day, I count my blessings, in this city of tragedy."

He managed a smile. "Miz Sophie, you'se sumpin' special. I guess we all plain lucky.

Later, Will didn't take the destruction of his property so philosophically. He flew into a rage, which had to work itself out.

"It's that gol-derned Carpenter, that's what it is. I swear I'll git him fer this, iffen it's the last thing I do." He clenched his fists, and his black eyes shot fire.

Sophie tried to touch him; he jerked away. "I don't see how you can be so bloomin' peaceful about this. Do you know how much that stuff would cost, today?"

His anger seemed to give her more strength. "Yes, Will, I know. But if it had been in our house, it would have also been destroyed, as everything our neighbors had. Except," her chin quivered, "they lost their lives."

Later, wondering why Will hadn't left for work, Sophie went to find him. Searching everywhere in the building, she discovered her husband in the storage room, cleaning a new revolver.

Aghast, she confronted him. "Will, what does this mean?"

He looked up, grim determination on his face. "That evil one ain't gonna go on 'till somebody gits hurt. I aim to stop him. Don't try to talk me out of it."

Sophie began to cry. "Oh, Will, you'll go to jail—what will I do?"

Her pitiful look touched him. He put his arm around her shoulder. "It's all right, Sophie. I'll not murder him. He's carryin' a gun, that's for sure, and when we're face to face, he'll draw. It's gotta be self-defense. See?"

She didn't see, but Will was firm. All he had to do was find Carpenter.

That wasn't so easy. Inquiring of fellow workers, he heard conflicting stories.

"No one knows; they say he's gone berserk." The fellow sitting on a log with his lunch box, bit into a sandwich. "There's talk he committed suicide. About the only place to look would be the river, and another body wouldn't mean much."

A little perturbed by the callousness of the man, Will moved to another. "Seems he's nowheres about. Some say he left town. Couldn't stand it here no more without his family. Cracked up."

One worker, however, echoed Will's idea. "Will, I think he's in hiding around here. You know, he instigated a lynch mob to get your daughter. He's nuts, and he's sure that your Shona's a witch. If I was you, I'd keep an eye on her. Sooner or later, he's going to try something."

At last, Will found someone who shared his view of Carpenter. The man was right about keeping watch on Shona.

* * *

Carpenter had been busy. After a long search, he had taken a room in a house on Prospect Hill, as "Josh Carns."

Sympathizing with his unemployment and the loss of a family, the housewife assured him that there would be a nourishing meal, when he returned from job-hunting.

With no intention of looking for work, Joshua found a place behind some shrubbery above the hospital, and settled down to watch.

Waiting was tiresome, but important. Hours passed with no sign of Shona. At times, he stretched and moved about, careful to keep out of sight from any direction.

His plan was well formulated. The witch must die, if not by hanging, then by drowning, as tradition dictated. She must be captured, trussed, and hidden until nightfall, when she would be moved to the river.

Days passed; one could be patient. Often, Shona appeared on the portico with Cassie for a noonday break. Helpless, he waited, sure that his time would come.

Another week went by. In the few times when she appeared, she was in the company of Plato or Will. Her father, ever vigilant, did not allow her to leave the building without one of them.

Eventually, however, so much protection began to crush Shona. She begged her father for some freedom. "Papa, let me go out by myself for a little while. Nothing's going to happen to me."

Grimly, he answered, "Come to my room; I've got something to say to you."

She obeyed with alacrity, wondering at his solemn attitude.

As she entered, Will broke into her thoughts as rudely as though they had been spoken. "Young lady, I tried not to git into this. Do you know jest what danger you're in?"

Before she could answer, he explained.

"Well, that so-called attempt at robbery, when both you and Plato was hurt, wasn't robbery at all. Them . . . those men were after you. They were goin' to lynch you. Think about that. You could be dead, right now."

Her face whitened, and a queer, cold feeling came over her. She sat down on a chair.

"Didn't you see the rope?" Will demanded, regretting what he had been forced to say.

"Of course I saw the rope. I thought it was to tie us up with. Oh, Papa, why would anyone want to hang either one of us?"

"It was *you* child—not Plato. You're supposed to be a witch, remember?"

Suddenly, it all came back—the taunts of the schoolboys, the death of her playmate, the town meeting, Miss McKay's contribution to the publicity . . . Everything seemed to be closing in on her. Perhaps she was, indeed, some sort of pariah. She closed her eyes.

Will came to put his arm around her shoulder. "It's all right, honey. We ain't goin' to let nobody hurt you. Don't worry."

* * *

Dinner at the Pensyl home consisted of roast chicken, stuffing, mashed potatoes, and other accompanying delicacies. The meal was served by Maggie, a pretty woman of about forty, with large, brown eyes and a chestnut braid around her head like a tiara.

Harry, her husband, and Joshua ate heartily. Harry savored each bite; Joshua gobbled without tasting the food or noticing the pretty cook.

His urgent purpose was the only thing to consider. To that end, he had decided he would need a cohort. Now, he could study Harry's excellent physique and gauge his mentality at the same time.

Here was a truck-gardener, not particularly bright, but with a quality of brawn that could probably match that of the indomitable Plato.

Now, he must discover how suggestible the man might be. While Maggie was in the kitchen, as he wolfed down a slab of apple pie, Joshua broached the burning subject.

"What do you think about witches?"

"Witches? I don't think about them. There hain't been a witch around here for years. Folks run 'em out of town, a long time since."

Delighted, Joshua pursued the matter.

"What would you say if I told you that there's one in the city right now?" He leaned toward Harry confidentially, and added, "She's the one who wiped out the city of Johnstown."

Harry put down his fork. "How do you know that?"

Joshua indicated the direction of the kitchen with his eyes. "Mebbe we could go out on the porch and have a talk."

Intrigued, Harry rose, lifting his voice. "Maggie, we're goin' to sit outside fer a bit."

"That's fine, dear. I'll join you after while."

He shot a glance at Joshua. "Iffen you got sumpin' to tell me, let's have it."

They were outside now, Harry sitting on the wooden swing, Joshua on the top step.

Carpenter cleared his throat. "Well, it's a long story. I gathered bits and pieces from things having to do with this Will MacDonald's daughter. I don't know whether she was kidnapped by the Hogback Witch or not—anyhow, they found her livin' with the woman. That woman hated everybody in this town."

"So . . . ?"

"Seems the old one died, and this youngster's been carrying on the witchery, or whatever they call it."

Harry appeared to be skeptical. "What d'ya mean, carryin' on? What did she do?"

"Do," exploded Joshua. "She darned near got my son killed. That's what. Oh, she didn't touch him. Her school friends got him and left him for dead."

"But, after all, she didn't . . ."

"Let me tell you what she *did* do. Killed her little playmate, right on the street. No one saw what happened, but that little girl dropped dead, just like that."

As Carpenter talked, he became more agitated. The act of recounting drew out the imbalance of his thinking. Unfortunately, by this time, Harry had become so intrigued, that Joshua's insanity escaped his notice.

He continued, angrily. "Furthermore, neighbors swore they saw her doing something to her little brother in his carriage. He died, too."

Horrified at these disclosures, Harry tried to think. All of it was confusing. He wasn't sure that Joshua had made his point.

"Joshua, how in tunket kin ya say this witch could have something to do with causing that big flood?"

His companion shot him a scornful glance. "She had everything to do with it. She and her boyfriend went up to the dam and must have done some kind of hex up there. They came down and told people that the dam was going to go."

"Lord, we've been hearin' that every year. Never meant nothin'."

Carpenter glared, Remember how this engineer, Montgomery, said the dam was safe, so long as it didn't go over the top?" Harry shook his head.

Playing his trump card, Joshua gave him a piercing, evil smile. "This time was different, it tore out the whole front end."

Perhaps it was that triumphant attitude, more than the logic, which finally impressed Harry.

"I guess you set me straight, all right," Harry agreed. He would have asked some questions, but Maggie appeared in the doorway.

She breathed the fresh air appreciatively. "Isn't it a pleasant night?" Harry grunted affirmation, and she came to sit beside him on the swing.

Carpenter saw his chance. "Didn't you folks lose anyone in the flood?"

It stung them both. Maggie dropped her head and couldn't answer. Harry spoke for her.

"We don't know. Our son, his wife and two children were livin' down on Washington Street. Before the dam broke, they was seen on a rooftop. After that . . ." His voice trembled; he went silent.

Maggie, now weeping, cut in. "We're not sure. Maybe they got away. It's just that—it's been so long—we don't know anything." She broke into uncontrollable sobs and rushed into the house.

"Guess ya shouldn't a brought that up. She's been holdin' up pretty good, but this . . ."

Josh got to his feet. "I'm sorry. Maybe you can see why I'm about to get this witch. I lost my wife and son."

Grimly, he stalked off to his room.

Harry sat on the swing, moving slowly, not noticing a slight rain blowing in on his face. Something caused him to reflect on the terror of that last day in May. The tears that had refused to come for weeks, burst now, wracking him with sobs.

Finally composed, he came to a conclusion. Whatever Joshua had planned, Harry was his man.

TWENTY-THIRD

Shona's life had lost its joy. It had become movement without meaning, work without purpose, existence without hope. The reason? She was only seventeen.

Cassie talked to Sophie about it. "She's mopin', Miz Sophie; you kin see—she eatin' like a l'il, sick bird."

"Of course, I can see." Sophie hadn't meant to be so abrupt. Seeing Cassie's injured expression, she softened. "I didn't mean to snap at you, dear. It concerns me that I *do* see this, and I've no idea what's causing it. Why don't you two have a conversation? She won't talk to me, knowing I worry."

Cassie managed a smile, moving away to help Jean in the instrument room, replacing sterilized utensils. She knew that questioning Shona would only drive her inward, unless it was on her own terms.

Strangely, a time for their dialogue came soon, almost as though Shona had sensed the need. Cassie had scarcely stretched herself on the bed for a rest, when someone rapped.

Raising herself on an elbow, she called, "Who is it?"

A familiar voice answered. "It's me—Shona."

Cassie sprang to open the door, thanking the Lord for quick response to a recent prayer. Now, though, seeing the girl's swollen, flushed face, her pleasure suddenly became alarm.

"Shona, what . . ." She had no chance to go on—Shona threw her arms around Cassie's neck and began to cry.

Together, they sat on the bed. Cassie pulled a clean handkerchief out of her apron pocket and handed it to Shona.

"Jes' tell me about it, chile."

She wiped her eyes and attempted to smile. "Cassie, I'm so miserable, I could die. There's no today for me—and no tomorrow. All I have is a depressing yesterday."

Cassie patted her hand and drew away. "How cum, honey?" It was necessary to denote interest without prying.

"Cassie, you know how much I love Michael."

Cassie nodded, and she continued. "I think Papa has said something to Michael. He doesn't come around at all; you see that."

Cassie frowned slightly. "Ah don' see why yo' Papa should get the blame. Mebbe Michael's done foun' someone else."

She shrugged that off. "I thought I knew what it was. Papa never wanted me to see Michael at all—said he's too old for me."

"Mebbe he's right. How ole's Michael, anyway?"

"Only ten years older. What's that got to do with it? If it weren't for Papa, Michael would ask me to marry him. I'm sure of it . . ."

Cassie struggled for the right thing to say, then just patted her hand.

Shona straightened up, wiping her eyes. Her nose was red;

her eyes, puffy. Cassie melted. "Why don' you go 'n talk to yo' Papa?"

She shook her head. "No use. I think he has something else against Michael. One day last week, I saw him coming up the walk. Papa ran down and talked to him."

"Well, that's a good sign."

"No, it was bad. They got into an argument; both of them were very angry. Michael clenched his fists, and must have made some nasty remark. Then he walked away. Cassie, I know he was coming to see me. He hasn't been here, since."

"Don' worry, honey. Didn't you ever hear 'em say, 'Love will fin' a way'?"

Shona's eyes lit with hope. "Do you really think so, Cassie? Do you believe he'll get Papa to like him?" At that moment, she retrieved some of her optimism.

She rose to go, and threw both arms around Cassie. "'S funny, you always know how to make me feel better."

* * *

The dining room at the hospital had a pleasant atmosphere—large windows, and six octagonal tables with snowy cloths. A great buffet stood on one side of the area, with a huge cut-glass pitcher and its accompanying glasses reflected in the mirror.

On the other side of the room, a massive china closet held all varieties of gilt-edged, ornate china—a personal collection of Dr. Galloway.

Shona had never paid particular attention to the room, except for seeing to it that the tablecloths were clean and properly placed. Now, setting dishes and silverware for the staff, two ambulant refugees, and her family, she stopped to gaze appreciatively.

Life seemed brighter this morning, like the reflection of the sunlight on the faceted glassware. Through her mind raced the new-found hope which Cassie had inspired.

"Love will find a way," she repeated, mentally, over and over. The words almost set themselves to a melody.

Her deep concentration collapsed as Cassie called from the kitchen, "Shona, chile, we' got some dishes ready, here."

She hurried to help. As she was serving, her thoughts began to dwell on the attitude of her father. She must discover what it was that her father held against Michael. Eventually, age barriers fall, but when her father became angry with someone, that was something else.

After the meal, when the others had gone, Shona waited, toying with her food. She noticed that Sophie, too, was eating slowly.

Shona took a deep breath, then plunged. "Papa, I need to

know. What is it that you don't like about Michael? That is, beside his age?"

Will picked up his knife. "Pass me that bread—my butter lapped over."

She looked from him to her mother, who was concentrating on her food. "Mama, you see, Papa won't tell me anything. Tell me what's wrong?"

Sophie avoided looking at either of them. "Honey, that's between your father and Michael. I have nothing to say."

She turned again to Will, casting liquid eyes which usually conquered him. "Papa . . ." she began.

Ignoring the look, he snapped, "See here—for the last time, I'm tellin' you. I don't want to hear his name around here, again. The man's no good."

Then, suddenly, he looked at his watch and jumped to his feet. "Lord, I fergot the time. There's a meetin' at the mill office—gotta go."

With no further notice of Shona, he kissed his wife and rushed away.

Shona eyed her mother. "Aren't you going to tell me?"

A strange look came over Sophie's face. "Please don't ask, dear. There are some things one doesn't discuss with a young girl. There, I'm afraid I've said too much already."

With that, she rose from her chair, taking her dishes to the kitchen.

Shona looked over at Cassie, who was hurriedly gathering the rest of the dishes on a tray.

"Cassie . . ."

"Don' know nuthin' chile—I swear." Then, she, too, hastened off.

Shona sat, reflecting. Apparently, there was some sordid story abroad about Michael. Not for a minute could it be true, but to protect him, she must find out.

It occurred to her that Michael couldn't stay away too long. Soon, he would be coming—he would tell her.

* * *

Joshua's waiting was becoming intolerable. Sitting on the porch step, early in the morning, he cleaned his gun, thinking dark thoughts. Harry found him there, and evinced shock.

"You're not goin' to shoot her?" There was alarm in the question. Such action would land both of them in jail.

" 'Course not—this revolver will keep any so-called heroes away, so that we can nab the girl."

"But, iffen it comes to that—if somebody sees us, we're in trouble ourselves."

"Don't be a fool." Carpenter glared at him. "We've got to keep our faces covered. Nobody is going to know who we are."

"There's one thing you ain't said," Harry ventured. "How are you plannin' to do it? I've heered they drive a stake through the witch's heart, or burn her. Wouldn't want nothin' to do with that—no sir!"

Joshua looked his scorn. "I'm not a barbarian. In the old days, people did those things, but in Salem, they hanged them. I had planned to do that, but it fell through. So, now, I figure drowning is the best way." He put the gun back in its holster.

"Why is that?"

"Because, we can weigh her down with a hunk of steel, and later, when the rope rots and the body comes up, it will be just another flood victim."

Joshua's cool delineation of purpose nearly deterred Harry's accord. Witch, or no witch, had the man not considered the enormity of his intention?

Then, the horror that had swept the city came back to him. He remembered futile attempts to contact his loved ones; the final acceptance of their possible deaths. If this creature had, indeed, caused such mayhem, it was only just that she should die.

He turned to go in, just as Maggie appeared.

"What are you two whisperin' about?" She said it lightly, with just a trace of curiosity.

Harry brushed past her, into the kitchen. "I didn't know we was whisperin'. Jest man-talk, honey."

They entered to a bountiful breakfast of pancakes and sausage—the kind of breakfast Carpenter used to enjoy. Eyeing it all, the memory of his wife came rushing back. With that recollection came anger, rising to such a pitch that he dashed out of the room and up the stairs.

Maggie called after him, to no avail. Puzzled, she looked at Harry. "Do you suppose he's sick? Surely, he'd be hungry—this is a late breakfast."

Harry looked up from his plate, sausage poised on his fork. "Maggie, sometimes I think the fellow's a bit queer. It's too bad. I did hear that some of these people down in the valley went plumb loco."

Almost frightened, she said, "Harry, do you think . . ."

"Naw, he's all right. Jest mad at the world, I reckon."

Flushed with anger and pain, Joshua seethed in his room, waiting impatiently for his partner to finish breakfast. There must be no slip-up; if a chance came to make the capture, Harry must be ready.

Little did he know how soon that time would come.

* * *

Shona was through with a stint at dishwashing. Hearing the sound of a horse's hooves, she pulled off her apron and ran out on the portico. It was Plato, seated on Lady, advancing with that elegant posture which she had always admired.

She ran out to greet him, innocently enough, to begin with. Then a thought flashed into her mind. Looking at the horse's feet, she pretended concern.

"Plato, do you see how Lady's limping? There must be a stone in that back hoof."

"I didn't notice nothin', honey." He turned the horse around and trotted her a few paces.

"Oh, yes, Plato, there's definitely something wrong. I think you should check."

Obligingly, he climbed down. "Which foot is it?"

In a few moments, she was on Lady's back. "I must have been mistaken, Plato. She's all right. I'll be back in an hour."

She was off, in a cloud of dust. He watched her go—an excellent horsewoman, Plato admitted to himself. Why had he ever taught her to ride?

Shona's first stop, of course was the Red Cross. While Michael had assumed many jobs, this was his dedication.

Tying Lady to a post, she saw Dr. Winston moving among the workers in the tent, and called to him.

He rushed up, his eyes lighted; the sight of Shona was always a pleasure. Grasping her hand, he said, "Shona, dear, we've missed you. I hope you've been well?"

Actually, he had never seen her looking better. If there was a trace of unhappiness in her eyes, it was probably his imagination.

She nodded. "I'm fine. Dr. Winston, have you seen Michael Stewart?"

Now, her mission was clear; it was Michael again. He answered with a touch of envy. "No, I haven't. That man is everywhere. There's some connection with the National Guard. Apparently, he has a commission."

Her agitation became evident. "I must see him, doctor. I have to find out something—right away."

She had no time to waste. Freeing the horse and mounting swiftly, she waved. " 'Bye. I'll see you again, sometime. Thank you."

In a flash, she was gone.

Unfortunately, Shona's ride proved to be so delightful that she almost forgot her mission. The loveliness of the day, and the warm, obedient body carrying her brought a kind of ecstasy which reminded her of happier days.

Wondering about that, the answer came simply. It was freedom, working its enchantment. Here, at last, she had actual, uninhibited leisure, so long denied her and cast off as unthinkable.

Forgetting caution, Shona relaxed today. Riding the forest trail with the captivating cover of green about her, and the pleasant scent of pine, she responded happily to the soft breeze lifting her curls.

Sure that she would see Michael at the National Guard barracks, she thrilled at the thought. Then, sharply, a stabbing pain in her head flashed a warning.

The pain had come quite some time ago, but she had learned to shut it down, when the omen seemed to be trivial. Somehow, today, there was danger nearby.

At once she drew Lady to a walk. That was her mistake. The change of pace caused the animal to hesitate for a moment. Just then, two men stepped out of the underbrush, one on each side of Lady, catching the reins. Alarmed, the horse reared, snorted, and then stood quiet.

Looking from one to the other, there was no means of identifying them. Both wore bandannas over their noses, and black hats pulled down just above their eyes.

The shorter man dragged Shona from the saddle. "You handle the horse. We're lucky to have it."

Now, his disguise meant nothing. Shona recognized Carpenter's voice. Anger and terror combined to give her an amazing strength. Kicking and striking, she nearly got away.

Holding both of Shona's hands with one of his own, Carpenter called to Harry. "Tie up that horse and get over here. Bring the rope."

Dutifully, Harry did as he was told. However, helping Joshua bind Shona's hand and foot, he began to wonder what he was doing. By this time, a dirty bandanna was gagging the girl, and her blue-green eyes flashed fire.

"Say, Josh, this is jest a purty kid. You sure she's what you say?"

"Listen, Harry, I told you, you can't judge by looks. C'mon now, help me get her on the horse."

They flung Shona across Lady's back like a sack of potatoes, and led the animal deeper into the forest, away from the trail.

Approaching the spot where they must cross open ground to the river, Joshua hesitated. "We can't chance it. We'll have to wait till dark."

"What good is that? We can't walk a horse in the open, with a body on its back. You must be crazy."

Any reference to his sanity infuriated Carpenter. "Don't be a fool We get rid of the creature. C'mon, we'll take her down, now."

They hauled Shona from Lady's back and laid her on the ground. Then, Joshua turned and gave the mare a slap on the rump. With a snort, she wheeled and headed for home.

For some time, the men sat on a log and looked at each other. Harry had a sick feeling which was growing stronger. He decided to try reasoning.

"Say, Carpenter, we got her all tied up now, and she won't

be too heavy for you to drag. How about lettin' me out? I jest don't feel good about this."

Joshua glared at him. "Want to welsh out? Well, it won't do you any good, if I'm caught. I'll darn well see to it that they get you, too."

"But, I did help you, didn't I? Why can't you let me go? I don't want to drown nobody. Maybe, we're wrong."

You're in it, and you're staying. You're already as guilty as I am, whatever happens."

Impressed with that certainty, and dismayed by its logic, Harry stayed with Carpenter. Both of them cast occasional glances at the girl. She seemed to be sleeping.

But, far from slumber, Shona was well aware of her peril. She could not help wondering why there had not been any real warning. Now, with her family having no idea of her whereabouts, rescue was unlikely. There was physical misery—the discomfort of the binding ropes and the suffocating rag in her mouth. And, along with that, alert to Carpenter's hate, there was fear.

* * *

Up at the hospital, a mystery reigned. Under the direction of Dr. Winson, Plato had traveled to the Guard barracks over the trail Shona would have taken. She had not arrived at her destination.

Plato talked it over with Sophie and Cassie. Fortunately, Will was working.

"The doctor said she was lookin' for Michael. Mebbe she foun' him. Do you want me to git the police?"

Sophie shook her head, trying not to cry. "The poor child has been so unhappy. Let's not add to her troubles. At least, we can wait a little while."

Later, Plato was weeding the flower bed edging the building, when he heard a familiar snort. There, just in view, was Lady, cantering up to him.

Now frightened, Plato caught the horse, inspecting its saddle, which had been dragged down to one side. Shona must have fallen.

He raced into the building, looking for Sophie. In the kitchen, she was peeling apples, alone. From the look on his face, she set the pan on the table and jumped to her feet.

"Miz Sophie, we' better git a search party. Lady's here, but somehow—she los' l'il Shona." His voice choked with emotion.

Hearing the story from a distraught Sophie, Dr. Garroway immediately called the police. They promised speedy action. Now, there was nothing to do but wait.

Sophie's mind raced. On top of the fact that something could have happened to Shona, she dreaded the fact that Will would soon be coming home. There was no way of knowing what course of action his anger would take. She could only hope that it wouldn't be directed to her daughter.

Just then, hearing his footsteps on the portico, she ran to meet him, trying to be natural. He gave her a perfunctory peck on the cheek, and settled himself in the alcove, just inside.

No one was around. Sophie perched on the arm of his chair. "Honey, I have something to tell you. I hope you won't be severe with Shona. She couldn't help doing—what she did."

"Jumpin Jehosophat, she did what—or, what was she doin'? Don't make a lot of sense, seems to me." He had picked up the newspaper, but dropped it to the floor.

"She borrowed Lady, and went to look for Michael." It all came out in a rush; tremulously, she watched his face to see what would happen.

As expected, Will's temperature began to rise. "Borrowed Lady? Who allowed that? Didn't I tell her not to see that man again? Why . . ."

Sophie cut in, hoping to stop his raving. "Actually, she got on the horse before Plato could do a thing. Don't be too upset, dear. Shona's been in love with Michael for a long time."

Will was more than angry. His face went red, deepening to a shade that was almost purple. Both fists were clenched. Sophie's explanation had not helped.

Glowering at her, he shouted, "Where is she? I swear, there'll be punishment for this. I demand to see her, right now!"

Sophie crossed to another chair and burst into tears. For a second, Will was ashamed. His voice softened. "It's not that bad. I ain't fixin' to beat her up—nothin' like that, but she's got some answerin' to do. Fetch her."

"I can't." Sophie's sobs increased.

"What do you mean, you can't? Where is she?"

She tried to control her emotion. "Lady came back—alone . . ." She dabbed at her eyes with a tiny linen handkerchief, and attempted to smooth her dark hair, which was streaming out of its combs.

Will leaped to his feet. "What about the police? Do they know? I'll get a . . ."

Sophie stopped him.

"Dear, they covered the area she was to travel. There was no sign of her. She did arrive at the Red Cross, but there was no sign that she ever got to the Guard post."

"Lord, do you know what this means?" Will's anger had become sheer fright. "That fellow could have her, right now. He vowed to kill her."

Sophie hadn't known, but she had worried about the man. She attempted to soothe her husband, but he grabbed his hat, which had been tossed on the table.

"I'm goin' out myself, and there better be no harm done to

the child, or I won't be responsible . . ."

Before she could say anything more, he was gone. Worse than that, he had a gun.

Arriving in the valley, Will realized that his light-weight, gray business suit wasn't suitable for the heat of the day. On seeing the Guard men, without coats, he envied them.

He moved toward the man who seemed to be in charge. "I'm Will MacDonald. I guess you've heered; my daughter's lost. Are you makin' up a search party?"

The smooth-shaven, pleasant officer extended his hand. "Pleased to meet you, Mr. MacDonald. I'm Joseph Wells, commandant of this outfit. Sorry about your trouble. Of course, we can't authorize a search, yet."

"What do you mean, you can't authorize a search? The police went out, right away."

"Right, Mr. MacDonald. They made a routine check, to see whether she might have been thrown from the horse. She could be on her way home, right now."

"Mr. Commander, or whatever, you don't understand. My daughter is under threat of death. It's jest possible that the fellow has her, this minute. Can't you do somethin' about that?"

It was as close to a plea as he could muster. Officer Wells smiled sympathetically. "I would, if possible. But, under exceptional circumstances, we may send out a search party in twelve hours. That's the best I can do."

Will gave up. He must go back and get Plato. Lanterns would be needed soon, for the dusk was beginning to fall. By now, his worry nearly amounted to panic.

Scarcely had he turned, when a voice near his ear startled him. "Mr. MacDonald, if you're going to conduct your own search, may I help?"

It was Michael. Frantic as Will was, this was no time to spurn a sincere offer of assistance. He attempted to be gracious, but his smile went awry.

"Sure could use some help. I'm goin' to get Plato, 'n some lanterns. Gotta get some of these clothes off, too."

They looked at each other. Not dressed for heat, they both had shining, wet faces, and sticky, damp hair.

As they hurried along, Michael wanted to know about Shona's disappearance. Somewhat annoyed, Will growled, "Iffen she hadn't been bound and determined to see you, she wouldn't be lost. I don't know what gits into that girl."

Michael spoke sadly. "She cares for me—just as I care for her. There's not much we can do about that, is there?"

"Mister, there's lots you kin do about that. You ain't much of a catch for a pure, young girl, I'd say. Don't hold with your shenanigans—no, sir."

Michael flushed. Even in the twilight, Will saw it.

"Mr. MacDonald, I've tried to explain why I was seen

entering Lizzie Thompson's place. I was commissioned to carry a message."

"Commissioned, eh?" Will's response was almost a sneer. "I guess you was paid to go up there."

"Yes. In fact, I had to serve a summons. Apparently, some contraband had crossed the border; hence the National Guard was involved. Actually, I made three trips to Frankstown hill before I could get the papers to her, personally."

There was no reason to doubt his sincerity. Will searched for a way out. "I had a feelin' that you was . . . were up there for other reasons. Didn't mean nothin'. Jest gotta protect my child."

Michael made no comment. What did it matter, if he had gained in some way, with Will? All that was important was Shona. Where was she? What might be happening to her?

* * *

At that moment, Joshua had found the ideal hiding place, not far from the trail, to be sure, but perfect, nevertheless.

An enormous stand of bramble bushes formed an impenetrable shield on three sides. The fourth, fell away sharply—a sheer drop of land, heavily forested.

Even if Harry did need to be prodded a bit, everything seemed to be working out. Together, they dragged their burden into a clearing behind the bushes. Here, they could see in all directions, with no danger of anyone noticing them.

Suddenly, below them, on the trail, they heard the sound of horses' hooves, and listened in alarm until the threat passed. Both men breathed relief. Now, the passage of society below could be noted without worry.

As for Shona, outwardly quiet, her thoughts moved in such chaos that it was impossible, at first, to sort them out.

Although for the first time in her life, she was aware of the fact that she could die, fear stood remote, in the background. Probably, her strongest emotion was remorse. A father's love had kept her prisoner; as a result, he could be plunged in grief.

She thought of him now, contrasting his devotion with the hatred of the men sitting nearby. The rope, not heavy, but harsh, cut into her wrists and ankles, and the rag in her mouth tasted like oil.

Sadly, she wished the family could have known her penitence. If she died, because of her rash action, everyone she loved would suffer. Indeed, most of their trouble since she had arrived, had been a result of her own action.

She peeked from half-closed eyelids to see what the men were doing. Carpenter was alert, watching in every direction, as though fearing discovery. The other man, a picture of dejection, sat with his knees drawn up and his arms resting on them, looking into space.

Did she hate Carpenter? The emotion was not clearly defined. It seemed to be something larger. This man, with his insane vendetta, had to be a victim, too. Prejudice, usually born of ignorance, had been the bane of countless lives. Unhappily, she realized that if she lived, she would know its poison for many years.

* * *

Twilight fell suddenly, almost as though someone had drawn a curtain across the sky. It was cooler, now; a west wind had sprung up.

Joshua roused, preparing to drag Shona from their hiding place. Impatiently, he nudged Harry. "C'mon, it's time to go."

The breeze seemed to clear Harry's mind. He made no move to comply. Tactfully, he tried reasoning. "Josh, you kin easy drag her across there, to the river. You don't need me. Maggie'll be worried sick. I gotta go."

To his shock and surprise, Joshua pulled his gun. "You're staying. I need you to prove that this is a proper deed—if anything happens. We're not criminals. We're just trying to bring some justice to this town."

Harry's eyes were riveted on the revolver. Above the gun's barrel, Joshua's glare fixed on him. His resolve faded.

"Are you gonna help, or not?"

Hastily, he tore loose the part of Shona's dress which had been caught on the thorns, holding her. "I'm with ya, Josh. No need to get rough."

He had finally recognized Joshua's condition as being a phase of insanity, but the gun had spoken.

They dragged her out. The new, blue voile frock which Shona's mother had bought for her, had lost any semblance of its shape. Torn to strips, and smeared with countless, tiny drops of blood, it gave mute evidence of her mistreatment.

Before they could move her further, the moon, which had been shaded by dark clouds, burst through. Harry tried to hold back.

"Do you think it's dark enough?"

Joshua dropped to relax on the ground. The protective screen was still around them. "Wait till that next big cloud crosses over the moon. There's no hurry. They won't be searching yet. How can they be sure she didn't run away?"

Harry sank down beside him. "Poor Maggie. She's prob'ly about crazy, by now."

If he had expected understanding, he should have known better. Joshua's concentration was on his mission, nothing else.

Now, in his warped mind, it wouldn't really matter if they were caught—after the job was done. The people of Johnstown would thank him for his courageous deed, which meant justice.

He would have effected punishment for a great crime.

Nevertheless, other minds near him, had opposing thoughts. Harry planned mutiny. Shona, trussed, scratched and miserable, had an idea of her own. Neither had any idea of support from the other.

* * *

Now the moon was hidden. To Carpenter's joy, the land sloped. It would be easy to drag the witch to the water. Impatiently, he waited for Harry to move.

He began to haul Shona by the shoulders, but somehow she had made herself a dead weight. "Harry, I need you. Get over here and help." He made little progress.

With no assistance forthcoming, Joshua discovered that he had been abandoned. He cast a nasty glance at Harry and gave Shona's body a jerk, which somehow loosened his grip.

She recognized that—this was the time to wrench herself form his hands, and roll—not to the water, but away from it, toward the mound.

Joshua leaped to grab her, but Harry got in his way. It happened so quickly that the two collided, and Harry fell.

"What's the matter with you?" Carpenter's anger had become incredulity. "I thought we had a bargain."

Harry got up and faced him. "Josh, I tried like all git out to tell you. This is a wrong thing. I don't want no part of it."

In disgust, with Shona rolling on, Carpenter took a circuitous route around his former partner. Just as he stooped to capture her, the crashing of something coming through the underbrush made him hesitate.

As indecision set in, someone caught him around the legs and threw him to the ground.

It was Michael, now standing over him like the avenging angel himself, thought Shona. Dazed, Joshua scrambled to his feet, shocked and bewildered.

Immediately, Will and Plato rushed up, setting down their lanterns. Something in Carpenter's chest tightened. Whether it was the strain of exertion, or sheer frustration, it froze him there.

Horrified, he realized the futility of his mission. It had failed. He would never be able to bring justice to the city, nor to himself.

Plato was advancing, the moonlight accentuating his gleaming bare chest and smooth, round muscles. Immobilized, Joshua stood quietly as his hands were bound behind his back.

A short distance away, Will worked with his pocket knife, cutting Shona's ropes, mourning over her wounds.

At her head, Michael had removed the gag, kissing her lightly on the hair. Then he rose, looking for Carpenter.

Joshua, saw vengeance there. He saw it again when Will stood up. Some distance away, Harry stood, cold and aloof. Their friendship, the only one he had in the world, was ended.

Now, lights were advancing. No one had expected the police, but suddenly, a siren sounded, and the police wagon came across the flat from the trail.

In a last show of defiance, he broke away from Plato and ran to the river bank. Without hesitation, he leaped. With his arms tied close to his body, he slid easily into the water. There was no struggle. Some bubbles came up, but he did not surface. Scarcely disturbed, the stream moved on.

Two policemen rushed up to the roiling, muddy water, but they had no equipment for rescue.

Harry stepped forward, hesitantly. "I'm Harry Pensyl. I suppose you'll want to arrest me."

The officer he had addressed, looked from one man to another. "Is there some reason for this man's detainment?"

Before anyone could answer, Harry explained. "I'm at fault, goin' along with him. He made it all seem so right—gettin' rid of something evil. I believed him. When I figured out that his mind was sick, I wouldn't help him any more."

Now, Shona was in tears. "He's telling the truth," she sobbed. "He didn't want to help; he begged to go, but Mr. Carpenter pulled a gun on him."

Listening, Will came to Pensyl's defense. "You kin take my daughter's word for it. That's the way it is. She don't—doesn't lie."

The captain put away the book he had opened. "I don't think we have any grievance with Mr. Pensyl. And I want to commend you men for a job well done. We might have been too late to save this young lady's life.

Hailing his fellow officers, he gave instructions for recovering the body—the next day. Somehow, it didn't seem to be imperative.

Will stood by, grudgingly, as Michael held Shona, smoothing her hair and wiping dust from her face with a clean handkerchief. There were small scratches on her face and arms, and red marks had been made by the ropes.

* * *

TWENTY-FOURTH

Without asking anyone, Plato gathered up Shona and began the journey back to the hospital. Safe in his arms, she began to relax and breathe normally.

The day had been hectic since her capture. Now, aside from bruises and scratches suffered through rough handling, a new type of mental exhaustion had drained her of emotion.

She cast a glance back at Michael's finely chiseled face, so intense in his caring for her. How she loved him!

Elation, and concern met them at the hospital. Not waiting to hear the story, Sophie and Cassie rushed Shona off for a bath and treatment of her injuries.

Dr. Galloway remained on the portico, where they had been waiting—interminably, it seemed. He met the news of Carpenter's suicide with relief.

"It's good to know that he can't threaten Shona any more. The fellow should have been locked up, long ago."

Will concurred, but Michael remonstrated. "He had suffered a great loss. Everyone knew he was unbalanced. As a result, no one paid much attention to his ravings."

As had been his custom with Michael, Will glared. "I sure paid attention. Why do you think I kept Shona under guard all the time?"

Michael glowered back. "I guess you had reason, but you nearly destroyed her. It was cruel—like caging a wild bird."

Their argument broke off with the advent of Shona, looking strangely different.

With curls matted and snarled, there had been nothing to do but cut them short. And, although scratches and cuts were less vivid, a large, purple bruise had developed on her forehead.

Defying Will, Michael jumped to take her in his arms.

"Oh, Michael, I look terrible." She buried her face against his chest.

He smoothed her damp hair. "You've never been so beautiful. Now, you're the little girl I fell in love with. By the way, have I ever told you that I loved you?"

She murmured back, "You didn't have to tell me. I knew it, always."

They had been whispering, but Will heard.

"See here, young fellow, I guess you're all right, but that don't mean my child's ready for—whatever you have in mind."

Shona could scarcely believe what she heard. Her father had forgiven Michael.

Forgetting Will, they sank down on the steps. The others rose to leave—that is, all but Will, who had no intention of doing so.

Finally, Sophie came to his chair and whispered something to him. With a grunt, he rose.

"See here, girl, you need to get some rest . . ." He stopped, then turned away.

Apparently, Shona couldn't hear. Michael was kissing her.

It was a perfect night for the lovers. Clustered white flowers around the portico breathed fragrance, and the moonlight surrounded them with something almost like a benediction.

With the beauty of it all, they remained in each other's arms until Sophie appeared at the door.

"Honey, your father's getting upset. It's time for you to come in. Please, dear."

Michael rose. "I'm sorry, Mrs. MacDonald. It's not Shona's fault. I couldn't let her go." With a peck on her cheek, he was gone.

Shona came to her mother, starry-eyed. "Oh Mama, he's so wonderful. He's been planning a lot of things. Tomorrow, there's something he wants me to see. I think it's some kind of a gift."

Her mother frowned slightly. "I hope it's not a ring. Your father has come a long way, but he still won't stand for talk of marriage for a long time.

Shona saddened. "Oh, no, he didn't as me to marry him, yet, but I know he will. Just the same, that's not what he's talking about I'm sure."

"Well, honey, let's get to bed. With all this excitement, I hope you can sleep."

As she spoke, she looked again. Shona, so tired and listless upon arrival, had become a young, vibrant person, conveying the impression that she could do without sleep, forever.

* * *

The next day, because of heavy activity at the plant, dawn was obliterated. The red glow in the sky was not Nature's weather warning. It radiated from the Bessemer mill, along with enormous clouds of black smoke.

Prosperity had come to Johnstown. Buildings were being erected, and orders included more than steel beams. Pipes, fixtures, fittings—all these and many other necessities being forged, were responsible for unprecedented prosperity.

Will left early. A great deal of responsibility rested on his shoulders, these days. He exulted in it. Somehow, this awesome obligation to his fellow man had become his reason for living.

As for Shona, back on the job, handing out medications, she was thinking about Peace, her friend. She made a series of small, silent prayers that Peace had not suffered a frightening death.

At noon, she did not have lunch with the nurses as usual. She made herself a ham sandwich and went into the garden beyond the building to meditate.

There was only light smoke now, and the skies had cleared. Around her, pastel-colored asters spread their charm. She sat on a concrete bench beside the pool. Points of gold flashed in the clear water, and the fragrance of a nearby honeysuckle permeated the air.

The sheer beauty of the spot inspired Shona. Why not seek this sanctuary more often, for contemplation?

She had barely relaxed, when a rustle in the grass startled her. There stood Burton Galloway, with an ingratiating smile.

"I'm sorry if I disturbed you, Shona. Just wanted to

apologize for being so bold. Tell me, Hon, is there a chance for me, with you?"

Snatched out of her reverie, Shona tried to be civil. "Burton, there's something you seem to overlook. You have a wife."

"Correction. I do not have, I have never had, a wife."

"But, Peace . . ."

"We never got around to it. There didn't seem to be any hurry. Besides, I didn't know what to do. You, know, parental permission—all that. We didn't have it."

"So?"

"So she ran away—went out west, somewhere."

Shona was so relieved, that she didn't try to lecture. Wishing he would go, she concentrated on the goldfish.

He sat down on the bench and put his arm around her. She twisted away, just as Michael came down the gravel path.

Seeing who is was, he jumped up to face his old teacher. "Mr. Stewart, I was only trying to get somewhere with Shona, here. For some reason, she doesn't like me."

"For good reason, I'd say. What about your wife?"

He sighed. "That always comes up." Without further explanation, he walked off.

Michael sat down and kissed her. "They told me I'd find you here. What an appropriate setting for my pretty girl."

Like magnets, they drew together. They kissed, in a gentle, searching movement, probing this sensation of pure joy, and lingering as though it were an exquisite melody which must not cease.

But, although seemingly lost in space, responsibility flashed to Shona. She pulled away from Michael and jumped up.

"Michael, I've been here too long. Jean asked for help with a patient. I promised to be there."

He sighed, standing with her. "Well, it was wonderful . . . See you this evening—I hope."

She pulled his face down to hers, kissing him softly. "If Papa gives you any trouble—I love you, Michael. Don't ever forget that."

Before he could respond, she was off, down the gravel path like a deer.

And a dear she was, Michael smiled to himself. How fortunate could a man be—but how much more patience would be needed?

That evening, Michael went to see Shona's father, alone. Will sat at a small desk in his bedroom, studying his books.

He seemed amiable enough, so Michael spoke with some confidence. "Mr. MacDonald, you know I want to marry Shona. All we need is your permission. I haven't asked her yet, but . . ."

"Of course, you haven't asked her." His face flamed, and his neck veins showed above his collar. "No decent man would ask a child to marry him. As for permission, fergit it."

With some effort, Michael spoke reasonably. "Mr. MacDonald, I believe I'm a thoughtful man. For years, I've held off, stayed away, because Shona was just that—a child."

"Now, it's time for you to realize that your daughter is a woman, with a woman's feelings. In a few months, she will be 18. How long do you expect to keep her as a child?"

Will snorted. "Mebbe you don't know the law. The law says she's an infant, till she's 21."

Michael tried to ignore that. He continued: "I love Shona, and she loves me. Neither of us has ever cared so much about anyone else. Are you going to break her heart, and also shred the bond between the two of you?"

Never in his life had Will allowed anyone to reprimand him in such a way. Yet, somehow, his anger sputtered and died.

"See here, young fellow, I ain't—I'm not a monster. All I care about is my child's—my daughter's happiness. Jest can't see my little girl as a woman."

Michael flushed. "Mr. MacDonald, I have something to tell you. Shona doesn't know. For a long time, I've been working on a place in Westmont. Saved every penny I could, with one goal—to marry Shona. Lately, when my things in the city were destroyed, my father helped replace clothing and other goods. But, I built the house."

"Pretty sure of yourself, wasn't you?" Will suddenly felt that he had been a pawn—that whatever was to happen had been foreordained.

Michael spoke gently. "Sir, for many years, I've had one dream. At first it was a hopeless, illogical vision which could never come to fruition. But, somehow, it held together to become more reasonable, as time went by. That was because Shona was growing up."

"You mean . . ."

"I mean that Shona was the whole focus of the dream. There can never be anyone for whom I could care so deeply. You may rest assured, I'll look after her."

Will stood up, vaguely uncomfortable. Without looking at Michael, he said, "We'll discuss this later," and stalked out of the room.

* * *

Unaware of Michael's meeting with her father, Shona decided to talk to him, first. As soon as she could be alone with Will, she approached the subject which had become all too familiar.

"Father, I'm sure Michael wants to marry me. If I promise to wait until I'm 18, will that please you?"

He frowned, and was about to reject the plea, when Sophie walked in. Shona, having seen Will's face, left without waiting for an answer.

Will braced himself. Now would come the tearful protest from his wife, the hardest of all to withstand. He still held the opinion that Shona was too young—and would continue to be too young for some time.

Before she could speak, he stopped her. "It's clear what you plan to say, before you say it. You know how I feel . . ."

She interrupted him. "Will, there's something that I don't think you remember. When we married, I wasn't quite 18."

He stared at her. "You're makin' that up. You was a grown lady. We wouldn't 've been allowed to marry so young. I know I was 24—you must have been about that, too."

"No, my father thought there was too much difference. He finally gave his consent—but not his blessing. How can you have forgotten?"

Now, he remembered, unhappy in the thought. What more could he say?

He was sitting at the window, in their room. With a sigh, he gazed out at the garden. "Tell Shona to come in, will you?"

Shona arrived so swiftly that it seemed as though she could not have had time to get the message.

Breathless, she ran to him, but he averted his face. "Guess you're lookin' for good news. Well, it's like this. If you wait till you're 18, there's no objections. Michael's a good man—I admit that."

She stood transfixed for a second, and he continued. "One thing, though."

"Anything, Papa."

"I don't want you makin' a public spectacle of yourself. No kissin' 'n huggin' in front of people. 'Tain't polite."

"Oh, Papa, I don't mind that. I don't mind anything, now. You're so good to me." She choked, kissed him, and flew out of the room.

Will couldn't help being pleased with himself. He had stood his ground—up to a point—and there had been no rift between himself and his daughter.

To Shona's dismay, Michael had gone. He left word with Cassie that he had an early morning commitment, and would see her the next day.

That was true enough, but there was another reason. He dreaded the need to console Shona, if things went wrong.

Pouting, Shona went to Cassie. Michael hadn't even waited to find out what had happened.

Cassie didn't sympathize. "Chile, seems like you could wait till tomorrow. Mr. Michael, he did seem tired."

Getting nowhere with her complaint, Shona retired. Too happy to let anything dampen the thrill, she went to bed with a joyous prayer of thankfulness.

***

After a morning in which Shona moved blissfully, yet seeming to have no actual body, late afternoon arrived. When Michael called to announce his leaving work early, she decided to meet him in the garden.

Here, in the October sunlight, asters were a mass of color, heightened by the dark stand of evergreens behind them.

Hurrying up the path, Michael scarcely noticed the beauty of the scene. Then his worry vanished, for Shona, coming toward him, was smiling.

There was no chance to ask. Shona rushed up to him and threw herself in his arms. "Oh, Michael, he promised not to object."

He gave her a quizzical look. "I can marry you? Some turnaround. Are you sure he said that?"

"Of course, I'm sure." Her smile faded somewhat. "I do have to wait till I'm 18, but Michael, that's in the Spring."

Suddenly, a happy thought struck her. Drawing away from Michael a little, she glanced up at the cobalt October sky.

"Why don't we get the horses and go up to Hogback? The mountains are so beautiful right now—I don't see how Heaven could be nicer."

The idea struck a chord with Michael. "I'll go you one better. Let's go all around the city, through the hills. It will be a long ride, but lots of fun."

"Well, we can ride through most of the forest, but that hillside at the Stone Bridge is almost straight up and down. Remember?"

Of course, he knew, but everything seemed to be changed. One's location, at times, could only be realized by a point of reference, such as the Stone Bridge. Michael grinned sheepishly.

"You're right. We'd have to be riding mountain goats."

Sophie liked their plan. The excursion gave her the opportunity to present Shona's new riding habit, which had been taking up her spare time. She apologized for its color.

"Honey, you do look pretty in green, but I guess it should have been red, or yellow, for visibility's sake."

Shona stared at the divided skirt, which, to her way of thinking, would have been more useful as pants.

Nevertheless, she forced enthusiasm. "Mother, I love it. And I'm not going hunting, for goodness' sake."

A few minutes later, she came out on the portico, dressed for the ride. Michael could scarcely stop gazing at her. The pale green at her ivory face was a perfect complement to the short, red-gold curls escaping around her small, black hat. Her eyes, sometimes blue, were now almost jade green.

Sophie saw them off, in thoughtful, mixed emotion. There was no worry about the mate Shona had chosen, but she had led a sheltered life. Sophie could not help wondering about the instructions she had been side-stepping.

* * *

Winding down into the town, it almost appeared as a different country. The new buildings, some of them already stocked with merchandise, as yet bore only a shadow of the mill dust to which they would be exposed. The boards which had made up the sidewalks had been replaced with carefully laid bricks, as were the streets themselves. Brick streets were an innovation—certainly an improvement over the cobblestones, now seldom used.

Using the bridge as their point of reference, they traveled Main Street for a short distance, then turned off, up to Bedford Street, into the heart of the mountain.

Shona glanced at Michael, so straight and strong, his fine features expressing complete pleasure. Her thrill was in the fact that she was the focus of his joy.

Crossing to the Hogback section, the horses followed an ancient Indian trail, expertly contoured to the rise of the mountain, allowing gradual ascent, rather than a steep climb.

Now, moving further into the forest, the colored leaves became even more brilliant. Shona realized that sunlight was not the only source of light. Much of it radiated upward from the brightness of the leaves on the ground.

As they traveled in the direction of the cabin, Michael had a flash of compunction. Loving animals as Shona did, there was something she should know about him.

He looked over at her, and drew up his horse. "Shona, do you remember the day you found me here, so badly hurt?"

"Dear, how could I ever forget?"

"I've never told you why I was walking in the woods."

The question struck her as odd. "Why does anyone walk in the woods?"

"I never wanted you know—I was hunting."

Shocked, she stared at him, but he went on. "I was so afraid that you'd find my gun and never want anything to do with me. It's probably around here, somewhere."

She caressed him with her eyes. "It doesn't matter. You didn't need to tell me. You were very young."

At that moment, they came to the clearing where the cabin had stood. It was gone.

The only clue to its existence was the blackened stone fireplace, which rose like a monument above a mass of golden bushes. Just ahead of them, a bright red sumac blocked their way.

They moved around it, to view the remains of the herb garden. There, young maples had taken over, their reds and yellows contrasting sharply with the deep purple of an oak, branching far above them. Through the yellow underbrush, sprays of pink flowers struggled up from neglected roots.

Silently, all this beauty seemed to cry out to Shona—a tribute to Kate, who had been mother, teacher, and friend in those early years. Michael noted her sadness, and somehow, he knew.

Off through the trees, he could see a tiny waterfall. He spurred his horse, starting off in that direction. Purposely, distracting her, he called, "Let's see what's over here."

Together, they followed the little stream, until they came to a pool below the falls, recently formed by raging waters. Some large rocks stood at the water's edge.

"Michael, it's beautiful." Shona tethered Lady to a tree and was upon a rock, almost before he had dismounted.

He studied her, golden hair glinting in the sunlit shadows, and love overwhelmed him. This was a perfect setting for one so lovely. Sitting very close, his arm around her shoulders, he indulged in a dream—not one of which Will would have approved.

* * *

Strangely, as joyous as she had been, in the curve of his arm, Shona's mood changed. Michael, didn't notice it for a time.

At that moment, Shona's thoughts were entirely foreign to her nature. Fears surrounded her like little imps, determined to destroy her happiness. She studied the limpid pool, and imagined being bound and thrown into it.

Her childlike joy vanished. A gray squirrel, its cheeks bulging with nuts, stopped to study her, then scurried off.

He's free, she thought. He can do anything, go anywhere, without accounting to anyone. Suddenly, the colors, which had been clear and bright, darkened. She shuddered, and Michael felt it. Bewildered, he held her steady.

To his silent question, she whispered, "Michael, I'm afraid. I've been so thrilled by the joy of our love, that I've missed something. Now, I realize that my most precious possession, so long denied, is my freedom."

Bewildered, he countered. "You're right, honey. But why are you upset? You're free."

Seeing that he was at sea, she said, "Yes, for the first time, I'm free. And I want to keep that liberty, forever. The Bible says, 'Where your treasure is, there will your heart be, also.' "

"What's all this talk of freedom? No one will deprive you of that. We'll be part of each other, always. What could be more wonderful?"

She gave him an intense look. "Just one thing: freedom is more wonderful. To have liberty; not having to account to anyone else."

Michael frowned. These words, so strangely disturbing, should not be coming from someone pledged to marry.

"Shona, what are you driving at?"

"Darling, I'm a bird, let out of a cage. For the first time in my life, I don't have to hide. I think I love my liberty as much as I love you."

Struck by belated awareness that persecution and capture had left their marks, Michael cast about for the right thing to say.

He grasped her by the shoulders. "Dear, there's no way I can keep you, unless you really want to be with me."

She stared at him, as though seeing him in a new light. "Michael, you would be my jailer—I would live like Mama, not daring to do anything against Papa's wishes."

He gave her a horrified look. Now that the way had been cleared for him, how could this happen? She was slipping away.

She had been looking intently at the squirrel. Maybe she had imagined that the little animal had his freedom. It was a long shot, but he took it.

"Shona, did you see that squirrel? I suppose you think he's free."

She stared at him. "Of course. He can go anywhere, or do anything he wants."

"That's where you're wrong. His mouth was full of nuts, to store for the winter. He has a family to feed."

Shona considered this, thoughtfully. She had not been thinking of family responsibilities—only of her fear for the future.

She couldn't look at him and say it. Turning her head away, she almost whispered, "Michael, isn't that even greater bondage? I can't bear the thought of little ones needing me—perhaps hopelessly, like Ian."

Now, almost in panic, Michael grasped her by the shoulders, forcing her to face him. "Shona, unless one is a hermit or hobo, there's no way to escape responsibility. You already have it, in your job. Is that so bad?"

Hopefully, he looked into her face, and was gratified to see the love reflected there—almost a radiance. In his joy, he was totally unprepared for the sudden change.

Impulsively, she threw her arms around his neck. "Oh, Michael, I want you so much. We don't have to get married, do we? Why can't we just go away—anywhere, and always be together? Both of us can be free. Think how happy we will be."

Michael gasped as though drenched by a sudden shower. In that moment, he realized that her father was right. Shona was still a child, with no concept of the society she faced. Only the very daring or the most naive of young women would even consider such action.

His horrified look caused the light to fade from her face. Now, he was wondering how to say the right thing.

"Dear, you've had bad times, but this is not the answer. You're as free as one can ever be. We can't flout moral responsibiltiy and expect to gain happiness."

Suddenly aware of the impact of her suggestion, Shona flushed with chagrin.

Michael saw it, hesitated, and went on. "Dear, your father has given you your first taste of independence. I can give you another. I'll request that we omit the word 'obey' from the ceremony."

She gasped, saw the pleading look in his eyes, and slowly discarded her cause. Leaning against his chest, her reply was muffled.

"How could I think of you as a jailer? You know how much I want you."

"Enough to look at me for the rest of your life?" He said it lightly, but his expression was grave.

She gazed up at his strong, sensitive face, and smiled. "I think I'd like that."

Joyously, he caught her up, kissing her until she was breathless with exhilaration. At last, there were no fears—no doubts. This was joy and peace.

As they prepared to mount their horses, the brilliant red sun suddenly disappeared. Above them, to the east, the feathery white clouds were now transformed, spreading pink and gold across the blue sky.

Michael smiled at Shona as she followed the direction of his gaze. "Looks almost like a sunrise, Honey. Seems, a new day is dawning for us."

For a moment, she drank it in, then turned for another kiss. Still clinging, she whispered, "I didn't think it would happen. But then, sunrise in Johnstown has often been late."

The End

BIBLIOGRAPHY

Vexler, Robert I., and Furer, Howard B. *Pittsburgh, A Chronological and Documentary History, 1682-1976.* Oceana Publications, Inc., New York, 1977.

Vexler, Robert I., and Swindler, William F. *Chronology and Documentary Handbook of the State of Pennsylvania, 1978.* Oceana Publications, Inc., New York, 1978.

O'Neal, William B. *Architectural Drawing in Virginia, 1819-1969.* School of Architecture, University of Virginia, 1969.

Ginsburg, Madeline. *Victorian Dress.* Holmes and Meier, Publishers, Inc., New York, 1983.

Walker, Joseph E. *Hopewell Village, 1900.* Printed by Joseph E. Walker, 1966.

McHargue, Georgess. *Meet the Witches.* J. B. Lippincott, New York, 1984.

Ebensburg *Mountaineer.* July 29, 1858.

Johnstown, Pennsylvania, 1856. (Copy taken from rough copy)

Thwaite, Mary F. *From Primer To Pleasure In Reading, 1963.*

Carpenter, Humphrey. *Secret Gardens.* Houghton Mifflin Company, Boston, 1985.

Townsend, John Rowe. *Written For Children.* J. B. Lippincott, New York, 1985.

Johnson. Willis Fletcher. *History of The Johnstown Flood.* Edgewood Publishing Company, 1889.

Frank Leslie's *Illustrated Newspaper.* "Johnstown," Issue. Juime Publishing Company, 1889.

McCullough, David G. *The Johnstown Flood.* Simon and Schuster, New York, 1968.

About the Author

No one knew exactly where or when I was born. After being adopted as an abandoned child, I was brought to Johnstown at about two years of age. Later, I chose my own birthday: March 4, Inauguration Day. That long word was so satisfactory.

I seem to be one of those rare persons who had no desire to discover the whereabouts of my original family. (Fate doesn't always accede to desires.)

A graduate of Johnstown High School and Cambria-Rowe Business College, I got a job in 1943, when positions were scarce. Having had Polio (the reason of my abandonment), there was a consensus amont the Powers that I was not suitable as a prospective stenographer.

Angrily, I visited the company (Pennsylvania Electric). After convincing someone that "I don't type with my feet," I was hired. Thirty-seven years later, I retired, content.

Retirement offered a chance to attend the University of Pittsburgh at Johnstown in daylight hours, to pick up the few credits necessary for a BA in Journalism. It was a bit late. *The Tribune-Democrat* would accept my submissions, but could not hire another reporter. Then, too, the column I had been writing for *The Observer*, died with the paper.

My column for that weekly paper was entitled, "Taking Notice." It covered everything from the lack of porches on apartments being built, to damage done by picketing strikers. A fellow-worker said, "Marie, if you're going to write like that, you'd better use a pen name. They'll blow up your house."

As for my writing, other than poetry, my first novel, *KELSEY*, a love story about a fashion designer, languishes in a closet along with some short stories, a science-fiction television play, and a history, *THE INDIANS OF JOHNSTOWN*. Basically, I'm a poet. Some day . . .

* * *